Showdown With The Devil

Anonymous

Copyright © The Bourbon Kid 2020

The right of the author (under the accredited pseudonym The Bourbon Kid) to be identified as the author of this work has been asserted by him/her in accordance with the Copyright, Designs and Patents Act 1988.

This novel is entirely a work of fiction. The names, characters and incidents portrayed in it are the work of the author's imagination. Any resemblance to actual persons, living or dead, events or localities is entirely coincidental.

All rights reserved. No part of this publication may be reproduced, stored in a retrieval system, or transmitted by any means, without the prior permission in writing of the publisher, nor be otherwise circulated in any form of binding or cover other than that in which it is published and without a similar condition including this condition being imposed on the subsequent purchaser.

Books by Anonymous –

The Book With No Name
The Eye of the Moon
The Devil's Graveyard
The Book of Death
The Red Mohawk
Sanchez: A Christmas Carol
The Plot to Kill the Pope
The Day It Rained Blood
Showdown With the Devil

'When I'm done with you, you'll find yourself back in Hell. When you get there, be sure you tell Scratch, I'm coming for him next.'

The Bourbon Kid to Dracula in *The Greatest Trick*

One

'Mom? Did you hear that

Sandy opened her e~~~~ ~~ ~~~~~~~~~~~~liately. The midday sun almost blinded her. She sat up and reached ~~~ ~~ the glovebox for her sunglasses. After fumbling around for a while she latched onto a pair of big, round, brown-lensed shades. She slipped them on, soothing the bright light from above and then relaxed back into the passenger seat. Her nineteen-year old daughter, Arizona, was in the driver's seat of her BMW. The roof was down and Arizona's long blonde hair was blowing around above her head.

'Sweetie, didn't I tell you to tie your hair back if you're going to drive with the top down?'

'Yeah. But we're on the way home now, so who cares?'

'I do, sweetie. You should always try and look your best. And why aren't you wearing your tiara?'

'Jeez, mom, take a chill pill.'

'What?' Sandy shook her head. Teenagers. She looked around. They were driving along a desert highway with no other cars in sight. 'Where are we anyway?' she asked, adjusting her seat to get a better look at the road ahead.

'I took a detour. I wanted to see the sights. But it's really windy here, so I took the tiara off and put it in the back.'

'You're putting it back on when we get home. I want the neighbours to see that my little girl won the regional.' It suddenly dawned on Sandy that they were listening to a newsreader on the radio. 'What's with the news?' she asked. 'I thought you hated the news?'

'I do, but did you hear what they just said?'

'No, honey. What did they say?'

'They said there's been an attempted kidnapping in Austin.'

'That's delightful,' said Sandy, her disinterest clear. She leant down and switched the station on the radio. She found the song, "Right Back Where We Started From" by Maxine Nightingale. Happy with that, she reclined back into her seat.

Arizona still wanted to talk about the news. 'They said the kidnapper wore a Ryan Reynolds facemask.'

'Who's Ryan Reynolds?'

'He was the guy in that movie we saw where he was buried alive.'

'I don't remember that. What was it called?'

'I don't know, but he was buried underground for the whole movie.'

'Buried?'

'Yes, underground, the whole time.'

'I don't remember it.'

'Well, Ryan Reynolds was in it. He was in Deadpool too.'

'Oh, him. Is he the one married to Blake Carrington?'

'Blake Lively, mom. But, listen, how creepy is this? The news says that a man in a Ryan Reynolds facemask is the main suspect in a whole series of kidnappings. He grabs women off the street, then three days later he dumps their dead bodies in the trash. But the latest woman he tried to grab off the street managed to escape. She had pepper spray. Got him right in the eyes.'

'Was his dad Burt Reynolds? Keep your eyes on the road, honey.'

'Burt Reynolds? Was he the one with the monkey?'

'I don't know. Just stay away from men in Reynolds masks.'

Arizona pointed at a road sign as they zoomed past it. 'Did you see that, Mom? Fifty miles to go.'

'That's lovely. I might just close my eyes again for a minute.'

'I think I know who it is.'

'Who what is?'

'The kidnapper in the Ryan Reynolds mask.'

'Oh yeah. Who is it?'

'Ryan Reynolds.'

Sandy pulled her sunglasses down onto the bridge of her nose and peered over them at her daughter. It appeared that Arizona wasn't joking. 'Sweetie, the kidnapper is wearing a Ryan Reynolds mask as a *disguise*. If it was *Ryan Reynolds* doing the kidnapping, he'd wear a different mask.'

Arizona took one hand off the steering wheel and wagged her finger at her mother. 'Aaah, but, you see, that's the perfect cover isn't it? No one would expect Ryan Reynolds to wear a Ryan Reynolds face mask. He's literally the only person the police would never suspect. It's the perfect crime. He's a genius.'

'He's not a genius, sweetie. He's an actor.'

'He's a kidnapper. I would love to be kidnapped by him. If we see anyone in a Ryan Reynolds face mask, I'm pulling over. Then I can prove to you I'm right.'

'Okay, honey. I'm closing my eyes now.'

Fifteen minutes passed before Sandy woke up again. The sound of a car door slamming made her bolt upright. Arizona had left the car and was walking along the side of the road. Sandy couldn't see much of what was going on because even with sunglasses on, the glare from the sun was right in her eye-line.

'Sweetie, where are you going?' Sandy called out.

'I'm just going to help this man,' Arizona yelled back.

Sandy opened her door and climbed out. 'What have I told you about walking barefoot on the road?'

Arizona was only wearing a pair of tiny blue denim shorts and a pink bikini top. Thankfully, she had followed her mother's wishes and tied her hair back in a ponytail, but she was crouching down in the dust and dirt at the side of the road, with no shoes on. As Sandy approached, Arizona looked up at her.

'I think this guy might be dead.'

'Get away from him then.'

The man in question was lying face down on the ground. He was wearing black pants and a sleeveless green undershirt. A blue baseball cap covered the back of his head. Arizona pressed her hand into his back and poked him in an attempt to wake him up.

'Is he okay?' Sandy asked.

'He still looks dead, but apart from that he's okay, I guess.'

The crunch of a boot on the ground behind her made Sandy jump. She spun around and saw a man in a mask, his eyes peering out through two small oval holes. Before she could ask what was happening, he reached out with a big muscular arm, hooked it around her chest, spun her around and pulled her hard against him. He pressed a white rag over her mouth and nose. The rag smelled like something sweet mixed with disinfectant. Whatever it was, it wasn't good. Sandy tried to hold her breath and wriggle free. It was no use. The man's arm was almost crushing her chest as he pressed the cloth against her face even harder.

Out of the corner of her eye she saw Arizona suffering a similar fate at the hands of the man she had been tending to at the roadside, who was now very much alive. Sandy renewed her struggle and tried in vain to call out to her daughter, but she managed nothing more than muffled groans. Her head felt heavy and everything seemed to be tilting to the side. As her attacker lowered her to the ground, she saw Arizona go limp in the other man's arms. Then everything turned black.

'Zona, baby! Arizona!'

Sandy awoke. She'd been calling out her daughter's name in her sleep. How much time had passed? How long had she been out? Her brain was swimming inside her skull. Her hands and neck were covered in the grit of dirt and sand. She sat up. She was at the roadside, not far from her car. Her eyes darted to where she'd last seen her daughter. Arizona was gone. In the back of her mind she heard her daughter calling for her, screaming the word, "Mom" over and over.

Climbing to her feet was tricky. After a few failed attempts Sandy crawled over to the car. The passenger door was still open. She grabbed the frame and heaved herself up. Nothing in her field of vision would stay still. Everything wobbled, zooming in and out of focus.

In the midst of it all she heard a car approaching. She tried to wave it down, but the sudden movement made her feel sick. She clung onto the side of the car. Through her rolling eyes she saw a station wagon park up behind her BMW. A door opened and someone rushed towards her.

'Are you okay, miss?' a man asked.

Sandy looked up. A pink-skinned man with a bushy moustache and dark sunglasses was looking down at her. His big white Stetson hat covered half the sky.

'My daughter's gone,' Sandy spluttered. 'They've taken her.'

'Who's taken her?'

'Ryan Reynolds.'

The man put his hands on her shoulders to keep her steady. 'Here, you should sit down,' he said.

Sandy lowered herself down onto her car seat. It helped to clear her head a little.

'Wait there,' the man said. 'I'll get you some water.'

He ran back to his car and returned a short while later with a plastic bottle of water. Sandy drank some. It made her feel much better. She felt around on the floor by her seat, expecting her hand to touch her leather purse. It was gone.

'Can I use your phone?' she asked the good Samaritan.

'Err, sure.'

He handed her his cell phone. Sandy typed in a phone number she knew off by heart. Two rings later a man answered.

'Who is this?' he asked.

'Mike, it's Sandy. Is he there? I need to speak to him. It's urgent.'

The man on the other end of the line sighed. 'Sandy, you can't keep calling like this. The President is in a meeting right now.'

Sandy held in the urge to vomit, and replied. 'Tell him his daughter's been kidnapped.'

Two

At a crossroads in the desert wasteland known as the Devil's Graveyard a twenty-something black man named Jacko was sitting atop a boulder at the side of the road, staring at the horizon. He was wearing a musty old suit that he'd owned since before his death. His job was to open the secret fourth fork in the crossroads for people who came to visit the Devil. Over the many decades Jacko had been watching over the concealed entrance, he had frequently gone months at a time without unlocking it for anyone, but in recent times he had been kept busy by the members of the Dead Hunters, the only visitors he had ever considered as friends. It had been the best time. That time was over now. The boss, Scratch, also known as the Devil, wanted the Dead Hunters dead, and if he ever found out about Jacko's involvement in a recent plot to deceive him, he'd want Jacko dead too.

It was early in the day and the sun was poking its head up on the horizon when a vehicle finally approached the crossroads. Jacko hoped to God it was the Bourbon Kid coming to free him from his duties on the crossroads. It wasn't. It was a pink transit van. The Kid had driven many vehicles in his time, but Jacko couldn't recall him ever having one that wasn't black. As for pink, well, pink just wasn't the Kid's colour at all. Maybe Jasmine would drive a pink car? Or Flake? Or Sanchez?

Jacko was playing his harmonica, sliding it back and forth across his lips with his weathered brown fingers. He pulled a pair of deep black sunglasses from the pocket on his suit jacket, and slipped them on so he could discreetly check out the approaching vehicle. The driver of the pink van was dressed in black and had a hood pulled up over his head. Maybe it was the Bourbon Kid after all?

No such luck.

The van stopped at the crossroads. Its driver's window was down and the song "No Tengo Dinero," by Los Umbrellos filtered out.

'Can I help you?' Jacko asked, raising his voice to be heard over the music.

The driver killed the engine and with it, Los Umbrellos. He turned his head towards Jacko. Beneath the dark cowl was a man with a yellow, thin-skinned face and dark red eyes. He ignored Jacko's offer of help and opened his van door. He stepped out onto the gravelly highway. This was one big muthafucker. When he straightened up, he was over eight feet tall. Jacko gulped. His spot on the boulder normally gave him a height advantage over any visitors. Not this guy. This fucker was at eye level.

'You are Robert Johnson,' the man said in a deep, croaky voice.

'Most people call me Jacko.'

'A deception,' the man replied.

'I beg your pardon?'

'I see everything.'

'That's nice. Can I help you with anything?'

'I have come to see Scratch.'

'Is he expecting you?'

'He is.'

'Then go on in,' said Jacko, trying to act blasé. 'Don't waste time talking to me.'

The giant man in black stepped closer to Jacko. 'I see every man's sins,' he said.

'I bet that gets tiresome after a while,' Jacko quipped, thankful that his new visitor could not see the anxiety in his eyes.

'You wear your dishonesty on your face,' the man replied. 'I see all of your treachery. Your master will know it too.'

Jacko gulped again, almost loud enough to be heard by some of the many dead bodies that were buried all around the nearby desert wasteland. 'Have you been here before?' he asked.

'I've been coming here since before you were born.'

'I was born a long time ago, y'know?'

'Nineteen-eleven.'

'Excuse me?'

'You were born in the year nineteen-eleven. I was coming here long before that.'

Jacko shifted uncomfortably on his boulder, his suit pants riding up his ass a bit. 'Umm, well, that's great. You probably have better things to do than stop here chatting with me then. And if you've been around that long, you probably know where to go from here, right?'

The man in the long black robe waved a hand towards the horizon. The secret road from the crossroads opened up as if he had pulled back a concealing curtain.

'You *have* been here before then,' said Jacko.

'You and I will meet again soon,' the man replied. 'Once Scratch is aware of your treachery, I will return to snatch the life from you.'

Jacko glanced down at the leather belt around the other man's waist. It looked like he had a lightsaber hanging from the belt. Either that or a rather poorly shaped metal dildo.

'The blade of Hellfire,' the man said, noticing Jacko was staring.

'The what?'

The tall man unhooked the tubular object from his belt. He wrapped his long bony fingers around it and pointed it at the sky. A bright red and gold flame burst from the end of the tube, like the blade on a lightsaber.

'This is the blade of Hellfire,' the man repeated. 'Made from the hottest flames in Hell. It destroys everything it touches.'

Jacko felt the heat from the blade even though it was ten inches away from his face. 'I like your van,' he said, changing the subject.

The flaming blade on the man's sword extinguished, and he replaced it on his belt. 'We will meet again soon, Mister Johnson,' he said.

With that ominous comment floating in the air, the man climbed back into his van and sped off down the secret road towards Purgatory.

A bead of sweat rolled down Jacko's forehead. He had heard many stories about the man he had just encountered. He'd assumed the stories were little more than rumours, legends created to scare children. Every story about this man had one common feature. None of them had happy endings.

Three

Scratch was sitting at a small round table in the bar area in Purgatory, drinking coffee and watching an episode of the TV show *Gatchaman* on his big-screen television. Even though he was enjoying the action, he was only watching it to kill time while he waited for a visitor, a man he had not seen in over a hundred years. He checked his watch for the third time in as many minutes. It was still only nine-fifteen in the morning. He'd been up since three o'clock when the bad news came through that his old friend Dracula had been killed by the Bourbon Kid. And the Kid had left Dracula with a message, *"When you get back to Hell, tell Scratch I'm coming for him next"*. The words had been running through Scratch's mind ever since.

Dracula's death hadn't actually come as a surprise. The old vampire had killed the Bourbon Kid's son, so the Kid's revenge was inevitable. That's why Scratch had spent the last few days orchestrating plans of his own. Plans to kill the Bourbon Kid and his friends. He'd put the word out to the best assassins and bounty hunters that money could buy. And also to the deadliest killer of them all. The man whose arrival was imminent. Scratch had put on his favourite red suit in readiness for the meeting. He needed to look like he was in control of things.

He paused the television and drummed his fingers on the table. Behind him he heard the tap-tap-tap of fingers on a keyboard. His top scientist and all-round technical wizard, Eric Einstein, was behind the bar doing some work on the computer system.

'Can you keep the noise down?' Scratch called back to him.

'It's all done,' said Einstein. 'Come see for yourself.'

Scratch stood up and carried his mug of coffee over to the bar. Einstein placed a laptop on the bar and twisted it round so Scratch could see the screen.

'What do you think, boss?' Einstein asked, peering over his round spectacles with a conceited look on his face.

Scratch hated Einstein. He was an arrogant middle-aged geek, and he had an eccentric, crazy haircut, the kind that made him look like he'd just been electrocuted. Unfortunately, he was incredibly useful, so Scratch had to put up with him and his banal conversation skills.

'What am I looking at exactly?' Scratch asked.

Einstein pulled a pencil from the breast pocket on his long white coat and tapped the computer screen with it. 'See this here? We are now connected to our very own phone network. As of this moment, you can make external phone calls and send text messages.'

'To people outside of the desert?'

'Yes.'

'Good.' Scratch waited for Einstein to give him some more news. When the scientist stayed silent, Scratch raised his eyebrows. *'Well?* Did you hack into the phones like I asked?'

'I did,' the scientist replied. 'We're hooked into everything that happens on the phones of Rodeo Rex, Elvis and Jasmine.'

'What about the Bourbon Kid?'

'I've got no number for him. Until we find out what his number is, I can't hack into it.'

'You useless cunt. Have you found anything interesting on any of their phones yet?'

'I have.'

Scratch took a sip of his coffee. 'Well? What have you got?'

'I found some great pictures of Jasmine.'

Scratch slapped him on the arm. 'Forget those. What about text messages? Is there anything that indicates their plans?'

'Not yet, but it's early days. Give me a few hours and I'll know everything they've been up to, any website they've visited, messaging apps they've used. All of it.'

'That's good,' said Scratch. 'I want my important visitor to see that we're on top of everything.'

To Scratch's annoyance, his other main sidekick, Zilas, the deformed hunchback, who was supposed to be sweeping the floors, poked his sweaty head up from the other side of the bar. 'Oooh, who's coming?' he asked.

'You'll know him when you see him,' Scratch replied.

'Can't you just tell us?' Zilas begged.

'I could, but I won't.'

Einstein turned back to the computer and continued his work, knowing that an inevitable bout of rage from Scratch was incoming. Zilas had a knack for angering the boss with his inane questions.

'So, it's someone we know,' said Zilas, scratching a puss-filled red spot on his chin as he tried to work out who the visitor was. 'Can we play ten questions to guess who it is?'

'Go on then,' Scratch replied, feeling smug, even by his own smug standards.

'Is it a man?' Zilas asked.

Scratch groaned. 'I already referred to him as a *he* for fuckssake!'

Einstein spoke up in Zilas's defence. 'That doesn't always mean it's a guy these days.'

'Fine,' said Scratch. 'Next question.'

'What's his name?' Zilas asked.

'You can't just ask his name!' Scratch ranted. 'CHRIST! The whole point of this game is that you ask *yes or no* questions and then you *guess his name!'*

'Oh, okay. Where has he been since he was last here?'

Scratch clenched his fists. 'Listen idiot, I just said you're only supposed to ask questions that I can give a *yes or no* answer to. I'm penalising you for asking stupid questions now. That's three questions wasted, you only have seven left.'

'Are you going to answer my question about where he's been?' Zilas asked.

'No, six questions left.'

'Did that count as a question then?'

'Yes, five.'

'Five what?'

'Questions left. Four.'

'Four what?'

'Questions left. You have four questions left to ask me about the identity of the visitor. So far all you've worked out is that he's a man. Stop wasting questions.'

Zilas took some time to think. 'Okay, he said eventually. 'Can we start again?'

'No! Three.'

'I've only got three questions left?'

Scratch leapt over the bar and grabbed Zilas around the throat. He lifted the hunchback off his feet. 'Christ you're annoying! You ruin everything with your bloody stupid questions all the fucking time!'

'What have I ruined this time?'

Scratch threw the scruffy hunchback onto the floor. 'Forget it. The man who's coming is Barazima.'

'Barazima?' said Zilas, sitting up and rearranging his raggedy, green, velvet outfit. 'Barazima who?'

A deep, booming voice called out from the bar entrance. 'You can call me Death.'

Zilas scrambled to his feet and peered over the bar top. Standing in front of the batwing doors at the entrance was a man dressed in a long black cloak, with the hood pulled up over his head. He stood over eight feet tall. Hanging from a leather belt around his waist was a metal object that looked like a lightsaber.

'Barazima!' Scratch yelled. 'So good to see you again!'

Zilas stared wide eyed. 'Holy fuck! The Grim Reaper's name is Barazima?'

Barazima ignored the hunchback and instead glowered at Scratch. 'Why have you summoned me?'

Scratch pulled a cigar from the top pocket on his jacket and chewed the end off before replying. 'I want you to help me kill a man named the Bourbon Kid.'

'You called me in to kill *one man?*'

'He has the blood of God in his veins, and he and his friends are plotting to kill me.'

Zilas scurried around the bar and stopped next to Scratch. He leaned back so that he could get a better look up at the Reaper's face. 'How come we've never seen you here before?' he asked.

The Reaper looked down at Zilas, his dark red eyes betraying a look of disgust. 'I've been on a world tour,' he replied. 'Not that it's any of your business, minion.'

Scratch saw an opportunity to impress his new guest. It was time to use the Eye of the Moon, the magical blue stone that he had concealed inside his stomach. The Eye had many powers and Scratch had been learning them all in readiness for what was to come. He stuck his cigar in the corner of his mouth and raised his right hand. His palm glowed red, like a ball of electricity. He thrust his arm at Zilas and a bolt of red lightning flew from his hand. It hit the hunchback in the chest and launched him across the room. He crashed into a jukebox by the wall and slid to the floor unconscious.

The Reaper nodded his approval. 'You have harnessed the power of the Eye of the Moon. I'm impressed.'

'I sure have,' said Scratch. 'It's secured inside my stomach where no one can get to it.' He hesitated a moment. 'I'm sorry, where are my manners? Can I get you a drink?'

'No. But you can answer me a question.'

'Anything. Go on.'

'I'm wondering why you keep the bluesman at the crossroads?'

'Oh him,' said Scratch. 'He's harmless enough. He controls who comes into Purgatory.'

The Reaper looked around the room. The disgust in his eyes did not fade. 'I know what he does,' he said. 'I looked into his heart. I know everything about him.'

'Then you know his real name is Robert,' said Scratch puffing on his cigar and blowing a smoke snake into the air.

'His name is not important,' said the Reaper, wafting the smoke away. 'He's been working against you since the day he signed a contract with you.'

Scratch froze, his cigar held inches from his mouth. 'Excuse me?'

'He was working with an old fortune-teller lady named Annabel de Frugyn. The two of them played you for a fool right from the start.'

'Annabel?' said Scratch, baffled. 'She's dead though. Dracula killed her last week. What's she got to do with any of this?'

'You remember Beth Lansbury?'

'Yes, the Bourbon Kid's girlfriend. We sent her back in time and left her there to die. What of her?'

'She was pregnant when you sent her back in time.'

'Yes, that's right. She had a son. We killed him.'

'No,' said the Reaper with a shake of his head. 'Beth gave birth to twins, a son *and* a daughter. The daughter was Annabel de Frugyn.'

Scratch felt his knees go weak. 'What? That can't be true? Annabel worked for me, predicting the future!'

'Exactly,' said the Reaper. 'She knew the future because her mother warned her of everything that was to come. And when you thought you'd killed the Bourbon Kid's son, you were wrong. Annabel tricked you. The son is still alive and well, living in Santa Mondega.'

Scratch needed a drink. 'What? But we killed the Bourbon Kid's son! Dracula did it, impaled him on a spear.'

The Reaper shook his finger at Scratch. 'Dracula killed a man named Melvin Melt who was tricked into taking the place of the Bourbon Kid's real son, Vincent Papshmir.'

'Vincent Papshmir?' Scratch staggered back against the bar and steadied himself against it. 'You mean the old preacher in Santa Mondega? He's the son of the Bourbon Kid?'

The Reaper nodded, 'And he's still alive.'

Four

Since the appearance of the Reaper, Jacko had been on edge. Normally he would pass the time by playing a tune on his guitar or harmonica, but for the first time in a long while he couldn't muster up the energy to play anything. His nerves were fried. He was sitting on his giant boulder, watching the road from Purgatory, knowing that at some point, either Scratch or the Reaper, or possibly both of them, would show up on it, heading towards the crossroads to confront him about what he and Annabel had done.

'You're feeling vulnerable, aren't you?' said a voice from behind him.

Jacko swivelled around on the boulder. A man in a long white robe was standing behind him. He had smooth white skin and curly blond hair. He also had a peculiar yellow glow around him. This day was getting weird.

'Who are you?' Jacko asked.

'I am the Angel Gabriel.'

'From the Bible?'

'That's me,' the man said with a smile.

There was something reassuring about Gabriel's manner. He looked and spoke just like Jacko imagined an angel would. With every step the man in white took towards him Jacko felt more at ease.

'Please tell me you've come to get me out of here?' Jacko said, sliding off his giant rock.

'You wish to leave the crossroads?' Gabriel replied.

'Fuck yeah, I do! You know, a guy just came through here, and I'm certain he was the Grim Reaper. I think he read my mind. If he tells Scratch what he knows, I'm in deep shit. I mean, *really fucking deep shit.*'

Gabriel stopped in front of Jacko and placed a reassuring hand his shoulder. 'You're in luck,' he said. 'Your old friend Annabel had a word with God. She pleaded with him to get you out of here. And she read his palm too, which she got totally wrong, but hey, God's got a sense of humour and he likes Annabel, so he says you may now pass through the gates of Heaven. Your life and your afterlife here in the desert have been honourable, and your unselfishness in helping your friends has not gone unnoticed. God has terminated your contract with Scratch.'

Every tense muscle in Jacko's body relaxed. 'Oh, thank God. You have no idea how much of a relief that is.'

Gabriel smiled. 'Go with God, my friend.'

'Wait, wait a second,' said Jacko. 'Can I say goodbye to the others?'

'The others?'

'Yeah, my friends, the Dead Hunters. They're the only thing that stopped me from going mad in this place. Well, them and Annabel.'

Gabriel offered a conciliatory smile. 'You'll get to see Annabel again very soon.'

'I know, and I'm looking forward to it, but I'd love to have one night with the gang. Whenever they're all here at Purgatory, it's just the best. I live for those nights.'

'I'm sorry,' said Gabriel. 'That's not how life and death works. Sometimes you don't get to say goodbye. You don't get one last night with your friends before you go. You should be grateful that God has accepted you into Heaven.'

Jacko understood, but even so, it was a crushing disappointment. 'Would you give them a message for me?'

'That depends. What's the message?'

'Just tell them all I'll miss them, and that they were good friends.'

Gabriel looked up to the Heavens as if he were silently conversing with God. Then he smiled at Jacko. 'I'll pass the message on when I think the time is right. Now go with God. Enjoy the rest of your afterlife.'

The angel waved his hand across Jacko and the bluesman vanished into the wind. His journey on earth at an end.

A sarcastic round of applause followed Jacko's disappearance. Gabriel turned around to see where it had come from. Walking towards him on the dusty road from Purgatory was a tall black man in a smart red suit.

'Scratch,' said Gabriel. 'Too bad you didn't get here a minute earlier. Jacko's gone for good. The Lord has reclaimed his soul.'

Scratch didn't look particularly bothered, which was surprising. He sauntered up to Gabriel with a relaxed look on his face. 'Jacko's betrayal was irrelevant,' he said with a shrug. 'He was small fry. I have much bigger fish to catch.' He stopped in front of Gabriel and smiled. 'Did you know, I found out the truth?'

The sunlight was surrounding Scratch's head, giving him a golden halo, which definitely didn't suit him. Gabriel took a step back.

'Jacko mentioned something about the Reaper,' he said. 'Have you really summoned Barazima?'

'I spoke with him just now, and he told me everything. I know all about Annabel and Vincent Papshmir, and how they deceived me. It was all very clever. Your friend Levian helped them as I understand it. You must be feeling very smug about now.'

This was a concern. If Scratch had found out everything, then Vincent Papshmir's life would be in grave danger. Gabriel intended to warn Papshmir, and his daughter Janis, that trouble was coming their way.

'It's been fun chatting with you, Scratch,' Gabriel said. 'But it's time I was going. My work here is done.'

'Not quite,' said Scratch.

'What do you mean?'

'Take a look behind you.'

Gabriel turned around. 'What the——'

The Grim Reaper loomed over him. It had been a long time since anyone had snuck up on Gabriel, but the Reaper had done it. There was a saying in the afterlife, "Death creeps up on us all". Well, that phrase was certainly true here. Gabriel had been caught completely off guard. The Reaper unleashed his sword of fire and swung it down from above his head. Its raging hot flames ripped through Gabriel's head, chopping him in half right down the middle. A normal sword would have passed right through Gabriel without touching him. But this was different. The Reaper's blade destroyed everything it touched, human, ghost or angel. Gabriel had time to let out one feeble cry for help before his existence in the afterlife was brought to an end. With one swing of the blade, his soul was obliterated, leaving only a plume of smoke behind. Gabriel was gone forever, never to exist again, even in the afterlife.

Scratch kicked some sand and dirt over the spot the angel had been standing on. 'That was magnificent,' he said. 'Goodbye Gabriel, you gloating prick!'

The Reaper extinguished his fiery blade and tucked the sword handle back into its place on his belt. 'Your enemies do not fear you,' he said to Scratch. 'You have become a laughing stock.'

'I beg your pardon?' said Scratch, irritated by the Reaper ruining the joyous moment.

'Your very existence is under threat,' the Reaper replied. 'And the reason why is obvious.'

'What?'

Barazima lowered his hood, revealing his grim, yellow-skinned face and blood-red eyes. 'Throughout history you've come up with dastardly plans to destroy your enemies, haven't you?' he said.

'That's true,' Scratch agreed. 'What's your point?'

'My point is, you surround yourself with idiots. You're constantly taking advice from idiots and then hiring idiots to carry out your plans.'

'What idiots?'

'The hunchback you have hanging around in Purgatory, *he* is a buffoon.'

'Zilas? Well, yes, of course he is. But I enjoy beating him up.'

'You also admitted to me earlier that you hired Dracula and a group of ninjas to try and take down the Bourbon Kid last week.'

'What's wrong with Dracula?'

'I know what happened to him when he tried to seduce the fat Mexican.'

'Aah, yes that,' said Scratch, remembering the incident that ended with Dracula being flushed down a toilet after Sanchez took a dump on him. 'That was unfortunate. It could have happened to anyone.'

'And the ninjas?'

'There was nothing wrong with the ninjas,' Scratch argued.

'Where did you get those ninjas from?'

'Zilas found them for me.'

'I've read Zilas's mind. He merely found some ninja outfits and gave them to a bunch of his friends.'

Scratch was livid. 'No wonder those ninjas looked so shit when they took the masks off!'

'You get my point?' said the Reaper. 'You employ idiots and they fuck things up. My suggestion is, use better people and your fortunes will improve.'

Scratch spotted a small bird a few metres away in the desert. It was pecking the ground trying to catch a worm. He aimed the palm of his hand at it and unleashed a bolt of electricity. It hit the tiny bird and set it on fire. Within seconds it exploded and vanished in a puff of smoke. It was a satisfying reminder of the Devil's new power.

'For your information,' Scratch said, returning to his conversation with the Reaper. 'I recently sent out a call to the best assassins and bounty hunters the world has to offer. They should be arriving here imminently. I've got cannibals coming too.'

'The Skinners?'

'Yes. Happy?'

The Reaper scratched his chin, pondering for a moment before giving his assessment. 'That's good. Because even though I expect to kill this Bourbon Kid fellow myself, I'm aware that he and his friends have, in the past, always found a way to defeat their enemies. The four horsemen of the apocalypse, Rameses Gaius, Cain, the Pope, all of these great evils have fallen at the hands of the Kid and his friends. They all underestimated him, but worst of all, they underestimated his friends.'

Scratch kicked some dirt at nothing in particular. 'You think I don't know this?' he said. 'I have plans in place to eliminate all of them. I've even arranged for Sanchez and Flake to become Mayor and First Lady of Santa Mondega.'

'Why?' asked the Reaper, unsure of the relevance.

'Why?' Scratch repeated in a mocking tone. 'I'll tell you *why!* Melinda Bone, the Chief of Staff at City Hall thinks Sanchez and Flake had something to do with the murder of her sister, Nora.'

'Why does she think that?'

'Because I told her they did. Consequently, she has arranged to have them both assassinated on their first day in office. I threw a small donation into her retirement fund as an incentive, of course.'

The Reaper was unimpressed. 'Couldn't you just kill them yourself?'

'Oh, I'd like to, but I don't have the proper authorisation. But the way I have it planned, their deaths will look like a classic case of cold-blooded revenge from Melinda Bone.'

'And the others?'

Scratch approached his old friend and put an arm around him, guiding him back onto the path to Purgatory. 'The idea is to *divide and conquer,*' he said. 'Take them out one by one, saving the Bourbon Kid for last. Once his friends are gone, he'll be much easier for you to kill.'

Five

Sanchez hated politics. He hated watching the news too. And until recently he'd hated the city mayor as well. But times had changed. Sanchez was about to become the new mayor, and Flake, his girlfriend, the new First Lady. It irked Sanchez somewhat that her title sounded better than his, but he was consoling himself with the knowledge that he was officially more important than her now.

He was sitting at a small round table in his bar, the Tapioca, eating a bowl of potato chips and watching the television, waiting for the news to start. As the clock switched to 8.30am, Flake came down the stairs behind the bar and walked into the drinking area. Her mousy brown hair was wet and hanging down by her shoulders. She was wearing a dark blue bathrobe and she smelled like strawberries. She pulled up a chair and sat down next to Sanchez. He sniffed the strawberry smell. Flake always smelled good. She always looked good too. People all over the city were puzzled as to how Sanchez, a chubby, middle-aged Mexican bartender with thinning dark hair and poor hygiene had managed to snag Flake, a petite, effortlessly beautiful, former waitress who was ten years younger than him, and lusted after by half the guys in town.

'Have they mentioned you yet?' she asked, helping herself to some chips.

'Any second now,' Sanchez replied, while discreetly moving the bowl of chips further away from Flake.

The SM News logo popped up on screen, accompanied by twenty seconds of shitty bongo drum music. Then came the good stuff. Sanchez rubbed his hands excitedly, and Flake leaned across to massage his shoulders as if she was preparing him for a ring walk into a prize fight, rather than just watching the news.

The newsreader, Gertrude Monkberry, a fifty-something lady with big hair and what Sanchez considered to be a dodgy eye, greeted the audience with a concerned look on her face, as if she was about to report on the end of the world. After a short pause, she launched into the top story.

"City hall today announced the identity of Santa Mondega's new mayor. Local man, Sanchez Garcia, known to most people in the city as the fat bartender at the Tapioca, is to take over from the much loved, but recently deceased, Tim Shepherd, as the Mayor of Santa Mondega."

'Much loved?' Sanchez scoffed. 'He was a fucking serial killer for goodness sake.'

'Ooh look,' said Flake. 'You're on TV!'

A photo of Sanchez appeared in the corner of the screen behind the newsreader. In it he was wearing a white T-shirt. His face looked sweaty and bloated.

'Wow,' said Flake. 'Is that a recent picture?'

'Shush, I can't hear what she's saying.'

The newsreader had moved onto some information about how Sanchez became the mayor.

'Local reporter, Simon Haller, joins us now from City Hall to explain how Mr Garcia was able to become mayor without being elected democratically.'

The screen cut to a hefty, drunken looking, grey-haired gentleman in a pale blue suit, holding a microphone, and standing on the concrete steps outside City Hall. The caption "Simon Haller" appeared on screen beneath him.

'Thank you, Gertrude,' he said. 'For the many members of the public querying how Mr Garcia became mayor, I can now explain the situation. It has come about due to an ancient anomaly in the law. It appears that back in the seventeen-hundreds, before the city had a mayor, a sheriff controlled not just law *enforcement*, but also the creation of any *new* laws. One of the inexplicable laws created during that time stated that anyone who murdered the local sheriff would have to take over the position. It was incorrectly believed at the time that this law would deter people from trying to kill the incumbent sheriff—or mayor, in today's words. Since Sanchez Garcia admitted to murdering Mayor Tim Shepherd, although he claims it was in self-defence, the law decrees that he now becomes the mayor. And so this great city finds itself under the rule of a tyrant!'

'Tyrant?' said Sanchez, seething. 'I'll have him executed for that. Cheeky bastard.'

'Quiet,' said Flake. 'Look, the updated opinion polls are coming in.'

On screen, Simon Haller continued, 'An opinion poll taken earlier today showed that Mayor Garcia has the lowest approval rating of anyone in the entire history of approval ratings. His numbers currently sit at minus *eighty percent*.'

Behind Simon Haller several protesters were on the steps of City Hall, waving banners with slogans such as "Black Lives Matter" and "Mayor Garcia sucks balls".

Sanchez picked up a remote and switched off the television. Flake kissed him on the cheek and reached across him to get another potato chip from his bowl.

'That's promising,' she said, crunching on the chip. 'I heard you were polling at minus eighty-five earlier.'

'Yeah,' Sanchez grumbled. 'I sneaked in some anonymous votes for myself.'

'Don't worry. Once we announce your policies tomorrow, your ratings will start to soar.'

'I have to have policies?'

A man's voice answered the question. 'Policies are simple!'

Flake and Sanchez both looked around in surprise, for they thought they were alone. Leaning against the bar was a tall black man with blond hair, wearing a long white dress with a slim brown belt around it. He had a kind face, hypnotic blue eyes and a million-dollar smile. He was known to both of them. His name was Levian and he was an angel. Flake liked him. Sanchez found him quite tiresome, and suspected he was a pervert because he kept showing up unexpectedly.

'Levian!' said Flake. 'What are you doing here?'

'I was looking for Rodeo Rex,' Levian replied. 'But having just seen the news, I thought I should congratulate you first. I must say though, I don't remember you killing Mayor Shepherd, Sanchez.'

'He didn't,' said Flake. 'Annabel did, but Sanchez took the credit for it to stop the police from asking too many questions.'

'Was there a reward?' Levian asked, his eyes tightening.

'A thousand bucks,' said Sanchez. 'But I gave it all to good causes.'

'Such as?'

'The local mini-mart was close to going out of business, so I spent a lot of the money on snacks in there. And I helped out the local bookmaker by laying some bets that didn't come in.'

'Might I offer you some advice?' said Levian.

'About what?' Sanchez asked, hoping it wasn't fashion advice. Angels wore such crap clothes.

'About how to win over the public.'

'Pffft,' said Sanchez. 'I can do that without you.'

'Okay, what are your policies?'

'Mind your own business.'

'That's what I thought. I want you to listen carefully. Of all the things going on in the world right now, the most important, which incidentally is being overlooked by many of the world leaders, is *climate change*.'

'Climate what?'

'Global warming.'

'What's that?' Sanchez asked with a groan.

Levian approached the table and pulled up a chair for himself. He sat down beside Flake, staring across at Sanchez with a grave look on his face. 'Global warming is a hugely important issue,' he said. 'The sea levels are rising all over the world, and in about fifty years' time this city and many others will be flooded due to the ice caps melting. I recommend that you erect some flood barriers all around the city. That will keep the oceans at bay when the floods come. Santa Mondega could be one of the few safe havens in the world. You can help to save the human race, give it a chance to flourish again when the sea levels eventually return to normal.'

Sanchez grabbed a handful of chips. 'I'll be dead in fifty years,' he said, shovelling a load into his mouth. 'Why should I care?'

'I think it's a good idea,' said Flake. 'It could be your flagship policy. And it'll create jobs for people, because let's face it, you'll need to employ a big workforce to erect the barriers. How high do they need to be?'

'At least thirty metres,' said Levian.

Sanchez waved a dismissive hand. 'You expect me to commission the building of a bloody thirty-metre wall all around the city? You must be mad!'

'This city is full of climate change protesters,' Levian countered. 'They'll back the idea once you explain it to them.'

'Are you really suggesting I try to win over a bunch of tree-hugging hippies with a slogan like, "Build a wall?"'

Levan smiled. 'Use your charm.'

'Use *your* charm,' Sanchez hit back, unconvincingly.

'I also have a gift for you,' said Levian. He reached into a pouch on his belt and pulled out a thin gold chain. Hanging on the chain was a large gold key. 'Wear this around your neck,' he said. 'This used to be given to the sheriff of Santa Mondega back in the dark days when the city was overrun with the undead.'

'What is it?' Sanchez asked, staring at it. 'A key? Pffft! What a crap gift!'

'It's the key to the city,' said Levian. 'If ever you're in a tricky situation, one that you cannot get out of, use this key. It will unlock any door in the city of Santa Mondega.' He handed the key to Sanchez, who took it and flicked some dust off it.

'This key is huge,' Sanchez groaned. 'I can't see it fitting into many locks in this city. And I'm not wearing it around my neck. I'll look like a pimp!'

'Just keep it anyway. You never know when you might need it. Now, about Rex. Is he here? Or Elvis?'

'They're all asleep upstairs,' said Sanchez. 'They were out half the night.'

'Doing what?'

'It should be on the news any minute now,' Sanchez replied. 'They murdered a bunch of devil worshippers at the Cherry Poppins brothel last night, so they're all pretty tired, I think.'

The happy glow vanished from Levian's face. 'You can't just murder people for being devil worshippers,' he whispered. There was menace in his tone.

'One of them was Count Dracula, the guy that killed Annabel. He got what he deserved, I reckon.'

'That's not the point. They can't do things like that without my authorisation.'

'Don't tell me,' Sanchez replied. 'Tell *them*.'

Levian shook his head. 'First of all, I'm going to have to tell God, and I don't think he's going to be very pleased.'

Six

'Let me do the talking,' said Vegas.

'You seem edgy,' Leonardo replied. 'Momma said this guy was okay, so what's there to worry about?'

'I'll tell you what's worth worrying about,' replied Vegas. 'The motorcycle parked over there. Either of you two noticed it?'

'I seen it,' said Renwar, anxious to be part of the conversation.

Vegas Bastard was the eldest of the three brothers. He'd been born six minutes before Renwar and twenty minutes before Leonardo. To the naked eye, all three men were identical. Three, thirty-five-year-old white males, all with two-day-old stubble, skinhead hairstyles and bulging muscles. They dressed more like bikers than truckers, in black jeans and matching sleeveless leather jackets. They even had matching tattoos on their arms. Each one had a picture of their mother's face tattooed onto their right bicep, and a tattoo of Hulk Hogan on their opposite arm. The brothers had been inseparable since birth, doing almost everything as a team. They had been hunting bounty for money for sixteen years. And they were damn good at it too. Their home was a blue and white branded "Cooler Cola" truck. The truck had taken them all over the world on their hunts. It was currently parked around the back of the building they were standing in front of.

Purgatory had a strange red and black cartoonish exterior that looked like something from a Japanese anime production set in the wild west. It sure was weird, and creepy.

Right now Vegas's attention was focused on the specially modified racing bike parked outside the bar. The owner was known to all three of the Bastard brothers for he was in the same line of work as them.

'What the fuck is *he* doing here?' Leonardo grumbled.

Vegas replied. 'My guess is, this isn't an exclusive job. It's a multiple hire. Sonofabitch.'

The three men standing at the threshold of Purgatory glanced at each other. They shared a nod of the head then walked through a set of batwing doors. They found the owner of the racing bike, a man named Stunky, seated at the bar nursing a glass of water. Stunky was known in bounty hunter circles as *The Flying Axe,* because he was an accomplished acrobat and he liked fighting with axes. He was in his early twenties and fairly new to the bounty hunting business, but he'd made a name for himself with his expertise in axe throwing. He had a thick, shaggy yellow beard, and a stars and stripes bandana that covered the top of his head. His black leather jacket was hung on the back of his stool. A pair of silver-coloured leather axes were sewn onto the back of the jacket as a reminder in case anyone forgot his nickname.

Next to Stunky was another bounty hunter, a slim bald man in his late twenties, known in bounty-hunting circles as "The Chinaman". He was Chinese, obviously, and his specialty was martial arts. Like most of the bounty hunters working the streets, towns, cities and states of the USA, he was a walking cliché.

There was a third person sitting at the corner of the bar, and none of the Bastard brothers had ever seen her before. She wore a raggedy, dark grey dress and a black cowboy hat. She looked pretty fucking old, *so old* that her skin had turned a sickly pea-green colour. She had an unsightly hook nose and straw-like purple hair.

But the man the Bastards had come to see was standing behind the bar, dressed in an expensive dark red suit with a matching bowler hat. He had black skin and yellow eyes and a smirk that made you feel like he knew your deepest, darkest secrets.

'You must be the Bastard brothers,' the man in red said with a broad smile. 'Three beers for you.'

He placed three bottles of Shitting Monkey beer on the bar top. Vegas pulled up a stool and grabbed one of the beers. His brothers followed suit, taking up seats on either side of him.

'What do we call you?' Vegas asked.

'You may call me Scratch,' the man replied. 'But for now, just enjoy your beers. We're waiting on the arrival of one more party, then we'll get down to business.'

'While we're waiting,' said Vegas, shooting a look around the room. 'You could do me one favour.'

'Go on.'

'Tell me who the fuck that green bitch is?'

'That's Trixie,' Scratch replied.

'I don't know her. And I didn't know this was gonna be an open job. We were led to believe it was an exclusive hire.'

'Well, it's not,' said Scratch. 'Now, you can do me a favour. Place your gun on the bar. I want to show you something.'

Vegas reached down to his hip and unholstered his pistol. He placed it on the bar, its barrel pointed at Scratch.

Scratch nodded at Trixie. The green-skinned woman lifted her right hand and waggled her fingers at Vegas's gun as if she were casting a spell on it. Nothing happened.

'Impressed?' Scratch asked Vegas.

'What did she do?'

'Pick up your gun.'

Vegas grabbed his gun. He couldn't lift it. He tugged in all directions but it wouldn't move. Sniggers from other patrons at the bar began to ring in his ears. Leonardo and Renwar tried to spare his blushes by pulling at his arms and at the gun. The result was the same. The gun wasn't moving.

'ENOUGH!' yelled Vegas, waving his brothers away. He glared at Scratch. 'What did she do?'

'She magnetised the bar top.'

'With what? I didn't see her press anything.'

'She didn't. You see, Trixie was born with a special gift.'

'I bet it wasn't her face,' said Renwar, nudging Vegas.

Scratch ignored them. 'She was born on the North Pole,' he said.

'That's stupid,' said Vegas.

'That's what everyone said to Trixie's mom when she decided to give birth there. But the unusual birthing site meant Trixie was born with the power to magnetize any item with metal in it, like the metallic paint on the surface of the bar. Perhaps if you apologise for calling her an old witch, we can move on?'

'I didn't call her a witch. I called her a bitch.'

'Then perhaps you'll apologise for that too?'

'Fuck that. Give me my fucking gun back.' Vegas tugged at his gun some more, his frustration growing.

Trixie made a gesture with her hand again, and almost immediately, the magnetic field ceased to exist. Vegas yanked the gun off the bar, but almost fell off his stool because he was pulling with more force than was needed. There was a smattering of muffled sniggers around the room. Vegas tucked his gun back in its holster and avoided eye contact with everyone.

'Good day to you!' Scratch called out cheerily.

Everyone looked around. Standing at the entrance were two men who looked like they had come from a tribe of ancient Mayan people. They were wearing Tarzan-style brown loin cloths and little else, other than a few shrunken skulls and animal teeth that hung from string chains around their necks. The younger of the two men had his hair scraped back in cornrows. His light brown skin was painted in ancient markings and tattoos. His body was so chiselled it looked like it was made from marble. The older man looked the same except he was bald, his scalp covered in tattoos, and his body, while not as solid as his comrade's, was bulkier, and his muscles bigger. It was he who spoke on behalf of them both.

'I am Snake Hawk, leader of the Skinners. This is my son, Albatross. I come on behalf of my people,' he said, bowing his head.

'Do come in,' said Scratch. 'Care for a drink?'

'No.'

'Excellent. Why don't you sit in the corner over there away from everyone else?'

Snake Hawk took a long, careful look at everyone else in the room. His stare was intense and unfriendly. When he'd finished evaluating the others, he and his son walked over to a table next to a window and sat down, facing the bar.

'Do they smell, or something?' Vegas asked.

'I don't think so,' Scratch replied.

'Then why do they have to sit over there?'

'They look hungry,' said Scratch. 'For the safety of everyone else, it's best they keep their distance.'

'We ain't scared of them,' Vegas said with a sneer.

The Chinaman, who had stayed quiet up to this point, spoke up in response to Vegas. 'They cannibal,' he said. It was hard to tell if he asking a question or stating a fact.

'Cannibal?' said Vegas. 'Bit grim isn't it?'

'They are from a great tribe,' said Scratch. 'They're called Skinners because they skin their victims alive as they eat them, piece by piece.'

'Well that's charming,' said Vegas, sharing a disgusted look with his two brothers.

'Quiet please, everyone,' said Scratch, addressing the room. 'Now that we're all here, let's get down to business. You have all been invited here today because I'm offering huge sums of money for the apprehension, or in some cases, murder of, four individuals with whom I've had a disagreement. If you turn around and look at the television screen on the wall you will see the individuals to whom I am referring.'

All of the bounty hunters at the bar twisted around on their stools to get a look at the television. On the screen were the faces of two men. One was a dead ringer for an early nineteen-seventies Elvis Presley, the other was a long haired, gruff looking, thirty-something, Hell's Angel. Vegas knew them both.

'That's Elvis and Rodeo Rex,' he said.

'Correct,' said Scratch. 'I'm offering five million dollars for each of them.'

Stunky, the axeman, raised his hand. 'Dead or alive?' he asked.

'Dead,' said Scratch. 'These two men both broke contracts with me. And their punishment is death and an eternity in Hell.'

'Nice,' said Vegas. 'Those two assholes are way past their prime. We can take them easy.'

'Actually, I'd prefer if you Bastard brothers focussed on the next target,' said Scratch. 'She's much more your kind of bounty.' He clicked his fingers and the picture on the screen switched to a video set in a bar.

'Who the fuck is that?' Renwar asked on behalf of everyone.

'That is Jasmine,' said Scratch. 'The FBI will pay a million dollars for her capture. I will add another two million to the prize fund, so a million apiece for the three of you.'

'Why do you want us to get *her?*' asked Vegas.

'Just watch.'

The bounty hunters sat in silence and watched an incident on the television that had become an internet sensation. It was one of the most viewed videos of all time on all the popular porn sites. In the clip, Jasmine was naked and performing somersaults, one of which saw her spring over a bar top and land behind a bartender who she then attacked. The attack involved her pulling his pants down and smashing his cock and balls with a club while a fat Mexican fellow held him down. Every now and then she would stop bashing the guy's genitals and massage them instead, getting him aroused before smashing him again with the club. The film ended with the fat Mexican guy pouring poison into the bartender's asshole. Scratch paused the footage.

'Jasmine is wanted for assassinating Pope John Paul George,' he said, checking to see if all three of the Bastards were paying attention. 'I don't have a remit to have her executed, so all I ask is that you capture her and hand her over to the FBI. On the other hand, if you were feeling particularly brave you could use her as bait to catch the others, but I seriously don't recommend that.'

'We'll get her,' said Vegas. 'That'll be fun.'

'And finally,' said Scratch. 'The last target is this man.' He clicked his fingers again and a picture of a hooded man appeared on screen. His face was partly concealed by the shadow of his dark cowl, but he had a chiselled jaw and three-day-old-stubble. Age, undetermined but somewhere in his mid-to-late thirties.

Someone muttered the name out loud, *'The Bourbon Kid.'*

'Correct,' said Scratch. 'Now, I don't want anyone going after this guy until the others are either dead or captured. He will be the hardest to catch. And in all honesty, I'm not sure any of you are up to it. I have other plans for him, but if any of you are feeling brave, he's worth ten million. But know this, going after him is suicidal. The man lives in the shadows. You never see him coming.'

From his table by the window, Snake Hawk called out to Scratch. 'What does that mean? He lives in the shadows?'

'It means,' said Scratch looking around at each person in the room. 'If you decide to go after him, check every dark corner of every house, every alleyway, every room you enter. He'll know you're coming, and he'll be there waiting for you, in the shadows.'

Snake Hawk's son, Albatross stood up and spat on the floor. 'We are hunters,' he snarled. 'We hunt in sunlight, we hunt in darkness. No man escapes us.'

His father tapped him on the arm and he returned to his seat, anger etched into his face.

'Well, that's very impressive,' said Scratch. 'And I believe it's true, but I just want you all,' he raised his voice to address the room again, 'to remember what I said, the Bourbon Kid lives in the shadows, in the darkness, and he has no mercy. Always, no matter where you are, watch your back, and each other's. Those of you who heed my words, may soon find yourselves a few million dollars better off. Good luck to you all.'

Seven

Sanchez was busy tucking into his breakfast at a table in the drinking area of the Tapioca when Jasmine came downstairs. She had a blue bath towel wrapped around her. Her long dark hair was still damp from having recently showered, and there were droplets of water running down the smooth brown skin on her arms. As she walked around the bar and approached Sanchez's table, he noticed that the towel she had wrapped around herself was nowhere near big enough. It covered her body from her boobs down to just below her belly button.

'Morning Sanchez,' she said, as she approached his table.

Sanchez was in the process of eating Flake's famous thirteen-item breakfast, but at the sight of Jasmine approaching in her pointless towel, he missed his mouth and hit himself in the face with a forkful of sausage.

'Morning,' he garbled, making a second attempt to aim the sausage at his mouth.

'Ooh, can I have a nibble of your sausage?' Jasmine asked. 'I'm starving and that looks great. Flake's such a good cook isn't she?' She snatched the fork right out of Sanchez's hand and sucked the sausage off the end of it. 'Mmmm, that's great,' she said, offering the fork back.

Sanchez snatched it away from her, seething at the loss of a chunk of meat, but also wrestling with the spectre of Jasmine sucking on his sausage while half-naked. 'Levian was here earlier looking for you lot,' he said, punctuating his statement by spearing another piece of sausage.

Jasmine walked over to the bar and leaned over it to pour herself a drink from one of the soda guns. 'Did he say what he wanted?' she asked.

'I can't remember.'

Flake walked out of the kitchen and into the serving area behind the bar. She was dressed as a waitress. Every morning she wore the same black dress with a white apron, purely for Sanchez's benefit. It reminded him of the days when she was a waitress at the Olé Au Lait café, and he'd spied on her from behind his newspaper while she made his breakfast.

'How's your breakfast, Sanchez?' she asked him.

'It's brilliant,' he replied, keeping his eyes on the food. 'You're the best, Flake.'

Flake soon worked out why he wasn't looking up from his plate. 'That's a small towel, isn't it?' she said, peering over the bar at Jasmine.

'It was the only one available,' Jasmine replied. 'Rex and Elvis took the bigger towels.'

'I bet they did. Where are they anyway?'

In answer to Flake's question, the thundering of footsteps on the stairs behind her indicated the arrival of the two men. Elvis appeared first, dressed in a slim red suit, his hair immaculately greased back into a quiff. He bounced off the bottom step and grabbed the soda gun Jasmine was using. He finished pouring her drink for her and replaced the soda gun in its holder. Jasmine leaned further over the bar top to share a kiss with him.

After an unnecessarily passionate bit of PDA, Elvis looked up. 'How's everyone?' he asked. 'All good?'

'Morning,' Sanchez called back, without looking up.

Rex rocked down into the bar behind Elvis. His brown hair was damp and hanging down by his shoulders. He was wearing black leather pants and a matching sleeveless vest. His huge biceps glistened with droplets of water from his early morning shower.

'Mornin' all,' he said, cheerfully. 'Too late for breakfast?'

'Not if you make it yourself,' said Flake. 'And Rex, in future, please let Jasmine have a bigger towel.'

'She was last out of the shower,' Rex replied. 'It's her own fault.'

Sanchez spat some egg out onto his plate. 'Did you all shower together?' he spluttered.

'Damn right we did,' said Elvis. 'From now on, no one uses a bathroom on their own. If you need to go shower, pee or poop you gotta go with someone else.'

'What the fuck are you talking about?' Flake asked, incredulous.

'We talked about it last night,' said Rex. 'JD killed Dracula and told him to warn Scratch that we're coming after him next. And you know what Scratch is like. He'll try to strike first. And he's got that portal that can take him into any bathroom in the world. That means no visiting the toilets on your own, unless you wanna get whacked.'

Sanchez felt his butt cheeks tense up. No using the bathroom without someone else present? What madness was this?

'Don't worry, Sanchez,' said Flake. 'I'll go to the toilet with you.'

Butt cheeks unclenched. Flake, what a saviour. Sanchez breathed a sigh of relief and carried on eating.

Jasmine walked over to Sanchez's table and sat down next to him, plonking a glass of lime and soda down on the table. She picked a piece of bacon from his plate and began nibbling on it.

'Sanchez says Levian was looking for us,' she called over to the others.

Elvis lifted up the bar flap and walked through it with a bottle of beer in his hand. 'What did the old fart want?' he asked, pulling up a chair and sitting down opposite Sanchez.

'I came with a warning,' Levian replied, appearing next to the bar. Once again, the angel had come out of nowhere, and once again, Sanchez—startled and dealing with too many interruptions during his breakfast already, poked himself in the face with a sausage that was intended for his mouth.

Elvis swivelled around on his chair to face Levian. The angel did not look amused.

'Wassup, Levian?' Elvis said, pretending like he hadn't just called the angel an "old fart".

Levian approached the table and stopped next to Elvis, looking down at him with an air of superiority. 'You should have spoken with me before you went on a killing spree at the Cherry Poppins,' he said.

'Those people got what they deserved,' Elvis replied.

'And if Scratch has his way, so will you,' said Levian. 'You do realise he has the Eye of the Moon in his possession, don't you? From what I've heard he's inserted it into his body so that no one can take it from him.'

'Up the anus?' Sanchez cracked, crunching into a slice of brown toast.

'I don't know,' Levian replied. 'But if Scratch knows how to use the Eye, and I suspect he does, then he'll be able to fire bolts of electricity and lightning from his hands. He'll be able to bring statues to life to carry out his bidding, and he can raise the dead, which means he can create a zombie army, if he feels like it.'

'The Eye is blue though,' said Elvis, interrupting what was looking like a long rant. 'And blue's not really Scratch's colour.'

'In the Devil's hands, the Eye turns red, did you not know that?'

'No, I didn't. I also don't care.'

'Fine,' said Levian, looking around at the others. 'I'm just warning you all. And you should also know, God is not pleased about what you did at the Cherry Poppins.'

'He's not?' said Jasmine, reaching for one of Sanchez's hash browns. He slapped her hand away in the nick of time and shifted the plate a little further away from her.

'You killed a whole bunch of innocent people last night,' Levian went on. 'So, no, God is not pleased.'

'What innocent people?' said Rex, walking through the bar flap into the drinking area. 'We killed a fucking army of devil worshippers!'

'Is that what the Bourbon Kid told you?' Levian asked. 'Because if he did, it was bullshit. Half of those people you murdered last night at the brothel were ordinary civilians, customers of the place.'

'They weren't devil worshippers?' Elvis asked, grabbing one of Sanchez's sausages and dunking it in a pool of ketchup on the side of the plate before chewing on the end of it. He ignored Sanchez's strangled cry.

'No,' Levian replied. 'Do I have to say everything twice?'

'Pardon?' said Sanchez, leaning over his breakfast in an effort to keep the others away from it.

Levian ignored him and chose to engage with Rex who was standing near him. 'You realise Scratch will already be plotting how he's going to have you all killed, don't you?'

'Yep,' said Rex. 'We've just been discussing it.'

'Me and Sanchez will be okay, won't we?' Flake inquired. 'We haven't done anything.'

Levian sighed. 'I don't know. Just don't use the bathroom on your own in case Scratch uses his portal to pay you a visit. Always go in groups and take some weapons with you.'

'We've already talked about this,' said Elvis.

'Exactly,' said Jasmine. 'We're being careful. Me and Elvis even let Rex join us in the shower this morning.'

Levian closed his eyes and rubbed his forehead in exasperation. 'That's not how to do it,' he said. 'One of you needs to stand guard. You can't all be in the shower together at the same time. Scratch could walk in and shoot you all dead.'

'Rubbish,' said Jasmine. 'Rex can catch bullets with his magnetic metal hand,' she winced and then added, 'when he's not washing himself with it.'

'Okay, fine, listen,' said Levian, taking on a more pragmatic tone. 'Just remember, this isn't the movies. You might be the good guys, but in real life the good guys don't always win.'

'The good guys don't always win in the movies either,' Elvis reminded him.

'Yes, they do,' said Levian. 'Name me one movie where evil triumphs over good.'

After a short pause where everyone tried to remember a movie they'd seen where the villains were victorious, Jasmine raised her hand. 'I know,' she said, brimming with excitement. '*Coming To America.*'

The answer was greeted with strange looks from everyone apart from Sanchez, who nodded in agreement.

Levian's shoulders slumped, and he groaned, '*Coming To America?* What do you mean, *Coming To America?* At the end of that film, Eddie Murphy gets the girl. How on earth is that the bad guy winning?'

Elvis reached over and rubbed Jasmine's back. 'Honey, are you sure you mean Coming To America?'

'Definitely,' she replied with great confidence. 'The bad guy in that film was Darryl, the Soul Glo guy, right?'

Everyone nodded or grunted in agreement.

'Well,' Jasmine continued. 'At the end of the film, Eddie Murphy ends up with Lisa the uptight, miserable older sister. But Darryl ends up with Patrice the younger sister, who's way more fun than Lisa.'

'Better looking too,' Elvis added. 'Jasmine's right. Patrice was a fuckin' babe. I'd pick her over Lisa any day.'

'Exactly,' said Jasmine, giving Elvis a peck on the cheek. 'When I was a kid I used to fantasise about being Patrice.'

Levian's irritation was visible for all to see. 'Why would you want to be Patrice?' he asked. 'She was vain and stupid!'

Sanchez put his knife and fork down and tried to respond but he had a mouthful of food that needed chewing first. He needn't have concerned himself because Jasmine had her answer all worked out.

'I still remember the first time I saw that movie,' she said, staring up at the ceiling. 'I was twelve years old. And there was a scene halfway through the movie where Patrice gave Eddie Murphy a handjob at a basketball game. Right then I knew I wanted to be like Patrice when I grew up!'

'Twelve?' said Rex, perplexed. 'And you wanted to give Eddie Murphy a handjob?'

'Oh yeah. I was in love with Eddie Murphy right up until he got fat.'

'Eddie Murphy never got fat!' said Sanchez.

'Yeah he did,' Jasmine replied. 'Haven't you ever seen that film where he was a professor? He put on loads of weight. And I know he lost it again afterwards, but he must have loads of excess skin hanging around under his shirt. That put me right off him.'

'You mean *The Nutty Professor?*' said Flake. 'He was wearing a fat suit!'

'Well d'uh,' said Jasmine. 'Of course he was wearing a fat suit. He was overweight!'

'Have you ever actually watched The Nutty Professor?' Sanchez asked.

Jasmine shrugged. 'No, but I've seen clips of it.'

Levian's patience snapped. 'Would you idiots shut up? The bad guy does not win in Coming To America. Patrice was stupid! Lisa was the much better catch, and she married the prince at the end. And Eddie Murphy was not fat. Why the fuck are we even arguing about this?'

Jasmine replied. 'You said the bad guys never win in the movies.'

'She's right,' said Sanchez. 'You did say that. Although I can't remember why.'

'I said it because I was trying to make the point,' Levian said, his face darkening with rage, 'that in *real life* things don't turn out like they do in the movies. Bad guys like Scratch win all the time in the real world.'

Rex nodded. 'I agree. Patrice was *way hotter* than Lisa. I'm with Jasmine on this one.'

'FOR FUCKSSAKE!' Levian yelled. 'Scratch told me you lot were annoying, but I never understood what he meant. You're driving me crazy. I'm trying to tell you your lives are in great danger, and you're fucking rambling on about Coming To America!' He glared at Jasmine. 'And would you put some clothes on! You're wearing a fucking tea-towel for God's sake!'

Rex was closest to Levian. He raised a defensive hand and tried to calm the angel down. 'Hey, relax. Just because Jasmine was right, doesn't mean you have to get in a mood. And I think you may have used the Lord's name in vain just then.'

'I'm allowed to. I'm an angel.' A hush descended over the room. Levian seemed to appreciate that he was losing his cool. 'Where is the Bourbon Kid?' he asked, changing the subject.

'He's over there,' said Sanchez, pointing his fork over at a darkened corner of the drinking area. Sure enough, the Bourbon Kid was sitting at a table in a shadowy corner of the room, smoking a cigarette and drinking a glass of bourbon. He was wearing a long black coat with the hood pulled up over his head. It looked like he hadn't shaved in a week.

'When the fuck did you get here?' Rex asked him.

The Kid replied in a gravelly voice. 'I've been here a while.'

Levian turned to face the Kid. 'You murdered a lot of innocent people last night. God is not pleased.'

'I don't care.'

Jasmine argued on the Bourbon Kid's behalf. 'Okay, so we murdered a bunch of innocent people. It happens sometimes. Don't stress about it, you'll give yourself an ulcer.'

'You stupid cow,' Levian growled. 'Don't you realise you can't work for God if you're going around killing innocent people!'

'Woah, wait a sec,' said Elvis, getting up from his chair and squaring up to Levian. 'You know, for an angel, you've got a real fuckin' attitude.'

Levian refused to back down. He looked mighty pissed. 'You idiots have been reporting into me for less than a week and you've already killed about fifty innocent people. Do you realise how bad that makes me look?'

'Is it quite bad?' Jasmine asked.

'IT'S VERY BAD!' Levian raged.

'You know,' said Elvis. 'You're starting to sound just like Scratch. He was always shouting at us and calling us idiots.'

'AND NOW I KNOW WHY!'

Levian stormed over to the Bourbon Kid's table. 'You're out!' he snapped. 'From now on, you're on your own. You're not part of this team. As far as I'm concerned, you can go back to work for the Devil, who incidentally wants you dead, and from what I hear is planning on sending every bounty hunter, vampire, werewolf, zombie, mummy, ghoul and freakshow in the world after you. You've got a bounty on your head so big, even blind people will be looking for you.'

The Bourbon Kid blew a smoke ring at Levian, but did not reply. Elvis did that for him, yelling across the bar at the angry angel.

'Hey, Levian.'

'What?' Levian replied, still eyeballing the Bourbon Kid.

'Why don't you fuck off?'

The angel spun around and switched his furious glare onto Elvis. 'Really?' he said. 'That's how you wanna play this? You're gonna reject God,' he pointed at the Kid, 'for *this* piece of shit?'

'Hey, hold on there, cowboy,' said Jasmine standing up. 'You can't come in here and tell us who is in the Dead Hunters and who's not. You either get on board with how we work, or, like Elvis said, you can fuck off.'

Levian looked around the room. Aside from Rex who seemed embarrassed by the whole situation, everyone else was giving him the "fuck off" eyes. The room was silent with the exception of Sanchez chomping away on his breakfast.

'Are you saying you don't want my protection?' Levian asked, eventually.

'It's not that we don't *want* it,' Elvis replied. 'It's that we don't *need* it, plus I think I speak for us all here when I say, we all think you're a bit of a cunt.'

'Fine,' said Levian, pursing his lips. 'If that's how you want to play it, that's up to you. But know this, the Devil is coming for all of you, and now you're on your own. I could have protected you. God would have taken care of you.'

'Fuck the Lord,' said the Bourbon Kid. 'You can tell him I said that.'

'I will,' said Levian. 'Enjoy your rest of your short life. That goes for all of you.'

Flake called out from behind the bar. 'Wait! Levian, I've got something for you.' She reached under the bar and then came up with nothing but her middle finger raised.

'Classy,' said Levian, disgusted.

A moment later the angel vanished into thin air.

'That's just great,' said Rex. 'Now we're fucked. Scratch is gonna send a whole army of assassins our way, and we've got no one on our side. It's just us.'

'We can deal with a few assassins, can't we?' said Flake.

Rex screwed up his face. 'Do you know how to spot a good assassin?' he asked her.

'Someone with a gun? Or a knife?' Flake suggested.

'The best assassins don't look like assassins,' Rex declared, addressing the whole room. 'That's why they're so good at what they do. No one sees them as a threat. That's how they get you.'

Eight

Arizona's stomach dropped. The truck had stopped again. That could only mean one thing.

Being kidnapped was nothing like she'd expected, and nothing like it was on television shows where the hostage ends up falling in love with her captor. She was tied up in total darkness. Her arms were bound together with rope that was attached to a pulley system above her head. She was allowed to sit on the floor when she was alone, but every once in a while the truck stopped and her kidnapper joined her in the back. Each time he paid her a visit she was hauled up on the pulley into a standing position with her hands above her head. What followed was always the same, her bikini was removed and she was sexually assaulted. Today was the third day of it.

The back doors opened and daylight flooded into the cramped space. The kidnapper climbed into the trailer and slammed the doors behind him, plunging everything back into darkness. The truck started moving again, and after a few seconds the light bulb hanging from the ceiling came on, causing her to wince. And there he was, Mister Pervert.

'How are you this morning?' he asked her as he removed her bikini top.

He'd gotten rid of her cut-offs on the first day, leaving her with just the pink bikini. The guy had an insatiable lust for her. He was visiting her six times a day to get his kicks. After dropping the bikini top onto the floor he began unbuttoning his pants. It was now or never for Arizona.

'I need to go to the bathroom,' she blurted out.

The kidnapper's face lit up at the news she needed the toilet. It made her skin crawl. Every time she'd had to pee so far, the freak had further humiliated her by forcing her to pee in his mouth.

'I was hoping you'd say that,' he said, standing in front of her, fastening his pants.

'I need to go number two.'

Her plan was for him to untie her. That was her only chance of escape.

'You need a shit, huh?' he said, grinning. 'It's about time.'

He peeled off her bikini bottoms, leaving her fully naked.

'Can you take me to a bathroom somewhere?' Arizona asked.

'I can do better than that. I'll bring the bathroom to you.'

Arizona's heart sank. Not only did she have visions of him lying on the floor beneath her, forcing her to squat over him, this seriously curtailed her escape plan. She wasn't ready to give up though. Surely he'd have to untie her for this?

He pulled a cell phone from a pocket on his cargo pants and made a call. Arizona knew he wasn't alone because someone else had to drive the truck while he was in the back with her.

'Yo,' he said into his phone. 'She's ready to poop.'

He ended the call without another word. Arizona closed her eyes. She had no idea what was about to happen, only that it would probably be awful, but also, it just might offer her a chance to escape.

The truck pulled over and stopped. The driver killed the engine.

'Can I go outside to use the bathroom?' Arizona asked.

'No.'

Arizona inwardly groaned. She had to find a way to make him untie her. The footsteps outside were getting louder. The back doors opened again and daylight flooded in once more. There were two men outside. One of them was carrying a bucket. They climbed into the trailer and one of them closed the doors.

All hope of escape vanished when the doors closed. The horror of her situation sank in. She hadn't been sexually assaulted by just one man these last few days. There were three of them. And they were identical in every way.

'Oh, my God, you've cloned yourself!' she said, staring at the three men.

The one who had undressed her shook his head. 'No, sweetheart. We're brothers. Identical triplets.'

The brother with the bucket approached her and placed it down next to the wall behind her. The three men lined up in a row in front of her, the same creepy look on each of their faces. The one who had undressed her tugged on the rope on the pulley, lowering her arms to her sides.

'Go on then,' he said.

Arizona looked down at the bucket behind her. It was filthy. It looked like it had been used as a toilet many times before, possibly by other girls they had kidnapped. There were stains all around the inside.

'You want me to go in that?' she asked, her eyes welling up, not just at the indignity of the bucket and the watching audience, but also at the knowledge that her hopes of escaping were gone.

'Come on, babe, we ain't got all day,' said one of the men.

'Can I have some privacy?'

'No fuckin' way. We've been waiting three days for this.'

The brother in the middle pulled out a cell phone and started filming her.

Arizona had tried appealing for mercy many times to what she thought was one man. Now that the three of them were together, she hoped for a different outcome. 'You know my dad will pay loads of money for my release,' she said. 'You could let me go. I won't say anything to anyone.'

'You promise?' one of the brothers replied, sarcastically.

'Yes.'

'What do you think we are, stupid?'

'My dad is the President.'

'So you keep saying.'

'He'll have people looking for me. If you let me go now, I can get him to call off the search.'

The brothers looked at each other and smirked. The one who did most of the talking, leaned in close.

'Look, missy. We know you're not the President's daughter. So, how about you stop peddling that lie, and start shitting into that bucket. We stopped the truck specially for this, so don't let us down.'

'Will you let me go after this?'

'Sure. We've got one more stop to make. We're going to a place called Santa Mondega to pick up another girl. Once we've got her, we won't need you anymore.'

A tear rolled down Arizona's cheek. 'Please don't kill me. I won't tell anyone what's happened here.'

The three shaven-headed thugs all laughed in unison.

'Seriously,' said Arizona. 'If you kill me, my dad will send the worst people in the world after you.'

The man with the phone ran his hand down her neck, stroking her soft skin all the way down to her breast. 'Sugar,' he said. 'We *are* the worst people in the world. We're the Bastard brothers, and we don't fear anyone.'

Nine

Sanchez checked his reflection in his bedroom mirror. In less than an hour he was due to appear at City Hall to take up his position as Mayor of Santa Mondega. He didn't own any suits, or smart clothes, so he'd picked out his trusty old red Hawaiian shirt and a pair of black pants that didn't have too many stains on them. He unbuttoned his top button and tried to look intimidating. It worked. He looked almost exactly like Tom Selleck in *Magnum P.I.* except he was a foot shorter and a stone heavier.

'Flake!' he called out. 'What do you think of this?'

Flake poked her head around the door. 'Ooh yeah, you look good. Very sexy.'

'Do you think it's appropriate though? You know, for the mayor?'

Flake stepped inside the bedroom. She was wearing her old blue cop uniform that Sanchez loved so much. Her days and nights seemed to revolve around wearing old outfits to keep Sanchez happy.

'You're the mayor,' she said, massaging his shoulders. 'You can dress however you like. You're the most important man in town.'

'That's true. How come you decided to wear the cop uniform today?'

'I'm the First Lady. I figure I can wear what I like too. Plus, I've got handcuffs. I always wanted to do it in the mayor's office.'

'Do what?'

'What do you think?' she said, squeezing his ample butt.

'Oh, right, yeah. Who's gonna wear the handcuffs?'

'That's up to you. You are the mayor, after all.'

A car horn beeped down below in the street. Flake peered through the blinds on the window to see who was responsible. There was a man sitting in a blue jeep on the opposite side of the road. He was wearing a red balaclava that revealed only his eyes and mouth. Flake was about to point him out to Sanchez, but then right below her she saw the car she was looking for. 'Holy shit!' she gasped. 'Your Limo is here. Take a look!'

Sanchez joined her at the window. 'That's not a Limo. That's a jeep!' he moaned.

'Squeeze your gut closer to the window,' said Flake. 'The Limo is right below us.'

Sanchez sucked his gut in and pressed his face up against the window. Flake was right. There was an enormous white Limousine parked right outside the front of the Tapioca. This was a great day indeed. Finally, the city of Santa Mondega was treating Sanchez with the respect he'd always deserved.

'Awesome,' he said. 'I hope they've got all the snacks I ordered.'

'You're so lucky,' said Flake. 'I wish I was going in the Limo.'

'I thought you were?'

'Well, I was,' said Flake. 'But while you were in the toilet just now, a woman called Melinda phoned. She's the Chief of Staff at City Hall. She told me I had to drive myself there because there's a special parking spot reserved for the First Lady in the underground parking lot. You get the Limo, I get the best parking spot.'

'You should take my ambulance,' said Sanchez. 'You can put the siren on and clear the roads, then me and my entourage can follow you across town.'

'Deal.'

Flake quickly tied Sanchez's shoelaces for him and sprayed some deodorant on him, then the two of them hurried downstairs to the bar area.

Elvis and Jasmine were sitting at the bar playing some kind of drinking game. Jasmine had one hand inside Elvis's pants and he had a hand inside her purple catsuit, which was unzipped down to her midriff.

'What are you two doing?' Flake asked.

'We're playing the cold hand game,' said Jasmine.

'Who's winning?'

'I am,' said Elvis.

'I'm pretty sure you're not,' said Jasmine.

'Hey, I've told you before,' said Flake. 'No jizzing in the bar!'

While Flake berated them, Sanchez noticed there was a new customer in the bar. Sally Diamond, a police detective, was sitting at a table in the corner with Rex. Sally had befriended Rex and Elvis recently when they were investigating a serial killer who turned out to be the previous Mayor, Tim Shepherd. Rex had taken quite a shine to Sally. She was his type for sure, a feisty redhead who liked a drink. She was wearing a pair of ripped black jeans, a white blouse and a tight-fitting yellow leather jacket. And she had big brown eyes. Rex was a sucker for those. Sanchez noticed that she had an empty wine glass in front of her.

'Hi, Sally,' he said. 'Can I get you another drink?'

'Red wine, please.'

Sanchez ducked down below the bar, cursing to himself. Red wine was one of the drinks that couldn't be confused with piss, so he had no choice but to actually pour her a glass of what she'd asked for. While he looked for the cheapest, nastiest bottle of red wine, Flake headed round to the drinking area with a box of tissues for Elvis.

Sally waved her down like she was hailing a cab. 'Hey, Flake!' she called out. 'What's with the cop uniform?'

'I used to be on the force,' Flake replied. 'Kicked some ass in my time. Thought I'd wear it to City Hall. Let people know I mean business.'

'It suits you. You should rejoin the force. We could use someone like you.'

Flake leaned back over the bar to check Sanchez wasn't peeing into Sally's wine. 'I'm First Lady now,' she called back. 'As well as personal chef to the mayor.' After seeing that Sanchez was in fact pouring a glass of red wine, she turned back to face Sally. 'I just don't have time to beat the streets anymore.'

'First Lady, huh?' said Sally. 'Good luck with that. It's a hard job.'

'I WIN!' Jasmine yelled.

Sanchez finished pouring the glass of red wine and slid it across the bar to Flake. She walked it over to Sally and placed it down on the table.

'Here you go,' she said.

'Thanks,' said Sally. She picked up the glass and took a big swig. 'Mmm, this is good stuff.'

Rex laughed. 'You don't have to be polite, we all know the wine tastes like shit in here.'

Sally blushed. 'Don't be so rude. I like this stuff.'

Flake rearranged some nearby chairs. 'You know, you two can come with us to City Hall if you like?' she offered.

'We'll be okay here, thanks,' said Rex. 'Elvis is coming though.'

'Yes, I know.'

'I'm coming too,' said Jasmine. 'I'm not missing a chance to go for a ride in a Limo. They're so classy.'

Elvis hopped off his stool. 'I'm just gonna go take a leak in the parking lot.' He planted a kiss on Jasmine's cheek. 'I'll catch up with you in a minute. Don't let the Limo go without me.'

'I'll come with you,' said Flake.

Elvis looked surprised. 'You wanna watch me pee?'

Flake rolled her eyes. 'No, my ambulance is parked out there, and I'm driving it to City Hall.'

'Yeah, right.'

Elvis made a hasty exit through the kitchen with Flake hot on his tail to make sure he didn't pee up against the side of her ambulance.

A minute later, Sanchez left the Tapioca and headed out onto the sidewalk where his Limo was waiting. A young Latino man in a black suit and tie was leaning against the vehicle. At the sight of Sanchez, he grabbed a peaked black cap off the roof of the Limo. He put the cap on and straightened up.

'Hello Mister Mayor,' he said, opening the back door of the Limo. 'My name is Manuel and I am your driver today and every day for as long as you run the city.'

'Brilliant. Did you get all my snacks?'

'Everything you requested is inside, sir.'

Jasmine walked out of the Tapioca and waltzed straight past Sanchez and Manuel. She climbed into the back of the Limo and made herself comfortable.

'Wow!' she said. 'There's barbecue ribs in here!'

Sanchez was about to dive into the Limo to save his snacks, but he felt a hand on his shoulder. He looked around and saw the hand belonged to Elvis.

'Hey, Sanchez,' Elvis said, pointing across the road. 'Do you know that guy?'

On the other side of the street was a stocky man with a red balaclava pulled over his head. He was wearing a pair of loose-fitting, grey sweatpants and a black, short-sleeved shirt that showed off a pair of bulky, white arms. It looked like he was ready to rob a bank, or mug an old lady. He was standing by a blue jeep, staring intensely at the Limo through the eyeholes on his balaclava.

'He's probably a fan,' said Sanchez, waving to the man. 'Now that I'm the mayor, it's only natural that people will see me as some kind of celebrity.'

Their view of the man was blocked off when Flake pulled up alongside the Limo in her ambulance. There was a big, wet piss stain all down the side of it. Flake wound down the window and shouted across to Sanchez and Elvis.

'Hurry up! We haven't got all day!'

She switched on the ambulance siren to reiterate her point. Sanchez took the hint and ducked into the Limo where he got straight into an argument with Jasmine about who was allowed to eat the snacks.

Elvis introduced himself to Manuel. 'Hey, man, I'm Elvis. Do us a favour and follow the ambulance. She's leading the way.'

Manuel bowed his head. 'Yes, sir.'

Elvis joined the others in the back of the Limo. Manuel closed the door behind him and hopped into the front. A minute later they were on the road, following the ambulance to City Hall.

On the other side of the street the man in the balaclava jumped into his jeep and followed the Limo.

Ten

The nightmare. The curse of the recurring nightmare. Vincent Papshmir's dreams played tricks on him. Every dream started differently. Whether it was a dream where he was playing in a field with his daughter, or one of those stupid dreams where he was giving a sermon with no pants on, every dream was hijacked and turned into a chase. Hijacked by the appearance of the Devil. At some point in every dream, Papshmir would look around and see Scratch behind him. Then he would run, and run, and run. The running went on forever, until he invariably awoke, covered in sweat and kicking the duvet around. For the last week it had happened every night. On one night it even happened twice. It had reached a point where Papshmir dreaded falling asleep. Unfortunately for him, he was over a hundred years old, so falling asleep was one of the things he did most.

On this particular morning he had risen at six a.m. and gone through his normal routine. Breakfast, newspaper, shower, get dressed. It was a Wednesday so he picked out his Wednesday suit, a black two-piece with red lining and a clerical collar. He checked his appearance in his bedroom mirror. Old man, old face. Old *saggy* face. Still had hair though. A decent head of it. Grey as a rat.

He headed out into the church hall and carried on the day's chores. He lit some candles around the hall, filled the font with water, blessed it to make it holy, filled a pump-action water-gun with water from the font, checked between the rows of pews for piss and vomit, and set everything out ready for the day ahead.

He hoped to spend the day talking to the residents of Santa Mondega, reassuring them about their faith and any other shitty life problems they had. At 10.30 a.m. he opened the arched wooden doors at the front of the church and let the light in. It was a good day. No one was waiting outside. He stared up at the sky to assess the day's weather. Cloudy and cool, hopefully no rain.

'Morning Vincent,' said a voice from behind him.

A shiver ran through his whole body. How had someone snuck in behind him already? He turned around slowly, wincing in expectation of someone walloping him with a weapon. What he saw was a man with shaggy dark hair and three-day-old stubble. He was wearing a long black coat with its hood down. Papshmir knew him well. It was the Bourbon Kid.

Unlike most people, the preacher breathed a sigh of relief at the sight of Santa Mondega's most prolific mass-murderer. He greeted him with genuine warmth. 'Good morning, sir,' he said. 'May I ask how you got in here?'

'Do you remember my brother?'

It wasn't the response Papshmir was expecting. Normally people made a little small talk before getting down to business. And as for remembering the Bourbon Kid's brother, yes, of course he remembered him. The poor kid had been dead a long time, murdered by a gang of vampires and werewolves.

'Uh, your brother?' Papshmir muttered, acting as if he was unsure for a moment, before adding, 'Oh, yes... of course, Casper. That's right isn't it? Charming young fellow. I liked him a lot.'

'Yeah, Casper, that's him.'

Papshmir gave a conciliatory nod of the head. 'Dreadful what happened to him. I was very sad to hear about it.'

'Yeah, sure.'

'Would you like anything to drink? We could go to my office if you like? Was there something in particular you wanted to discuss?'

The Bourbon Kid didn't move. 'A long time ago, my brother told me you helped him to make a piece of cloth with my initials on it. I was wondering if you still had it?'

'Err, no I....' Papshmir hesitated, confused by the question. 'I gave it to him, and I assumed he gave it to you.'

'He did.'

'Oh, okay. So, *you* should still have it then?'

'I lost it. Wondered if you had another?'

Papshmir's throat tightened up and he felt himself becoming unduly anxious. 'I wouldn't have thought so,' he said. 'Why don't you take a seat?' He gestured at the rows of pews.

The Bourbon Kid sat down on the edge of a pew and gestured for Papshmir to take a place on a pew on the opposite side of the aisle. The priest walked over to it and sat down, twisting sideways to face his visitor.

'You were good to my brother,' the Bourbon Kid said, his eyes staring deep into Papshmir's. 'I used to think it was strange that you paid him so much attention when he was a kid. You know, I asked him a hundred times if you'd tried to do anything weird with him. But he was adamant you were his best friend. I used to think that was strange. You're a good man, Vincent.'

'Thank you, that's very kind of you.'

'Your mother would be proud.'

Papshmir missed a breath. 'My mother? Umm, yes, I hope she'd be proud, yes,' he mumbled.

'Have you packed your stuff up yet?'

'Excuse me?'

The Kid leaned across the aisle. 'Me showing up here like this,' he said, raising his eyebrows. 'It's your sign to get outta town.'

'What?'

'Do you need me to spell it out for you?'

Papshmir was baffled. The emotion of the moment had stifled his thinking. 'What are you saying?'

'My guess is you've been watching your back your whole life. When you turned around just now, I was there. Who's it gonna be next time?'

Papshmir knew the answer. It was the man in the red suit who had been haunting his dreams. Just thinking about him sent a shiver through his body. He took a breath before giving his answer, as if it was a million-dollar question on a quiz show. 'I guess it could be a big guy in a red suit,' he said. 'A fella, goes by the name of Scratch.'

The Kid sat back. 'That's right. I'm here because I pieced all this stuff together. You're a smart guy, Vincent. If I can work it out, how long do you think it'll be before Scratch does?'

'Not long, I suppose.'

'You need to get as far away from here as possible, and take Janis with you.'

'Janis? You know about her?'

'I know. I figured it out, which is why you gotta assume that Scratch has figured it out too. Or he will do soon.'

Papshmir choked up. His eyes filled with water. 'What should I do?'

'Start packing. Right now,' the Kid replied. 'You need to be gone, *yesterday.*'

'Will you be coming with us?'

The Bourbon Kid stood up. 'No. Say goodbye to Janis for me. And neither you or her must try to contact me. No texts, no calls. If either of you gets a text from me, don't reply to it.'

'Why not?'

'Because it won't be from me. Same goes for texts from Elvis, Rex and all the others. Any message you get, treat it like it's a fake.'

Papshmir rubbed his forehead. This was a lot to take in. 'What are *you* going to do?' he asked.

'Stay here and finish what you and Annabel started. I know the sacrifices you've made. It's time you went and lived your life. And it's time for me to find a way to kill the Devil.'

'That means I might never see you again.'

'Yeah.'

Papshmir leapt to his feet and grabbed the Bourbon Kid, embracing him, squeezing him tight. It was his first ever hug with his father, and it had been a long time coming. He felt the Kid squeeze back for a moment before he pulled away. The two men looked into each other's eyes.

'You did real good,' said the Bourbon Kid. 'Tell Janis,' his voice trailed off and he hesitated for a moment, then added, 'she's cool.'

Papshmir's bottom lip quivered. He'd waited his whole life for this moment, but it hadn't gone anything like he'd expected. He wiped some tears away from his eyes. 'I'll tell her,' he said.

The Kid wished his son good luck and headed out via the front doors. As Papshmir watched him leave, a thought crossed his mind. He called out to his father. 'Wait!'

The Bourbon Kid stopped in the middle of the arched doorway and turned around.

'You never told me how you got in here,' Papshmir said. 'Have I left a window unlocked, or something?'

The Kid smiled. 'You dig tunnels, remember?'

Once again, it wasn't the answer Papshmir was expecting. By the time he figured out what it meant, his father was gone.

Eleven

The Limo ride to City Hall was over far too quickly. Sanchez, Elvis and Jasmine managed to eat almost all of the snacks. All that remained was a handful of chicken nuggets. Sanchez tucked a few into the pockets on his shirt and shoved one last handful of chips into his mouth before joining Elvis on the sidewalk outside City Hall. His new driver, Manuel, assured him that the remaining snacks would be kept warm in readiness for his next trip in the Limo.

Jasmine was the last one to exit the car. She had polished off two glasses of champagne and was already looking a little unsteady on her feet. She stared up at the ancient yellow-bricked building. There were rows of high windows all the way up, many with gargoyles sprouting out of the walls next to them. And there was a lot of bird shit everywhere.

'Wow,' she gasped. 'This place is huge. And Sanchez is now running it?'

'Not just the building,' Sanchez reminded her. 'I run this whole city now.'

'That's crazy,' said Jasmine.

Manuel tapped Sanchez on the shoulder. 'Excuse me, Mister Mayor,' he said. 'This lady coming down the steps is Melinda. She will show you to your office. Good luck, sir.'

The woman coming down the concrete steps at the front of the building was in her early fifties, with poufy brown hair. She was wearing a smart blue suit jacket and a pencil skirt.

Elvis greeted her as she stepped onto the sidewalk. 'Nice to meet you,' he said, taking her hand and kissing it.

'You must be Elvis,' said Melinda, the disdain on her face impossible to conceal. She looked Jasmine up and down. 'And you must be Jasmine.'

'Yes, how did you know that?'

'It's my job to know.'

'What exactly is your job?' Jasmine asked.

'Thank you for asking,' said Melinda. 'I am Melinda Bone, the Chief of Staff here at City Hall. I keep everything in the building running smoothly so that the mayor and First Lady can get on with all the important business. I had an *excellent* relationship with the last mayor.' She pointed at Sanchez and added, 'before you killed him.'

'Yes, well, he was asking for it,' said Sanchez, waving his hand, gesturing for her to lead the way up to the building. 'Take me to my office please, Belinda.'

'It's *Melinda*,' she replied. 'But first of all, before we enter the building, I'm afraid we're going to have to get you a new suit.' She waved her hand up and down at his clothes. 'This just won't do. You'll be making your first public appearance today, so it's vitally important that you create a good impression.'

'I always make a good impression,' said Sanchez, pulling a chicken nugget from his top pocket and taking a bite out of it. 'People just naturally warm to me.'

Melinda disagreed. She clicked her fingers at Jasmine 'You, Jasmine, you have slightly better taste in clothes. Be a love and head to Parker's clothes store. Pick out a suit for the mayor and bring it back here. We'll need it within the hour, so don't dilly-dally.'

'Dilly what?' said Jasmine.

Melinda reached into a small leather pouch on her belt and pulled out a set of car keys. She tossed them to Jasmine who managed to catch them just before they hit her in the face.

'What are these for?' Jasmine asked.

Melinda pointed across the street. 'They are the keys to the silver truck that's parked over there in the No Parking zone,' she said. 'I take it you know how to drive?'

The truck Melinda was pointing at was huge. It looked like a garbage truck, but with a long metal shaft sticking out of the top of it.

'What kind of truck is that?' Elvis asked.

'It's a salt truck,' Melinda replied. 'We bought it some years ago when the city was covered in snow for a week. By the time it arrived here the snow had melted so we've never actually used it.'

'I'll make it my first job as mayor to sell it then,' said Sanchez. 'That'll bring some money into the coffers.'

'We tried that,' said Melinda. 'No one will buy it because unlike normal salt trucks this one has a stupid rotating shaft on the top that sprays salt everywhere. It's totally impractical.'

'Then I'll fire the person who bought it,' said Sanchez.

'We already did that.'

Jasmine looked at the keychain she had been given. There was a laminated paper tag attached to it. Two words were typed onto the tag, "THE BUM".

'The Bum?' said Jasmine, reading it aloud. 'What does that mean?'

'It's the name of the salt truck,' said Melinda.

'Why is it called The Bum?'

'Because it lives on the streets, day and night. All the public vehicles in this town have a name. It makes them easier to keep track of.'

'What's the Limo called?' Sanchez asked.

'It's called the Limo,' Melinda replied, frowning. 'You were just in it.' She turned back to Jasmine. 'Now young lady, remember, I want you to take the salt truck and get the mayor a suit from Parker's. Tell Mister Parker to send the bill to my office.'

Jasmine tugged at Elvis's sleeve. 'You gonna come with me?'

Elvis didn't look keen. He leaned over and whispered in her ear. 'I would, honey, but I wanna have a look at something in the building's archives. I'll tell you about it later.'

'Fine.' Jasmine gave him a kiss on the neck. 'I'll go for a ride in The Bum on my own.'

Sanchez stepped across Jasmine, blocking her from crossing the street. He lowered his voice so that Melinda couldn't hear. 'Get me a suit like the one Arnold Schwarzenegger wore at the beginning of True Lies, you know, the flashy suit he wore when he was doing the tango?'

'I've never even seen that film!' Jasmine complained.

Sanchez was livid. 'How have you not seen True Lies?'

'Because I haven't.'

'Fine, listen. Forget Parker's clothes store. Go to Domino's Party Store instead. It's only a couple of doors away from Parker's. Tell the guy in there what I want. He'll definitely have one.'

Jasmine rolled her eyes. 'Fine! Jeez, why do you have to make everything so difficult?'

'Because I'm the most powerful man in the city.'

Jasmine reached into Sanchez's top pocket and helped herself to one of his chicken nuggets. 'Seeya later,' she said, popping it in her mouth.

She sprinted across the street, causing two taxicabs to crash into each other.

'Right, can we go now, please?' said Melinda.

Elvis and Sanchez followed her up the steps to the main building. They were halfway up when Flake bounded up behind them.

'Hey guys, where's Jasmine going?' she asked.

'She's getting a suit for the mayor,' said Melinda, her impatience clear. 'I'm Melinda, by the way. We spoke on the phone earlier. Did you find your parking spot?'

'Yeah, a nice security man showed me where it was.'

'Excellent. Now, *please* can I show you all into the building?'

Melinda led them to the top of the steps where they had to pass through a set of doors into a secure passageway with metal detectors on either side. The detectors went crazy as Elvis walked through.

'Wait one moment, please,' said Melinda.

A tubby Mexican security guard with a thick black moustache approached Elvis. 'Our detector shows you have a gun and a knife in your possession, sir,' he said. 'I'm afraid you're going to have to give them up. They will be returned to you when you leave.'

'He's with me,' said Sanchez. 'And I'm the mayor.'

'That's all well and good, sir. But at the present time, the law states no one is allowed to bring weapons into City Hall.'

'Can I change that law?' Sanchez asked Melinda.

'You can,' she replied. 'But the law was brought in to stop people from entering the premises with the intention of assassinating the mayor.'

'We should probably keep that law then,' Sanchez agreed. 'Hand over your stuff, Elvis.'

Elvis shook his head and made a noise of disgust, but complied. He opened his tight-fitting red jacket. He had a dark red shirt underneath, with a gold Desert Eagle discreetly holstered under his arm. The security guard relieved him of it and placed it in a cloth bag. When the guard looked up again, Elvis had pulled a large, jagged edged knife on him.

'Don't forget this,' Elvis said with a smile.

He offered the security guard his knife, handle first. The guard took it and placed it in the bag. 'You may now enter the reception hall,' he said, his voice shaking just a little bit. 'Have a nice day.'

The reception hall was impressive. It had marble flooring and a ridiculously high ceiling. It was a busy place too. There were members of the public bustling around and queuing at various desks to complain about all kinds of shit.

'I'm gonna head for the archives,' said Elvis. 'I got some digging around to do.'

'I'm sorry,' said Melinda in a patronising voice. 'But that area is restricted. I'm afraid members of the public aren't allowed down there without a special pass.'

'I'll be okay,' said Elvis. 'I've been there before.'

'Not since I've been in charge of the building,' Melinda replied with a fake smile.

Flake resolved the situation. 'You have my permission, Elvis. I'm First Lady of this shithole town, so unless Sanchez overrules me, you can go anywhere you like in this building.'

Melinda looked like her face was about to explode, so Sanchez stepped in to smooth things over as diplomatically as possible.

'Belinda, Flake's the top bitch in this building. What she says, goes. Got it?'

BEEEEEEEEEEP! BEEEEEEP!

In the streets down below, a bunch of drivers were honking their horns at something. The sound drowned out Melinda trying to remind Sanchez what her name was. Sanchez ignored her and rushed over to a set of windows to see what the commotion was all about. Pretty soon everyone in the reception had joined him to see what was going on.

Down at ground level, the salt truck, known as "The Bum" had pulled out into traffic. It was spraying salt in all directions from the revolving metal shaft on its roof. The salting was accompanied by the cacophony of beeping horns and abusive yelling from members of the public as everyone within a twenty-metre radius got covered in salt.

'Stupid bitch,' Melinda muttered under her breath.

Sanchez enjoyed watching lots of innocent pedestrians and drivers get covered in salt. The angry looks on all their faces was highly amusing. Cars were stopping or swerving to avoid the flying salt. Jasmine was driving down the street seemingly oblivious to the chaos she was causing. At the end of the street she took a left turn, bringing an end to all the fun, but leaving a trail of destruction in her wake. A blue jeep followed her around the corner, seemingly unfazed by all the flying salt.

Twelve

Jasmine had great fun driving around town in the salt truck. It took her twenty minutes to find Domino's Party Store because she took a wrong turn, which led to another wrong turn, and then another. She salted almost half the roads (and people) in the city before she finally parked the salt truck around the corner from Domino's. She headed into the store in a buoyant mood.

Domino's was a colourful store, filled with masks, hats, costumes and crazy gadgets. It was the kind of place Jasmine would have enjoyed working at. She saw a Tarzan outfit on one of the shelves. It looked perfect for Elvis. It was basically just a loin cloth. She held it up and tried to imagine Elvis in it. She came to the conclusion that it would look better on *her* than him. She was contemplating trying it on when the store owner came over to see if she needed any assistance. He was a short, fat, middle-aged man with curly blond hair. It looked like he was wearing one of his own outfits. He had on a light blue vest and a pair of blue shorts that were at least one size too small. He greeted Jasmine with a yellow-toothed smile.

'Hi, I'm Dick. Can I help you with anything, miss?'

'Your name is Dick?'

'Dick Domino, I own this store.'

'Oh, great. Nice to meet you, Dick. You know, I love that Thurman Merman outfit you're wearing. It totally suits you.'

'What?'

'Nothing.'

Dick looked confused. 'Was there something specific you wanted?' he asked.

Jasmine held up the Tarzan loin cloth. 'Do you have this for a lady?'

'We have a Jane outfit, if you like?'

'Jane who?'

'Jane from Tarzan and Jane.'

'Is that the monkey?'

'No, Jane was Tarzan's girlfriend. She wore a short brown skirt and top.'

Jasmine weighed up the idea. 'Are they see-through?'

'Oh, goodness no,' Dick replied. 'They're sturdy enough to preserve your dignity.'

'Dignity?'

'Huh?'

'Never mind. I'm actually here for someone else. I need to get a suit for the mayor. I'm his new secretary.'

Dick looked surprised. 'We have a new mayor already?'

'Yes, Sanchez Garcia, do you know him?'

Dick's face twitched like he was about to have a fit. He spoke through gritted teeth. 'That man once rented a Batman suit from me,' he grumbled, 'and when he returned it there were skid marks in the pants.'

'That sounds like him. Well, this time he wants an Arnold Schwarzenegger suit. From a movie.'

'Which movie?'

Jasmine's mind went blank. 'Shit. What was it? I remember it began with T.'

'The Terminator?'

'No, it wasn't The Terminator, or Terminator 2. It was something shorter than that.'

'Twins?'

Jasmine tried to think back to the moment Sanchez had told her what he wanted. She'd been too excited about the idea of driving in the salt truck, so she hadn't been paying enough attention. 'Hmm, *Twins*,' she said, thinking out loud. 'It might have been. What kind of suit did Arnie wear in Twins?'

'It was a plane beige suit. We have two in stock. They come with a green and white shirt and a pair of sunglasses.'

'That sounds perfect,' said Jasmine. 'Ideal for the mayor, don't you think?'

'If the mayor is Sanchez, then yes. Is he still seeing Flake Munroe?'

'He is. Do you know her? She's the new First Lady.'

Dick spat on his fingers and then ran them through his hair. 'When you see her could you tell her Dick said hello?'

'Hello? Just hello?'

'Yeah.'

'Have you got the hots for Flake?'

Dick's cheeks burned red. 'No,' he said defensively.

'Too bad,' said Jasmine. 'You're just her type.' She looked at the clothes hanging up around her. 'Do you have any skimpy costumes? I'm looking for something that shows a lot of skin.'

'The loin cloth you're holding is probably the skimpiest we have,' said Dick.

'That's too bad,' Jasmine groaned. 'I wanted something more revealing.'

Dick stroked his chin as he tried to think of a skimpy outfit. Eventually a lightbulb went off in his head. 'How about Harry Potter's Invisible cloak?' he suggested. 'I do have one of those. It comes with a pair of round spectacles.'

'Great! Can I see it?'

'Come up to the counter and I'll see if I can find it for you.'

Dick led her up to the counter. While Jasmine waited, he ducked into a store room out back. He returned a short while later with a pair of round spectacles and a transparent plastic coat.

'How's this?' he asked.

Jasmine's jaw dropped. 'Oh my God! That's perfect! My boyfriend will love it if I wear that.'

'Is he the guy across the street?'

'What guy?'

Dick pointed through the shop window at a man on the other side of the street, loitering outside David Blowie's Hair Salon. 'See him, over there. The guy in the balaclava.'

Jasmine walked over to the front of the store and peered through the window. On the other side of the street a short, stocky man in a black shirt, grey sweatpants and a red balaclava was staring at the store. As soon as he saw Jasmine looking at him, he turned away and ambled along the street, glancing back occasionally.

'Shit!' said Jasmine. 'Do you think he was following me?'

'I'm not sure,' said Dick. 'But he was definitely staring at you. Kinda creepy with that balaclava, don't you think?'

'I'm going to have to make a phone call. Can I use the changing room?'

'To make a phone call?'

Jasmine waved her hand up and down her catsuit. 'No pockets,' she said. 'My phone is kind of, you know, tucked away in a private place.'

Dick raised one eyebrow and curled his top lip. He muttered something and pointed at a yellow curtain near the back of the store. Above it was a sign that read, "CHANGING ROOM".

'Thanks,' said Jasmine. She handed Dick the Tarzan loin cloth and headed for the changing room. She pulled the yellow curtain aside and stepped into a small room with mirrors on all sides. She turned around to close the curtain and saw Dick sniffing the loin cloth. She called out to him. 'Hey, Dick, can you keep an eye on that guy for me?'

Dick stopped sniffing Tarzan's underpants and called back to her. 'Yeah, no problem.'

Jasmine pulled the changing room curtain across and unzipped her catsuit. She pulled it down past her knees so she could retrieve her phone from the private place she kept it. Her heart was beating fast. Who was the man in the balaclava? An assassin, a stalker? Nobody? She brought Elvis's number up on her phone and made the call. It went straight to his voicemail.

'Shit.'

Next on her list was Rex. She called the big guy up and he answered straight away.

'What's up, Jas?' he said.

'Rex, I'm at Domino's party store. I was picking out a suit for Sanchez, but there's a guy outside wearing a balaclava. I think he might be following me.'

Rex reacted exactly how she hoped. 'Wait there,' he said. 'I'm on my way. Stay in the store if you can. And don't turn your phone off. That way I can track you if you leave.'

'Got it. Hurry up, please.'

Thirteen

Elvis knew his way around City Hall. He'd been there many times in the past, often to visit the archives. City Hall's basement was an enormous room full of public records. Back in the days when Elvis was a hitman, he'd dug up information on many of his targets and clients in the boxes of information that were readily available down there. To gain access to the records, all that was usually required was a small bribe for the person in charge of the area, then it was free access to everything.

He walked through a set of double doors into a huge hall that looked like a library, only with boxes on the shelves instead of books. The boxes were filled with paperwork, and they were stacked up all the way to the ceiling.

An elderly man in a grey suit was sitting at a reception desk in front of the aisles. He was tapping away on a computer, peering at the screen through a pair of thick black-rimmed spectacles. At the arrival of Elvis, he stopped typing and looked up. His wrinkled face was filled with surprise.

'Elvis?'

'Hey there, Bob. How's it going?'

'I heard you were dead.'

'You heard wrong.'

'I have a file on you in here that says you died some years back. Nailed to a ceiling.'

'I faked it. But that's another story. Are your rates still the same?'

'It's ten bucks these days.'

Elvis pulled a roll of banknotes out of the breast pocket on his jacket. He peeled off a twenty and handed it to Bob. 'I'm looking for some information on a cop.'

'Got a name?'

'Sally Diamond.'

Bob laughed. 'I shoulda known.'

'What's so funny?'

'The last person who came in here wanted exactly the same thing.'

Elvis frowned. 'Information about Sally Diamond?'

'Yeah.'

'Who was it?'

'I didn't ask.'

'Can you describe him?'

'It was a woman. Lucky for you, she's still here.'

'She is?'

'Aisle seven. If you're quick you might get to her before she packs all the files away.'

'Thanks, Bob.'

Elvis cruised over to aisle seven, keen to see who else was looking for information on Sally Diamond, and why? For Elvis, looking up Sally's public records was simply a part of his job. He was doing his bit, checking up on her because she was getting rather friendly with Rex. But there was no understandable reason why someone else would be doing the same thing.

There were twenty aisles of records in the archives, all stretching about eighty metres to the back of the hall. Elvis found aisle seven and poked his head around it. The woman he was looking for was halfway down, dressed all in black and wearing a motorcycle helmet. The visor on the helmet was open but he couldn't see her face. Judging by her physique he guessed she was in her mid-twenties. She was flicking through paperwork in a brown box. Elvis moved stealthily into the aisle, and made his way along it, trying not to be noticed, but also trying to look casual. As he closed in on the woman she looked around. Their eyes locked for a moment. Elvis froze. Neither he or the woman spoke or moved a muscle for several seconds. Eventually Elvis broke the silence.

'Janis?'

'Hey, Elvis. How's it going?'

'What the fuck are you doing here?'

'Same thing as you, I bet.'

'Looking up Sally Diamond?'

Janis nodded. 'Yup. SLAG!'

Elvis puffed out his cheeks. He'd almost forgotten about Janis's awful Tourette's outbursts. 'Why are you looking up Sally D? And where the fuck have you been? I haven't seen you in years. Why are you in Santa Mondega?'

'Jeez, ask many questions, do ya?'

'Okay, one at a time. Why are you looking into Sally Diamond?'

'Like I said before, same as you, probably. Gotta make sure she's on the level. ASS! MOTHERFUCKER! SHIT! CUNT! FUCK! BIG TITTIES! BUTTBOY!' She took a deep breath to compose herself. 'If she's hanging out with Rex, we've got to make sure she's not gonna shop him to Scratch, right?'

Elvis leaned back a little. 'How the fuck do you know about Scratch?'

Janis rolled her eyes. 'What do you think I was doing in the Devil's Graveyard back in the day?'

'You were in the singing contest, weren't you?'

'TWAT! I was, yes. But come on, I can't fucking sing. I was just there to help Jacko win the show, and to try and stop you and Sanchez from getting yourselves killed.'

Elvis was baffled. 'What the fuck are you talking about?'

Janis lowered her voice to a whisper. 'Elvis, can you keep a secret?'

'Sure.'

'Annabel was my aunt. I helped the Bourbon Kid escape from Coldworm Abbey the other day.'

'What? He never mentioned that!'

'That's because it was a secret.' Janis suddenly twitched like she was going to kiss herself on the shoulder. 'SHIT BALLS! EAT MY ASS!' She regained some composure and carried on as if nothing had happened. 'Do you remember the preacher lady with the blue hair at Loomis's funeral?'

'Who's Loomis?'

'Jesus, Elvis. You were at his funeral a week ago! Loomis, the guy who was impaled on a spike! He was supposed to be the Bourbon Kid's son, *remember?*'

'Oh yeah, that.'

'I was the preacher with the blue hair that conducted the funeral.'

Elvis raised his eyebrows. 'The fat chick?'

'It was a fat suit, DUMBASS!' She lowered her voice again. 'I was in disguise so that no one, especially Scratch, would know who I was.'

Elvis scratched his head. 'And just exactly who are you? I'm confused as fuck. And did you know that Melvin Melt was in Loomis's coffin?'

Janis groaned. 'Okay, listen. You can't tell anyone this. Melvin Melt was just an asshole that we used to trick Scratch. You and Rex broke him out of prison, you remember that, right?'

'Yeah.'

'Well, after you broke Melvin out of prison, I took him to Coldworm Abbey and made him take the place of Brother Loomis, the monk that ran the abbey. That night, Scratch had Loomis executed because he thought he was the Bourbon Kid's son, but he'd actually killed Melvin Melt.'

Nothing Janis said made much sense to Elvis. 'You'd better run that by me again,' he said. 'Who was the Bourbon Kid's son?'

'HALFWIT!'

'All right, calm down.'

'*Papshmir* is the Bourbon Kid's son.'

'Vincent Papshmir?'

'Yes.'

'But what's all that got to do with you?'

Janis removed her biker helmet and placed it between two boxes on a nearby shelf. She shook her head from side to side, freeing her long brown hair, ensuring she rid herself of any potential helmet haircut, then admitted the truth to Elvis. 'I am Papshmir's daughter.'

Elvis closed his eyes. 'Fuck.'

'NUMBNUTS!'

'Wait a sec.' Elvis reopened his eyes. 'Does that mean you're the Bourbon Kid's granddaughter?'

'Give the man a prize!'

'Does Scratch know this?'

'No. And neither do you. You can never tell anyone, okay.'

'Okay, fine. Shit.'

Janis held up some paperwork she had pulled from a box. 'As for Sally Diamond,' she said. 'I think she's clean. With the exception of a few drunk and disorderly incidents when she was younger, her record is spotless.'

'What about her family? Anything of interest there?'

Janis put her finger to her lips and whispered, 'Shush.'

'What?'

She whispered again. '*Listen.* I think someone's here!'

'So?'

Janis crouched down, and even though Elvis had no idea why, he did the same. He cocked an ear to try and work out what Janis had just heard. He soon realised she was onto something. Voices were coming from the reception area. A man with a Chinese accent was talking to Bob the archivist.

'Where he go?' the Chinaman asked.

'Aisle seven,' Bob replied. 'Hey what are you doing?'

A loud crack followed.

Janis clutched Elvis's arm. 'Bob just had his neck broken,' she whispered.

Elvis grabbed her bike helmet from the shelf and handed it to her. 'This could be dangerous. You should go. Get outta here, and *be quiet*. Try not to yell anything.'

Fourteen

Jasmine zipped up her catsuit and left the changing room. Dick was behind the counter packing a suit into a big brown bag.

'Is the creepy guy still out there?' Jasmine asked him.

'He's gone. I think I scared him off,' said Dick. He placed two bags on the counter for her. 'Here you go. The mayor's suit is in the bigger bag and your invisible coat and glasses are in the other. How would you like to pay?'

Jasmine walked over to the window and looked out. 'Can you bill it to the mayor at City Hall?' she asked as she studied the streets for any sign of the man in the balaclava.

'I can do that,' said Dick. 'Perhaps you could do something for me in return?'

Jasmine turned around. 'Sure, what do you want?'

'Well, you see, I don't have a photo of anyone wearing the invisible cloak, and it would be nice to have one to go in the shop catalogue.'

Jasmine walked back to the counter. 'Are you asking me to do some modelling for you?'

Dick looked a little embarrassed. 'Umm, well, not exactly. But I've put my card in the bag. It has my phone number on it. Perhaps you could take some pictures of yourself in the invisible cloak and text them to me?'

'Yeah, I can do that,' she said. 'Do you need any pictures of Sanchez in his suit?'

'No. Just you in the invisible cloak will be fine, thanks.'

Jasmine picked up the bags. 'No problem.' She headed for the door. 'If my friend Rex shows up, tell him I'm around the corner in the big salt truck. Have a nice day.'

'You too, Miss, and don't forget the photos!'

Jasmine opened the shop door and headed out into the street. There was no sign of the balaclava man. She started walking back to the salt truck, while keeping an eye out for any creepy men in the street. There were loads of them.

The roar of a Chopper engine signalled the welcome arrival of Rodeo Rex up ahead. He cruised down the middle of the street on his Harley, but even though he saw Jasmine, he made no attempt to pull over. Instead, he winked at her as he went past, then nodded at something further along the street behind her. Jasmine glanced over her shoulder and saw the stocky man in the balaclava was twenty metres behind her on the sidewalk. He was following her.

Rex parked up further down the street. Jasmine assumed he had a plan, one that probably involved him sneaking up behind the stalker. She took a casual turn into a dark alley to lure the balaclava man into a trap. The alley was damp and stank of piss and rotten food. The walls were graffitied and plastered in posters advertising music concerts from months' back. Jasmine walked past them all, trying to get a sense of whether she was being followed. The sound of footsteps behind her confirmed the stalker was on her tail.

She stopped next to a dumpster and placed her bags on the ground. She bent down and pretended to tie the laces on her sneakers. The shadow of a man soon loomed over her.

'Excuse me Miss,' the man said in a monotone voice.

From her position close to the ground, Jasmine launched an attack. She swung her arm across the back of the man's ankles and swept his feet out from under him. He fell backwards and landed on the ground on his back, staring up at the sky. Jasmine got up and kicked him hard between the legs, the laces of her sneakers making a good connection with the guy's nutsack. He wailed in pain and grabbed his crotch with both hands.

Jasmine reached down and yanked the balaclava off his head, revealing the face of a man in his twenties with wavy brown hair. 'Why are you following me?' she demanded.

'Oh, my fuckin' balls!' the man groaned as he writhed in agony.

Rex rounded the corner at the end of the alley and ran towards them. As soon as he saw Jasmine had the situation under control he slowed down to a leisurely walk, and smiled at her.

'Who is it?' he called out.

'I'm about to find out,' Jasmine replied. She lifted the lid of the dumpster and dropped the balaclava into it. When she turned back to the man on the ground, he had rolled over onto his front and started to crawl away. Jasmine crouched down and grabbed his sweatpants with both hands. In her attempt to pull him back, she ended up tugging his pants down to his ankles. He wasn't wearing any underwear. She yanked his sweatpants off over his sneakers, leaving him very exposed. He rolled over onto his back and held his hands up.

'Okay, okay!' he said. 'I'm not moving.'

Jasmine had to be sure. She tossed his pants aside and took a run up, smashing her foot into his balls again. He let out an anguished cry and lay on the ground in a crucifix pose, his battered junk on display for all to see.

Rex arrived on the scene and leaned over the poor bastard. 'Who the fuck are you?' he asked the man. 'And why are you following my friend?'

'Mind your own fucking business,' the man groaned.

Rex grabbed a handful of the stalker's hair and hauled him to his feet, then he slammed him against the dumpster in order to get a better look at his face.

'Any idea who he is?' Jasmine asked Rex.

'No. Are you okay?'

'Yeah I'm fine. This loser never laid a glove on me.'

'Good.' Rex pressed his face up against the other man's and wrapped his metal hand around his throat. 'Who sent you?'

'No one,' the man blubbed.

Jasmine leant down on one knee and threw an uppercut punch into the guy's balls. She hit them so hard that he started dry heaving over Rex's hand.

'I'll ask you one more time,' said Rex. 'Who sent you? Was it Scratch?'

The man stopped wincing and looked up at Rex. Then he unwisely spat in the giant biker's face. 'Fuck you! I'll never tell!' he cried defiantly.

Jasmine grabbed the man's dick and lifted it up, pressing it against his stomach, then she punched him in the nutsack again like she was hitting two miniature speed bags.

'OOOOOWWWWW! OH SHIIIITTTT!'

'Hurts doesn't it?' said Rex. 'Now I'll ask again. Who sent you?'

'I'll take it to my grave,' the man mumbled through a face full of tears.

'Fine.' Rex took out his phone and held it up to take a photo.

'What are you doing?' Jasmine asked.

'Sending a picture of him to Alexis Calhoon. If he's anyone serious, she'll know who he is.'

Rex snapped a picture of the man's face, then punched him in the gut and let him slide down to the ground on his knees, sobbing. He texted the picture to General Alexis Calhoon, the head of the US Government's Phantom Ops department. Calhoon was a trusted ally of the Dead Hunters, a fifty-something black woman who took no shit from anyone, and who also had access to secret files on every taxpayer in the country.

Jasmine crouched down and grabbed the prisoner's swollen balls. She squeezed them as hard as she could, digging her fingernails into the soft skin on his sack, and warning him that any attempt to escape would result in further punishment. While she was doing that, Rex followed up his text message to General Calhoon by phoning the General on her cell.

She answered the call straight away. 'Hey, Rex. What's with the photo you just sent me?'

'I need to know who the guy is?'

'Looks like a pervert to me. Give me a minute and I'll run it through my database.' A minute ticked by, during which Jasmine continued squeezing her prisoner's balls, enjoying the way he writhed in agony. Rex trod on one of the guy's feet to keep him down. By the time Calhoon returned to Rex's call, the guy in the black shirt was sobbing like a toddler.

'Hey Rex, you still there?' said Calhoon.

'Yeah, still here.'

'Okay, sorry to take so long. I'm working from home.'

'That's okay. What'cha got?'

'I've got nothing on this guy, Rex. He's got no criminal record. I can't even bring him up using facial recognition. The guy's totally clean.'

'You're sure?'

'Yeah. Out of interest, what's he done to upset you?'

'He's been following Jasmine.'

Calhoon laughed. 'He probably *is* just a pervert then!'

Rex crouched down and studied the sobbing man's face. 'You know what,' he said to Calhoon. 'I think you're right. Can you hang on the line a mo? I'm just gonna check something.' He placed his phone down on top of the dumpster and studied the man's face. 'I know you,' he said, tapping the man on the forehead. 'What's your name?'

'Fuck you,' the man replied. 'I'll never talk.'

Rex grabbed the man by his hair again and hauled him back to his feet. Jasmine released her grip on the guy's gonads, and stood up too. Rex pushed the sobbing man up against the dumpster. Before he could restart his interrogation, Jasmine stepped in front of the prisoner and slammed her knee into his balls. He made a loud "ooof" sound then slumped forward. His face landed on Jasmine's chest.

'Wait!' said Rex. 'Don't hit him anymore.'

'Why not?'

'I know who he is.'

A couple of middle-aged men stopped on the sidewalk at the end of the alley, intrigued by what was going on. One of them yelled down to them. 'Hey, is everything okay down there?'

'Yeah, it's okay,' Jasmine called back. 'This guy wouldn't pay me, so my pimp is beating him up.'

Rex sighed. 'Wouldn't it have made more sense to tell them the truth?'

Jasmine shrugged and pushed the drooling idiot's head away from her chest. The back of his head slammed against the dumpster again. 'Who is this guy then?' she asked Rex.

Rex flicked the man on the nose. 'Tell her who you are,' he ordered.

'Never!'

'Can I hit him again?' Jasmine inquired.

Rex shook his head. 'Not yet.' He placed his metal hand around the man's throat again. 'Listen, you punk,' he said. 'I just wanna know if Scratch got to you. If you tell me the truth, I'll let her hit you in the nuts again.'

The man swallowed hard as he pondered his response. Drool slid out of his mouth.

'Wait a second,' said Jasmine. 'I'm confused. Did you say I should hit him again if he tells us *the truth*? But if he lies, I do nothing?'

'Yeah, that's right.' Rex tightened his grip on the man's neck. 'Do you know who Scratch is?' he demanded.

The man groaned. 'I don't know what you're talking about.'

'Do I hit him?' Jasmine asked. 'He's getting a boner, you know.'

'Yeah, I know. This guy isn't here to hurt you.'

'He's not?'

'No. This is Agent Sack-Whack.'

Jasmine looked up at Rex. 'Agent *what?*'

'I knew I recognised him. You're Agent Sack-Whack aren't you?'

The drooling man nodded. 'Yeah.'

Jasmine punched the guy hard in the nuts again, which made him choke like he was going to vomit, but he also smiled, which creeped Rex out. He released the man and stepped away.

'Stop hitting him,' he said. 'It's what he's here for.'

Jasmine wiped some ball sweat off her hand onto the guy's shirt. 'I'm totally confused,' she complained.

Rex ignored her. 'What's your *real* name, boy?' he asked the sobbing weirdo.

'Bradley.'

'Can someone please tell me what's going on?' Jasmine asked.

Rex replied, 'This guy Bradley is known on the internet as Agent Sack-Whack. He's been onto every porn site that has that video of you on it, and he's been posting in the comments asking if anyone knows who you are. I think it would be an understatement to say this guy is a fan of yours, and also a fan of being punched in the nuts.'

'He's been *enjoying* it?'

'I'd say so,' said Rex, glancing down at the man's swollen genital area.

'I suppose I've enjoyed it too,' Jasmine admitted. 'Even though he's a bit sweaty.'

Rex shook his head. 'I can't believe I left Sally at the Tapioca for *this*.' He tapped Bradley on the forehead again. 'Look, buddy, just tell us what you want with Jasmine?'

Bradley took a moment to catch his breath. 'All I wanted was a selfie,' he said. 'But this has actually worked out so much better than I hoped.' Through the tears in his eyes, he gazed at Jasmine with nothing but admiration. 'You see, Miss, umm, Jasmine, I'm a really big fan of yours.'

'Awww, that's so sweet,' said Jasmine, beaming.

'You're so much prettier in person too.'

Jasmine fluttered her eyelashes at Bradley, and by way of thanks for the compliment she slammed her knee into his nuts again. He bent over in pain, mumbling something that sounded like, *"thanks, that's awesome"*.

By now, a crowd of people had gathered at the end of the alleyway, all watching the action with a mix of different reactions. Some were appalled, some highly amused and some were filming it for their social media pages, or porn sites.

Bradley slid down to the ground with his back up against the dumpster. He had a satisfied look on his face, albeit one that was hidden behind a sea of tears.

Jasmine ruffled his hair. 'If I'd had my high heels on, I would have given you a real sack-nailer,' she said, apologetically.

Rex was well aware of the people filming them, and recognised the need to get moving. 'Forget this loser. We should get going.'

'Hang on a minute,' said Jasmine, raising a quizzical eyebrow. 'How did you know this guy has been commenting on my porno vid?'

'What?'

'You said you'd seen him on loads of porn sites, commenting on my video. How would you know that?'

Rex tutted. 'It's my business to know who's stalking my friends.'

Jasmine's eyes sparkled. 'You've been watching my porno on loads of different sites, haven't you!'

'No I haven't. I mean, I've been trying to get these sites to take the video down. That's the only reason I know about this guy.'

'Pah! Bullshit! Admit it, you like watching my porno.' She gasped. 'It all makes sense. You want me to punch you in the nuts, don't you!'

'No, I do not!'

'I do,' Bradley piped up from the ground by Jasmine's feet.

'Pipe down, bitch boy, you've had enough,' Jasmine replied, before subtly standing on his massively swollen scrotum and twisting her foot from side to side.

Rex grabbed his phone from the roof of the dumpster and returned to his call with Alexis Calhoon. 'Hi, Alexis, sorry about that. We're all a little bit paranoid here at the moment. A lot of shit has gone down just recently, and the end result is that we don't work for Scratch anymore.'

'You're not working for Scratch?' Calhoon sounded surprised.

'That's right. And we parted on bad terms, so we're all on edge, hence this phone call.'

'I understand,' said Calhoon. 'Is there anything I can do?'

'There is one thing,' said Rex. 'If you hear of any assassins that might be heading for Santa Mondega, it'd be real useful if you could give us a heads up.'

'No problem,' said Calhoon. 'Just one thought though. If at any time in the future, we speak, and I say the words *sack-whack*, it means I've been compromised, so you should disregard anything I say.'

Rex snorted a laugh. 'Sack-whack! Ha! That's good thinking. I'll let the others know too. Thanks, Alexis. Talk to ya later.'

Rex ended the call and put his phone away. Jasmine was still doing the twist on Bradley's ball sack, so Rex picked up the bags Jasmine had put down by the dumpster.

'What's this?' he asked, looking inside the bags.

'One is an invisible coat and the other is a suit I picked out for Sanchez. I've got to take the suit to City Hall because he's got an important meeting later today.'

'I can take it for you, if you like?' Rex offered.

'Nah, it's okay,' Jasmine replied. 'I'll take it in The Bum.'

'In the what?'

'The Bum, the council gritter.'

'You've lost me.'

'The salt truck.' Jasmine pulled a set of keys out of her cleavage and held them up. 'I borrowed it from City Hall. I've been salting the roads while I drive it.'

Rex slapped himself on the forehead. 'I wondered why everyone I saw was covered in salt.'

'I don't actually know how to turn the salter thing off,' Jasmine said.

'I can take a look at it for you, if you like?'

'Nah, it's okay. You should get back to Sally. I'm sorry if I ruined your date.'

'She'll be fine.'

Jasmine gave Rex a peck on the cheek and took the shopping bags from him. 'Thanks for coming anyway. I really appreciate it.'

She kicked Bradley in the nuts one last time as hard as she could, which was enough to leave him curled up in a ball, sobbing in pain and declaring his undying love for her.

****

Back at the bar in Purgatory……

'Bingo!'

Scratch looked up to see what Einstein was "bingo-ing" about. The mad scientist was sitting at a table not far from him, tapping away on his laptop computer.

'What's with you?' Scratch asked him.

'Rex has just made contact with General Calhoon.'

Scratch downed the last remnants of a glass of cognac and rushed over to see what Einstein had discovered.

'Here,' said Einstein. 'Listen to this.' He played back a recording of the phone call between Rex and Calhoon.

Scratch fist-pumped. 'This is just what we needed,' he beamed. 'Where is Calhoon right now?'

'She's at her home, a ranch in Montana.'

'Set the location on the portal. I'll go pay her a visit.'

Fifteen

Janis put her helmet on and flipped the visor down to muffle any verbal outbursts she might have. Elvis ushered her through a gap between the aisles and blew her a kiss goodbye. Janis was light on her feet and didn't make a sound as she made her escape.

The intruder who had killed Bob the archivist was light on his feet too. Elvis listened out for any footsteps, but there were none. Either he was going deaf, or everyone else in the archives was wearing slippers.

He was pissed about not having his gun or knife. But if the City Hall rules were consistent then the person who had just killed Bob ought to be unarmed too. Elvis preferred not to find out, so his priority was to get out of aisle seven before he was spotted. He ducked through a gap that took him into aisle eight. He stayed low and crept back towards the front of the hall. Part of the way along the aisle he spotted a small gap between two boxes on the bottom shelf. He crouched down next to it and spied through it into aisle seven. Someone was walking barefoot along the aisle to where he and Janis had just been. Elvis held his breath and waited for the shoeless person to pass by.

'I see you,' a voice whispered.

Elvis stayed still.

'Do you know who I am?' the voice whispered again.

Elvis had a poor view between the boxes, so he stood up a little and peered through another gap. The intruder was a short man, probably Chinese. He wasn't looking at Elvis, all his talk about "I see you" was just bluffing. This asshole was still on the hunt for his target.

'There's no escape,' the man whispered. 'Your time is up, *Elvis.*'

Elvis's view was obscured, but it looked like the whispering assassin was wearing a yellow outfit, like pyjamas, or karate slacks. Whatever it was, he looked like a badass *Bruce Lee, kung-fu motherfucker.*

Elvis ducked down again and pussyfooted his way along the aisle back to the reception. His escape was going pretty well until his phone suddenly rang.

Shit.

He pulled it from his pocket, and even though it was a call from Jasmine, he switched it off. But the game was up. The man in the next aisle had heard the phone and was making some moves.

Elvis sprinted for the end of the aisle, but so too did the kung-fu motherfucker, and he was way quicker. Just as Elvis thought he was going to make it to the end of the aisle, a flying Chinaman in yellow pyjamas leapt through a gap in the aisles and landed on his toes in front of him. Elvis hit the brakes and casually pulled a lever arch file from the shelf next to him and held it up, smiling at the Chinese man.

'Found it!' he said. 'This place is a maze, I tell you.'

The Chinese guy had short cropped dark hair and a spiteful look on his face. 'You Elvis?' he hissed, his two front teeth very prominent when he opened his mouth.

'Nope.'

'Bullshit.' The man pointed his finger up and down at Elvis's red suit. 'You Elvis!'

'Okay, you got me. What the fuck do you want?'

'Five million dollar reward!'

Elvis had heard stories of a Chinese bounty hunter, known in the hitman universe as *The Chinaman*. The Chinaman had a reputation for being able to kill folks in less than five seconds, using only his hands, or sometimes his feet, elbows or knees.

'Do you wear that suit to bed?' Elvis asked, stalling for time.

The Chinaman shook his head. 'You no funny. Your suit shitter.'

'My suit what?'

'SHITTER!'

One thing Elvis couldn't tolerate was people dissing his suits. It was time to take things up a notch. 'Are you by any chance the Chinaman?' he asked.

The other man squinted. 'You heard of me?'

'Yeah. I always wanted to know, did *you* give yourself the nickname *the Chinaman?*'

'Fuck you. Other people, racists give me nickname Chinaman!'

'Maybe if you didn't keep missing words out of your sentences when you're talking, you wouldn't seem like such a cliché? Then perhaps you could get a different nickname? I'm thinking like, I dunno, say, Pyjama man? The Yellow Assassin?'

The Chinaman's face stiffened. 'Yellow assassin?'

'Yeah, I was referring to the colour of your suit.'

The Chinaman pointed an angry finger at Elvis. 'You stalling for time! No more time for you. Time to die!'

'Fucking great. Let's dance.'

Elvis put his lever arch file back on the shelf and took up his best karate stance. He'd done a fair amount of martial arts in his day, but his day was kinda fifteen years ago, and his skills were liable to be a bit on the shite side. The Chinaman on the other hand was in his late twenties, peak physical condition, and really limber. He took up his own kung fu pose. It was a fuckload more impressive than Elvis's. His knees weren't creaking for starters.

Elvis decided to goad him, in the hope of luring him into a mistake. 'Come on then, Mister LaRusso,' he said, beckoning the Chinaman towards him.

It worked. The Chinaman leapt into the air and spun around at a speed faster than Elvis's eyes could keep up with. His legs whizzed around like propellors before one of his feet kicked Elvis flush on the side of the head. The King lost his footing and crashed into a shelf packed with boxes, before tumbling onto the floor.

The Chinaman loomed over him. 'Too easy,' he gloated. 'Five million dollar, here I come.' A horrible angry grin appeared on his face. Elvis was too dazed to defend himself. His opponent screamed out a high-pitched "death cry" and raised his right hand above his head.

SMACK!

The Chinaman turned cross-eyed and his arms dropped to his side. Half a second later he fell forward like a domino, landing on top of Elvis, and hugging him like a sleeping child.

Janis was standing over the two men, dusting off the motorcycle helmet she had just smashed the Chinaman over the head with.

'That oughta be the end of that,' she said.

Elvis pushed the Chinaman aside and staggered to his feet. 'What took you so long?'

'I wanted to see if he was as badass as he looked. SWEET AND SOUR BASTARD!'

'Jeez, that Tourettes really brings out the racist in you doesn't it?'

'You're the one who called him yellow.'

'I was referring to his clothes.'

'Yeah, right.'

Elvis looked down at the Chinaman. 'Do you think he's dead?'

Janis crouched down next to the unconscious Chinese assassin and lifted her helmet above her head. With a violent swing she smashed it down onto the Chinaman's skull six or seven more times. Blood and brain splattered all over the aisle as each blow from the helmet splintered away more pieces of his head. When she was finished she stepped back away from the body and wiped some blood from her forehead with her sleeve while pondering the body.

'That good enough for ya?' she asked.

Elvis nodded. 'Yeah, I think you got him.'

'No shit, I did.' Janis had a sudden twitching fit and started yelling, 'FUCKER! I KILL YOU! THERE WILL BE MURDER!' She took a deep breath and composed herself. 'Anyway, I'd better get going. It was nice seeing you again.'

'Woah, hey, what's the big hurry?' said Elvis. 'I haven't seen you in years. How about you stick around for a minute and fill me in on what you've been up to? Keep me company while I look through Sally Diamond's files?'

'Sally's clean. I already looked through her records.'

'Yeah, but I didn't.'

Sixteen

Calhoon was in her lounge at home, sitting in her favourite armchair, drinking a mug of coffee and watching the news on TV. Her husband was out of the house visiting a friend, but she had her two Alsatians for company. They were asleep by her feet, contented because they had just been fed.

She had been having a relaxing morning away from work, but the recent call from Rodeo Rex had unsettled her. She had just agreed to deceive the Devil in order to help Rex. She liked Rex and knew if ever she were in trouble, he and Elvis would drop everything to come to her aid, so she wanted to help them. But she also knew Scratch. She'd met him once, only briefly, but she had found the whole incident quite terrifying. Scratch hadn't tried to intimidate her, in fact he'd been quite charming, but he was the Devil, and so by default he was as evil as evil could be. Thinking about him put her on edge. In an effort to take her mind off him she flicked through the channels on the television to look for something light-hearted.

There were all kinds of shows and movies, none of which sounded like they would help her to unwind. *Constantine, Lucifer, Devil's Advocate, Little Nicky, Problem Child, The Cosby Show,* none of it seemed appropriate in the circumstances. She eventually settled on an old episode of *Moonlighting*. It had been on for less than a minute when her Alsatians both looked up and growled.

'Good day to you, General Calhoon.'

The dogs whimpered and bowed their heads, cowering back into their sleeping positions. Calhoon recognised the voice that came from behind her. She put her mug of coffee down and attempted to stand up. A large hand pressed down on her shoulder, pushing her back down into her seat.

'Don't get up on my account,' said Scratch.

'How did you get in here?' Calhoon asked, in the politest way possible.

'I came in through your bathroom, which I might add is exquisite.'

'Thank you.'

Scratch walked around her chair and stopped in front of the television. It switched itself off just before Bruce Willis could say anything funny in response to a telling off from Cybil Shepherd.

'Lovely dogs,' said Scratch before abruptly ending the small talk and getting right to the point. 'I take it you know why I'm here?'

'I can't say that I do.'

'Yes, you can. Sack-whack is the password, is it not?'

Calhoon slumped back in her chair. 'It is,' she admitted. Her mind was racing, her blood pumping. Was she about to suffer an awful fate at the hands of the Devil? 'Can I fix you a coffee, or something?' she asked, not because she wanted to fix him a coffee but because she needed to say something to end what was close to becoming an awkward silence.

'No,' Scratch replied. 'Now that we've agreed you will not be using the password *sack-whack* to warn the Dead Hunters that you have been compromised, let's discuss how you can help me to kill them.'

Calhoon sighed. 'Okay.'

'Good. Now here's the thing, *Alexis,* I have access to all of your communications. I see everything you do on your computer and all your other devices. From this moment forth I will communicate directly with you through your phone, either on calls or text messages. And you will do everything I ask, or I will see to it that your two lovely dogs suffer terrible, tragic accidents. Are we on the same page?'

Calhoon nodded. Normally, if someone threatened her beloved dogs she'd find a way to have that person's legs broken, or worse. But this was the Devil. Nothing she could do would have any effect on him. 'What do you want me to do?' she asked, reluctantly.

'First of all, I think it's about time Jasmine was arrested for the murder of the Pope. She's gotten away with that for far too long, wouldn't you agree?'

'Yes.'

'Good.' Scratch took out a cigar and sucked on it. It lit up instantly. He took a few puffs on it and blew a smoke ring before addressing Calhoon again. 'As I understand it, you know the Bastard brothers, is that correct?'

'I know them, yes.'

'Yes, you do. They do jobs for you from time to time. I don't care for them much myself, vulgar fellows. But when I found out that they do lots of bounty hunting for your department, I thought, *"What the hey? Let's give these clowns a chance."*

'That's very good of you.'

'Yes, it is,' said Scratch, puffing on his cigar again and looking at a photo on the wall. The photo was of Calhoon and her husband, Roger, taken when they were hiking through mountains. Scratch promptly blew some smoke at it. 'Anyway,' he went on, 'I have arranged for the Bastard brothers to hunt Jasmine down, but I would like you to assist them. You are able to keep tabs on her location by tracking her phone, are you not?'

'Yes, I am.'

'Good. You will feed information of her whereabouts to the Bastards, keeping them updated on every move she makes. Now, just so you're clear, if there are any complications, if she loses her phone, or you lose track of it, or you're struck down by lightning, I will consider that an act of sabotage on your part, and your dogs will be executed, understood?'

Threatening the dogs again. What a piece of shit.

Calhoon hid her true feelings and nodded. 'I understand,' she said.

'I should also remind you that not only do I have complete access to all of *your* communication methods, I'm also tapped into the Dead Hunters phones, and also the phones belonging to Flake and Sanchez.'

Calhoon shifted uncomfortably in her chair. 'Not to be snippy, but, if you have access to all of their phones, why do you need me?'

Scratch chewed off a piece of his cigar and spat it on the floor to show his disgust. 'I'm not wasting my time sitting around checking people's phones all day,' he said. '*And*, as has been pointed out to me already today, I am surrounded by idiots in Hell, so therefore, I'm hiring you to do it for me, because you, General Calhoon, are exceptional at what you do.'

'Thanks, I guess,' said Calhoon. 'Just one thing though. I am wired into the phones for Rex, Elvis and Jasmine, but not the Bourbon Kid. I think he changed his number a while back.'

Scratch took another puff on his cigar. 'The Bourbon Kid is a little more paranoid than the others,' he said. 'But if you can find a contact number for him, or provide any information that leads to his execution, I will see to it that you are handsomely rewarded. I could make you the next President, if that's what you desired.'

Calhoon picked up her mug of coffee. She held it in both hands, and while she contemplated taking a sip, she made Scratch an offer. 'I'm no fan of the Bourbon Kid,' she admitted. 'He's responsible for regular spikes in my murder rates. Cost me my annual bonus twice. If, as you say, there's a handsome reward involved, I think I know the one man in the world who could possibly kill him for you.'

Scratch tapped some ash onto Calhoon's previously immaculate wooden floor. 'You know someone who could *kill* the Bourbon Kid?'

'Falco Logan.'

'Who?'

'Falco Logan.'

'I've never heard of him.'

'No one has. That's how good he is.'

'Tell me about him.'

'Well, first up, I'm fairly certain Falco Logan isn't his real name. And second of all, he's so good at what he does, that no one, aside from me and two others in my unit even know of his existence. He's the guy we send when we have to kill someone, and the President can't know about it.'

'I'd like to meet him.'

'So would I. But it's not possible. That is to say, I can't arrange it. If I could, I would have met him myself, but I haven't. No one has.'

'Then how do you contact him?'

'A secure messaging app. Used only by the world's top assassins. He's on it, but only on the proviso that he's never included in group messages unless he's blind copied. None of the other assassins believe he exists. He's a myth, a ghost. In fact, I'm calling him a *he*, but for all I know, Falco could be a woman, or a space alien. I really don't know anything about him, and with someone that good, that's how I like it.'

Scratch sucked hard on his cigar for a significant amount of time. Eventually he blew out a puff of smoke shaped like a question mark. 'Okay,' he said. 'Who has he killed for you in the past?'

'For me, he's killed six times. Now I know that might not sound like much, but these were my six most wanted. Some were top names in the terrorist world, a couple were leaders of countries that weren't complicit with our international policies, and one had some serious dirt on people in high places, if you know what I mean?'

'The President?'

'I can't say.'

'You can,' said Scratch, 'But I admire your discretion and your ethics. How do you pay this Falco Logan character?'

'Cash, in a suitcase, at a place of his choosing. The money is left at the location. He collects it when he's ready.'

'Can you give me a phone number for him?'

Calhoon shook her head. 'Uh uh. Like I say, I send him a message in the secure app. His number is scrambled. He never acknowledges the messages, or replies to say he's accepted the job. But every time, no matter where he is in the world, he kills the target within seventy-two hours.'

Scratch walked up to Calhoon and perched his backside on the arm of her chair. 'Okay,' he said. 'Let this Falco Logan person know that the Bourbon Kid is up for grabs.'

'How much should I say you'll pay?'

'Five million dollars.'

Calhoon shook her head. 'He won't do it for that. It has to be at least twenty million. That's why I've only hired him six times. He's kind of expensive.'

Scratch's eyes shone bright at the notion of having to pay twenty million dollars. He leapt off the arm of her chair and beamed a huge toothy smile at her. 'I like the sound of him,' he announced. 'Give him the job. Price, twenty million. And I'll let the Bastard brothers know you're a trusted ally, working for me. From this moment on, you can start giving them updates on where Jasmine is.'

Scratch exited the way he had come in, via Calhoon's bathroom. She breathed a sigh of relief. What a fucking morning this was turning out to be.

Seventeen

Jasmine drove the salt truck back to City Hall, spraying masses of salt over every road, sidewalk and pedestrian she passed on the way. She parked the truck back in its regular spot and raced up the steps to the main building, carrying the bag containing Sanchez's suit. After a brief stop at reception where the creepy security guard with the thick black moustache carried out a rather unnecessary body search, she was greeted by Melinda, the Chief of Staff.

'Where have you been?' Melinda asked, tapping her watch.

'It's a long story,' Jasmine replied. 'I got side-tracked in a back alley. Had to kick a guy in the balls for a while.'

Melinda snatched the suit bag from her. 'That sounds lovely,' she sneered, peering into the bag. 'What is this?'

'What does it *look* like?' Jasmine replied, with a hefty dose of sarcasm. 'It's a suit!'

Melinda scowled at her. 'No, it's a *beige* suit,' she said, tutting. 'It's not what I would have picked, but it'll have to do, I suppose.'

'That's a load off my mind,' Jasmine said, pretending to care. 'Where is Sanchez now? Can I see him try on the suit?'

'I'm afraid not. You're not suitably dressed for this building,' she said, pointing at Jasmine's catsuit, 'and the mayor is going to be very busy for the rest of the day. But he'll be on the news later. You can see him then. Goodbye.'

Melinda turned and marched over to a set of elevators at the back of the reception hall. Jasmine didn't like Melinda, the old bag was kind of rude and condescending, and seeing as how she hadn't asked for the keys to the salt truck back, Jasmine decided to keep them. Riding round town in The Bum was fun.

'Hey, Jas!'

She looked around and saw Elvis strolling towards her across the reception floor. A slim, brown-haired woman in a black leather outfit was walking by his side. She was carrying a motorcycle helmet.

'Hey, honey. Who's your biker friend?'

'This is Janis,' said Elvis. 'Janis, this is Jasmine.'

'We met before,' said Janis. 'FUCKING WHORE!'

Jasmine glowered at Elvis. 'What have you been telling her?'

'Nothing,' Elvis replied. 'She has Tourette's.'

'She can read minds?'

'No,' Janis replied. 'It's a condition I have. It means I yell shit out at inappropriate times. I never actually meant to call you a whore just then. SLAPPER!'

'Have we really met before?' Jasmine queried. 'I think I'd remember you.'

Elvis clarified things. 'You remember the funeral we went to at Coldworm abbey the other day?'

'Yeah.'

'Janis was the preacher lady with the blue hair who conducted the ceremony.'

Jasmine scratched her head. 'Really? You've lost a lot of weight since then. Have you been on the *Nutty Professor* diet? You look much younger now too.'

'I was wearing a fat suit,' said Janis. 'DUMB CUNT!' She cleared her throat. 'Sorry about that. What I meant was, I was in disguise. It was a mask and a fat suit. COCKSUCKER!'

There were a number of other people in the reception hall, some worked there, others were members of the public visiting to register complaints about the new mayor. All of them were distracted by Janis's very vocal swearing. Lots of strange looks were aimed in the direction of the threesome in the middle of the hall. Elvis dealt with it by addressing the whole reception hall.

'WHAT THE FUCK ARE YOU ALL LOOKING AT?' he yelled, glaring at anyone who was still looking their way. It had the desired effect. Anyone who was anyone knew who Elvis was, so within a few seconds everyone was going about their business as usual, with the exception of the security guard who had taken Elvis's weapons from him earlier. He stared at the three of them, shaking his head in disgust.

'Hang on a minute,' said Jasmine, thinking out loud. 'Is this the Janis you met in the Devil's Graveyard?'

'Yeah, that's right,' said Elvis.

'The one you fucked in the back of Annabel's bus?'

'I really should get home,' said Janis, slipping her helmet back on. 'My dad will be wondering where I am. I'll see you guys later. Have a nice day. IN THE ASS!' She slid the visor down on her helmet and had a twitching fit, which involved an outburst of swearing that was mostly muffled out by the visor.

'Nice to have met you,' said Jasmine. 'I really like your helmet.'

Janis waved goodbye to them both and hurried out of the building, pausing only briefly to punch the security guard in the gut. She caught him unawares and by the time he realised who had hit him, she was long gone, leaving him looking embarrassed, and holding his gut like he'd just eaten some dodgy takeaway.

'She seems nice,' said Jasmine. 'Does she work here?'

'Nah,' Elvis replied. 'She was here for the same reason as me. I found her in the archives going through Sally Diamond's files.'

'What files?'

'Personal stuff. Seeing as Sally's a cop in the city, I figured they'd have a file on her down in the basement. I thought I'd check it out, see if she had any dark secrets we should know about.'

'Dark secrets? Like kinky stuff?'

Elvis shook his head. 'No, nothing like that. But, you know Rex likes her, right? Well, I thought it would make sense to do a check on her, you know, make sure she's not, *you know*.'

'A man?'

'*No*. I just wanted to make sure she was *on the level*. I didn't want Rex hanging out with someone who might be an undercover agent or something.'

'You're so weird.'

'Yeah, well, you know what else? I got attacked by a Chinaman while I was down there. He must have been following me, or something. Luckily Janis smashed his skull in with her helmet.'

'I got followed too!' said Jasmine, excited that they had something to share. 'But it was just a fan who wanted a sack whack. Who was your Chinese stalker? And why was Janis looking at Sally's files? That doesn't make sense to me. Did you arrange to meet her down there? Are you having an affair?'

Elvis rolled his eyes. 'Why would I have an affair? I've got you, and you're awesome. And what's this about a sack whack? What fan? What happened?'

It was Jasmine's turn to roll her eyes. 'Jeez, calm down. It turned out okay. I tried calling you, but I guess you were busy with Janis. Anyway, Rex came to help me. We should head back to the Tapioca and tell him about your Chinese stalker. Come on, I'll take you in The Bum.' She waved her keys at him. 'You can tell me all about Janis on the way. Does she really live with her dad?'

'Her dad is Vincent Papshmir.'

'No way!'

'Wait 'til I tell you who her granddad is.'

As they headed for the exit, the security guard stepped forward with his arm out to stop them. 'Do you know that woman who assaulted me just now?' he asked.

Elvis replied by punching him in the stomach, just like Janis had done. The guard doubled over in pain holding his gut with both hands. Jasmine kneed him in the face for good measure, which busted his nose. He folded on the floor in a heap, groaning and weeping.

Elvis retrieved his gun and knife from a box of confiscated items by the doors, then he and Jasmine walked out of City Hall arm in arm, setting off the metal detectors as they went. As they walked down the steps to the sidewalk, a dark shadow closed in over the city. The sunlight vanished behind an enormous gathering of black clouds. Within a few seconds the streetlights came on, lighting the city up like it was Christmas.

'That was weird,' said Jasmine.

'We should get moving,' said Elvis, upping his walking pace. 'This could be Scratch. If he's here and he's got the Eye of the Moon then he could be responsible for this sudden darkness. After the dark comes the snow.'

'Snow? Why would it snow?'

'Some years back a mummy named Rameses Gaius used the Eye to darken the skies over Santa Mondega. It brought all the undead out from their hiding places. I wasn't actually here, but I know when the skies went dark, it started snowing.'

'Lucky we've got a salt truck then,' said Jasmine.

Snow started falling before they reached the bottom of the steps. And by the time they'd crossed the street and hopped into the salt truck, it was pelting down hard and fast.

'Scratch is here,' said Elvis.

Jasmine started up the engine. 'Where? I can't see him.'

'I don't know where. But he's somewhere in the city. Shit's about to get real.'

Eighteen

Sandy had been sitting in her hotel room watching her phone all day. She had barely slept a wink since her daughter Arizona had been kidnapped. It had been almost three days. Three days without any positive news, no leads, nothing. She had put her faith in Arizona's father, the President of the United States, and his top security advisor, Mike Raffone. She had trusted them to deliver her daughter back to her. Mike hadn't even returned her last call. Asshole. She was beginning to regret not calling the police. Every minute that went by she was more tempted to do it, even though Mike had made it clear she was not to involve anyone else.

She sat down on her bed and dialled Mike's number again. His secretary, Denise, answered. Sandy butted in before Denise had even finished saying hello.

'I need to speak to Mike right now. I'm not hanging up until he tells me what's going on.'

'Please hold.'

Almost a minute went by before Mike came on the line. 'Hello, Sandy. How are you?'

'How the fuck do you think I am? My baby is missing and you're not returning my calls!'

'Sandy, we talked about this. You need to stay calm. I'm doing everything I can. The President is very concerned too. It's his number one priority, I promise you.'

'Can I talk to him?'

'No. He's on a flight to Brussels at the moment.'

'Oh, for God's sake! Come on, tell me something. Have you got *any* leads yet?'

'I already told you, Sandy. We've got our best people working on it, round the clock. She'll be found soon. Just try to stay calm.'

'I wish you would stop telling me to stay calm. *You* try staying calm when *your daughter* is kidnapped. I want hourly updates from you Mike, or I'm going to the press.'

A silence followed. When Mike spoke again, his voice was less sympathetic, bordering on intimidating. 'Sandy, we've talked about you not saying things like that. This isn't the time to be making threats that you might regret.'

'Well, you'd better do something!'

'Okay, okay, calm down.'

'I told you, stop telling me to be calm!'

'You're right,' Mike's voice switched back to soothing and reassuring. 'Listen, Sandy, this is confidential, I shouldn't even be telling you, but I'm meeting this afternoon with a top secret, special ops team. These guys won't just get Arizona back for you, they'll do some serious damage to the people who took her. All this will be over in less than twenty-four hours. Just trust me, okay?'

Sandy felt just the tiniest amount of reassurance. 'Okay,' she said, the anger fading from her voice.

'Good, now I gotta go. I'll call you later.'

Over in Washington DC, Mike Raffone replaced the receiver on his desk phone and sat back in his chair, grasping at his thick silver hair. Special Agent Rick Chelios was sitting on the opposite side of the desk. Chelios was a big dude in his early fifties with white hair and big glasses. He was wearing military slacks, and he was ready to spring into action at the drop of a hat.

'Want me to put a couple of people outside her building?' Chelios asked.

Raffone grabbed an elastic band from his desk and listlessly pulled it back and forth in his hands. 'Yeah,' he said, eventually. 'If Sandy goes anywhere, I want her followed. And if she goes anywhere she shouldn't, I want her out of the picture. This dumb bitch and her daughter will bring this fucking government down if we don't resolve this situation.'

'Yes sir.' Chelios stood up to leave Raffone's office, but he hesitated.

'What is it?' Raffone asked.

'How are you going to find the daughter in less than twenty-four hours? Are you going to use Calhoon's people?'

Raffone flicked his elastic band at a painting of Abraham Lincoln that was hanging on the wall. It hit Lincoln's silly hat and bounced onto the floor. Raffone looked at Chelios, who was unimpressed by the band flicking.

'Get me a car,' said Raffone. 'Calhoon's working from home this week, so I'll pay her a personal visit.'

Nineteen

'This isn't bad is it?' said Flake, admiring Sanchez's new office.

Sanchez had made himself comfortable in a big, soft, brown leather chair behind his new desk. The chair had wheels, so he was practising rolling around the room in it while Flake checked out all the boring stuff on the shelves, and the crappy pictures on the walls.

'This is an exact replica of the Oval Office in the White House,' Flake said, running her hand along the wall. 'How cool is that?'

'It's stupid,' said Sanchez. 'There aren't any corners. I wanted an office like J.R Ewing had in Dallas. This one doesn't even have any of those swinging cradle balls on the desk. That needs to be rectified as soon as possible. What am I supposed to play with?' He rolled back behind his desk and pulled open some drawers. They were all filled with paperwork. 'And where are the snacks?' he grumbled.

Flake ignored him. She was staring out of the window at the city. 'What time is it?' she asked.

'Hammer Time,' Sanchez replied.

'No, seriously. What time is it? It's gone dark outside. It's like night time out there. And I think it's snowing.'

There was an old-fashioned red phone on Sanchez's desk. He grabbed it and pulled it towards him. He lifted the receiver and pressed a button on the keypad that had the word "SECRETARY" on it. The phone rang once before a woman answered.

'Hello, Mister Mayor,' she said.

'What time is it?' Sanchez asked.

'It's five past eleven, sir.'

Sanchez hung up the phone. 'It's five past eleven,' he repeated for Flake's benefit.

'Isn't that weird?' said Flake.

'Not really. It ties up perfectly with how long we've been here.'

'No, I mean the snow. Last time we had snow was when Rameses Gaius tried to take over the city. I wonder if Scratch is in town with the Eye of the Moon?'

'Did I ever tell you I hate snow?' said Sanchez.

Flake turned away from the window. 'Lots of times, Mister Mayor.'

Sanchez raised an eyebrow. 'Mister Mayor, eh? Sounds sexy when you say it.'

Flake manoeuvred herself around his chair and sat down on his knee, placing her arms around his chubby neck. 'Call me the First Lady,' she said in a sexy voice.

'First Lady, hmm. If you're First Lady, I ought to be President. Can we get that changed? Mayor is a rubbish title. President is much better.'

A knock at the door was swiftly followed by Melinda walking in with a large brown shopping bag. She marched across the room and placed it down on the desk in front of Sanchez.

'Your strange friend in the catsuit returned just now with your suit, Mister Mayor,' she said. 'Would you like to try it on?'

Flake slid off Sanchez's knee and stood beside his chair. 'Is Jasmine here?' she asked.

'I sent her home. Her clothing was not appropriate for this building.'

Flake moved away from Sanchez and leaned against the desk, giving off a casual, *"I've settled in nicely, thanks"* kind of vibe. 'Hey, Melinda, do us a favour while you're here,' she said. 'Tell us how we go about changing the law so Sanchez can be called Mister President instead of Mister Mayor?'

'I don't think you can do that,' Melinda replied, giving off her own, *"Tough shit, I run this place"* kind of vibe.

'I think we can,' Flake retorted. 'On the news this morning they said that a long time ago the mayor used to be known as the sheriff, so how did they change the name back then? It must be possible.'

Melinda sighed. 'Then I suggest you look it up in the Santa Mondega historical logs.'

'And where would we find them?' Flake asked.

Melinda pointed to a set of shelves built into the wall on one side of the office. The shelves were full of thick hardback books that looked like old encyclopaedias. 'The historical logs are over there,' she said. 'Those are the only copies in existence so be careful with them because they're irreplaceable.'

'Great, I love a good book,' said Flake.

'Good,' said Melinda, stepping away from the desk. 'I'll leave you now, Mister Mayor, so you can put your suit on. Please don't delay. Your first public engagement is in less than an hour. I'll call you when your bodyguard shows up.'

Melinda left and closed the door behind her. Sanchez leapt up from his chair and picked up the bag with the suit. 'Did you hear that?' he said. 'I get a bodyguard! How cool is that?' He handed the suit bag to Flake so she could open it for him.

'A bodyguard, wow,' she said, looking in the bag. 'I suppose it's to protect you from all the protestors who think you're unfit for office.' She pulled out the suit and held it up for Sanchez to see.

'What the fuck is that?' he groaned.

'That's what you get for letting Jasmine choose your suit,' said Flake, staring at the beige suit. 'It's okay though, isn't it? The shirt looks like your kind of thing. And it looks like a good fit.'

'It's not the suit from *True Lies* though is it,' said Sanchez. 'It's the suit from *Twins,* for fuckssake.'

'Try it on. Let's see how it looks.'

Sanchez took off his Hawaiian shirt and handed it to Flake. He emptied all the crap out of the pockets on his pants and placed it all on the desk, then pulled his pants down and handed those to her too. Amongst the shit he'd placed on the desk was his hip-flask and the gold key that Levian had given him earlier in the day.

'You brought your hipflask? Flake groaned. 'Please tell me it's not full of piss?'

'Of course it's full of piss. What else would be in it?'

'You're the mayor now. You can't be tricking people into drinking your piss anymore. You should be above that sort of thing.'

Sanchez held his arms out. 'You never know when you're going to need some piss. Now, come on, hurry up and put my suit on me. I can't stand here in my Y-fronts all day!'

Flake put his arms into the green and white checked shirt and buttoned it up, then helped him into the beige pants and jacket. The final piece of the outfit was a pair of dark sunglasses. She slid them over his eyes and stepped back to take a look at him.

'Wow, you look *exactly* like Schwarzenegger did in *Twins!*' she said. 'This really suits you.'

'You think?'

'Definitely. It looks very presidential.'

'Excellent. Do we have a mirror in here?'

'Hang on,' said Flake. She moved around the desk and sat in Sanchez's chair. She ran her finger over a series of buttons on the edge of the desk and eventually pressed one. To Sanchez's amazement, a section of one of the walls swivelled around 180 degrees revealing a full-length mirror. He walked up to it and took a look at himself.

'I do look good,' he agreed. 'Jasmine does have good taste after all.'

Flake grabbed Levian's big gold key. 'Don't forget this,' she said, tossing it to him. The key hit Sanchez on the chin and fell to the floor. He bent down to pick it up.

'You'd better give me my hip-flask too,' he said, straightening up and slipping the key into his pocket.

'No way,' said Flake, grabbing the flask and vacating Sanchez's seat. 'I'm holding onto this.'

Sanchez muttered something under his breath and then returned to his chair. He shifted around in it, trying out various official-looking poses for greeting visitors, while Flake headed over to the bookshelves and started pulling out all the historical logs. She blew the dust off a few of them and found they were impressive handmade hardbacks that had been kept in good condition. She dropped a pile of them down on Sanchez's desk. A cloud of dust blew up in his face causing him to cough and splutter.

He was still waving dust away from his face when there was a loud knock at the door.

'You may enter,' Sanchez called out.

The door opened and Melinda stepped into the room again. 'Your bodyguard is on his way up, sir. It's time to pick a bull for your initiation ceremony.'

'A bull?' said Sanchez. 'What are you on about?'

'Oh, I'm sorry,' said Melinda. 'I assumed you knew. It's tradition for the mayor to go to Mutner's farm on his first day in office to choose a bull for his initiation.'

'What's the bull for?' Flake asked.

Melinda faked a smile. 'It's an old tradition. The mayor has to pick his favourite bull from the farm and give it a name. Then tomorrow, the bull takes part in a bullfight with the city's best Matador, in your honour.'

'In my honour?' said Sanchez. 'That sounds like a good idea.'

'This will be great fun, won't it?' said Flake. 'I've never been to Mutner's farm before.'

'I'm afraid this event is for the mayor only,' said Melinda. 'You will have to stay here. But, if you like, I can arrange for your personal shopper to come and measure you up for an outfit for tomorrow? After all, you can't keep coming into City Hall in a policewoman's outfit, can you?'

'I guess not,' said Flake. 'And I could do with a new outfit, or two.'

'Excellent,' said Melinda. 'I'll arrange it for you now.'

A heavy-set gentleman in a grey suit appeared in the doorway behind Melinda. He almost filled the whole door frame. He had slicked-back, black hair and he wore big sunglasses, which gave off a real gangster vibe. Melinda introduced him.

'Mister Mayor, this is Frank, your new bodyguard. I'll leave you to get acquainted.'

Frank stepped aside, allowing Melinda to leave and return to her own office.

'Come on in,' said Flake.

'With all due respect, ma'am,' said Frank. 'We're running short of time. The mayor's driver is downstairs waiting. And with the weather changing like it is, the sooner we get going the better.' He peered over his sunglasses at Sanchez and added, 'Nice suit.'

'Thank you,' said Sanchez, pleased that his bodyguard was showing the correct levels of respect.

'It makes you look just like Danny DeVito from that *Twins* movie,' Frank continued.

Sanchez was livid. He looked nothing like Danny DeVito. For starters he had slightly more hair, and he was also good inch taller than Mister DeVito. 'I'm supposed to be Schwarzenegger,' he said, glaring at Frank.

Frank pointed at Sanchez and let out a hearty laugh. 'Hahaha, yeah, great gag, sir. Schwarzenegger! Hahaha!'

Flake could tell Sanchez was seething. 'Don't forget this,' she said, handing him his hipflask, and winking at him.

Sanchez accepted it and slipped it into a pocket inside his jacket. His anger melted away. 'I love you, Flake,' he said.

'I know you do.' Flake kissed him on the cheek and smiled at Frank. 'How long will this bull-choosing thing take?' she asked him.

'Oh, don't worry, ma'am,' Frank replied. 'What we've got planned won't take long at all.'

Twenty

Dark skies, thick black clouds, snow settling on the gravestones outside the front of the church. Vincent Papshmir had seen it all before. The memories of the last time it had happened, several years prior, were still with him. In the midst of all the snowfall back then, the church had come under attack from a bunch of vampires dressed like clowns, and if that wasn't bad enough, a young Sunflower Girl had taken a dump in his confessional box.

He was standing at the front entrance of the church, impatiently waiting for his daughter to return home. The streets outside were rapidly emptying of people. Papshmir guessed that many of the residents of Santa Mondega also remembered what had happened before and they were all heading home.

'This is it,' he muttered to himself. 'He's coming. Where the fuck are you, Janis?'

She'd been gone longer than expected. He'd tried calling her but all he'd got was voicemail. Kids, who'd have them? Ever since Janis was old enough to walk she'd been hard to keep track of. She'd loved a game of hide and seek. If it hadn't been for her outbursts of Tourette's, Papshmir would never have found her. As an adult, she was even more elusive.

Papshmir's anxiety had been increasing ever since the Bourbon Kid showed up earlier that morning. He'd had the emotional embrace with his father that he had waited his whole life for, but now like never before, he recognised the perilous nature of his situation. It was time to skip town, but not without Janis.

The roar of a motorcycle engine lifted his spirits. As she had done many times before, Janis rode past the gates at the front of the church. She cruised around the side of the building to park up at the rear.

Papshmir closed the church doors, and slid a long metal bolt across them, sealing them shut. He heard Janis enter through a door at the end of the west wing. The pitter patter of her boots on the stone floor grew louder as she approached the main hall. Papshmir headed down the aisle towards the altar. He was halfway down when Janis appeared, hurrying past the front row of pews, carrying her helmet in her hand.

'Have you seen the weather?' she asked.

'Is that blood on your helmet?'

'I killed a Chinese guy. I'll tell you about it later. We gotta go.'

'No fucking shit we gotta go! Where have you been?'

'Murdering a Chinese guy. Keep up, YOU FUCKER!'

'I've got news too,' said Papshmir. 'I just had a visit from the Bourbon Kid.'

'SNIFF MY HAIRY ASS! What?'

Papshmir was so used to Janis's outbursts he barely heard them. 'He dropped by to tell me he knew who I was. *And you.* He knows *everything*, and he says we need to leave town.'

'So let's leave!'

'I'm already packed. Is there anything you need to get?'

'Have I got time?'

'If you're quick. This is the fire drill we've been waiting our whole lives for. You remember the routine?'

'Yeah, yeah, of course I do.'

'Good, so get packing. Grab only what you need. You've got two minutes!'

'Two minutes?'

'One fifty-five.'

'All right. Hang on. Let me get some holy water first.'

Janis ran over to the church font and pulled a silver water pistol from inside her jacket. She dunked it into the water in the font to let it fill up. As she was holding it underwater she looked around.

'Did you hear that?' she asked.

'What?'

'Listen.'

The two of them stood totally still, barely breathing, listening for further sounds. At first there was nothing, then all of a sudden someone started banging on the front doors.

'Shit,' said Papshmir. 'It's probably just someone wondering why we're closed.'

'But what if it's not?'

There was a statue of a gargoyle head protruding out of the wall behind Janis. Papshmir pushed past her and poked his fingers into the statue's eyes, pushing them back into its head. A secret compartment in the wall slid out above the gargoyle head. He reached into the compartment and hauled out a heavy-duty water gun that was shaped like an M32 grenade launcher. It was already loaded with holy water. He closed the compartment and turned away. Janis was in the aisle, facing the doors with her water pistol pointed at them, ready to shoot if necessary. Seeing him armed and dangerous, she lowered her gun.

'I'm gonna go grab my stuff,' she said. 'Are you gonna wait here?'

'Yeah. Go, hurry up. And be quiet.'

Janis kissed her father on the cheek. 'I'll be back real quick.'

She ran down the aisle, staying low to avoid being seen through any of the stained-glass windows. When she reached the end of the aisle she darted down the east wing.

Papshmir moved cautiously towards the front doors, his trigger finger twitching, just in case. He flipped open a spy hole in one of the doors and peeped out. There was no sign of anyone outside in the churchyard. The spy hole didn't cover all angles though, so even though it looked like no one was there, someone could be hiding out of sight. He turned away from the doors and scanned the hall, checking that he hadn't forgotten anything. It looked like everything was in order, but then suddenly it wasn't.

A tall, burly, black man in a dark red suit strolled around the corner of the west wing. He was wearing a red bowler hat. Papshmir's heart sank. The Devil was in his church.

'Good day to you,' said Scratch. He stopped at the altar and picked a thick hardback Bible from the pulpit. He flicked the book open and looked around the church, admiring the architecture. 'Nice place,' he said. 'Vincent isn't it?'

'What do you want?'

Scratch turned a few pages of the Bible and cast his eyes over the text. 'Do your flock grow tired of the tedious, banal passages littered throughout this monstrous book?' he asked.

'The book offers them comfort in times of need.'

'HA! Really? Let's see, shall we? I'll read a passage, and you tell me if it offers you comfort? Here we go, "*Matthew 10:28, Do not be afraid of those who kill the body but cannot kill the soul. Rather, be afraid of the One who can destroy both soul and body in Hell.*"

Papshmir kept his water gun down by his side. He grasped the crucifix he wore on a chain around his neck, and held it up. 'Be gone, for this is God's place!' he bellowed at the top of his voice. 'You have no business here.'

Scratch closed the Bible and tossed it to the floor. 'I take it you know why I'm here?' he said, ignoring Papshmir's bellowing.

'No. Be gone with your wickedness!'

'*Be gone with my wickedness?*' Scratch laughed. 'That's rather trite and old fashioned, wouldn't you say? I think a more modern way of conveying what it is you're trying to say would be something simpler, like, I don't know, "*Fuck off*"?'

'Okay, *fuck off then.*' Papshmir let go of his crucifix, fearing it wasn't deterring Scratch. He lifted his water gun and held it in both hands, pointing it at his enemy. 'You're not welcome here.'

'Oh, I'm aware of that,' said Scratch taking a playful step towards him. 'You know, normally I wouldn't be here. I'm not a fan of churches. They're kind of boring, and they're usually run by paedophiles. You know what's great about that?'

'What?'

'Most priests end up in Hell. See, the great thing about you guys is that barely any of you actually believe a fucking word of the Bible. You just use it to get to the kids.'

'You're disgusting. I'm giving you five seconds to get out of here, or I blast you with holy water.'

'I know you're one of the good ones, Vincent. Can I call you Vincent?'

'I don't care what you call me. You've got two seconds.'

'So shoot!' said Scratch, a sly grin on his face. 'But before you do, I just wanted to know something. Are you aware that your father, the Bourbon Kid, signed a contract with me? A contract promising me the souls of any offspring he might have? That was irresponsible of him, don't you think?'

'Okay, your time's up.'

Papshmir's hand was trembling. He wanted to blast Scratch with his holy water gun, but he was crippled by doubt. What if the gun didn't fire? What if it did and he missed? What if the holy water had no effect on Scratch? If you're going to shoot the Devil, you'd better not miss.

CRASH!

Papshmir jumped. Behind him, the double doors at the front of the church were knocked off their hinges. Papshmir didn't exactly want to take his eyes off Scratch, but he had no choice. Someone or some*thing* had showed up behind him. *Please be the Bourbon Kid. Please.* He looked back over his shoulder.

Damn.

Standing in the doorway, wielding a sword with a blade made of Hellfire was a man dressed in a long black robe. Not the Bourbon Kid. This man was eight feet tall, and the skin on his face was yellowed with age. He began moving towards Papshmir, his sword raised.

A huge grin broke out on Scratch's face. 'Hot diggity!' he cried joyously. 'Have you met the Reaper before?'

Papshmir made a snap decision. To Hell with Scratch! The Reaper was looking like the bigger threat right now. Papshmir turned away from the smirking Devil and directed his water gun at the Reaper. He squeezed the trigger and a thick burst of holy water spat out towards the incoming foe. But one swipe from the Reaper's flaming sword evaporated every drop of water before it came anywhere near him.

'BRAVO!' yelled Scratch. 'GOOD SHOW!'

Twenty One

The Oval office was a lonely place without Sanchez. Flake laid out the Santa Mondega history books on the desk and sat down in the mayor's leather chair. There were twenty-two books in all, so looking for information on how to change Sanchez's job title was a daunting prospect.

There were three books with the words "Sheriff's Log" embossed in gold on the cover. The rest were entitled, "Mayor's Historical Records", so Flake deduced that the title of Santa Mondega's most powerful man had changed from sheriff to mayor somewhere in book three. She opened the third tome and ran her finger down the chapter headings to look for something indicating the change. Halfway down she found what she was looking for. Two names with dates and page numbers next to them.

> *Sheriff Jack McLafferty - 1812 to 1814   Page 192*
> *Mayor Nuno Marquez - 1814 to 1832   Page 266*

She flicked through the book's pages until she found page 266 and the arrival of Nuno Marquez.

> *After the murder of Sheriff Jack McLafferty, Nuno Marquez was voted into the position of sheriff by a committee of six local officials.*

Flake paused momentarily and let the words sink in. Nuno Marquez was *voted* into the position of sheriff after the murder of Jack McLafferty. That wasn't consistent with what she had heard on the news. The reporter had claimed that in accordance with an ancient law, anyone who murdered the sheriff, or mayor, would inherit the title and take over the ruling of the city.

She read a little further on and found what she was looking for. Sheriff Nuno Marquez had proposed the change of his title from sheriff to mayor, and then approved it himself, like a dirty little dictator. Sanchez would be pleased when he heard how simple it was.

One thing was still bothering Flake though. What had become of the person who murdered Sheriff Jack McLafferty? She turned back a few pages to look for information about it. The last paragraph of McLafferty's chapter detailed his death.

> *In February of 1814 Sheriff Jack McLafferty was killed by an immigrant gunslinger named Kansas Bill Rigby.*

Flake stopped reading. Who the fuck was *Kansas Bill Rigby?* And if Rigby had murdered McLafferty, why didn't he take over as the new sheriff? She read on and found the answer.

As punishment for the crime, in accordance with Samarenti's Law of 1713, Kansas Bill Rigby was taken to Mutner's Farm and beheaded. The head of a bull was placed on his shoulders, and his body was paraded through the city as a warning to others not to attempt to kill the sheriff in future.

Flake slammed the book shut. Her heart was punching her in the throat, and her head was spinning. *Sanchez was on his way to Mutner's farm!* The farm was only a ten-minute drive away and he'd already been gone for ten minutes. She ripped her cell-phone from her belt and made a call to him. She didn't even get a dialling tone. The call went straight to a recorded message informing Flake that the number she was trying to reach was out of service.

She grabbed the phone on the desk and pressed the button with the word SECRETARY on it. The phone rang once before a woman answered.

'Hello, sir,' she said.

'Hey, this is Flake, the First Lady. Can you tell me, is there a phone in the mayor's Limousine? I need to make a call to Sanchez. It's urgent.'

'You can call him from the video phone on the desk,' the secretary replied.

'How the fuck do I do that?'

'You should see a grey button on the mayor's desk. It's marked, "Video phone". Just press that and wait while I connect you.'

'Okay.'

Flake wasn't entirely sure what was about to happen. She put the phone down and scoured the desk for the grey "Video phone" button. It was easy enough to find because it was right in front of her. She pressed it. Almost immediately, the pile of history books on the desk started moving. They were pushed aside by a small monitor that rose up out of the centre of the desk. Three words flashed up on the screen in black letters.

CALLING MAYOR'S LIMO

After about ten seconds, with Flake on the verge of storming out of the room and beating the secretary to death, the screen buzzed into life. There was no sign of Sanchez. The only thing visible on the screen was the seat in the back of the Limo and an information bar at the bottom of the screen indicating the vehicle's current location.

MUTNER'S FARM

Flake yelled at the monitor. 'Sanchez! Are you there? Can you hear me? SANCHEZ!'

Twenty Two

Every drop of water Papshmir fired at the Reaper evaporated before it even touched the raging hot blade of his sword. The preacher had to think fast. He was sandwiched in between the Grim Reaper and the Devil, in the aisle of his own church, no less. The Reaper was closing in on him from one side, whereas the Devil was on the other side, slapping himself on the thigh and laughing at his own jokes. It made the choice simple. Go for the Devil. It was hard to believe that such a thing could ever be the best option. Papshmir spun around and turned his water gun on Scratch, hoping for a different outcome. He blasted holy water at the smirking man in the red suit. Unlike the Reaper, Scratch didn't have a flaming sword to swat the water away with. It hit him, spraying all over his jacket, and his neck and face.

Success!

Every part of Scratch's body that came into contact with the water went up in flames. It gave Papshmir a renewed sense of hope. He marched toward the Devil, spraying more water at him.

The success was short lived. The fire was little more than an irritation to Scratch. The Devil raised his hands. He had a glowing red light in each of his palms. He thrust his hands towards Papshmir, shooting bolts of red electricity from them. The electricity moved so fast, Papshmir had no time to react. The bright red bolts struck him in the chest, lifting him off his feet. The power launched him across the church hall, over the pews, past the Reaper, and into the wall by the doors at the front of the church. Papshmir slumped to the floor, every bone in his body shaking. His water gun bounced away from him across the church floor.

The flames that had engulfed Scratch only moments earlier had already fizzled out, leaving a few blackened marks on his suit, but not a single burn on his skin. A few puffs of smoke floated up to the ceiling above his head.

'Do you know what that was?' Scratch cackled. 'That's the power of the Eye of the Moon! Your pathetic holy water is no match for me. The Eye and all its powers live within me!'

Papshmir was too dazed to take in everything Scratch was saying. He was seeing stars, and he had a ringing sound in his ears.

Scratch dusted himself down. 'Another suit ruined,' he sighed. He looked up at the Reaper and waved him away. 'Go on then, go and get him.'

The Reaper retreated back down the aisle to where Papshmir was crumpled in a heap on the floor. Scratch strolled casually along behind his giant comrade.

Papshmir scrambled to his feet, still dazed by the blast of electricity and the impact of smashing into the wall. There was only one thing for him to do. *Run.* Lead them away from the church. Away from Janis.

Papshmir's legs didn't get the memo. His attempt to make a run for it faltered as his legs staggered in different directions, like Bambi on ice.

The Reaper closed off Papshmir's route to the exit and loomed over him.

'DO IT!' Scratch yelled.

The Reaper lifted his sword high above his head and swung it down at the hapless preacher. Papshmir held up his arm to defend himself. The scream that followed was like music to Scratch's ears. The Reaper's blade of fire chopped Papshmir's left arm off at the shoulder. Blood spurted out like water from a fire hydrant. Papshmir's eyes almost popped out of his head. He staggered back, his balance hampered by the loss of his arm. His brain was frazzled and incapable of rational thought.

The Reaper lowered his sword and stepped back. Scratch strolled past him, clicking his fingers and wiggling his shoulders as if he were dancing (badly) to some disco music that was playing in his head.

'That looks pretty painful!' Scratch said, smirking at Papshmir. 'Annoying isn't it? You shoot someone with your clever holy-water-rifle thing and nothing much happens. Then someone cuts your bloody arm off! Hahahaha! Can you feel the resignation flowing through your veins? The knowledge that you tried to kill the Devil and it didn't work because, y'know, it's the Devil. What the fuck were you thinking trying to kill *me*, huh?'

Papshmir steadied himself against the wall, unable to respond to Scratch's gloating. Some of the blood shooting from his arm speckled over Scratch's face. The Devil licked it up with his long, juicy red tongue.

'Any last words?' Scratch asked.

Blood oozed from Papshmir's mouth when he opened it to talk, but he still forced a smile at Scratch, which took the Devil by surprise. Then with all his strength he mustered up the energy to yell two words.

'JANIS! RUN!'

Scratch ignored the yelling. He stepped closer to Papshmir and arched his hand, curling his fingers into gruesome clawed weapons. His fingernails were long, gnarly, yellow and sharp. He lunged at the injured preacher's face, sticking the sharp nails on his index and middle fingers into Papshmir's eyeballs, gouging them out. Papshmir cried out, his agony excruciating.

Scratch had an eyeball on the end of both fingers. He slid them into his mouth one at a time, sucking the eyeballs off. It had been a long time since Scratch had eaten a person's eyeballs. Papshmir's tasted good. He chewed on them, savouring the taste while the holy man slumped onto his side, all the fight draining from him, along with his blood.

A woman at the other end of the church hall screamed, 'DADDY!'

Scratch swallowed half an eyeball, almost choking on it. Had he really just heard someone cry out, *"Daddy"*? The word raced around his mind. The answer soon accompanied it. *Papshmir had a daughter.*

Scratch looked down at the floor. His red ankle boots were standing in a pool of Papshmir's blood. He swivelled on his heels and looked around for the woman who had shouted. There she was, standing in front of the altar.

'Janis!' Scratch whispered to himself as he swallowed some more eyeball. As soon as he set eyes on her, he knew who she was. He had seen her once before, many years earlier. The daughter of Vincent Papshmir was a Janis Joplin impersonator who had taken part in the last ever *Back From the Dead* show. It all made sense. Papshmir's daughter, Annabel's niece, the granddaughter of the Bourbon Kid. *The youngest in the bloodline.*

Scratch spat some eyeball onto the floor. 'JANIS!' he chuckled. 'How very nice to meet you again.'

Janis reached inside her leather jacket and pulled out two pistols. She pointed one at Scratch and one at the Reaper. The one she fired at the Reaper was a holy water pistol. The water barely had enough power or velocity to trouble the Reaper. He had plenty of time to swat it away with his sword of fire.

The other gun was loaded with bullets. Janis fired off every round she had at Scratch, her aim true. The bullets peppered his chest. But any impact they had was soon negated by the power of the Eye of the Moon. The Devil's wounds healed straight back up, leaving just the fresh holes in his suit to add to all the fire damage. When Janis ran out of bullets, Scratch smiled at her, then he clicked his fingers. The Reaper heard the message loud and clear.

Go get her.

The giant in the black robe marched down the aisle towards Janis, his flaming sword raging hot, ready to strike her down. Janis lowered her guns, then dropped them to the floor, tears streaming down her face. Her father's voice cried out one last time with every ounce of strength he had left.

'JANIS, FUCKING RUN!'

Her father had warned her many times that this day would come. She may not have been entirely ready for it, but he'd told her enough times what to do. And he had just emphatically reminded her. Janis turned away from the incoming Reaper and sprinted down the east wing corridor.

Scratch leaned over Papshmir, and whispered into his ear. 'This is tragic isn't it? I didn't even know about her. She gave herself away by shouting, *"Daddy"*. This day is just getting better by the minute.'

Twenty Three

Being driven around the city in his own Limo was everything Sanchez had hoped it would be. His bodyguard, Frank, had chosen to sit up front with the driver, Manuel, which left Sanchez alone in the back, gorging on free snacks. He switched on a television monitor in the back of the driver's seat and flicked to an obscure satellite channel called *Smudge TV,* so he could watch his favourite show, *Topless Weather.* The show featured women in sexy uniforms stripping while they predicted the weather for the rest of the day.

Topless Weather wasn't due to start for another minute, so while the commercials ran, Sanchez wound his window down an inch and peered out. The snow had eased up a little, but the dark clouds were still overhead. The Limo was cruising down a dirt track towards a big farmhouse that was surrounded by fields covered in thick white snow. There was no sign of any crowds of well-wishers to greet the new mayor though, which made him wonder why he'd needed a new suit for the occasion. Sanchez knocked on the blacked-out glass partition screen between him and the front seats.

'Excuse me, driver,' he shouted through the glass. 'Where are all the people?'

Manuel did not respond. Nor did Frank. Sanchez knocked on the glass a few more times but they either couldn't hear him, or they were ignoring him. Eventually he gave up trying to get their attention and instead made a mental note to get Flake to fire them both when he got back to City Hall.

He sat back in his seat and ripped open his third bag of peanuts. As was often the case for Sanchez, the bag split and the peanuts flew everywhere, mostly landing on the floor. A few landed on his gut, and one nestled in the breast pocket of his new shirt. He ate those first and then leaned down to pick up the rest of the nuts that were strewn across the floor.

'Sanchez! Are you there? Can you hear me? SANCHEZ!'

It didn't matter where he was, Flake always seemed to be yelling at him. But where the hell was she?

'Flake?' he called out, while rolling his head around.

'Sanchez, thank God. Where are you? Oh, wait. I can see your ass. What are you doing?'

Sanchez scraped together a handful of peanuts and sat back up on the seat so he could eat them while he worked out where Flake was yelling from.

'Sanchez! Thank God you're okay. Are you on your own?'

He finally spotted her. Her face was in the middle of the television screen. 'Are you reading the weather?' he asked, bewildered.

'What?'

'You know they make you strip on that show, don't you?'

'Would you shut up!' Flake hissed. She lowered her voice. 'Are you on your own? Can anyone hear us?'

'I'm on my own in the back of the Limo,' Sanchez replied. 'Why? Are you gonna do the dirty weather?'

Flake squinted her eyes like she was doing the Superman "laser-eyes" thing, something he'd seen her do many times before. It usually meant he was in trouble. 'Shut up and listen,' she whispered. 'I've been reading the City Hall history books.'

'Oh,' Sanchez groaned. 'Find anything interesting?'

'Yes. They're not taking you to Mutner's farm to pick out a bull to represent you in a bullfight. I looked it up. In the past when someone murdered the mayor they were taken to Mutner's farm and beheaded. Then they put a bull's head on you and parade you through the city. It's to deter other people from murdering the mayor.'

Sanchez waved a dismissive hand at the screen. 'Would you listen to yourself? That doesn't make sense. If someone beheads me, then *they* would *also* have to be beheaded for murdering me, because I'm the mayor.'

'Christ, Sanchez! Shut up! You need to get out of there. Can you jump out of the car?'

'Are you crazy? I'll ruin my new suit. There's snow and mud everywhere round here. Plus I can see some massive cow pats sticking out above the snow.'

'Sanchez, they're going to ki—'

Flake was cut off in mid-sentence as the TV switched itself off, and the Limo came to a stop. The blacked-out partition screen between Sanchez and the front seats buzzed and rolled down. Manuel's face was visible in the rear-view mirror. He was looking at Sanchez.

'Hey boss,' he said. 'Sorry, I had to shut the television off. We've arrived at our destination.'

Sanchez wound his window down further to get a better look outside. The farm was deserted, with the exception of one animal loitering in the field at the front of the farmhouse. It was a bull with a huge set of horns, and even bigger bollocks.

'Christ,' said Sanchez. He leaned forward and tapped his bodyguard, Frank, on the shoulder. 'Have you seen the sack on that thing?'

'Let me go check it out for you Mister Mayor,' said Frank. 'Wait here a sec.'

Frank climbed out of the Limo, leaving Sanchez to make small talk with Manuel.

'So, Manuel, how long do they give you for toilet breaks?'

Manuel said nothing. He was engrossed in watching Frank. The bodyguard was approaching the bull pen. When he was close to it he checked something on the gate, then turned around and gave Manuel a thumbs-up sign.

'What's that about?' Sanchez asked.

'He's going to stun the bull,' said Manuel. 'We should go and watch. I'll get your door for you, sir.'

'You can call me Mister President if you prefer,' Sanchez replied.

Manuel didn't reply. He exited the car and opened the back door. Sanchez slid along the seat and climbed out. The snow was cold beneath his feet and made a pleasant crunching sound as he set foot on it. Manuel slammed the door shut.

'Where are we going first?' Sanchez asked, wincing at the light snowfall. 'Have they put some food on for us?'

'We'll head on up to the farmhouse,' said Manuel. 'We can watch Frank stun the bull from up there. It'll be safer than staying in the car. I'll walk behind you so if anyone sees us, they'll know how important you are.'

'Good thinking.'

'On you go then, boss,' said Manuel. He prodded Sanchez in the back, ushering him onto the track that led up to the farmhouse.

'How will he stun the bull then?' Sanchez asked. 'Zap it in the nuts with a taser, or what?'

'It will probably be something like that, Mister President. By the way, I really like your suit. It makes you look like Arnold Schwarzenegger.'

Sanchez decided not to have Manuel fired after all. The driver was finally beginning to show him the proper levels of respect. And now that they were bonding, it seemed only appropriate for Sanchez to introduce Manuel to his special brand of humour.

There was an enormous cow pat on the edge of the track, neatly concealed beneath a layer of snow, but not quite enough to escape Sanchez's keen eye. He casually veered across the track towards it and slowed his walk down so that Manuel almost bumped into the back of him. As soon as Sanchez felt Manuel's breath on the back of his neck, he put his plan into action.

'Hey, what's that?' he said, pointing over at the horizon.

Manuel turned his head to see what Sanchez was pointing at. While he was distracted, Sanchez ducked down and curled into a ball. It worked perfectly. Manuel stumbled over him and fell face-first towards the ground.

'Shhhiiiitttt!'

The unfortunate Limo driver face-planted into the giant cow pat. The steaming pile of excrement engulfed his whole head, accompanied by a lovely splatting sound.

Sanchez leapt back to his feet. 'GOTCHA!' he yelled, pointing at the fallen driver. He was about to kick some snow at Manuel when he spotted a rapidly expanding patch of blood around the stricken Limo driver's torso. Then he saw the reason why. There was a huge silver blade sticking out of Manuel's back. It was covered in blood. The Limo driver had impaled himself on it when he fell.

'Oh, shit!' Sanchez winced. 'Sorry, man. I didn't realise you were carrying a.....' He stopped in mid-sentence as Flake's warning flashed in his mind. Was it possible she was right about the whole beheading thing? What the fuck was Manuel doing with something that looked like a giant machete?

The Limo driver twisted his head to look up at Sanchez. There was shit all over his cheeks and lips, and blood was dribbling from his mouth. He mumbled two words.

'You *dick!*'

As it turned out, they were his last words. Manuel's head fell back into the giant turd with another loud splat, which was music to Sanchez's ears.

The whole situation was pretty awkward though, and Sanchez hoped Frank hadn't seen it. He looked around. Frank was in the large, fenced off pen with the bull, but he was staring at Sanchez. He looked furious. He stormed out of the bull pen and rushed over to see what had happened.

'He did it to himself,' Sanchez lied.

Frank stared in horror at the blade sticking out of Manuel's back.

'*You* did this!' he said, his face contorted with fury. He reached inside his jacket and pulled out a Glock pistol.

'It was an accident,' Sanchez protested, raising his hands in surrender and backing away from Frank. 'I didn't mean to do it.'

Frank took aim with his gun, pointing it at Sanchez's heart. 'I always hated you, you fat piece of shit!' he raged.

'I'll get you a pay rise,' Sanchez offered.

'Fuck you.'

BANG!

The bullet flew out of the gun barrel. It fizzed through the cold air and hit Sanchez in the chest. The brute force of it lifted him off his feet and sent him sprawling onto his back in a pile of mud and snow. Blood sprayed up onto his face. An agonising dull pain seared through his upper body, robbing him of oxygen, making it hard to breathe. Sanchez stared up at the cloudy sky. Through his blurred vision he saw a million tiny snowflakes falling down from above, and he saw Frank moving in for a second shot.

The bodyguard stopped beside Sanchez and pointed the gun at his face. 'Manuel was my brother,' he said, a tear rolling down his cheek. 'You killed him. Now I kill you, *asshole.*'

Twenty Four

After a fun ride in The Bum, Jasmine and Elvis arrived back at the Tapioca. Jasmine parked the salt truck across the street and Elvis jumped out onto the sidewalk, his feet sinking into six inches of snow. The blizzard coming down from above almost turned him into a snowman by the time he'd walked around the truck to help Jasmine down from the driver's side. He took hold of her hand and the two of them fought their way across the road to the Tapioca.

'It's like a ghost town around here,' said Jasmine, breathing in a flurry of snow every time she opened her mouth.

Elvis did not respond. He pounded his fist on the front doors of the Tapioca and waited for someone to let them in. No one did.

'Is anyone in?' Jasmine asked.

Elvis walked over to a window and wiped some snow off with his sleeve. He peered in through the space he had cleared. 'It's empty!' he grumbled. 'Can you call Rex and see where is?'

'Not right now,' Jasmine replied, snuggling up to him and peering through the window to see for herself.

'Why not?'

'I don't have any pockets on this catsuit, so I tucked my phone inside myself.'

Elvis stopped peering through the window and gave Jasmine a quizzical look. 'That's it, I'm getting you a belt.'

'What for?'

'For starters, we should all be wearing gun belts now anyway. You need a gun by your hip in case of emergencies, and in your case you also need a holster for your phone.'

'But it's only a small phone, and I like keeping it tucked away,' Jasmine replied, giving him a playful shove.

'Is it on vibrate?'

'Yeah.'

'I might call you later then.'

'Call me now. Warm me up.'

'Hang on. I can see Rex.'

Rex was inside the Tapioca after all. He approached the front doors, unbolted them and then pulled one door open. He greeted Elvis and Jasmine with a smile.

'You made it then?'

Jasmine brushed past him. 'Yeah, fucking freezing out there though.'

'What took you so long?' Elvis asked, as he stepped inside the warmth of the Tapioca.

'Me and Sally were in the kitchen making sandwiches.'

'Are there any left?'

Rex closed the door and slid the bolt back across to keep it shut. 'Nah. We ate 'em all.'

'Bullshit. You weren't making sandwiches.'

Jasmine shook all the snow out of her hair and off her shoulders and walked into the bar area. Sally Diamond was sitting at a table on her own, nursing a glass of red wine. There was a bottle of Shitting Monkey beer on the table too. The jukebox was easing out some background music in the form of "Come Away With Me" by Norah Jones, which gave the place a relaxed atmosphere for a change.

'Hi, Sally,' said Elvis. 'How were the sandwiches?'

'What sandwiches?' Sally replied, puzzled, before hastily adding. 'Oh, yeah they were great.'

'I might make myself some.' Elvis headed through the bar area and out into the kitchen. Jasmine followed him but stopped behind the bar to pour herself a drink.

'Hey, Jas,' Sally called out. 'I hear you've been kicking one of your fans in the nuts this morning?'

'Yeah,' Jasmine replied. 'Rex recognised the guy from a bunch of ball-busting porn sites. Did he tell you?'

'No, he didn't mention that part.'

'Oh, well, just so you know, I think he's into that sort of thing.'

'I am not,' said Rex, returning to his seat at Sally's table. 'Jasmine's just teasing.'

Sally nodded. 'Yeah, sure.'

While Jasmine poured herself a glass of vodka, lime and soda, Elvis returned from the kitchen, sidled up behind her and wrapped a gun belt around her waist, clipping it together at the front. It had a holster on the hip with a small pistol tucked into it.

'You're so thoughtful,' Jasmine said, leaning back to give him a kiss.

Sally called over to them. 'You guys make a real cute couple.'

'We keep things pretty fresh,' said Jasmine.

'Yeah, I guess you must have learned a trick or two when you were a hooker,' said Sally, before taking a sip of her wine.

Elvis patted Jasmine on the ass and whispered in her ear, 'I don't think she meant that the way it came out. She's just had a few too many.'

'Hey, I don't mind,' Jasmine whispered back. Then she yelled over to Sally, 'Has Rex tried to grope you with his metal hand yet?'

Elvis left her and headed through the bar flap into the drinking area. 'Sally, you don't need to answer that,' he said.

'No, he hasn't groped me with his metal hand,' said Sally, answering the question anyway. 'But I don't think my ass could take a metal fist anyhow, unlike some people.'

Jasmine grabbed a bottle of beer from a shelf behind her and hurled it across the bar. It looked like it was aimed at Sally's face, but Elvis breezed past and caught it in his stride as he approached the table. He snapped the lid off with his teeth and pulled up a chair next to Rex.

'It's all about the lubricant,' he said.

Rex slid his arm around Sally's shoulder. 'Let's talk about something else,' he suggested.

'Whadda you make of all this snow then?' Elvis asked.

'It's a bad omen,' said Rex. 'It means Scratch is coming.'

Jasmine walked through the bar flap with her drink and was about to join them when she spotted the Bourbon Kid sitting at a table in the farthest corner away. He was basically a fixture there, to the point they forgot he was there most of the time.

'Hey, JD, do you wanna join us?' she hollered.

The Kid was having some time alone with a bottle of bourbon and a whiskey glass. He declined Jasmine's offer with a shake of his head.

'What the fuck is that?' Jasmine asked.

'I think he wants to be left alone,' said Rex.

'Not him,' said Jasmine, pointing at something near the Bourbon Kid. 'That, *there!*'

Not far from the where the Kid was sitting, one of the tables was shaking. Something below it was causing one of its legs to move up and down, as if it was enjoying the background music.

The Bourbon Kid jumped up from his seat and hurried over to the table. The sight of him springing into action alerted the others to the possibility of some imminent danger. The Kid wasn't prone to overreaction so to see him jump up and head for the moving table was a big deal. He lifted the table leg up and moved it aside. The section of floor beneath the chair leg rose up. As the others arrived and drew their guns ready for some conflict, a secret trapdoor camouflaged in the floor swung open. A young woman dressed in black leather poked her head out. She stared up at the group of people pointing guns at her. She looked terrified.

'Janis?' said Elvis.

The Bourbon Kid reached down and grabbed Janis by her arm and hauled her out of the hole in the floor. She was shaking and visibly flustered.

'What's happened?' the Kid asked her.

Janis had tears streaming down her face. 'It's my dad. I think they killed him!'

'Who did?'

'Scratch, he's at the church with this other huge guy. I think it's the Grim Reaper. FUCK, ARSE, BEARDY TWAT! He had a sword made of fire!'

'Who is this?' Rex asked. 'And what the fuck is she on about?'

The Kid placed his hands on Janis's shoulders and looked into her eyes. 'Is your father definitely dead?' he asked.

Janis's bottom lip trembled. No words came forth. She buried her head in the Bourbon Kid's chest, threw her arms around him and bawled her eyes out.

Rex was exasperated. 'Can someone tell me what's going on?'

'She's Papshmir's daughter,' said Elvis. 'The rest, I'll tell you later.'

The Bourbon Kid stroked Janis's hair. 'Is Scratch still there?' he asked.

Janis pulled away from him and nodded. 'I think so.' A tear rolled off her chin and she yelled, 'FUCK!' as loud as she could. No one could tell if it was intentional or a Tourette's outburst.

The Kid ushered her over to Jasmine and Sally. 'Stay here with these guys. I'll go see what's what.'

Jasmine took Janis over to a nearby table and sat her down while Sally ran behind the bar to get her a glass of water.

Rex stared at the hole in the floor. 'Where the fuck did this tunnel come from?'

'Papshmir dug it,' the Bourbon Kid replied. 'It's an escape tunnel, for days like this.'

'Man, that's crazy,' said Rex.

The Bourbon Kid lowered his foot onto a metal rung in the wall beneath the trapdoor and started to climb down into the tunnel. Rex grabbed his arm. 'Wait,' he said. 'Me and Elvis will come with you. Just give me a minute to tool up.'

The Bourbon Kid shook him off and pointed at Janis. 'See her? She's my blood, the last of my family. Stay here and make sure nothing happens to her. I'll check out the church on my own.'

With that, The Kid pulled the hood up on his coat and lowered himself into the tunnel.

Rex looked at Elvis. 'What the fuck? Shit, man. I think this is gonna be a fucker of a day.'

Twenty Five

Flake panicked. Her video call to Sanchez had abruptly ended before she could fully warn him of the danger he faced. There was only one thing to do. She had to get to Mutner's farm as soon as possible.

She kicked her chair back and stood up to leave. She was halfway across the room when the red phone on the desk started ringing. She hoped it would be Sanchez calling her back, so she dashed back and answered it immediately.

'Sanchez?' she said, hopefully.

'No, this is Ross from security. Am I speaking with Flake Munroe?'

'Yes.'

'Good. Miss Munroe, I've been informed that you are the owner of an ambulance in the underground parking lot, registration number—'

Flake cut him off in mid-sentence. 'Yes, it's my ambulance. What about it?'

'I'm afraid I have some bad news. Someone has crashed into your vehicle. As a matter of urgency, would you be able to head down to the parking lot and exchange insurance details with the other party?'

'Erm, yeah, yeah, sure. I was heading down there anyway.'

'Great, thanks. I'll let the other party know.'

Flake slammed the phone down. She had no intention of swapping insurance details with anyone. She just needed to get the ambulance and drive like the wind to Mutner's farm. She bolted for the door, but as she reached for the doorknob she hesitated. Something felt wrong. Was she being led into a trap? She'd seen something like this before in a movie. Images raced through her mind. Al Pacino, Sean Penn. *Carlito's Way!*

In the movie, Sean Penn's character took a phone call from security telling him his car had been pranged, or something like that. Flake's recollection was a little hazy. The call resulted in Sean Penn heading for the elevator to go check on the damage to his car. It was all part of a ruse that ended with him being stabbed in the chest by an assassin when the elevator arrived.

Flake was unarmed. If there were hitmen waiting in the elevator for her, she'd be in big trouble. *Damn,* this whole First Lady thing had made her so paranoid. She scoured the room for a weapon. Her eyes settled on a gold-plated letter opener on Sanchez's desk. She ran back and grabbed it, and tucked it inside her belt where it couldn't be seen. She left the office and walked briskly past several rows of desks manned by council employees. She wanted to run towards the elevator, but she was trying not to draw attention to herself.

One person did notice her, a heavy-set, oily-skinned man, with mafia-style greased-back black hair. He was wearing a brown suit that matched the leather sofa he was sitting on in the visitors waiting area. He was reading a tabloid newspaper, but he looked up as Flake marched past. She couldn't see his eyes because he was wearing sunglasses. Who the fuck reads a newspaper indoors while wearing sunglasses? Assassins, that's who!

The man stood up and tucked his newspaper under his arm. 'Can I help you, Miss Munroe?' he called out.

'I'm just heading down to the parking lot,' Flake replied, without breaking stride. 'Someone's hit my ambulance.'

'I'm Norman,' the man said, approaching her. 'I'm your personal bodyguard. I'll go with you.'

'That's not necessary,' said Flake, hurrying on towards the elevator.

'My job requires me to escort you to the parking lot,' Norman said, lengthening his stride to catch up with her.

Bastard. This had the feel of a set up. Flake didn't like it one bit. She quickened up and when she reached the elevator she pressed a grey button in the wall to call it. Norman mooched up and stood alongside her. He smelled of expensive after-shave. A definite giveaway that he was an assassin. Probably.

Flake checked her watch. 'Actually, you know what? I think I'll take the stairs,' she said.

'You can't at the moment,' said Norman. 'The cleaners are giving them the monthly washdown.'

'I don't care about that.'

PING!

As Flake made a move for the stairs, Norman grabbed her arm just above the elbow, wrapping his huge hand around it.

'Elevator's here,' he said. 'Come on. Twenty seconds is all it'll take. In that time I can give you a rundown on all our security procedures. By the end of the week you won't wanna go anywhere without me.'

Norman's grip was firm, not enough to call it threatening, but firm enough for Flake to be troubled by it. He stepped into the elevator and pulled her in with him.

'Sorry to manhandle you,' he said, releasing her arm and pressing a button on the lift's keypad. 'But, you know if someone attempts to shoot you or the mayor, I have to grab you and pull you to safety, so it's not a bad idea for you to get used to being grabbed. I'll always try to go for the arm if I can, but different situations call for different measures, you know?'

'Right.'

The carriage doors closed in front of them and the elevator began its descent to the underground parking lot.

'How are you enjoying being the new First Lady?' Norman asked, while checking his appearance in the mirrored walls of the lift carriage.

'It's okay, I guess.'

Norman had a gun tucked into a holster inside his jacket. Flake tried not to stare at it, but it was constantly there in her peripheral vision. There weren't supposed to be guns in City Hall. Or maybe bodyguards were exempt from that rule? She wished she knew.

Norman spat on his hand and wiped it through his hair, slicking it down as he continued to check his appearance in the mirror. Flake was sure she'd seen a gangster in a movie do the same thing right before he pulled his gun and shot someone. She just couldn't remember which film.

The display on the keypad showed they were passing through floor 4. Different scenarios were playing out in Flake's mind. Would Norman make his move while the elevator was still moving? Or wait until they were in the parking lot where there was less likelihood of being interrupted?

Fuck it! Why wait for the meathead to make his move at all?

Flake slid her hand down to her belt and discreetly clasped the handle of the gold letter-opener. There was no time to waste. She pulled it out and leapt up onto Norman's back, wrapping her arm around his neck and her legs around his waist. It certainly caught him off guard. He staggered back, possibly intending to slam her into the back wall.

'What are you doing?' he spluttered.

Flake plunged the letter-opener into the side of his neck. Blood squirted out all over her hand. The further in she pushed the sharp gold object, the faster the blood spurted out. A stream of it leapt across the elevator, splattering onto the mirrored walls. Norman made some pretty grim choking and gurgling sounds. In a state of panic, he tried desperately to reach up and grab a hold of Flake. She used every ounce of strength she had to stay on his back, like someone riding a bucking bronco. All through the struggle she continued stabbing him repeatedly in the neck, spraying more and more blood all over the walls. As the elevator went past the ground floor, Norman slumped to his knees, his attempts to fight her off waning with each passing second.

PING!

They arrived at the basement and the doors slid open. Flake released her grip on Norman and climbed off his back. Her hand was caked in his blood, and she had a feeling there were specks of it on her neck and face too. The letter-opener was absolutely dripping with the stuff. She considered stabbing him with it again, but soon realised there was no need. Norman's head thudded against the floor between the open doors and his body crumpled into a curled up position. A pool of blood began to surround him on the floor.

Flake leaned down and wiped some blood from her hand onto Norman's jacket then relieved him of his gun. She spotted a hanky in his pocket and used that to wipe her fingerprints off the handle of the letter opener, then she dropped them onto the floor beside him. The elevator doors started to close, so she stuck her arm out to stop them before they hit Norman's head. She poked her head out into the parking lot and checked both ways, ready to shoot anyone who came at her.

The parking lot was gloomy and badly lit like something out of a scary movie. With both hands on her gun, she stepped out of the elevator. The doors tried to close behind her but thudded into Norman's head, then reopened again. As Flake moved past a row of cars towards her ambulance at the far end, she stayed alert, constantly checking for any eyes watching her from the shadows. The only sound above Flake's breathing came from the elevator doors, which were thudding repeatedly into Norman's head as they tried to close.

As she neared the ambulance, which was parked with its back doors facing a wall, she asked herself the question, *"If some guy has really crashed into the ambulance, then where the fuck is he?"*

The tip-tap of footsteps interrupted the repetition of the lift doors. A small, hunched figure appeared from behind the ambulance. In the poor light Flake struggled to see a face on it. But as it came closer, she saw it was a little old lady in a skirt and cardigan, with her hair up in a bun, and a handbag draped across her, hanging by her side. The woman raised her right hand, possibly to shield her eyes from one of the dim lights.

'Hello, is this your ambulance?' she asked, reaching into her bag with her free hand.

There was no time to hesitate in this kind of life and death situation. Flake remembered some advice Rex had given her earlier. *"The best assassins don't look like assassins,"* he'd said. *"That's why they're so good at what they do. No one sees them as a threat."* Flake wasn't about to make that mistake. She took aim with her gun.

BANG!

A bullet ripped into the chest of the assassin lady. She let out a whimper and promptly fell to the ground in a heap. A set of car keys clattered onto the ground beside her. Flake scampered over and pointed her gun at the face of the fallen assassin.

The woman on the ground choked up some blood. She was old, maybe seventy, maybe older. Too old to be driving around underground parking lots on her own, Flake decided.

'Who sent you?' Flake snarled at her.

The woman didn't reply. She just kept blinking.

'Didn't think I'd be ready for ya, huh?' said Flake. 'Are there any others?'

The woman choked up some more blood. Flake scoured the surrounding area. There were no other assassins in sight.

'This is real clever,' Flake whispered. 'Send an old lady who looks harmless. Very sophisticated. Didn't work though, did it?'

The woman spluttered some words. 'I'm sorry, I reversed into the ambulance.'

Flake glanced at the front of the ambulance and saw that one of the headlights was broken.

'Oh, you're good,' she said, nodding to herself. 'You smashed one of my headlights for extra authenticity. Nice try. Well, this has been fun, but I can't hang around to chat.'

Flake kicked the assassin in the ribs for good measure, then jumped into the ambulance. She pulled the key from her pocket and slid it into the ignition. She hesitated. What if the ambulance exploded when she turned the key to start the engine? That had happened in loads of movies. Fuck it. It was a chance she had to take. She turned the key. The engine roared into life. Nothing exploded. The song "So Far, So Good" by Sheena Easton kicked in on the radio. Flake released the parking brake, hit the gas, drove over the old lady, reversed back over her just to make sure, then sped out of the parking lot towards Mutner's Farm.

Twenty Six

The Bourbon Kid climbed a ladder in the wall of the tunnel and pushed open a hatch at the top. He poked his head up through it. He was in Papshmir's study. A door that led out into the church was wide open. The sound of voices in the corridor outside floated in. Two men were bickering about something. He recognised one of the voices. *Scratch.* The Devil was here. The other voice, deep and abrasive, had to be the man Janis thought was the Grim Reaper.

The Kid climbed out of the tunnel, careful not to make any noise. He unholstered his Headblaster gun and edged towards the open door. The bickering of the two men stopped suddenly. All that remained was the sound of the wind blowing into the church hall from outside. A cold draft was running all through the building.

The Kid crept out of the study into the east wing corridor. There was no one around. He moved silently along the corridor to the next door, which was also open. He poked his head around it. It was an empty bathroom. Scratch and the Reaper had most likely exited the church that way, through Scratch's portal. But what of Vincent Papshmir?

He found his son near the entrance to the church. The front doors had been demolished. And so had Papshmir. His corpse was mutilated almost beyond recognition. His eyes had been gouged out, and one of his arms cut off. His clothes were ripped to shreds, his chest torn open. Scratch had shown no mercy.

The Bourbon Kid crouched down next to the body. It was hard to look. He closed his eyes and rubbed his head in frustration. Oh, Vincent, why were you still here? You knew Scratch was coming. You should have been packed and halfway to Barbados.

He opened his eyes again and took a long look at what the Devil had done to his son. He had to remember it, imprint it in his mind, use it as motivation, as a reminder of what he would have to do to Scratch by way of repayment, way of revenge. And he was going to have to perform some kind of cremation. Janis could never be allowed to see what had become of her father.

****

A black van had been parked across the street from the church for much of the morning. Sitting behind the wheel was a man with a thick, shaggy yellow beard. Stunky, the axeman had been watching, waiting for the possible arrival of any members of the Dead Hunters, who, if his research was correct, were frequent visitors to the church. It had been an eventful wait too. He'd seen an eight-foot tall muthafucker in a black bathrobe turn up and obliterate the front doors at one point. It piqued his curiosity. He had to know what was going on inside.

With the doors no longer blocking the view into the church, Stunky exited his recently hired van and trudged through the wind and snow up to the gates at the front of the churchyard. He concealed himself behind a gatepost so he could watch what went on inside the church. He witnessed the destruction of Papshmir, and the bickering that followed when the preacher's daughter escaped.

When Scratch and his giant friend headed to the other end of the church, Stunky hung around to see if they came back. They did not. Something better happened. Stunky struck gold. His eyes lit up with dollar signs. A man dressed in black showed up inside the church. Not just any man. *The Bourbon Kid.* The man worth ten million dollars. *Ten million.*

Scratch had warned all of the bounty hunters of the suicidal nature of going after the number one target. Stunky had intended to heed the advice and just go after one of the easier targets like Elvis. But the Kid was all alone. There would never be a better time. The Flying Axeman made his move.

He unhooked two wooden-handled axes he had strapped across his back and crept up the path through the churchyard, keeping low to avoid being seen. His prize, the Bourbon Kid, was crouched down next to the decimated body of the dead preacher. As Stunky snuck through the entrance, the Kid looked up. The two men made fleeting eye contact.

Stunky wasn't one for introductions, or wasting time. He hurled one of his axes at the Kid's head. Perfect throw. In all of his days of throwing axes he had never missed his mark. But the reactions of the Bourbon Kid were something he had never encountered before. The hooded man plucked the axe out of the air, an inch away from it hitting him in the forehead.

'Impressive,' said Stunky. 'Now we both have an axe. Care to tango?'

'Maybe I'll just shoot you,' the Kid replied.

'Reach for your gun, and you're a dead man. You're quick, but not that quick.'

The Bourbon Kid ran his finger along the blade of the axe he had acquired. He was obviously impressed by the craftmanship. He wrapped his other hand around the handle, getting a feel for the weight of the weapon.

Stunky glanced at the remains of Father Papshmir. 'Scratch killed your preacher friend, huh? How does that feel?'

The Bourbon Kid did not respond verbally. With his free hand he beckoned Stunky towards him.

'You wanna dance, eh?' said Stunky, a smile breaking out on his face. 'Okay, let's rock.'

Fighting with an axe was all about the angles. And Stunky, with his skills as an acrobat knew how to attack from up above, down below, from the side, or a mix of all three in a rapid-fire combination. And he liked to strike first. He sprinted, not towards the Kid, but up onto a row of pews. He slammed his foot down on the top of a pew and launched himself high into the air, attacking the Kid, not only from above, but also from the side furthest from his opponent's weapon. As Stunky descended he swung his axe down at the Kid's head.

The sound of an axe ripping through flesh was like music to Stunky's ears.

Usually.

It had never been *his* flesh before though. His axe hit nothing but air. The Bourbon Kid sidestepped and swung his own axe upwards with devastating speed. The axe ripped through Stunky's genitals and kept going. It sliced him open from groin to chin, like someone cutting open a bag of sand. The famed axe-man landed on his feet, but he wobbled as he looked into the eyes of the man who had just cut through him.

Stunky's torso exploded. Blood and entrails vomited out. His knees buckled, but before he could collapse to the ground like an empty banana skin, the Bourbon Kid grabbed a clump of the axeman's hair and dragged him over to a section of the wall next to a stained glass window. The axeman's innards slid out of him, sloshing onto the floor like slime. The Kid held Stunky's head against the wall and took a sideways step, lining up like a tennis player ready to serve an ace. He swung his axe at the other man's head. With a splendid whoosh, the blade chopped horizontally through Stunky's face, right across the bridge of his nose. The blade embedded itself in the wall with the top half of Stunky's face resting on it, his dead eyes staring back at his killer. The Kid let go of the handle of his axe and stepped back. The axe stayed in the wall. Every part of Stunky's face and body that was below the blade slid to the ground. Guts, bones, gristle and organs slathered across the floor. The stench was epic.

The Kid looked into Stunky's eyes and asked him a question.

'How does *that* feel?'

Twenty Seven

Flake turned on the ambulance siren and blazed a trail across town, jumping red lights, ignoring stop signs, driving on the wrong side of the road, driving on the sidewalk, breaking speed limits, overtaking school buses and occasionally making rude hand gestures at people she didn't like the look of.

If there was a record for driving from City Hall to Mutner's Farm, Flake beat it easily, even in the snow. The ambulance skidded and bounced around as she completed the last part of the journey, the drive down the dirt track that led to Mutner's farmhouse. As she neared it she was greeted by a sight that turned her blood cold. Two bodies were lying motionless in the snow outside the farmhouse. One was Manuel, the Limo driver. He had a machete sticking out of his chest. The other was Sanchez.

Flake stopped the ambulance and jumped out. Her boots sank into the deep snow. The wind and falling sleet blew into her face, slowing her progress as she trudged along the dirt track to reach her soulmate.

'Sanchez!'

No response. When she finally got to him, she slid down to her knees by his side and placed her hand on his chest. There was blood on his jacket and face, and a bullet hole that went right through the top pocket on his blazer. She touched his neck with her fingers to check for a pulse. Tears welled up in her eyes.

And then as if by some kind of miracle, Sanchez opened one eye, and looked up at her.

'You're alive!' Flake gasped.

'I've been shot,' he said.

'I know. I can see the bullet hole! You've lost a lot of blood.'

Flake leant down and kissed him. His face was wet, and his lips tasted sour and vinegary. She recoiled and wiped her mouth. She sniffed her fingertips, then tasted them.

'This is piss,' she said.

Sanchez sat up. He lifted open his jacket and pulled his hip-flask out of the inside pocket. There was a big dent in it and the lid was missing. 'God bless the hip-flask,' he said. 'It took a bullet for me.'

Flake wiped her eyes. 'You're not hurt then?'

'Apart from being knocked off my feet and covered in my own piss, I think I'm okay.'

Flake looked around. 'Who shot you? Was it Manuel?' she asked, pointing at the dead Limo driver with the machete sticking out of his back.

Sanchez scoffed. 'Him? Pah! He wishes. That snake tried to attack me from behind with the machete. Lucky I have good reflexes. I saw the attack coming and pulled off a karate move. Threw him over my shoulder onto his own blade.'

Flake wasn't convinced. 'Sanchez, is that bullshit?'

'Yes, he fell into a big pile of it. I've got some on my suit too. Go careful, that stuff is everywhere. Huge piles of it. That bull is a dirty bastard.'

'I'm confused. You've got blood on your suit. Whose is it? And who shot you?'

'My bodyguard, Frank,' Sanchez shook his fist at the sky. '*The turncoat!*'

Flake looked around. 'Where is he? Is he still here?'

Sanchez glanced at his watch. 'He should be back any second now. Quick, lie down, play dead.'

'What?'

A rumbling sound was heading their way, coming from behind the farmhouse. Sanchez grabbed Flake and pulled her to the ground with him.

'Don't move,' he whispered.

'Am I lying in shit?'

'Probably, but don't move, whatever you do.'

Sanchez had reverted to his previous position, flat on his back, pretending to be dead. Flake was lying next to him, looking over at the farmhouse to see who was coming. The rumbling noise grew louder and louder. There were high-pitched screams too.

'What *is* that?' she whispered.

'Don't let him see you.'

Frank the bodyguard reappeared from around the side of the farmhouse. He was yelling all kinds of obscenities. And it was obvious why. Flake followed Sanchez's lead and stayed completely still on the ground. The rumbling noise wasn't being made by Frank, not directly anyway. It was actually coming from the hooves of a bull that was charging around the farmyard with Frank impaled on one of its horns. The horn had ripped right through his pants and penetrated deep into his asshole. The raging bull thundered past Flake and Sanchez, with the screaming bodyguard bouncing up and down on its head. Flake watched it charge around the outside of the bull pen it was supposed to be standing in. As the bull faded into the distance, so did Frank's anguished cries.

Flake whispered out of the side of her mouth to Sanchez. 'What the fuck happened here?'

Sanchez twisted onto his side and pointed at Frank's distant figure. 'That idiot unlocked the bull pen, then left it wide open while he tried to kill me. He was just about to shoot me in the face when the bull ran out of its pen and rammed its horn right up his butt. It's been running around the perimeter of the farm ever since, with him stuck on its head, yelling like a bitch.'

Flake sat up on her knees. 'Is that *his* blood on your suit then?'

'Yeah, once that bull's horn went up his ring-piece, it spurted everywhere.'

'I love you, Sanchez.'

'I love you too,' he replied, attempting unsuccessfully to sit back up.

Flake climbed to her feet and offered him her hand. He took it and she pulled him up into a seated position again.

'You know what?' he said, pausing for breath. 'I don't think I want to be the President anymore.'

'It's only your first day. It'll get better.'

'Yeah, but it's not as much fun as I thought it would be. I mean, I know exactly how JFK must have felt when he was assassinated. Although, *he* was lucky because he didn't end up covered in piss and cow shit, or blood from some guy's butt-hole. I had it much worse than him.'

'Do you want to go back to the Tapioca?'

Sanchez nodded. Flake grabbed his arm with both hands and hauled him to his feet.

'I think I prefer just hanging out with you and the gang, y'know?' said Sanchez, flicking some shit off his jacket.

Flake kissed him on the cheek and then wiped some piss off her face. 'City Hall's not a safe place for us,' she said, mulling over all that had happened in the last twenty minutes. 'Someone wants us both dead. It could be Scratch, but then again, it could be someone at City Hall. Melinda springs to mind.'

Sanchez looked surprised. 'Why would she want us dead?'

'I don't know. But while we try to figure it out, how about I drive us back to the Tapioca and cook you some breakfast for dinner?'

Sanchez smiled. 'I think I'd like that.'

Twenty Eight

Comforting Janis was tough. Jasmine had never known her own parents, so she didn't know what it was like to lose one. She helped Janis out of her leather jacket and set it on the back of her chair. Janis slouched over and buried her head in her hands, sobbing. Jasmine sat down beside her and gave her a shoulder to cry on, but it was hard to know what to say to someone whose father had just been murdered by the Devil and the Grim Reaper.

'I like the pattern on your shirt,' Jasmine said, referring to a flowery design on Janis's top.

Sally came back from the bar with two drinks. A glass of water for Janis, and another glass of red wine for herself. She placed the glass of water on the table in front of Janis and sat down beside her. She didn't seem to know what to say either.

Elvis was standing by the hole in the floor, waiting for the Bourbon Kid to return. Rex was pacing up and down, muttering to himself.

Janis wiped some tears from her face and looked over at Elvis. 'The Chinaman was just the beginning,' she said, her nose bunged up with snot. 'We're all going to die.'

Rex stopped pacing around. 'What Chinaman?' he asked.

Elvis answered him, 'Me and Janis ran into a bounty hunter earlier at City Hall, a guy called the Chinaman. You know him?'

'I know *of* him,' said Rex.

'Yeah, well he was there to kill me, but Janis clocked him with her bike helmet.'

Rex pulled at his long brown hair. 'And you're only telling me this now?' he said, clearly irked. 'Did the guy say anything to you? Was he sent by Scratch?'

Elvis shrugged his shoulders. 'It's gotta be Scratch, right? Who else would have sent him?'

'Shit, this is bad. How the fuck did the Chinaman find you anyway? Are we all being followed?'

'He followed me down into the archives. He could have been following me all morning for all I know.'

'The archives?' said Rex. 'At City Hall?'

'Yeah, I was there this morning, while Sanchez was being inducted as mayor.'

A perplexed frown broke out on Rex's face. 'What were you looking for in the city archives?' he asked.

Elvis looked uncomfortable. 'Huh?'

'What were you looking for?' Rex repeated. 'And why was Janis down there with you?'

Jasmine decided to act as peacemaker. 'Look, Rex, it's no big deal. They were just checking Sally out, to see if she was okay. And she is.'

Sally looked crestfallen. 'What? You were looking through my records?'

'It was just due diligence,' said Elvis. 'You're hanging out with us a lot these days, so I just thought, seeing as I was at City Hall, I'd have a look at your public records.'

Rex had a look of thunder on his face. 'And what did you find exactly, while you were snooping on Sally's private life?'

'Nothing,' said Elvis. 'She's totally clean.'

'But I drink, right?' said Sally, her disappointment with Elvis clearly evident.

'Hey, Sally, we all drink here. It's no big deal.'

'If you wanted to know anything about me you could have just asked,' Sally replied.

Jasmine cleared her throat. 'Do you mind? Can't this argument wait until later? I mean, *hello!*' she said, with a fluttery wave of her hand towards Janis.

Sally understood. She turned away from the argument and rubbed Janis's back. 'We all know how tough it is to lose someone,' she whispered. 'It's never easy.'

Janis forced a polite smile and then picked up her glass of water. She took one sip, but as soon as she swallowed it she winced and put the glass back down on the table. 'Is there vodka in this?' she asked, looking like she might vomit.

'Yeah, sorry,' said Sally. 'I just thought it would help take the edge off things for you.'

Janis kicked her chair back and stepped away from the table. She grabbed her stomach and leaned forward, then she threw up on herself, and over the table. Jasmine and Sally moved out of the way.

'That's my fault,' said Sally, backing away towards the bar. 'I'm sorry. I don't know what I was thinking. I'll get a cloth and clean that up for you.'

Janis had puke on her hands and down the front of her shirt. Jasmine put her arm around her shoulder and guided her away from the puke.

'Come with me,' she said, 'I'll get you cleaned up. Elvis, can you get her some clean clothes from upstairs?'

'Yeah, sure.'

Elvis left the bar area and headed upstairs to find something of Flake's for Janis to wear. He was probably relieved to get away from the argument he'd been having with Rex and Sally.

Jasmine guided Janis over to the Ladies washroom to get cleaned up, but Rex grabbed her arm as they walked past him.

'Hey, Jas, wait a minute. You should stay away from the toilets,' he reminded her.

'I've got my gun,' Jasmine replied, slapping her hand against the pistol that was holstered on her belt. 'And I'll leave the door open.'

Rex let go of her arm. 'Okay, but make sure you holler if anything looks weird.'

The two women carried on to the washroom. Jasmine whispered in Janis's ear. 'Don't mind him. He's a big fusspot, is all. Worries about everything.'

Janis's head twitched to the side. 'Wanker,' she whispered.

Jasmine pushed open the door of the Ladies washroom and used a small waste bin to prop it open. There were five cubicles on one side of the room and four washbasins and a row of mirrors on the other. Jasmine helped Janis over to the nearest washbasin. Janis leaned over it and retched like she was going to be sick again. Even though her lungs were burning, nothing came out and she ended up just spitting into the sink a few times. Jasmine grabbed some paper towels from a dispenser on the wall and pulled Janis's hair away from her face so she could wipe some orangey puke from around her mouth.

'I'm really sorry about what happened to your dad,' Jasmine said. 'I only met him a few times, but I really liked him. He was cool.'

'He was the best,' Janis spluttered.

Jasmine wetted a paper towel and wiped down the front of Janis's flowery shirt. 'You know, everyone here is an orphan,' she said. 'You're welcome to stay with us for as long as you like. We got a real good group of friends here, and we look out for each other.'

Janis forced a smile. 'Yeah, thanks.'

The paper towel Jasmine was using got mucky pretty quick. She disposed of it in the bin by the door, and was about to grab some more towels when she felt a vibration in her crotch. 'Oh Jesus,' she said, squirming. 'Someone's texting me.'

Janis looked up into the mirror. 'Don't mind me,' she said. 'You text away. I'm okay.'

'I'll just pop into a cubicle to read it,' said Jasmine, still squirming.

'Why?'

'I don't have pockets on this catsuit, so I keep the phone inside me.'

Janis looked puzzled. 'You what?'

'I'll just be a minute. Give me a shout if you need me.'

Jasmine ducked into the nearest cubicle and unbuckled her belt. She placed it on the floor then unzipped her catsuit. She retrieved her phone quite quickly, knowing that time was precious. The display on the phone showed she had a text message from an unknown number, which was highly unusual. She opened the message. It read -

"GET OUT OF THERE!"

Jasmine frowned and whispered the message out loud to herself. *'Get out of there?'*

What the fuck did it mean? It took a couple of seconds before a hot flush washed over her. She zipped up her catsuit and grabbed her belt.

'Janis!' she whispered as she put the belt back on.

Janis did not reply.

'Janis, we've got to go.'

'JASMINE!!!'

Jasmine burst out of the cubicle, dropped her cell phone and unholstered her pistol in one magnificent, swift move. She pointed the gun in the direction of Janis's cry for help. She was greeted by a horrific sight.

Janis was being dragged towards a bright red light that was glowing from a strange opening in the wall at the back of the washroom. Dragged by a burly black man in a red suit. *Scratch.* He had one arm wrapped around her neck and another around her waist. The opening in the wall he was dragging her towards was the portal that led back into Purgatory.

'OH SHIT!' Jasmine yelled in a state of panic. 'REX!'

Scratch's eyes shone, his pupils flickering between red and gold. He had a twisted grin on his face, which was in total contrast to the look of unbridled terror on Janis's face. Janis kicked and screamed as she tried to free herself from his grasp, but her feet couldn't touch the floor, so she had nothing to grip onto.

'HELP ME! JAS, HELP ME! PLEASE!'

Jasmine aimed her gun at Scratch's head. There was no time for reasoning, or pleading with him. This was Scratch, the Devil, the most unreasonable cunt in the universe.

BANG!

Her shot was clean, her aim totally on the money. With little to aim at, she managed to blast a hole through Scratch's head, just above his right eye. It rocked him back a step, and blood spurted out of the wound in his forehead, but he kept a firm grip on Janis who was fighting for her life with no success.

To Jasmine's dismay and horror, the bullet hole in Scratch's head healed up almost immediately. A fair amount of blood had popped out of his head, but he was completely unaffected by it. Jasmine yelled again.

'REX!'

Rex burst into the washroom. He had a Mare's Leg shotgun in one hand, primed and ready for action. He pointed it at Scratch's head, but he hesitated. He couldn't fire off a shot without hitting Janis. The Mare's Leg was all wrong for this situation. He scoured every inch of the available target. It couldn't be done.

Scratch winked at them both.

'I'll be back for you soon enough,' he said.

In spite of Janis's frantic attempts to bite Scratch's hand to free herself from his grip, he carried her back through the hole in the wall into Purgatory, using her as a shield to stop Rex from blasting him with his shotgun. And then came the moment Jasmine and Rex would never forget. Scratch pressed his sharp nails into the flesh just below Janis's ear and ripped through the skin from one side of her neck to the other. Janis looked like she tried to scream, but all that came from her lips was a muffled choking sound.

Blood squirted out of her throat, all over Scratch's hand, some of it spraying onto the floor of the washroom. The look of terror in her eyes wilted as the life drained out of her. The portal entrance closed up, replaced by a plain white wall. Scratch was gone, with the ominous promise he would return.

Janis was gone too, never to be seen again.

Twenty Nine

For Flake, driving back from Mutner's Farm was a much more relaxed affair than when she had driven to it. The snow had eased up a little but in some parts of town it was almost a foot deep. The roads weren't as bad as the sidewalks because thankfully someone had driven a salt truck around half the city that morning.

With their mood much more optimistic, Flake and Sanchez were singing along to *"Let It Snow"* by Vaughn Monroe. Halfway through the song, Flake stopped the ambulance at a red light, which was unusual for her. She slapped Sanchez on the arm.

'What's that for?' he asked.

'Look at those idiots,' she said, pointing through the windscreen.

Sanchez tried to get a good look, but with the snow coming down, and the windscreen wipers moving back and forth it was hard to focus.

'What am I looking at?' he asked.

'Over there, in the County Motel. Look!'

Sanchez leaned back and stared out of his passenger side window. He finally saw what Flake was pointing at. A snowball fight was taking place in the County Motel parking lot. A young, very athletic blonde woman in a pink bikini was hurling snowballs at a muscular but very naked man with a shaved head. It looked like they had jumped out of a *Cooler Cola* trailer truck that was parked behind them with its back doors open.

'Wow, they must be fucking freezing,' Sanchez said, a chill running through him at the sight of the woman in the bikini.

'He definitely looks cold,' said Flake, leaning across Sanchez to get a better view.

'And her snowballing technique is appalling,' said Sanchez. 'She's not taking enough time to pat the snow into a solid ball, so it's falling apart as she throws it. What an idiot.'

The snow in the motel's parking lot was almost up to the woman's knees. As the naked man closed in on her, she looked around and saw Sanchez staring at her through the ambulance window. She waved at him with both hands. Sanchez waved back. 'She's very friendly,' he remarked.

The traffic lights turned green and Flake drove the ambulance on. 'What are they doing now?' she asked, keeping her eyes on the road.

'He's just tackled her,' Sanchez replied. 'Now he's carrying her back to the Cola truck. She's waving again.'

'Maybe we should try naked snowballing later?' Flake suggested.

'I don't think so,' said Sanchez. 'I've had enough of snow for one day, thank you.'

Flake spent the rest of the ride back to the Tapioca trying to convince Sanchez that snowballing was fun, but he wasn't having any of it. Eventually, with the argument unresolved, Flake parked up at the back of the Tapioca, and the two of them headed inside via the back door into the kitchen. As soon as they walked into the bar area it was obvious something was amiss. Elvis, Rex, Jasmine and Sally Diamond all started yelling and pointing guns at them. Flake froze, while Sanchez raised his hands in surrender.

'Oh, thank fuck it's just you two,' said Rex, lowering his shotgun.

The other paranoid lunatics lowered their guns too and breathed a collective sigh of relief.

'What's with you lot?' Flake asked.

'Scratch was here,' said Rex, tucking his gun into the holster on his belt. 'He killed Janis.'

'What?'

'We've had quite a day too,' said Sanchez, lowering his hands. 'My bodyguard and chauffeur both tried to kill me at Mutner's Farm. Fortunately I killed one of them with a bit of karate, and the other one got impaled on a bull's horn, *right up his asshole.*'

Elvis sniffed the air. 'What's that smell?' he asked, turning his nose up. 'Is it bullshit?'

'Yes it is,' said Flake. 'Sanchez has got some on his jacket. Forget about that though. What are you guys talking about? Who's Janis?'

Elvis answered. 'Sanchez, you remember Janis who had Tourettes?'

'Yeah.'

'She was here, and—' Elvis tailed off because he'd seen the Bourbon Kid climbing back out of the trapdoor in the floor. The hood on his coat was down and he had blood on his face.

'Why is there a hole in my floor?' Sanchez asked. Flake elbowed him in the ribs to shut him up.

'Where is Janis?' the Bourbon Kid asked, looking around, his mood darkening with every passing second.

'She's gone,' said Elvis. 'Scratch came out of the wall in the toilets and took her.'

Sally backed him up. 'It all happened so quick, there was nothing we could do.'

'Who is Janis?' Flake asked for the second time.

The question was greeted with silence and a lack of eye contact from everyone. Eventually, a tearful Jasmine responded.

'She was Papshmir's daughter. JD's granddaughter.'

Flake looked at Sanchez to see if he knew what Jasmine was talking about. He shrugged, then leaned down to grab a bag of peanuts from under the bar.

Elvis called over to the Bourbon Kid. 'Was Papshmir okay?'

The Bourbon Kid shook his head, then he pulled his hood up, cloaking his face in shadow. He walked over to his usual table in the corner. His bottle of bourbon and a whiskey glass were still there from earlier in the day. He sat down and filled the glass with bourbon, then he downed the contents in one and slammed the glass back down.

Jasmine called over to him. 'I'm so sorry. It was my fault. It all happened so fast. She was sick on herself and wanted to freshen up, so I took her to the Ladies room, but my phone went and.....'

The Kid interrupted her. 'What did he do to her?'

Rex took a few steps towards the Kid's table to try to smooth things over. 'It's not Jasmine's fault, man. None of us could have stopped him.'

'What did he do?' the Kid repeated, while refilling his glass with bourbon.

'It was quick,' said Rex.

The Kid did not reply.

Sensing that he was waiting for more information, Jasmine spoke up. 'He grabbed her and dragged her through the portal into Purgatory,' she said, chewing the nail on her thumb. 'I managed to fire off a shot. I hit him in the head but it didn't hurt him. Rex came in too, but there was nothing we could do. And then, as the portal was closing..... he killed her.'

The Bourbon Kid took a sip of his drink. 'How did he do it?' he asked, still not making eye contact with anyone.

Jasmine was afraid to say any more about it. She looked to Rex for help. He answered for her.

'He cut her throat.'

'If there's anything I can do....' said Jasmine.

The Bourbon Kid picked up his drink again. Without taking his eyes off it he replied to Jasmine. 'You could get out of my sight. That would be a good start.'

Jasmine wiped some tears from her face. 'Someone sent me a text that said *"Get out of there."* Someone was trying to help us.'

Elvis stroked Jasmine's hair. 'Any idea who sent you the text?' he asked her.

'I don't know.'

'But how could someone know you were in the toilets at that moment?' Sally asked, baffled by everything that was going on.

'Cameras,' said the Bourbon Kid.

'Cameras?' said Jasmine, horrified. 'You mean there are cameras in the toilets?' She looked at Sanchez. 'Why would you do that?'

Sanchez was appalled at the accusation. 'I'm no Chuck Berry!' he retorted. 'It was probably Rex.'

Rex groaned. 'For fuckssake. Can't you see? Scratch put them there. He's probably got hidden cameras everywhere. He could be watching us right now. From this moment on, we all have to assume Scratch can see everything we do in this place. That's how he knew Jasmine and Janis were in the Ladies room.'

'That still doesn't explain how someone texted me,' said Jasmine.

'Maybe Jacko texted you?' Elvis suggested. 'He would want to help. Does he have your number?'

'I don't know,' Jasmine replied, looking at the message on her phone. 'Should I reply to this message and ask if it's him?'

The Bourbon Kid spoke up. 'Why don't you do us all a favour and text him from the Ladies room?'

The hurt on Jasmines face was clear for all to see. She knew exactly what the Kid meant, but she couldn't muster a response. Elvis took hold of her arm and shepherded her away to the other side of the bar.

Rex stepped closer to the Bourbon Kid's table. 'Hey, look. We're all real sorry about Janis, man. She seemed really cool. I liked her.'

'Good for you.' The Kid pulled a cigarette out of a pack he'd placed on the table. He put it between his lips and sucked on it, lighting it up. He took in a lungful of smoke, then exhaled in Rex's direction.

Sally walked up behind Rex and tapped him on the shoulder. 'I think I should be going,' she said. 'This isn't any of my business, and I don't think anyone wants me here.'

'You're right about that,' the Bourbon Kid muttered under his breath.

Rex hesitated as if he was going to say something to the Bourbon Kid, but instead he chose to leave things to settle. The Tapioca wasn't a great place to be right now. The atmosphere was all kinds of wrong.

'I could use some fresh air,' Rex said eventually to the whole group. 'I'm gonna walk Sally home. Call me if you need me.'

Thirty

'Zilas, put something on the jukebox. I'm in the mood for dancing!'

Scratch was buzzing. The look on the faces of Jasmine and Rex when he killed Janis was something to be savoured. He carried Janis's corpse over to the bar and propped her up against it. He grabbed a clump of her shirt to hold her upright and with his free hand he ripped her head off her shoulders. Blood squirted out all over the bar and the floor of Purgatory. He let go of her body and it slumped to the floor like a rag doll. Right now all Scratch wanted was to serenade Janis's lovely head.

Zilas took Scratch's jukebox request a little too literally. He selected the song "I'm In the Mood for Dancing" by The Nolan Sisters. Scratch hated the song, but it was ideal for the current situation, not that he would ever admit that to Zilas. He danced around the bar area in Purgatory holding Janis's head up and staring into her vacant, lifeless eyes. He sang along with the Nolan Sisters even though he only really knew the chorus. He was in such a good mood he didn't even care that people were watching him.

Eric Einstein took a break from tapping away on his laptop to enjoy the show from his stool at the bar. Trixie, the witch was a few stools down from him, chewing the foot off a dead rat that had been served to her on a plate. And Snake Hawk, the leader of the Skinners tribe, was next to her, drinking a Bloody Mary. He was more impressed by Janis's bleeding head than he was by Scratch's attempts at singing and dancing. He also had his eye on Janis's decapitated corpse that was spreadeagled on the floor. The only other person inside Purgatory was the Grim Reaper. He was standing in the corner, looking livid.

When the Nolan Sisters stopped singing, Scratch turned to his audience and waited for a round of applause, which didn't come. He didn't let it bother him though. *Fuck 'em* if they couldn't appreciate a good song and dance routine. He had an idea for something else they might like though. He pulled Janis's head up to his face. Her tongue was hanging out of her mouth, drooping down over her chin. Scratch loved the taste of a woman's tongue, and the temptation to savour the taste of Janis's was too great. He wrapped his lips around it and sucked it into his mouth. Admittedly, with her being dead, her tongue had turned deathly cold. It still tasted sweet and wonderful though, possibly because of how pleased Scratch was with himself. After sucking on it for a while, enjoying it like it was an ice lolly, he lost all restraint and with one glorious chomp he bit into it. Blood oozed out all down his face. He had eaten Papshmir's eyes earlier in the day as a starter, Janis's tongue was the main course. The Bourbon Kid's heart would make for a perfect dessert later in the day if everything continued to work out as planned.

Snake Hawk cleared his throat to grab Scratch's attention. He pointed at Janis's body. 'You gonna eat that?' he asked.

'Maybe,' Scratch replied, through a mouthful of tongue, which was proving to be chewier than expected. He swallowed some of it and then clarified his response to Snake Hawk. 'You and your men need to stay hungry. I have something better lined up for you.'

'Good,' said Snake Hawk. 'Because the boys are getting bored out there.'

The *boys* he was referring to were outside on the forecourt, hanging around with a bunch of crazy-ass skeletons that had recently been exhumed from the shallow graves in the deserted wasteland around Purgatory. The skeletons were braindead idiots, of course, but Scratch liked the look of them. He would have brought some zombies up, but cannibals and zombies don't mix well together. He knew from previous experience that the dumb fuckers only fight and try to eat each other.

Einstein raised his hand. 'Boss, there's something you should know.'

'What?' Scratch snapped at him.

'Just before you went through the portal to grab Janis, someone sent a text to Jasmine's phone, warning her that you were coming.'

Scratch dropped Janis's head and kicked it across the room. It bounced off the wall and rolled across the floor, landing next to the jukebox.

'How could someone text Jasmine to warn her about my plans?' Scratch asked. 'No one knew what I was doing!'

Einstein grimaced. 'The text was sent from here.'

'What?'

It didn't take Scratch long to figure out who the culprit was. Zilas was edging away from the jukebox, towards the front doors, looking decidedly nervous.

'You piece of shit!' Scratch snarled. 'Why the fuck would you do that?'

'Do what?'

'Come here!'

Zilas lowered his head, but continued backing away until the Reaper grabbed him by his collar, lifted him off his feet, and marched him across the room. He dropped the hunchback in front of Scratch and returned to his corner so he could go back to looking livid.

Zilas cowered in front of his master. 'I'm sorry,' he mumbled.

Scratch gritted his teeth. 'What the fuck? Why are you helping my enemies?'

'I'm not,' Zilas said, trembling. 'I just, you know, I like Jasmine. I didn't want her to get hurt.'

Small puffs of smoke blew out of Scratch's ears. 'GODDAMMIT! YOU FUCKING CLOWN!' He launched into a full on assault, kicking Zilas hard in the stomach. The thunderous kick lifted the hunchback off the floor. His feet rose up behind his head just before he landed on his face with an almighty slap, then lay there groaning while Scratch continued kicking him in the head and ribs, or wherever else he felt he could do some damage. Beating up Zilas was a great stress reliever, far better than any of those squeezable rubber things handed out by psychiatrists.

'I fucking told you before, Jasmine *isn't* going to be killed!' Scratch ranted. 'Christ! How many times do I have to explain everything? The plan is to capture her and hand her over to the FBI. Then they can sentence her to death by lethal injection or whatever they choose.' He stopped kicking Zilas and stepped away to give the hunchback a chance to admit his mistake.

'I'm sorry,' Zilas cried. 'Jasmine's always been nice to me. I was thinking maybe you could let her live with me as punishment for whatever she did?'

'Live with you?' Scratch bellowed a hearty laugh that went on for an inappropriately long time. On several occasions it looked like he was finished laughing, only for him to start up again like he'd just heard the best joke ever.

When eventually he did stop, the smile vanished from his face completely. He kicked Zilas in the face, breaking his jaw into a million tiny fragments. He bowed down over the sobbing hunchback to taunt him some more.

'If you ever, ever side with anyone against me again, I'll see to it that you suffer unimaginable pain for every second of the rest of eternity. And I'll start by taking your fucking phone and RAMMING IT UP YOUR PEE HOLE!'

Before Scratch's ranting could get any more unpleasant, he was interrupted by Eric Einstein.

'Boss! Boss!' the crazy-haired scientist called out. He was tapping the screen on his laptop while waving his other hand in the air, excitedly.

'Yes. What?'

'Rodeo Rex is about to leave the Tapioca. Without the others!'

Scratch clicked his fingers at Snake Hawk. 'Bring a few of your men in. It's time for them to get fed.'

Thirty One

It looked like night-time in Santa Mondega even though it was only early afternoon. Since Rex and Sally had left the Tapioca, the snow had eased up and now the city had more of a fairy-tale look to it, much different to the wild blizzard from earlier in the day.

The walk to Sally's apartment block took them past the city harbour. The snow crunched beneath their feet as they walked together along the promenade, admiring the view and enjoying the peacefulness. They had the seafront to themselves.

In the years that he'd been a member of the Dead Hunters, Rex hadn't had time for any romance in his life. It had been non-stop assignments for Scratch, hunting the undead, killing them, and then hunting some more. But since meeting Sally he'd begun to realise how much he missed having a female companion to hang out with. Sally was just his type, slim, athletic, fiery red hair, pretty face, good sense of humour, liked a drink, and on top of that, she didn't take any shit from anyone. In Rex's mind she was kind of like Flake, but with better taste in men, he hoped.

'You know, for all the horrible stuff that happens in this city, it's a beautiful place,' he said, stopping and pointing out to the sea. 'Look how peaceful it is out there.'

Sally gazed at the horizon and leaned against Rex's huge bicep. 'Let's face it,' she said, 'Without the great sea views I don't think anyone would live here.'

Rex slid his arm around her shoulder. 'If you could live anywhere in the world, where would you wanna go?' he asked.

'South of France.'

'South of France? How come?'

'I dunno. You asked, and it was the first place I thought of.'

'I'd wanna go somewhere like Norway.'

'It'll be cold in Norway.'

'It's cold here.'

'I'll tell you what,' said Sally, jabbing him gently in the ribs. 'When we get to my place I'll warm you up by cooking you one of my world-famous veggie burgers. How's that sound?'

Rex removed his arm from her shoulder and recoiled in mock horror. 'Veggie burger?'

'Yeah. What? You don't like veggie burgers?'

'I don't get why they even exist. Either have vegetables or have a burger. What *the fuck* is the point of a veggie burger?'

Sally stepped back and blinked several times. 'Have you ever *had* a veggie burger?' she asked, her eyebrows raised.

'No, why the fuck would I?'

'Well for starters, if you'd had one, you could comment on why you don't like them. You're just dissing something you haven't even tried.'

'I don't need to try a veggie burger to know it's shit.'

'Fine. Don't have one then.'

Sally turned her back on him and started walking along the promenade again. Rex allowed himself a wry smile and followed after her, walking briskly to catch up. Sally looked back and saw him following, so she started running, pretending to flee. Rex wasn't really in the mood for running through deep snow, so he carried on with his brisk walking. Sally stopped when she reached, of all things, a burger stall. The stall was closed but she banged her fist on the side as if to try and wake someone inside.

'Hello! Anyone there?' she bawled. 'If veggie burgers are better than meat burgers, please stay silent!'

Rex slowed his walk to a stroll and eventually rocked up beside her. 'You're funny,' he said sarcastically.

'Here look,' said Sally, pointing at a menu on the front of the stall. 'See, veggie burgers are cheaper than cheeseburgers and they have less calories. Look at the pictures here, and tell me the veggie burger doesn't look better than *every other burger on here*.'

'The veggie burger looks like shit,' said Rex.

Sally stared into Rex's eyes and smiled. He knew what it meant. This was his cue to kiss her. He moved in, but to his surprise and disappointment, Sally backed away.

'What's the matter?' he asked.

'Nothing.'

Sally glanced at something over Rex's shoulder. He twisted his head to see what had caught her eye. Across the way from them, outside a set of public toilets was an old woman with purple hair and a sickly green complexion. She smirked at Rex, revealing a set of black, oily teeth.

'Can I help you?' Rex asked her.

The woman raised her right hand as if she was about to do a Jedi force-pull. She stared at the burger stall and wiggled her fingers at it, like a puppeteer. The result of her wiggling fingers didn't seem to do anything to the stall, but it made Rex's hand quiver. Before he could figure out what was happening, the burger joint had been transformed into a giant magnet. Rex's metal hand snapped back towards the stall.

He tried to keep control of it, but it moved with an unstoppable force. His hand slammed into the stall just below the menu. He tried to pull it free, but it was glued solid. The gun holstered to his hip sealed itself against the side of the burger stall too.

'What the fuck?' He looked at Sally. 'This burger joint seems to be magnetised.'

'I'm sorry,' said Sally, backing away some more.

A bellowing laugh from nearby sent a tremor through Rex's veins. He looked back to where the old purple-haired woman was standing. Behind her, Scratch had stepped out from the public toilets. And he was not alone. Three heavily tattooed, olive-skinned men in loin cloths followed him out. Their bodies were adorned with hunting trophies, such as teeth, shrunken skulls, finger bones and other unspeakable things. And now they had their eyes firmly set on Rex.

'Hello, Rex,' said Scratch, cheerfully. 'I see you've met Trixie. She's a bit of a whizz when it comes to magnetising things. And these three fellas behind me, they're the Skinners. In case you hadn't guessed, they're cannibals. They tend to enjoy hunting their prey before eating it. But I wanted to introduce them to the concept of fast food. Today's menu, the Rodeo burger.'

Rex whispered out of the side of his mouth. 'Sally, *run.*'

'Oh, don't worry about Sally,' said Scratch. 'She's with us. You didn't really think she liked you, did you?' He launched into one of his inappropriately long laughs.

Rex looked forlornly at Sally, hoping that she would deny it all. 'What the fuck is going on?' he asked her.

Sally couldn't look him in the eye. 'I'm sorry Rex,' she said. 'I had no choice. They said they'd kill my mom.'

Rex's heart missed a beat. 'What? You shoulda told me. We could have protected you!'

Sally shook her head. 'No, you couldn't. I'm sorry.'

Scratch waved Sally away. 'It's time for you to go, my dear. You won't want to watch this.'

The three Skinners closed in on Rex. Each of them was brandishing a sharp wooden dagger that was impervious to the magnetic pull of the burger stall. Like typical hunters they came at him from different angles. One from each side and one from the front. Rex swung out with his free hand and kicked out with his leg, but this was a fight that could not be won.

He pleaded with Scratch. 'Hey wait, let's talk about this!'

'I don't think so,' said Scratch. 'I'll see you back in Hell, *when you get there.*'

The cannibals leapt on Rex like wild animals, ripping at his skin with their knives, and biting at every part of his body with their jagged teeth. He struggled in vain to prize his metal hand or his gun away from the magnetised burger stall. To no avail. He succumbed to the cannibals attacks and slid to ground with the three of them swarming over him, his metal hand the only thing visible above the carnage.

Scratch clicked his fingers at Trixie. 'Come,' he said. 'Let's leave them to it.'

The witch released her magnetic spell on the burger joint and followed Scratch back into the public toilets that led back to Purgatory.

Rex's metal hand slid down into the snow along with the rest of his body, the hand being the only part of him that the Skinners had no interest in feasting upon.

Further down the promenade, Sally Diamond fled, the sound of Rex's fading screams in her ears.

Thirty Two

The Tapioca was a sombre place to be, especially for Jasmine. And when Elvis nipped outside to take a dump in the snow rather than risk using the toilets, she was left with a choice of hanging out with Sanchez, who was watching an episode of *The Mysterious Cities of Gold* on the bar's television, or join Flake in the kitchen. It wasn't a tough decision. Even though Sanchez's cartoon looked quite entertaining, she chose the kitchen because Sanchez smelled of piss and cow shit, and Flake was better company, obviously.

Flake was cooking a fried breakfast, and she had quite a system going on. Even though it was only Sanchez who had expressed an interest in eating sausages, bacon, eggs, hash browns, tomatoes, mushrooms and fried bread, Flake appeared to be making enough for everyone, and doing it on her own looked like hard work.

'Can I help with anything?' Jasmine asked.

'I've got it all under control,' Flake replied. 'It might look like chaos but I've done this a million times, including once already this morning.'

'How do you get the timing of everything right? I mean, when I tried to do this for Elvis once I burned half the stuff before I'd even put the eggs under the grill.'

'You put the eggs under the grill?'

'To crisp them up a bit.'

Flake grabbed a damp towel and wiped some sweat from her brow. 'You know, you should go talk to JD. He's on his own out there and he's probably calmed down a bit by now. I know he was a bit shitty with you, but he was upset, which is understandable, isn't it? I'm sure he's realised by now that what happened to Janis wasn't your fault.'

'But what would I say to him?'

'Ask him if he wants a bacon sandwich.'

'I'd like a bacon sandwich.'

'Good, because I'm making you one, with sausages. Go on, go ask JD if he wants anything. I always find food is a good conversation starter. You'll see, he won't be mad at you forever.'

Jasmine smiled. 'He never really talks to me, y'know. I think, like, he thinks I'm stupid or something.'

Flake turned over some bacon rashers on the grill. A big puff of smoke blew up in her face. She stepped back and waved it away. 'Go show him you're *not* stupid then.' She grabbed a pen and a small notepad from the sideboard and handed them to Jasmine. 'Write his order down on here for me.'

Jasmine kissed Flake on the cheek. 'Thanks, Flake. You always know the right things to say.'

Flake rubbed Jasmine's arm. 'Just make sure you don't fuck up his order.'

Jasmine left the kitchen, pen and paper in hand, and headed over to the Bourbon Kid's table in the corner of the drinking area. He had a cigarette hanging from the corner of his mouth, and he was staring into a glass of bourbon. When Jasmine arrived at his table, he ignored her.

'I'm taking food orders,' she said. 'Flake's making breakfast for everyone. What would you like?'

The Kid did not reply, so Jasmine pulled up a chair and sat down opposite him. In her nervousness she wasn't sure what to say, and his silence was making things even more awkward. She eyed up his glass of bourbon.

'Can I try some of that?' she asked.

Still no reply. Jasmine put her pen and notepad down and reached across the table. She grabbed the glass of bourbon and took a sip. It was a sour taste. She slid the glass back to him.

'How do you drink that shit?' she asked.

'On my own.'

Jasmine spluttered a nervous laugh. 'You like me really,' she teased. 'I know you do.'

The Kid took a drag on his cigarette, then tapped the ash into an ashtray. He picked up his glass of bourbon and took a big sip, then placed it back down on the table and exhaled smoke from his nostrils.

Jasmine tried again. 'You know, we've got lots in common.'

The Kid closed his eyes and let out a weary sigh. 'Like what?' he asked.

'We've both lost a lot of people that we care about.'

He glanced up at her. 'Did you kill *your* parents too?'

It was true, the Kid had murdered both of his parents, for reasons that he didn't generally talk about. Jasmine hadn't killed hers, not that she knew of anyway.

'No. I never knew my parents,' she admitted. 'I grew up in a brothel and when I was old enough, I had to work there.'

'I've never heard you say a bad word about that place.'

'That's true,' she agreed. 'I did like it, but I didn't know any different. I didn't know that I would one day have *real* friends, people who like me for who I am. You know, you're probably the only guy that's never tried to get me into bed.'

'I bet Sanchez has never tried.'

'He's afraid of Flake, so he doesn't count.'

'What do you want, Jasmine?'

'Do you remember the first time we met?'

'What?'

'It was on a plane. You and Rex and Elvis brought me and Jack Munson back from Romania.'

'Yeah, so?'

'Well, I was really nervous because you guys were pretty scary. And I wanted a cigarette, but Rex wouldn't let me smoke on the plane. But then you lit one up and gave it to me.'

'Is this your weird way of saying you want a cigarette?'

'No. I'm saying that when I was nervous and I thought you guys were going to kill me, you were the one who put me at ease. You were the first one to welcome me into the group.'

The Kid took another drag on his cigarette, and stared at his drink. 'I was probably trying to annoy Rex.'

'Deny it all you like, but *you like me.* I know it. Remember that other time when that psychopath murdered Jack and then cut off his face, and wore it as a mask while he tried to rape me?'

'If you're looking for a grief counsellor you're talking to the wrong guy.'

Jasmine brushed off the sarcastic remark and forged on. 'When Rex and Elvis told you what Mozart did to me, you pulled out a gun and blew him away. You didn't hesitate, not for one second, even though Rex had specifically told you *not* to kill him because he had information we needed.'

'Again, probably trying to annoy Rex.'

'Look, what I'm saying,' Jasmine continued, 'is that I never had a friend like you before. You never talk to me. You pretend like you don't like me, but when I'm in trouble, you always step up. You and Elvis and Rex, you're the best friends I ever had. And I know I annoy you because I'm dumb sometimes, but *I like you.* You're like the dad I never had.'

'*The Dad?* Are you fucking kidding me?'

Jasmine grinned and pointed at him. 'I made you smile.'

'You did not.'

'I did. Look at you! You love it that I made a joke and you found it funny.'

'It better be a fucking joke.'

There was no denying it though. His eyes gave it away. He had smiled, kind of.

'Did you ever see my porno?' Jasmine asked.

The Kid sucked on his cigarette and the end lit up bright gold. He washed the smoke down with another mouthful of bourbon then exhaled through his nostrils. 'What?' he said, as if only just registering what she'd said.

'My porno. Everyone else has seen it. You've never mentioned it. Did you ever watch it?'

'What the fuck? Just now I was your fucking dad. Now you want me to watch you in a porno?'

'It's not exactly a porno. Sanchez is in it too.'

'I don't wanna see it.'

'You should. Remember the bartender that drugged you on Blue Corn island? Well, in this short porn film, I got naked and then me and Sanchez killed him. I smashed his dick and balls to pieces, then Sanchez poured poison in his ass. And I did some somersaults. Do you wanna see it? It's on my phone.'

The Kid sighed. 'If I watch it, when it's finished, will you leave me alone?'

'Scouts honour!'

'Go on then.'

'Great!' Jasmine stood up and took off her belt, then started unzipping her catsuit.

'What are you doing?'

'I keep my phone in my pussy.'

The Kid winced and stubbed his cigarette out in the ashtray before asking, 'Why?'

'They don't have pockets on this thing. Plus, the phone vibrates when people text me, and I kinda like that.'

'You have pockets on your belt,' he reminded her.

Jasmine shrugged. 'Pocket, shmocket.'

She pulled the catsuit down to her waist and was about to reach for the phone when the Kid reached out and grabbed hold of her wrist.

'Show me the video another time.'

'Are you sure? I mean, my phone's right here.'

'I don't wanna see you pull it out.'

He let go of her wrist and she zipped her catsuit back up. 'You are so weird,' she said, shaking her head.

'Yeah, I'm the weird one. *You*, your perfectly fucking normal.'

It felt like her chat with him had worked. His anger, or hatred was no longer so obvious. And she had sort of made him smile. She felt a burst of excitement. Then another one.

'Oh my God!'

The Kid groaned. 'What now?'

'My phone's ringing. I really do have to get it out.'

Thirty Three

The three Skinners, Snake Hawk, Dancing Lizard and Red Sky used their wooden knives to peel the skin and flesh from Rex's body, licking up his blood like it was red wine. A feast in the snow was a rare treat. In between cutting slices from his arms and torso, they also lunged in and bit at him with their jagged V-shaped front teeth, which made the kill feel more primal, more animalistic. The V-shaped front teeth were a trademark among the Skinners. A coming-of-age ritual in the tribe that involved having the teeth filed down into jagged V shaped fangs in order to strike fear into their enemies.

Snake Hawk had a passion for eating eyeballs. And hearing Scratch bragging about eating Papshmir's eyeballs had only increased his hunger for them. He thrust the end of his knife into Rex's left eye and gouged it out. Rex moaned, but it was hard to know if it was from the eye-gouging or the general flesh-flaying that was taking place.

Snake Hawk stood up and stepped back away from the slaughter. Rex's eye was skewered on the tip of his blade. He bit into the eye as if it were an apple. Goo squirted out of it and dribbled down his chin. He licked it up with his long black tongue and smiled at the delightful sight of his comrades ripping their meal apart.

Rex had initially put up a brave fight considering he had one arm pinned against the burger stall, but the three pronged attack quickly proved too much for him. Ever since the witch had left, and her magnetic spell on the stall ended, the three cannibals had been pulling Rex's body around in the snow, picking off the best fleshy parts from his arms and torso. Eating flesh from a victim who was still breathing had a special feel about it. For Skinners, feasting on a living being was the ultimate rush. The three of them became so engrossed in the feeding frenzy that they didn't hear the muffled footsteps approaching them.

Red Sky was on his knees in the snow, ripping away at one of Rex's arms with his knife when, without warning, he fell onto his side in the snow. A splat of blood hit the burger stall behind him. Snake Hawk froze and stared his fallen brother, confused by what had happened. Blood was spilling out of a hole in Red Sky's head, turning the snow into Merlot.

Dancing Lizard was holding Rex's other arm. He let go of it and looked up at Snake Hawk. His mouth opened as if to speak, but then suddenly his head split in two and he fell back onto Rex's ravaged body, Claret spilling from his skull onto the snow.

Snake Hawk instinctively swallowed a chunk of eyeball, almost choking himself on it. What the fuck was going on? His two brothers had been slain in a matter of seconds, both their heads obliterated by an invisible force.

Except it wasn't invisible.

It was Elvis.

Snake Hawk's fate was sealed long before he turned to face his killer. Elvis moved in real close, his Gold Desert Eagle pistol almost touching the tip of Snake Hawk's nose. The Chief Skinner turned cross-eyed as he stared at the barrel of the gun. Elvis pulled the trigger. A bullet exploded out and took Snake Hawk's nose on a ride through his brain and out through his skull before it fizzed off into the night sky for some fresh air. Snake Hawk's legs did an impressive Irish jig for a few seconds before they received the memo that they were now part of a corpse. His body fell sideways into the snow, Sangria pulsing out of the remains of his head.

Elvis tucked his gun away and slid to his knees by Rex's side. He pushed away the body of one of the dead cannibals and placed his hand on Rex's bloodied neck, trying desperately to stem the flow of blood. But there was *so much blood*, and so many wounds it was seeping from.

'Look at how they messed with my friend!' Elvis cried aloud.

It was hard not to panic. He was alone on a snow-covered promenade with three dead cannibals and his friend, *his best friend*, who was half-eaten by the cannibal motherfuckers. Elvis had to make a phone call. Get some help. He ran his bloodied hands up and down his jacket, trying to remember where he kept his phone. He found it in the same pocket it was always in. As he stared at it in his hand, he saw Rex's blood all over his fingers, his palm, his wrists, and now his phone.

"Block it out. Block it out."

He was on autopilot, his fingers tapping away on the phone without any assistance from his brain. Then he heard Jasmine's voice, her beautiful, reassuring voice.

'Hey sweetie.'

'Rex is in trouble! On the promenade. Get Flake to bring the ambulance. We gotta get him to a hospital. He could be dead already. Hurry! Quick!'

Her response was a blur of words, comforting, decisive words. She took control of the situation. The last thing he heard her say was, "Stay on the line. We're on our way."

Elvis dropped his phone into the snow and grabbed Rex's head. 'Rex, can you hear me? Hang in there, buddy. Everyone's coming. It's gonna be all right. Don't fucking die on me, man.'

In his frazzled state of mind, Elvis grabbed clumps of snow and dropped them onto the horrific wounds on Rex's body as if covering the skinless, bleeding areas would help them to heal. Then he sat down in the snow next to Rex and cradled his friend in his arms, talking to him, doing anything he could think of to keep him alive.

****

Jasmine burst into the kitchen. 'Flake! We've gotta go! Rex is in trouble! Elvis says he's been attacked on the promenade and he's gonna die. We gotta take the ambulance and go get him. NOW!'

Flake turned off the gas on the stove. 'Grab Sanchez!' she said, her calm authority evident immediately. 'He's got the keys. Go with him and start up the ambulance. Wait for me, I'll be right behind you.'

Jasmine turned and bolted out of the kitchen to grab Sanchez. Flake switched off all the cooking appliances and moved everything efficiently into safe places. She'd done many a fire drill when working as a waitress at the Olé Au Lait café, so it was all carried out with minimal fuss to the backdrop of Jasmine switching off the television and dragging Sanchez with her out to the ambulance.

Flake dried her hands on a dishcloth and hustled out of the kitchen. The Bourbon Kid was still sitting at a table in the corner. He looked like a man who had drunk too much, his eyes were concealed behind a pair of sunglasses, and he was refilling his glass with bourbon.

'Did you hear what's happened?' Flake asked him.

'Yeah.'

'Are you coming with us then, or what?'

'What do you need me for?'

Flake stopped, stunned by his response. 'We *don't* need you,' she said. 'But don't you wanna come anyway?'

'I'm fine right here.'

'Don't be a dick.'

'What?'

Outside in the parking lot the ambulance's engine kicked into life. Red and blue flashing lights filtered in through the windows.

Flake stared into the Bourbon Kid's sunglasses. 'You're so fucking stupid,' she said. 'You're sitting there feeling sorry for yourself because you lost a family that, until a few days ago, you didn't even know you had!'

The Kid's gun was on the table in front of him. He pushed the handle with his finger, aiming it at Flake. 'You should go,' he said in a gravelly, unpleasant tone.

'I'm sorry that Papshmir and Janis are dead,' said Flake, 'but until just recently, you didn't give two shits about them. You're mourning a family you never really knew, while Rex is out there somewhere in the cold and snow, *dying*. Could you live with yourself if he dies and you did nothing?'

'Yeah, I could live with it.'

Flake shook her head. 'Good for you, but you know, one day you're gonna wake up and realise there's another family that you didn't know you had. And you were *too stupid* to care about them. Rex is part of that family. And right now, we're all you've got left.'

'I still have bourbon.'

'Good for you. I hope you enjoy it.'

Thirty Four

Sally Diamond hurried back to her apartment block, shaken and tearful about what she had done. Seeing Rex taken down, then hearing his screams, the sounds and the images would haunt her, possibly forever, but certainly for the foreseeable future. The only way to get through the night would be with the help of her friend, Chardonnay. She'd had enough of the cheap red wine Sanchez served up in the Tapioca. It was time for something refreshing to wash away the taste.

A feeling of paranoia accompanied her as she walked through the gardens at the front of her building. She lived on the fourth floor of an eight storey high-rise. Normally the sound of music floated out of the other residents' windows, but with the cold air and frequent bouts of snow, no one's windows were open. To make matters worse, a man dressed in black was loitering near the building's entrance. *Paranoia overload.*

Sally kept up a calm exterior, but inside she was reeling. The ridiculous feelings of anxiety were overwhelming her. She had done a deal with the Devil. Her part of the transaction was complete, but the deal was with the *fucking Devil.* The same Devil who always double-crossed people in TV shows and movies.

As she walked up to the entrance, the man in black threw a glance in her direction. She prepared herself for a possible confrontation but the man graciously stepped aside for her, allowing her to slide her keycard into the door. She kept him in her peripheral vision the whole time, just in case he made a move. But he didn't, and thankfully he made no attempt to follow her in. The whole uneventful experience left Sally wondering if this was what life was to be like from now on, constantly watching her back, worried that every stranger, every person who looked her way, was one of the Devil's people, or Rex's buddies looking for revenge. Doing a deal with Scratch was going to be a lifelong regret.

A ride in an empty elevator was followed by a panicked sprint along the corridor to her apartment. Stupid really. There was no one else in sight, but she just couldn't wait to be back in the sanctity of her lounge, holding a cold Chardonnay, drinking it, drinking more of it, forgetting, slipping into oblivion. And a deep, deep sleep. She'd already polished off a fair amount of red wine in the Tapioca, so mixing it up with some white ought to knock her right out.

She locked the door behind her, breathed a sigh of relief, walked into her lounge and took her jacket off. She threw it onto the arm of the sofa and headed into the kitchen.

'JESUS!'

Sally had a brief flash of what a heart attack might feel like. Her fridge door was open and a man was poking around inside it. *A man in a red suit.*

Scratch.

Another man was standing behind him, an even bigger man, aged in his early thirties with a mop of floppy brown hair. He was dressed all in black like the guy she'd seen outside. His skin-tight T-shirt showed off bodybuilder muscles, not as big as Rex's, but big enough.

Scratch straightened up and smiled at Sally. 'I'm sorry,' he said. 'Did we startle you?'

'A little bit, yeah.' Sally pressed her hand against her chest. Her heart and lungs were chugging away like a set of bagpipes. 'What are you doing here?' she asked, wheezing the words out.

Scratch gestured at his companion. 'This is Steve. He's the head of your new personal security team.'

'Hi, Steve.'

Steve offered a nod of acknowledgement but nothing more. He was a very serious looking individual.

Scratch reached into the fridge and pulled out a bottle of Chardonnay. 'I assume you were coming for this?'

Sally accepted the bottle and stayed put, holding it, breathing short breaths, wondering what was next. As it turned out, Scratch opened one of her cupboards. He pulled out a big round wine glass and handed it to her.

'Thank you,' she whispered.

'Anything else I can get you?' he asked.

'No.'

'Come then. Join us in the lounge.'

Sally stepped back into the lounge. Scratch followed her in, but Steve hung back in the kitchen.

'Please, sit down,' said Scratch. 'Make yourself comfortable. It's your home after all.'

Sally sat down on the sofa and placed her empty wine glass on a coffee table in front of her. She unscrewed the lid on the bottle, and with a trembling hand she poured some wine into the glass. Even though she wanted to fill it to the top, she stopped when it was only half full, rather than embarrass herself by spilling any.

Scratch pulled out a chair from her dining table at the back of the room and twisted it around to face her before he sat down on it. Steve, the meathead, walked in carrying a red suitcase. He placed it down on the coffee table next to her glass of wine, and opened it up so that she could see what was inside. It was money. Lots and lots of dirty fifty-dollar bills.

'A million dollars,' said Scratch. 'All yours. You did what was asked of you, and this is your reward. Let it ease your conscience.'

'Thank you.' She picked up her wine and took a sip. The ice-cold drink slid over her tongue and hit her throat, which was tight from all the anxiety and cold weather. Sally's nose filled up with fluid. Her eyes almost popped out of her head. There was no stopping what came next.

Coughing fit! In front of the Devil. What a nightmare! Oh, the shame!

When the coughing fit came to an end she placed the glass back down. Her face was hot and burning red, her eyes bulging. She wanted to down the entire bottle, but as the first sip had shown, drinking in front of the Devil and his henchman was no way to relax. She wished they would fuck off, but she couldn't let them know that, and she hoped to God Scratch couldn't read her mind because, well, *fuck*.

'This concludes our business,' said Scratch. 'I want you to know that there will be no further demands from me. Should you feel any guilt or remorse for what you have done this evening, I suggest you go to church and ask the local preacher to forgive you for your sins. That confessing stuff actually works. I don't know why more people don't do it. But don't go to the Church of Saint Ursula because the preacher there recently had a nasty accident and he's a bit dead.'

Sally nodded along like a dog in the back seat of a moving car. 'Okay,' she mumbled.

'One last thing,' Scratch continued. 'Steve here has two colleagues patrolling the grounds outside. The three of them are assigned to protect you from any possible acts of vengeance from the Dead Hunters. Here, take this.' He reached into his pocket and handed her a small black device, a pager that fitted snugly in the palm of her hand. 'If at any point you feel unsafe or worried about anything, strange noises, nuisance phone calls, or someone breaks into your apartment, you just press the button on that pager. Steve and his two friends each have a device just like it. As soon as you press the button on yours, theirs will vibrate, alerting them to your need for help. Within thirty seconds they will be outside your door. Tell her, Steve.'

Steve finally spoke, his voice gruff, reassuringly so. 'Press the button on your pager now,' he said.

Sally squeezed her thumb against the button on the pager. Steve reached into his hip pocket and pulled out an identical pager. It buzzed very faintly and a small red light on the side of it flashed on and off. He held it up for Sally to see.

'When you activate your pager,' he said, staring intently at her to make sure she was listening, 'me and my buddies are gonna be in here like Crockett and Tubbs, and another guy. We'll kick the door down if we have to. And believe me we can do that in a matter of seconds. If there's anyone in here threatening you,' he tapped a gun holstered on his hip, 'we shoot him dead. We do not hesitate. You got that?'

'Yep, got it.'

Scratch gestured for Steve to exit. The bodyguard left the apartment via a door at the end of Sally's entrance hall, the door he had just promised to kick down in an emergency.

'I hope he's reassuring?' said Scratch.

'Definitely.'

'Good. Now, before I go was there anything else you were worried about?'

'Umm, I suppose, I was wondering what happened to Rex? Did he die?'

'I would think so,' said Scratch. 'Being eaten alive generally does result in death. He's probably arrived back in Hell by now, so don't worry, you won't ever see him again. He's gone for good.'

'But the others, Elvis and Jasmine, they'll come after me, won't they?'

Scratch smiled. 'Drink your wine, Sally. By the end of the night, you won't have to worry about Elvis or Jasmine, or anyone else for that matter. You're a wealthy lady. Try to enjoy it. Adiós, it's been fun.'

He winked at her, then walked into her bathroom, which was just off the hallway. The first time she had met him he had come in through the bathroom, armed with ten thousand dollars and a request that she double-cross Rex in exchange for another million. She had agreed, but it had put her right off using the bathroom.

She took a few sips of her wine and started to relax a little. After a few minutes she got up to check the bathroom. Scratch was gone. Relief!

Her suitcase filled with money was still on the table though. The money was real. She flicked on the television and started watching an Adam Sandler movie called *That's My Boy*. It wasn't long before she began to feel better about everything. She had booze and money. Lots of money. And three bodyguards outside.

Thirty Five

Elvis waited an eternity for the ambulance to arrive. A five-minute eternity. The longest five minutes ever. Rex was the one bleeding to death, and Elvis felt like he was dying alongside him. He was shaking, not just from the cold but from the shock of seeing so much of his best friend's blood. The snow all around him was red. Rex's arms, face and clothes were caked in blood, and Elvis had a bucketload of it on him too. There sure did used to be a lotta blood in Rex's body.

The ambulance pulled up close by. Jasmine leapt out of the passenger side before it had even stopped. She raced over to Elvis and Rex, and slid down onto her knees.

'Holy Shit! What the hell happened?' she asked, a stunned look on her face.

Elvis couldn't respond. He'd been talking to Rex just fine, but now that the others were here, the panic and shock had stolen his voice.

Flake jumped out of the driver's side. She stopped and stared at the three semi-naked corpses strewn across the promenade. 'Who the fuck are these guys?' she asked.

'Cannibals.' The word fought its way past Elvis's lips, opening the way for his voice to return. 'When I got here they were all over him. We've got to get him to hospital.'

Jasmine covered her mouth. 'Oh God, where's his eye!'

'You don't wanna know.'

The back doors of the ambulance opened and Sanchez fell out into the snow. A long stretcher tumbled out behind him and bounced off his head onto the ground. Flake trudged round to the back of the ambulance and helped Sanchez to his feet.

Elvis whispered to Jasmine. 'He was set-up.'

'What do you mean?'

'Those cannibals didn't follow him here. They must have been lying in wait for him.'

Jasmine reached down to Rex and stroked some hair away from his bloodied face, then she gave Elvis a puzzled look. 'I'm not sure what you're saying.'

'I think Sally led him here, on purpose.'

Jasmine still looked confused. 'You followed Rex and Sally here. How come?'

'Gut instinct.'

Flake and Sanchez arrived with the stretcher and set it down in the snow beside Rex.

'We'll grab his legs,' said Flake. 'You two take his top half.'

Between them, the four friends lifted what was left of Rex onto the stretcher, then each of them grabbed a corner and lifted him up.

'I want you three to take him to Saint Jude's hospital,' said Elvis as they started carrying the stretcher towards the back of the ambulance. 'There's a nurse there called Ingrid. She knows Rex. She'll make sure he gets the best treatment.'

'Got it,' said Sanchez.

'Aren't you coming with us?' Flake asked.

'No, I'm going to see someone. I won't be long.'

'You're going to find Sally, aren't you?' said Flake.

'Yeah, I gotta see her, find out if she was involved, *if* she's still alive.'

Jasmine furrowed her brow. 'I don't get it. You went to the archives and checked her out this morning.'

'I did.'

'And she was clean.'

Elvis glanced back at the dead cannibals. An image of them attacking Rex flashed through his mind. He blocked it out by shaking his head. 'Sally's a cop,' he reminded Jasmine. 'Cops don't hang around with the likes of us, not unless they're working undercover, or for someone like Scratch.'

They reached the back of the ambulance and propped the stretcher onto the back, then slid it in. Sanchez climbed in after it and took a closer look at Rex's face.

'Is he breathing?' he asked, wincing.

Flake climbed into the back to hurry things up. Between them she and Sanchez secured the stretcher against the wall to ensure it didn't slide around during the forthcoming trip to the hospital.

Elvis turned away. He'd had enough of looking at Rex's injuries. He looked into Jasmine's eyes instead. She stroked his arm and gave him a comforting smile.

'I'll come with you to Sally's place,' she offered.

He shook his head. 'Go to the hospital with these guys. That's where you're needed right now.'

Flake jumped out of the back of the ambulance. 'Come on, we gotta go,' she said.

'Drive like the wind, Flake,' said Elvis. 'I'll catch up with you down the line.'

Flake yelled at Sanchez. 'Keep talking to him!'

Sanchez was settling into a plastic seat opposite Rex, ready to tell him some jokes. He gave Flake a thumbs-up sign. She slammed the doors shut and patted Elvis on the arm.

'Good luck,' she said. 'And be careful, because if you go after Sally, you know you're walking into a trap, don't you?'

'I know.'

Flake threw a look at Jasmine. 'I'm gonna turn the ambulance around. Say your goodbyes and be ready to jump in.'

With that, Flake raced around to the front of the vehicle and climbed into the driver's seat. She started the engine and then set about turning the ambulance around, which was no easy feat in the snow on the promenade.

Elvis reached behind his back and pulled out a small pistol. He showed it to Jasmine. 'Sally left this at the Tapioca,' he said. 'It gave me the perfect excuse to follow her and Rex back to her place. But I was being too cautious. I let them walk way too far ahead because I was trying not to be seen, and because of that, I didn't see what was happening until it was too late.'

Jasmine wiped a tear from his cheek. 'But why would Sally hand him over to a bunch of cannibals?' she asked. 'And why would a cop leave her gun in a bar? That's pretty careless.'

'It is,' Elvis agreed. 'But she had been drinking.' He tucked the gun down the back of his pants again. 'You know, what I don't understand is, how did these three punks get the drop on Rex? Normally he can fight three guys at once without any of them laying a mark on him. Something else has happened here, and I need to know what. If Sally is still alive, she'll be able to explain exactly how this whole shitstorm played out. Then I'll know if she was involved.'

The sirens blared out on the ambulance, an unsubtle hint from Flake that it was time to go.

Jasmine ran her hand down Elvis's arm. 'Do you even know where Sally lives?'

'I know everything about her. At least, I thought I did.'

'Forget her. Stay with us. Safety in numbers, right?'

Elvis looked at the blood on his hands, Rex's blood. 'Don't worry, Jas. If anything doesn't look right when I get to her apartment, I'll turn around and go straight to the hospital.'

Elvis grabbed Jasmine and kissed her, a passionate, *I might not see you again,*" kind of kiss. When they parted, Jasmine had tears in her eyes.

'Don't get yourself killed,' she said.

He gave her a reassuring smile. 'Hey, it's me. I've done this sorta thing a thousand times.'

The ambulance pulled up alongside Jasmine. The passenger door swung open.

Flake yelled at her. 'COME ON!'

Jasmine turned away from Elvis and climbed into the ambulance. She buckled up in the seat next to Flake, then blew Elvis a kiss. He blew one right back. Then Flake hit the gas and the ambulance sped off in the direction of Saint Jude's hospital.

Elvis watched it go, then he headed for Sally's Diamond's apartment.

Thirty Six

Alexis Calhoon's week of working from home was turning out to be every bit as stressful as being in the office. One thing she'd learned very early in her career was that going out for a walk in the fresh air with her dogs was a great way to relieve stress. She put her walking gear on and walked out onto the front porch with her two excited Alsatians. It was as far as she would get.

A vehicle on the horizon was coming her way. A black Mercedes G-wagon. Gut instinct told her it would be work related. She watched the G-Wagon cruise along the highway, praying that it wouldn't make the turn onto the dirt track that led to her home. It did. She knew it would. Fucking hell.

She took the dogs back inside, which pissed them off. They'd watched with great excitement when she put on her walking boots and her green wax jacket. That was supposed to mean it was time for some fun in the woods. Instead they had to watch from behind the kitchen door as Calhoon walked back out onto the front porch without them.

The G-Wagon rumbled on down the dirt track to the front of Calhoon's house. The driver parked up, and a man exited from the passenger side. He was dressed in an expensive white suit and a matching panama hat. He was well tanned and in impeccable shape for a man in his fifties. Calhoon knew him, but had only ever met him on two occasions. His name was Mike Raffone, and he was the mouthpiece of the US government's security operation. A visit from him was most likely bad news. This was a man who reported directly to the President, and no one else.

'Hello Mike,' said Calhoon. 'Can I get you a coffee?'

'No time,' he replied, marching up to her. 'Can you take me for a walk around your fine ranch, please?'

'Of course.' She regretted taking the dogs back inside. Now she was going for a walk without them. 'Would you like to see the horses?'

'I surely would, General. Lead on.'

Calhoon stepped off the porch and walked across the grassy fields towards the horse pen. Raffone walked alongside her, his shoes probably not best suited for a country walk. He politely looked around and pretended to be impressed by the sights for about ten seconds. He even asked Calhoon how her husband was. She responded with a curt, "He's fine, thanks," and then they got down to the serious business.

'We have a major situation, General. A very sensitive matter. We've tried to fix it ourselves, but time is running out, so I suggested to the President that we utilise those very useful but highly secretive assets of yours.'

'Yes, sir.'

Raffone stopped walking, so Calhoon had to stop too. She turned to face him. He looked like a man who had just found out his winning lottery ticket was fake.

'Alexis, two weeks ago a nineteen-year-old woman went missing in Dallas. She was found three days later in a dumpster in Austin. She'd been drugged, sexually assaulted and beaten to death, in that order. The day after she was found, another girl, aged seventeen, went missing in Austin. She turned up three days later in a dumpster in San Antonio. She was also drugged, sexually assaulted and beaten to death.'

Calhoon took a guess at what was coming next. 'And now another girl has just gone missing?' she ventured.

'That's right. This latest girl is aged nineteen, with very similar physical traits to the other two, slim, blonde, you know the drill. She went missing in San Antonio fifty-seven hours ago.'

'That's a very small window for finding her alive.'

Raffone nodded. 'The woman who's gone missing, her name is Arizona Petersen. That mean anything to you?'

'No.'

'Good, no reason why it should. But here's the thing, and this is the crutch of why I'm here at your lovely ranch today. Arizona Petersen is the illegitimate love-child of the President of the United States.'

Calhoon's heart sank. She was about to be given the impossible task of finding the poor girl, who could already be dead. 'How can I help?' she asked, knowing exactly what was coming.

'Well, as I'm sure you've realised already, we've wasted the first forty-eight hours of this operation. The only thing we've achieved is that we've realised, several years too late that the person, or people, who kidnapped Arizona have been travelling around the country repeating this same process of three-day kidnaps for at least four years now. They don't occur every week. Sometimes the killer doesn't strike for over six months, but then when he does, it becomes a pattern again. He's constantly on the move, so we've been looking at things like travelling circuses, salesmen, that kind of thing. But we just don't have the amount of available time to follow up all the leads before it's too late for Arizona. If she dies, and her body turns up in a dumpster, then some cop somewhere is going to be assigned to look into the murder, and we wouldn't want that, because, well, *you know.* The President wants this girl found without anyone in the press finding out that she's even missing. This is a top, top secret investigation.'

'I understand. Do you have a picture of her?'

'I'll send you one. Do you think you can help your President out? Can some of those faceless assassins and bounty hunters that you utilise so well be assigned to this case with immediate effect?'

Calhoon inwardly sighed. She could hardly tell Mike Raffone that she was actually in the middle of another job where she was reporting into the Devil, who, as things stood, still probably outranked the President. 'I'll get a message out to my best people, right away,' she said.

'You have my permission to tell them who Arizona Petersen really is, but make it clear that if any of them decide to leak that information, they can expect the full force of the US law enforcement to hunt them down.'

'Yes, sir.'

'Oh, and Alexis. You can incentivise your people by telling them there is a ten-million-dollar reward for whoever brings her home in one piece.'

'I will tell them that,' said Calhoon. 'But, if I may speak slightly out of turn, you should know that my people, if they find her, they will expect to be paid in full. Any reneging on our side will most likely result in both you and I winding up at the bottom of a lake somewhere.'

Mike Raffone's demeanour changed from angsty to pissed. 'Are you threatening me, General?'

'No, sir. I'm just letting you know, *my people*, they're not good people. They're not the kind of people you ever want to meet. I just wanted to be clear about that.'

'Fine. Give me the name of one of your people, something I can give to the President, let him know we've got our best people on it.'

'I can't give out names Mike, you know that.'

'Just one. Tell me, who's your best guy?'

Calhoon sighed. Raffone was a nuisance, a jumped up, bullying prick who never took "no" for an answer. 'Falco Logan,' she replied eventually.

'Falco Logan? Who is he?'

'Mike, I could get killed just for telling you his name. Fortunately, I don't think that *is* his real name, but it's all you're getting. Oh, and you should know, if he's the one who finds Arizona, his price is twenty-million.'

Raffone looked aghast. 'Twenty million?'

'It's the minimum amount for him. The others will all do it for the ten, no quibbles.'

160

After a pause, Mike accepted that this was no time for an argument. 'That's fine,' he said. He shook her hand, indicating he was about to leave, but then added. 'You report into me on this one. I want hourly updates. The clock is ticking, General.'

Thirty Seven

Sally was halfway through her bottle of Chardonnay, and despite feeling better about things, every now and again the memory of Rex screaming would pierce her brain. How could she switch that noise off? How could she ease her conscience? The answer was on the coffee table, right in front of her. Money. Money solves problems. She had lots of money now. Her worries were over. She could move to a better neighbourhood, a better city, a better state.

Glorious sight though it was, the suitcase filled with cash was also a constant reminder of what had happened earlier in the evening. It was also *evidence of her involvement*. It had to be moved. She took one last look at the bundles of notes, then zipped the case shut and picked it up. A million bucks was pretty heavy. She carried it over to her bedroom and slid it under the bed where she could no longer see it, and just as importantly, *no one else* could see it. She closed the door and headed back to the lounge.

'Holy Fuck!'

She pressed her hand against her chest and stopped in the doorway. There was a man in a red suit climbing in through the window behind her lounge dining table.

Elvis.

He had lifted up her sliding window and let himself in. Men in red suits really seemed to have a thing for breaking into her apartment these days.

Her eyes darted towards the coffee table. The pager Scratch had given her was next to her wine glass. She could run for it, pick it up, press the button, *and,* if what she'd been told was true, she'd have three bodyguards kicking her door down in under thirty seconds. But at this point, she had no idea what Elvis's intentions were. She'd already concocted a story for him in case he showed up, a story she had been rehearsing in her head since her first meeting with Scratch when she had agreed to lead Rex into a trap.

'Oh Jesus, Elvis, you scared the crap out of me,' she said, breathing a fake sigh of relief. 'Is Rex okay? I swear to God, I didn't know what to do. He told me to run and lock myself in at home. I've been waiting for him ever since.'

'Shut up,' said Elvis. 'You're babbling, and it's pissing me off.' Now that he was fully in the room, he closed the window and turned to face her, dusting some snow off his shoulders onto her carpet.

'You're alive then?' he said. 'I wasn't sure you'd be here. You know there's a couple of unsavoury looking fellas hanging around outside your building?'

'There's always weirdoes hanging around outside here,' Sally replied, as casually as possible. 'On a cop's salary you can only afford to live in amongst the crooks.'

Behind the cool facade, Sally's mind was whizzing through her options. Her gun, *she didn't have it*. She'd left it at the Tapioca because Scratch had warned her not to have any metal on her when the attack on Rex took place. If she'd had the gun with her, she would have ended up stuck to the burger stall with Rex when it was magnetised.

Elvis pointed to her sofa. 'Sit down. We need to talk.'

So far he didn't seem angry. He didn't look as relaxed as usual though. And he had specks of blood on his face and neck. What did that mean?

Sally made her way over to the sofa and sat down. Had Elvis seen the pager? Would he even know what it was for?

'Is Rex okay?' she asked again.

Elvis ignored her. He grabbed a chair from the dining table and placed it down on the other side of her coffee table. He sat down on it, blocking her view of the television. Sally had done many interrogations in her time and from the way Elvis was sitting, making himself comfortable, this was going to be a lengthy questioning. At this point it wasn't clear if he was going to play it sweet or sour.

'I'll just switch the TV off,' she said, reaching out to the remote on the coffee table.

'Leave it.'

Sally pulled her hand away. 'I just thought it was a bit loud.'

'I like a bit of background noise,' said Elvis, his voice almost drowned out by Adam Sandler laughing at something. 'Explain to me exactly what happened after you and Rex left the Tapioca. Don't leave anything out. I wanna know every detail. Take your time.'

'Uh, well, there was this burger stall. We were just walking past it, and we were talking about burgers. I said I'd cook Rex a veggie burger, but he wasn't having any of it. But then, out of nowhere he suddenly got stuck. His metal hand stuck to the side of the stall.'

'The burger stall? It was magnetic?'

'Yeah.' Sally picked up her glass of wine and took a sip. Elvis didn't seem to notice. He just stared into her eyes the whole time. She wondered if she could reach out and press the button on the pager without him noticing. Maybe pick it up, put it in her pocket and press it? All these thoughts were spinning through her mind while she told him her modified version of what happened to Rex. 'And then these people showed up. They came out of the public toilets. Rex knew some of them.'

'What did they look like?'

'There were these three horrible-looking men, like jungle savage types, you know? Loin cloths, tattoos.'

'Yeah, I know. Who else?'

'There was a big black guy in a red suit. Him and Rex knew each other. I never got his name, but I think it was that Scratch fella you guys have been talking about.'

'Good guess. And what did Scratch say?'

Sally rubbed her head, glancing down at the pager, laying there on the table, enticing her to grab it. 'I don't really remember exactly what Scratch said, but he introduced this woman he had with him. Her name was Dixie, or something like that. No wait, *Trixie!* That was it, Trixie. She looked like a witch. She had like a green complexion and purple hair. She was horrible. It was her who magnetised the burger stall, I think.'

'Can I have some of your wine?' Elvis asked. 'Just a sip?'

'Er, yeah, sure. I'll get you a glass from the kitchen if you like?' Sally moved to stand up, but Elvis grabbed her arm, and guided her back down onto her sofa. He picked up her glass of wine and took a sip. Sally noticed some patches of dried blood on his hand. How had she not seen them before?

Elvis swilled the wine around in his mouth before swallowing it. 'Good stuff,' he said, placing the glass back down on the coffee table. 'Carry on with your story.'

'Oh God,' said Sally, choking up, not for effect, but because remembering what had happened to Rex was still genuinely upsetting. 'The guy in the red suit, Scratch, he set the three savages on Rex.'

'Did he say anything to you? Scratch, I mean.'

She shook her head. 'No, he totally ignored me. They all did. Rex yelled at me to run. He said, go home, lock yourself in.'

'And you did?'

'Yeah, I feel terrible about it, but I was so scared. I mean, that guy Scratch, he's the Devil isn't he?'

'Yes he is.'

'When I got back here, I thought about calling you, or Jasmine, but I was afraid. I mean, isn't the Devil all seeing? He would know if I tried to call you, wouldn't he?'

'You think the Devil has your phone tapped?'

'Umm, well, no, I guess not. I think I'm in shock. Is Rex okay? Have you heard from him?'

'It's the darnedest thing,' said Elvis. 'You know what? *He survived,*'

Sally felt like the bottom of her world had just dropped out. She tried very hard to channel her shock into concern. 'Oh, thank god! I was—'

Elvis interrupted her, as if he hadn't even heard her. 'But he's lost a lot of blood and it'll be a while before he can talk and tell us his version of events.' Elvis held up his hands, showing Sally his palms. There was more blood on his fingertips. 'See this,' he said. 'That's Rex's blood. I tried to wipe it all off in the snow, but some of it's gonna stick. Feels like it's gonna stay there forever.'

Sally finally noticed the rest of the blood on Elvis's tight-fitting red suit jacket. It hid the stains well, but they were definitely there. 'You can use my bathroom to wash that off if you like?'

Elvis stood up, which Sally hoped meant he was going to take up her offer of using the bathroom. 'Look, Sally, I'll be honest with you,' he said, looking around the lounge. 'I don't think Scratch is gonna come after you, *but,* and this is entirely up to you, if you want, you can come hang with me and the gang? I can't guarantee your safety. I don't know if it's safer for you to be here or with us. But I know Rex would want us to take care of you. He likes you. I haven't seen him this keen on a woman in a long time.'

'I like him too.'

Sally's heart was pounding. If Rex survived, Elvis and the others would soon know of her betrayal. She blinked and threw a side glance at the pager.

'I need to wash my hands,' said Elvis. 'I'm not keen on bathrooms, but I'll use your kitchen sink if that's okay?'

'Yeah, sure, help yourself.'

'I'll be back in a tick. Don't go anywhere.'

Elvis left the lounge and walked into the kitchen. As soon as Sally heard him turn on the faucet, she grabbed the pager and pressed the button, then returned it to its place on the table. She took a long swig of wine and started a countdown from thirty in her head.

Thirty Eight

Owning an ambulance had many benefits. Flake liked jumping red lights, while Sanchez liked seeing other drivers pull over to let him pass when he was in a rush to get home for his dinner. It was also handy when it came to parking, particularly at the hospital. Flake parked it right outside the front entrance of Saint Jude's main building. In no time at all Rex was taken from the ambulance by the hospital staff and rushed into an emergency room where the doctors and nurses got to work on him.

Sanchez, Jasmine and Flake moved to a waiting room on the ground floor. Sanchez hated waiting rooms, and he was still livid about missing out on the epic breakfast Flake had cooked him for dinner. He fidgeted around in an uncomfortable plastic seat for about fifteen minutes, listening to Flake and Jasmine fretting about Rex, before his patience finally snapped. His hunger pains were unbearable.

'I'm gonna go look for some food,' he said, standing up. 'Flake, have you got any money?'

Flake reached into a purse on the belt of her cop uniform and pulled out a five dollar bill. 'That's all I've got,' she said. 'Don't waste it on candy.'

Sanchez took the money and headed off to find somewhere that sold food, even though he was miffed that Flake had been a bit miserly with the five bucks. Hospital food was bound to be overpriced. And rubbish.

After wandering around and almost getting run over by some selfish people in wheelchairs, he finally found a battered old vending machine on the second floor. He approached it with great excitement, only to be disappointed when he found it was full of healthy snack bars and shakes. Fucking hospitals, trying to make people eat healthier. Sanchez was disgusted. He was about to kick the machine and march off to reception to make a complaint when he spotted a solitary candy bar on the top row of snacks. It was one of his favourites too, a delicious chocolate, nougat, caramel and biscuit extravaganza known as a *Chubby bar*. The sight of it had him drooling. He slipped Flake's five dollar bill into the machine and typed in the code for the Chubby bar. After a delay that nearly merited him kicking the machine, the Chubby bar started moving forward on a set of revolving rings. Just as it looked set to fall, its wrapper snagged on the end of the rings. When the transaction came to an end, the Chubby bar was left dangling tantalisingly over the edge.

'PIECE OF SHIT!' Sanchez yelled. He kicked the machine, almost breaking a few of his toes. That was followed by a lot of cursing and a one-legged dance in front of some bemused hospital staff. To make matters worse, he then spotted a sign on the machine that read, "NO CHANGE". He'd lost five bucks and didn't even get the change with which to have another try.

Over the course of his life, Sanchez had been stitched up by vending machines more times than anyone else in the history of the world. However, in recent years he had found a solution to the problem of thieving vending machines. The solution was called Flake. The love of Sanchez's life knew exactly how to shake a machine back and forth until the offending item dropped out. Her freakish strength was a wonderful asset. All Sanchez had to do was go get her. After checking that no one was lurking around to make a sneaky run at his Chubby bar, he ran back down to the waiting room. He found Flake and Jasmine talking with a member of the hospital staff, a slim, dark-haired woman in green scrubs. Sanchez tapped the woman on the shoulder.

'Excuse me, nurse. I've got my Chubby stuck in the vending machine, and it's stolen my five dollars.'

Flake glowered at him. 'Sanchez, this is Doctor Selvi. She's giving us an update on Rex.'

'And?'

Jasmine broke the news down for Sanchez. 'Apparently, Rex is having a blood confusion.'

'Transfusion,' said Dr Selvi. 'We have him hooked up to a blood bag and some saline. He's in for a rough ride. The next hour will be crucial.'

'Can we see him?' Jasmine asked.

'Yes, but only for a short time,' Dr Selvi replied. 'He's in a private room on the second floor. If you'd like to follow me I'll take you there now.'

She led them back the way Sanchez had just come from. When they walked through a set of doors on the second floor, Sanchez saw the vending machine at the end of the hallway, mocking him. Dr Selvi led them towards it, only to then stop outside a room halfway along the corridor. She opened the door to the room and showed them inside. Rex was in a bed against the wall. His head and shoulders were covered in bandages like he'd been mummified. His lower half was beneath the bed covers. He had an oxygen mask over his mouth and there were some tubes attached to his arm, feeding him blood and saline from a pair of transparent bags on a stand above the bed.

'Can he hear us?' Jasmine asked.

'Possibly,' the doctor replied. 'But he can't respond. I'm afraid his chances of survival are not good. He's lost a lot of blood and so much of his skin was cut off he's liable to get any number of infections. The best we can do for him at the moment is to give him his own room.'

'His eye looks pretty grim,' said Sanchez, noting the gaping black hole where Rex's left eye once was.

'Oh, goodness yes,' said Dr Selvi. She reached into her pocket and pulled out a black eye patch on an elastic strap. 'I've just acquired this eye patch for him.'

'Can I put it on?' Jasmine asked.

Dr Selvi handed it to her. 'By all means, but be careful.'

Sanchez tutted. 'I think Rex needs it more than you do, Jasmine.'

'It *is* for Rex, you idiot!' Jasmine replied. 'I'm not going to put it on myself, am I? I'm not stupid, y'know.'

She shook her head at Sanchez, then walked over to Rex's bedside. She wrapped the elastic around his head and secured the patch over his eye, then stepped back to admire her work.

'It looks good, don't you think?' she said.

'You've put it over the wrong eye,' said Flake. 'It's supposed to cover the missing eye.'

While Jasmine corrected her mistake, Dr Selvi retrieved a cloth bag from the end of the bed. She handed it to Flake.

'This bag contains Rex's personal belongings,' she said. 'His gun has been confiscated though. Hospital rules, I'm afraid.'

'That's okay, thanks,' said Flake.

'I'll leave you all with him for a while,' said the doctor. 'Visiting time is up in ten minutes.'

With Doctor Selvi gone, Sanchez tried to grab the bag of Rex's belongings from Flake in case there were any snacks inside. She was too strong for him and when he gave up, she opened it herself.

'What's in there?' Sanchez asked.

Flake held it open and showed him. It contained no snacks, just Rex's phone, some keys, a wallet and some loose change.

'We should call Alexis Calhoon,' said Jasmine. 'Her number is in Rex's phone.'

'What have we got to call her for?' Sanchez groaned.

'To let her know what's happened. She might be able to help us somehow.'

'Like how?' Flake asked.

'I don't know, but she might know a special doctor that treats these kinds of injures. Just ring her and tell her. It can't hurt.'

Flake typed the code 1,2,3,4 into Rex's keypad to unlock his phone. 'He's still not changed his PIN,' she said, shaking her head as she flicked through his contacts. She found Calhoon and made the call.

'Oh, hey, wait a sec,' said Jasmine. 'If Alexis says the words, "sack whack", it means you have to ignore everything she just said.'

'Sack whack?' said Sanchez. 'Why sack whack?'

Flake shushed him. 'Hello is that Alexis Calhoon?' she asked, speaking to a woman who had answered the call.

'Yes. Who is this?'

'It's Flake Munroe. I'm with Jasmine and Sanchez at Saint Jude's hospital in Santa Mondega. Rex has been attacked by a group of cannibal people. He's in a coma. Jasmine thought we should call you and let you know.'

Calhoon groaned. 'Okay, thanks for letting me know.'

'Is there anything you can do to help?' Flake asked.

'I'm afraid not, but thanks for calling. I've got to go. Sorry, bye.'

The line went dead. Flake looked at Jasmine. 'Pfft, that was a waste of time. That bitch doesn't give a shit. What a cunt.'

****

Alexis Calhoon ended the call with Flake, then sat back in her armchair and closed her eyes. This was really turning into a shitty day. She still hadn't taken the dogs for a walk, and now she was going to have to do something else she really didn't want to do. Scratch and his cronies were tapped into her phone, so they would have heard every word of her conversation with Flake. It left Calhoon with no choice but to pass on the details of the conversation to her best assassins. She brought up their group chat on her phone and typed in a message.

UPDATE: *Rodeo Rex injured and rushed to Saint Jude's hospital. Jasmine at same location.*

Within seconds she received three notifications. All three of the Bastard brothers had read the message. And then just as she was exiting the application, a fourth notification popped up. Her number one hitman, the elusive Falco Logan had read the message too.

Thirty Nine

Twenty seconds had passed since Sally pressed the button on her pager. She'd been counting down in her head. Her palms were sweating so much that when she picked up her wine glass it almost stuck to her hand. In ten seconds Steve and his other bodyguard buddies would arrive and kick the front door down. Ten more seconds. *Nine.* Nine more seconds. *Eight.*

Elvis walked back in from the kitchen. He was drying his hands on a paper towel.

'That was quick,' said Sally.

'Yeah. This blood's not coming off any time soon,' he replied.

He screwed up the paper towel and rolled it into a ball, before tossing it across the room. It landed in a waste basket by the window.

'Nice shot,' said Sally.

Elvis grabbed the chair he had been sitting on while he interrogated her, and carried it across to the bathroom. He propped it up against the handle on the bathroom door.

'What are you doing that for?' Sally asked.

'In case Scratch shows up here. Bathrooms aren't safe, remember?'

'Shit, yeah. Sorry, my mind's all over the place.'

'We should get moving,' said Elvis. 'I've been thinking. Scratch will most likely send someone here to kill you. You're a loose end, and Scratch doesn't do loose ends.'

Sally picked up her wine glass and poured the last mouthful down her throat. 'Do I need to pack?' she asked, standing up and wiping her mouth.

'No. It's only short term, but I think we should go out the way I came in.'

'Out of the window?'

'Yeah. Come on, let's move. I'm worried about the guys I saw outside. It'll be safer going down the fire escape.'

Sally wasn't a fan of the fire escape, a set of rusty metal stairs that stunk of piss. It was only ever used by the local bums and junkies. Now wasn't the time to complain about it though.

'Okay, just give me a minute,' she said, stalling for time.

'Uh, uh, no way. We gotta go now.'

'Okay.' In her head, Sally had counted past thirty. *Fuckssake Steve! Where are you?*

Elvis turned his back on her and headed for the window. This was her chance. She picked up the pager from the coffee table and concealed it in her fist. She squeezed the button again.

Bzzzz, bzzzz, bzzzz.

Three pagers buzzed in unison.

Nearby.

In her lounge.

Sally froze. Elvis turned around. Their eyes locked. He was no longer in a hurry to leave. He reached into his hip pocket and pulled out three pagers exactly like the one in her hand. He dropped them one by one onto the floor.

'You should probably sit back down,' he said.

Sitting down was easy because the strength had vanished from her legs. She slumped back onto the couch. 'I...I...,' The words didn't come. This wasn't part of the script. Things weren't supposed to turn out this way.

Elvis walked back to the sofa and glowered at her. 'Your three friends. Did you really think they were gonna stop me from getting in?'

'I don't know what you mean.'

Elvis didn't move, didn't speak. He waited for her to tell the truth.

'I only met one of them,' she admitted. 'I don't even know them really.'

'But you just tried paging them all?'

'I just did what they told me to. I think this place is bugged. I was going to signal you.'

'Sure you were.' Elvis pointed down the hall to her bedroom. 'The red suitcase you took in there before I came in, I'm guessing that was full of money, right? Blood money, from Scratch?'

The game was up for sure. Elvis knew everything.

'I didn't want the money, I swear,' Sally blustered. 'I was scared. The Devil came into my apartment. What was I supposed to do? I'm not like you guys.'

'You were supposed to tell Rex, and tell me. We would have protected you. You were part of the group. We welcomed you in, and whether you believe it or not, we would have dealt with it.'

'How do you deal with it when it's the Devil?'

'Because that's what we do. *You* could never have been one of us. We value things like friendship, loyalty and honesty.'

'So do I. But it wasn't that simple. Scratch said he'd kill my mom. I had no choice, I swear.'

Elvis reached back and pulled out a pistol that was tucked down the back of his pants.

'Is that mine?' Sally asked, recognising it.

'It is,' Elvis replied. 'At least now I know why you left it at the Tapioca.' He released the magazine from the gun, showed her it was empty, then placed it down on the coffee table. 'Last thing you'd want is to get yourself stuck to the burger stall when it turned into a magnet, right? Oh, and your mom, you say Scratch threatened to kill her?'

'He did, I swear.'

'Sally……….. your mom died twelve years ago.'

'What?'

Elvis walked around the table, stopping in front of the television. 'Those archives at City Hall, they've got it all. Everything you wanna know about a cop, it's all there. You didn't really think I was gonna let my friend Rex go out with a cop and not check her out thoroughly? I know everything about you. I know that the wine you buy from the local store is a French Chardonnay. I know you've been officially reprimanded for drinking at work, twice. I know the janitor of your building is called Bill. And I know that the drug dealer on the second floor of this building pays you hush money every month. And in case you weren't sure, I did kill your three bodyguards before I came up the fire escape. I slit the first guy's throat. The second guy, knife through the brain. And the third guy, well, I didn't have to be so quiet with him, so I bashed his skull in on the steps outside the front of the building.

'Oh God.'

'You know what else I figured out when I was on my way here? There were no cameras in the Ladies room at the Tapioca. Scratch knew Janis and Jasmine were in there because someone texted him. That someone was you.'

'No, no, I didn't, I swear. I don't even have Scratch's number.'

'You're not a good liar, Sally.'

'I'm not lying!'

'Janis is dead because of you. I'd say you're pretty lucky I found you before the Bourbon Kid did.'

Sally's voice was cracking. 'I didn't text anyone. You've gotta believe me!'

'I don't gotta believe anything,' Elvis replied, the look on his face darkening with every passing second. 'Now, Sally, I'm assuming, that with you being a cop an' all, you've seen my criminal records? Am I right?'

Sally felt the warm fuzz of acid erupting from her stomach into her throat. She swallowed hard to rid herself of it and then replied. 'I have read your file, yeah.'

'Did you read about what I did to Marcus the Weasel?'

'Yes.'

'What did I do?'

'You cut off parts of his body and fed them to him.'

'That's right,' Elvis agreed. 'I cut him open and fed his intestines to him, which was a messy job I can tell you, but it had to be done. You know why?'

Sally nodded. 'The report said you thought Marcus had killed Sanchez's brother.' Nausea floated out of her mouth with every syllable.

'Yup. See, Sanchez is my friend, and I liked his brother Thomas too.' Elvis reached inside his shirt and pulled out a hunting knife from a holster by his ribs. The knife had blood on it already. 'So, now you know what I do to people who mess with my friends. And you also know that Rex was my *best friend*.'

Sally leapt to her feet and made a run for the door. Elvis swung an arm across her throat, clothes-lining her before she'd taken two steps. It knocked the wind right out of her. She fell backwards and landed back on the sofa in a heap, choking as she tried to catch her breath. Elvis's shadow loomed over.

'I hope you're hungry.'

Forty

'Rex, can you hear me?' Jasmine asked.

She was sitting on a plastic chair beside his bed, stroking his bandaged head. Flake was with her, sitting on the end of the bed by Rex's feet. It was a waste of time waiting for Rex to respond. He was a million miles away from consciousness. Sanchez could certainly see it, even if Flake and Jasmine couldn't.

Sanchez was standing in the doorway, keeping tabs on the vending machine at the end of the corridor. So far, no one else had used it, so his Chubby bar was still hanging on a hook, calling to him, begging him to come get it. All he needed was Flake to shake the bloody machine, but she wanted to sit by Rex's bedside with Jasmine, whispering stuff into his ear, telling him everything will be all right.

'He can't hear you,' Sanchez warned them.

'I think he can,' said Flake. 'They say your hearing is the last thing to go.'

'Who's *they?*' Sanchez asked. 'I heard the last thing to go was your bowels. You have a big clear out right as you take your last breath, apparently.'

Flake glared at him. 'We've only got a few minutes with him before visiting time is up. Don't you want to say anything to him?'

Before Sanchez could come up with anything, Dr Selvi returned. She poked her head around the door.

'Visiting time is up, I'm afraid,' she said. 'You can still hang around in the waiting room downstairs if you like, but not in here.'

'Did you hear that?' Sanchez said assertively. 'The doctor says we've got to go.'

Dr Selvi patted Sanchez on the arm to show her appreciation for his respect of the rules. She whispered a quiet "thanks" to him then excused herself and moved further down the corridor to annoy some other visitors.

Sanchez moved over to Flake and gently tugged at her sleeve. 'Do you think you could go to the vending machine with me and help me get my Chubby out?'

Flake touched Rex's hand as a way of saying goodbye, then turned to face Sanchez. 'All right, calm down, would you? Stop thinking about your gut all the time!'

Sanchez recoiled, shocked at the anger in Flake's voice.

Flake ignored him and tapped Jasmine on the shoulder. 'Are you coming?'

Jasmine whispered something in Rex's ear before planting a kiss on his bandaged face, then she looked at the others. 'Do you think it's safe for us to leave him here on his own?' she asked. 'Should we put a hat on him or something? You know, to disguise him?'

'He'll be fine,' said Sanchez. 'We'll only be downstairs in the waiting room. We can see the reception from there, so we'll see anyone coming in. And Elvis will be here soon.'

'We should take it in turns to stand guard outside Rex's room,' said Jasmine, standing up. 'You never know if another assassin is going to show up.'

'Good thinking,' said Flake.

'I actually need to use the Ladies room,' said Jasmine. 'Sanchez should stay here and watch Rex first. Can you come with me, Flake?'

'Yes, of course,' said Flake.

'Fuckssake,' Sanchez groaned. 'What about my Chubby? Can't you women ever go to the toilet on your own?'

'We'll only be a minute,' said Flake. 'Besides, we *have* to go together.'

Sanchez was livid because Flake was right. It wasn't just because women always went to the toilet together, it was also because Scratch might come out of the toilet walls and try to kill them. 'Fine,' he said. 'But don't be ages. I'm starving.'

'We won't be long,' said Flake. She gave him a kiss and walked out into the corridor with Jasmine.

Sanchez followed them out. 'What if the doctor lady comes back and tells me to leave?' he complained.

'Tell her, *"no"*.'

'You can handle the scary doctor lady, can't you?' said Jasmine, teasing Sanchez.

'I'm not afraid of her.'

'Good,' said Jasmine. 'And you won't be afraid of any assassins either, will you?'

Sanchez gulped. 'They won't really come here, will they?'

'Hopefully not,' said Jasmine.

Flake offered a better answer. 'Sanchez, just pretend you're like Al Pacino in *The Godfather*. Remember when he was in the hospital protecting Marlon Brando from being assassinated? You can do that, can't you?'

Sanchez was fairly confident he could do anything Al Pacino could do. 'I suppose so,' he replied, casually.

Flake spotted a set of headphones on a trolley in the corridor. She grabbed them and offered them to Sanchez. 'Here, put these on. They're tuned into the hospital radio.'

Sanchez snatched the headphones from her. 'You promise to get my Chubby out when you come back?'

'I'll think about it. Just stay here. We won't be long.'

Sanchez put the headphones on. A deejay introduced a song called "Green Bird" by Yoko Kanno and the Seatbelts. 'Typical,' Sanchez muttered to himself, 'Japanese music.'

While Sanchez was busy tapping his feet to the music, Jasmine and Flake headed along the corridor in search of the Ladies toilets.

'I hate hospitals,' said Jasmine. 'They're like a big maze. We should leave a trail of breadcrumbs or something so we can find our way back.'

'It's all right,' said Flake. 'I know my way around.'

'Have you seen any toilets since we've been here though?'

'There were some downstairs by the reception.'

'Good. I want to get my phone out so I can call Elvis.'

'Can't you keep your phone on your belt like a normal person?' Flake asked as they approached a set of double doors.

Jasmine kung-fu kicked the doors open, smashing them into the face of a young bald-headed boy on crutches who was coming the other way. The boy lost his balance and fell sideways through an open window behind the door. His crutches clattered onto the floor.

Jasmine picked one up. 'These could be a handy weapon you know,' she said. 'I could definitely swing this at someone.'

'Chuck it out of the window,' said Flake. 'That poor kid won't be able to walk without it.'

Jasmine leaned out of the window to check where the boy was. He had landed safely in a patch of thick snow on top of a long trailer-truck with a logo on the side for *Cooler Cola*. Jasmine dropped both of the crutches down to him. In return the young boy made a rude hand gesture at her.

'Jeez, that kid's got an attitude,' said Jasmine. 'Ungrateful little shit.'

The two women made their way down a flight of stairs to the ground floor. At the bottom of the stairwell two shaven-headed male nurses in blue scrubs were having an argument about something.

'Excuse me,' said Jasmine. 'Coming through!'

The two men stopped bickering and stepped aside to let her pass. One of them smiled at her.

'Hey, Miss,' he said. 'Could you help us? We're looking for a Doctor Phil Good. Do you know him?'

'Doctor Phil Good?' said Jasmine, puzzled. 'I think I've heard of him.'

'They're kidding,' said Flake. 'It's a joke.'

'It is?' Jasmine took a closer look at the two nurses. The men shared more than just the same haircut, they were identical. 'Are you two twins?' she asked.

'Triplets actually,' one of the men replied.

'Huh?'

A third nurse, identical to the other two, stepped out from behind the stairwell. He snuck up behind Flake and wrapped a drugged cloth over her mouth and nose. It caught her unawares but she reacted quickly, stamping on his feet and elbowing him in the ribs. It was no use. He was too strong for her, and the chemicals in the cloth were filling up her lungs. He dragged her backwards and lifted her off her feet so she couldn't stamp on him anymore. The drug made its way into her bloodstream and within seconds she was unconscious.

Jasmine's attempt to help was thwarted before it even began. One of the two nurses sucker-punched her, smashing his giant fist into her cheekbone. The blunt force of it knocked her sideways into the wall, dazed and incapable of defending herself.

'Cover her face with the rag!'

Leonardo Bastard snuck behind Jasmine and pressed a rag against her face. His brother, Vegas grabbed her legs and lifted them off the floor. The attack on Jasmine and Flake was over in a matter of seconds without anyone in the hospital witnessing it. With both women unconscious, the Bastard brothers carried them outside to their trailer-truck and threw them in the back.

Renwar Bastard jumped into the driver's cab and started the engine. The truck pulled out of the hospital parking lot and drove off.

Forty One

Purgatory had rarely, if ever, been busier. It was like a nightclub, if indeed a nightclub had ever existed with a clientele made up of savage cannibals, brain-dead skeletons, the Devil, the Grim Reaper, a green-skinned, purple-haired witch, and Zilas the hunchback who was back serving drinks behind the bar--for the time being.

The only sensible person in the place was Eric Einstein. The tech genius was at a corner table on his own, tapping away on a laptop. He was bugged into Alexis Calhoon's phone. From there he was keeping tabs on everything that was happening with the Dead Hunters. And stuff was definitely happening. After ten minutes of trying to catch Scratch's eye, he finally succeeded. The Devil finished a conversation he was having with Albatross, son of Snake Hawk, and breezed over to join Einstein.

'Any news on Rodeo Rex?' Scratch asked, sitting down in a chair next to the scientist.

Einstein grimaced. 'It's not good.'

Scratch glowered at the techie nerd. 'Why? What's happened?'

'Ten minutes ago, Alexis Calhoon took a call from Flake Munroe. It seems that Rex survived the cannibal attack. He's in Saint Jude's hospital.'

The right side of Scratch's face twitched. 'What happened to Snake Hawk and the others?'

'They're dead. I saw it for myself. I hacked into a security camera on the promenade. After you left, Elvis showed up and killed them all. Then the others came and took Rex away in an ambulance.' Einstein lifted his laptop off the table, knowing what was coming next.

'FUCKERS!' Scratch slammed his fist down on the table. The table legs snapped and splintered off in different directions. The top of the table split in half and clattered onto the floor, leaving Scratch and Einstein sitting on wooden chairs opposite each other without a table in between them.

The smashing of the table sent the whole bar into a hush. Everyone looked at Scratch, then looked away again when they saw how angry he was.

'Shall we move to another table?' Einstein suggested.

Scratch stood up and addressed the room by waving his hand in the air like a Roman Emperor gesturing at the peasants. 'Carry on everyone,' he said. 'Nothing to see here.'

The assortment of oddballs went back to muttering amongst themselves, while Scratch and Einstein moved to a table out of earshot of everyone else.

'I want a full update,' said Scratch. 'Which of the targets are dead?'

'The only two dead so far are the ones you and the Reaper killed,' Einstein whispered. 'The others are all still alive. Stunky and the Chinaman are dead. And the hit on Sanchez and Flake appears to have failed, although at this point I'm not sure how.'

'Christ! Is there any good news?'

'Yes. Flake and Jasmine have just been snatched by the Bastard brothers at the hospital. Vegas texted Calhoon to confirm it.'

The news did placate Scratch somewhat. 'Well, that's something, I suppose.'

Einstein glanced across at the bar. 'Should we tell Snake Hawk's son that his father was killed? He keeps looking over here. I reckon he knows something's wrong.'

'Of course he knows something's wrong,' Scratch groaned. 'It's bloody obvious.' The Devil stroked his goatee beard for a while as he pondered what to do. Eventually he beckoned Albatross over from the bar.

'What's this guy's name?' Einstein asked as the heavily tattooed cannibal approached.

'Albatross.'

'Albert Ross?'

'No, Albatross, you ass! Don't get his name wrong while he's here. He's very tetchy about it. Apparently he hasn't yet earned his second name.'

'Huh?'

Albatross arrived at their table and bowed his head. He was a heavy-set fucker in his mid-twenties with his hair scraped back in cornrows. 'You have news of my father?' he asked.

Einstein spun his laptop around and showed Albatross a live feed from the security cameras on the Santa Mondega promenade. The footage showed his father and the two other members of the Skinners tribe laid out dead in the snow. Albatross's eyes burned with rage.

'What is this?' he asked.

'Your dad's dead,' Einstein replied. 'So are his two friends. And Rodeo Rex escaped.'

Albatross looked like he was ready to kill Einstein, just for telling him what had happened to his father. Scratch stood up and ushered the angry cannibal away from the table. 'Listen Albert, here's what we're going to do.'

'What did you call me?'

Scratch threw a filthy look Einstein's way, blaming the scientist for planting the name Albert Ross into his subconscious. Einstein looked bewildered by the angry stare.

'Albatross, that's what I called you,' Scratch said, returning to his conversation with the cannibal. 'Now listen, Rodeo Rex, the man your father tried to kill, he's in Saint Jude's hospital. If you wish to finish what your father started, I will be happy to send you there.'

'My whole tribe will go with me,' Albatross replied. 'And I will earn my second name by avenging my father's death.'

'Excellent,' said Scratch, the smile returning to his face. 'I will arrange for you to travel through the portal immediately. When you get to the hospital you and your men can do whatever you like with the people you find there, just as long as you kill Rodeo Rex. When he is dead you will be handsomely rewarded, all of you.'

'It will be done.'

Albatross marched off to round up his cannibal brothers. There were close to fifty of them still hanging around in Purgatory.

Scratch returned to Einstein's desk and clipped the scientist around the back of the head. 'Oi, you tactless gimp,' he said. 'Switch the portal location to the hospital, *now.*'

'It's already done.'

Scratch rubbed his hands with excitement. Even though things hadn't worked out exactly as planned, everything would soon fall into place.

The Grim Reaper had watched everything from his bar stool nearby. As Albatross hurried around gathering up his men, Barazima stood up, his eight-feet high frame casting a shadow over Scratch as he approached.

'Yes?' said Scratch. 'What do you want?'

'I will go with the Skinners,' said the Reaper. 'It is the only way to ensure the execution is carried out properly this time.'

'Marvellous!' said Scratch, pulling a cigar from his top pocket.

Barazima shook his head. 'I expected better from your people,' he said. 'This should have been finished by now.'

'Can we talk about this another time?' said Scratch, sucking on his cigar and lighting it up. 'Go forth and do thy killing. When it's done, come back and we will kill the Bourbon Kid together.'

The Reaper made a grunting noise under his breath, then turned away and headed over to the Men's toilets to wait for the Skinners.

Einstein tugged at Scratch's suit. 'Psst, boss,' he whispered.

'What?' said Scratch, slapping his hand away and blowing some smoke at him.

'I have some more news,' said Einstein, ducking away from the smoke and pointing at his laptop screen. 'The three bodyguards you assigned to protect Sally Diamond are dead.'

The smile vanished from Scratch's face. 'How are they dead?'

'My guess is it's Elvis,' said Einstein. 'I'm just looking for some camera footage to confirm it.'

Scratch put his hands together and drummed his fingers against each other. 'This is actually perfect,' he said. 'As soon as the Skinners have gone through the portal to the hospital, you will change the portal location to Sally's apartment.' He looked around Purgatory. His eyes settled on Trixie, the witch, and a group of skeletons. 'I will go there with Trixie and a bunch of those skeletons. It's time Elvis got what was coming to him.'

Forty Two

Sanchez kept checking his watch. Waiting around in a hospital was about as much fun as a Saturday night spent watching Plant World and Cooking World. The only thing stopping him from going nuts was the music coming through on his headphones. Even though most of it was cheesy stuff, when the song "Put a Little Love in your Heart" by Jackie DeShannon came on, he found himself singing along to it, even though he hated it.

By the time he'd heard five songs, his stomach was making gurgling sounds because he was so hungry. With no sign of Flake and Jasmine returning, he finally lost patience. Waiting around outside Rex's room was just too boring, so he headed off to the vending machine to have a crack at shaking his candy bar free. There was no one else around on the second floor, so he pulled off some discreet dance moves as he grooved along the corridor. The dancing came to an abrupt end when a pretty young nurse rounded a corner up ahead and sprinted towards him. He transitioned the dance moves back into a casual walk, styling it out as best he could. The nurse looked panicky, like she had a patient in desperate need of a bedpan, and she couldn't find a clean one anywhere. Sanchez smiled at her as she sprinted past him. She responded by shouting something that he couldn't hear on account of the chirpy, upbeat music coming through his headphones.

More doctors and nurses sprinted past the end of the corridor, all of them screaming stuff at each other. Whoever it was that needed the bedpan had probably shit the bed by now, Sanchez imagined. No wonder so many people died in this hospital every year, the doctors and nurses couldn't stay calm in a crisis. Sanchez considered the idea of having them all fired for incompetence, seeing as how he was technically still the mayor.

When he arrived at the vending machine he was relieved to see his Chubby bar still hanging over the edge of the top row of snacks. He checked both ways along the corridor. The panicking doctors and nurses had all disappeared, so he banged the machine with his fist to try and loosen the Chubby. The banging made his hand ache, but the Chubby didn't move.

'Fucking hell,' he grumbled.

No wonder people didn't like going to hospital. There was never a doctor or nurse around when you needed one to help shake a vending machine. Sanchez scratched his butt while he tried to remember how Flake usually dealt with corrupt vending machines. Brute strength was the only possible answer. And even though Flake was infinitely stronger than him, Sanchez felt determined. This could be done.

Two minutes earlier

Albatross, son of Snake Hawk, entered the hospital through the toilets on the ground floor, followed by fifty of his cannibal brothers. Carnage ensued. The Skinners, armed with their sharp knives and jagged black teeth, grabbed the first people they saw and started stripping them of their clothes, and slicing off their skin. Patients, visitors, janitors, doctors, nurses, no one was spared the wrath of the cannibals, who were still furious at the loss of their leader. Men, women and children were pinned to the floor and ravaged.

To begin with, the strongest and bravest of the doctors and nurses tried to fight back, but when the Grim Reaper showed up and started lifting people off their feet and ripping their heads off, it was soon a case of every able bodied person making a run for it. Bravery and honour led only to decapitation, or sometimes a slower, more painful death.

Albatross, his blood on fire, his heart raging at the world, was desperate to find Rex. Everyone else in the hospital was merely fodder, food for the others. He marched into the reception area and set his sights on a young male doctor who was trying to push an elderly wheelchair-bound gentleman to safety. Albatross grabbed the doctor and pulled him away from the wheelchair. He pinned the doctor against a wall, and pressed a knife against his throat.

'Where is Rodeo Rex?' he hissed.

'I don't know!'

Albatross dug the blade into the doctor's neck, drawing blood and a scream from his terrified prisoner. 'Try again,' he said, showing his teeth.

'Second floor,' the doctor squealed. 'Room twenty-four, I think.'

'Thank you.'

Albatross ran his knife across the man's neck, ripping his throat open. Blood gushed out, pouring down the doctor's previously spotless white coat. The new Chief Skinner licked the blade of his knife clean and let the dying doctor slide to the floor in a pool of his own blood. Next stop, second floor.

Albatross sprinted around the ground floor until he found a staircase. He bounded up it, scaring the shit out of a group of doctors and nurses who were on their way down. Some dived over the bannister, others turned and ran back up. Albatross didn't care about any of them.

He wanted Rex. He intended to cut the Hell's Angel's heart out and eat it in front of him as a way of revenge for his father's death.

When he rounded the steps at the top of the staircase he burst through a set of double doors into a long corridor. He saw a Danny DeVito lookalike at the opposite end of the corridor, kicking and shaking a vending machine. The stupid fool was listening to music through a set of headphones and hadn't a clue what was happening. Albatross disregarded him almost immediately. The man was definitely not a threat, and didn't look appetizing at all.

Albatross jogged down the corridor, checking the numbers on the doors, looking for Rex's room. He found room twenty-four about halfway down. The door was already open. He peered inside and saw a heavily bandaged man lying in a bed. Even though the room was dark, he knew right away that it was Rex. The sound of the double doors at the end of the corridor being smashed made him hesitate. He looked back and saw the Grim Reaper had kicked the doors off their hinges, and was walking along the corridor towards him.

Albatross yelled at the Reaper. *'I've found him! He's in here!'*

The Reaper nodded, to show he understood, but he didn't quicken his step. In fact, one of Albatross's fellow Skinners, a seasoned killer named Indigo Blue, sprinted past the Reaper. Blue had his eyes on Sanchez, who was still oblivious to everything that was happening.

Albatross looked down at the knife in his hand. It had been given to him by his father who had given it the name, *Gut-spiller*. It had taken the lives of many men.

Albatross entered Rex's room and walked over to the bed. This was it. Revenge would be sweet, and deserved. He raised his knife above his head and pulled the sheet back on the bed, revealing Rex's partially bandaged and badly mutilated torso. The Hell's Angel did not stir.

'Say hello to the Gut-spiller,' Albatross said, saliva drooling down his chin.

He plunged the knife down into Rex's chest. At least, he *almost* did. Out of the darkness, a hand grabbed his wrist, a strong, firm hand that prevented Albatross's blade from reaching its target. Albatross's hand twitched. No matter how hard he pushed he couldn't force his knife down that last inch. It hovered just above Rex's chest, unable to finish the job. It took Albatross a moment to realise what was happening, but then he remembered something Scratch had said when the Skinners arrived at Purgatory. The Devil had given them an explicit warning, and repeated it several times. Five words. That was all it was. Five words Albatross should have paid more attention to.

He lives in the shadows.

Forty Three

For the second time in a short while, Elvis was washing his hands in Sally Diamond's kitchen. On the first occasion he'd been washing away the blood of her three bodyguards, and a bit of Rex's blood. This time the blood was Sally's. He'd wanted to make her suffer the way Rex had suffered, but time wasn't on his side. He was well aware that Scratch could show up at any minute, so he'd given Sally a scare by intimating he was going to cut her open and feed her internal organs to her. But with time limited, he had to settle for beating her to death. He made it as quick as possible, pushing her onto the floor and using the heel of his boot to cave her face in. He drowned out her anguished cries by switching the TV to a music channel and turning up the volume. Death by AC/DC's "Highway to Hell".

He finished washing his hands, dried them on a paper towel and returned to the lounge. It was a mess. Blood and gristle from Sally's mashed-up head had seeped across the floor. The carpet was ruined. It would take a while to get rid of the smell too, he supposed.

The window across the room was beckoning him to use it for a hasty exit. But there was also the small matter of the suitcase filled with money that Sally had moved into another room. Did Elvis have time to grab it and carry it down the fire escape? He barely finished asking himself the question before the answer came.

It was an emphatic no.

He heard footsteps inside Sally's bathroom. And voices.

Fuck!

Elvis leapt over Sally's corpse and bolted for the window. The bathroom door quivered behind him. The chair he had placed up against it wouldn't keep it closed for long. He lifted the window up and climbed through it onto the emergency stairwell. As he pulled the window back down, the bathroom door blew off its hinges. It crashed into Sally's coffee table and then fell down on top of her.

Scratch walked out of the bathroom, followed by a woman with green skin and purple hair.

The first thing the Devil did was look right at Elvis. The two men locked eyes for a moment. A broad grin broke out on Scratch's face and he made a move towards the window.

Elvis hotfooted it along the grilled metal landing to a flight of stairs that led down. As he set foot on the first step down, he saw something below that made the hairs on the back of his neck stand up. Skeletons, swarms of them, bounding up the stairs towards him. There were more of them at ground level, making their way into the building through other entrances. The whole building was surrounded.

Shit.

There was only one way to go. *Up to the roof.* Elvis turned and scampered back along the landing. Up ahead, a big black hand reopened the window on Sally's apartment. Scratch poked his head and shoulders through it. Even though Elvis didn't want to antagonise the Devil any more than was necessary, there was only one option available to him. As he raced past the window he balled his fist and punched Scratch in the face. The punch connected perfectly and knocked Scratch back into Sally's apartment.

'SUCK ON THAT!' Elvis yelled.

He scrambled up the next flight of stairs, re-enacting the punch in his mind. He even made a promise to himself. If he could survive being hunted down by Scratch and an army of skeletons, he would spend the rest of his life *boring people shitless* with the tale of how he "chinned" the Devil.

Scratch's furious cries were almost drowned out by the sheer number of skeleton feet pounding on metal stairs, as they chased Elvis up to the roof. By the time Elvis reached the top of the stairs, his feet were killing him, his knees were aching, his lungs were burning, and his heart was close to exploding. But there was no time to take a break, or even slow down. He sprinted across the building's flat roof, trying desperately to think of a viable escape plan. Judging by the sounds of skeletons cackling behind him, he had a matter of seconds to come up with something.

There was only one way off the roof, and it was going to involve some kind of jump. Elvis had a brief, magical vision that involved Jasmine showing up in a fucking helicopter with one of those rope ladder things. But Jasmine didn't own a helicopter, knew fuck all about how rope ladders work, and also didn't know dick about being a pilot. It was never gonna happen.

Elvis looked around. Was there a jump that could realistically be made? There was nothing to his left. Nothing straight ahead either. To the right there was another building, but it was a few storeys higher than the one he was on. The only other direction was back the way he came and that was no kind of option at all. All the options were bad. The decision therefore became, "which of the options is the least shitty?"

He angled his run towards the taller building on his right. *"This is it. I'm about to jump from the roof of one building into side of another!"* The decision made no sense. He knew that. *"Even Wylie Coyote wasn't this fucking dumb!"*

He glanced back over his shoulder. Scratch was already on the roof, and so were a whole bunch of his dirty skeleton people. The bony fuckers were making all kinds of noise, their feet rattling on the small stones on the rooftop as they bounded across it. Scratch, on the other hand, he played it cool, strolling along as the skeletons swarmed past him.

"Man, this is a shit plan!" Elvis muttered to himself.

With all the energy he had left he sprinted to the edge of the rooftop and planted one foot down on the ground. He pushed down hard and launched himself through the air. He kept his legs moving in a running motion, as if that might somehow help. He'd never run across thin air before, but now was the time to see if it was possible.

It wasn't.

Forty Four

He lives in the shadows.

Albatross's arm trembled as he fought to slam his Gut-spiller knife into Rex's chest. It should have been easy, but to his great frustration he wasn't strong enough to finish plunging it into the man he blamed for his father's death. A hooded man dressed in black had appeared out of the shadows of the hospital room and grabbed his wrist. Albatross glanced at the face under the dark hood and saw the eyes of a man more ruthless than anyone he had ever encountered. A man who killed, not for food or survival, but for revenge, or hatred, or in some cases, *for no reason at all.*

The Bourbon Kid had such a firm grip on Albatross's wrist that the Skinner's arm was paralysed, quivering an inch above Rex's chest. The two men were locked in a test of strength, one that Albatross was not winning. The test came to an abrupt end when his opponent grabbed him around the neck and dragged him away from Rex's bed. The assassin was about to become the assassinated.

Albatross was spun around. The wall of the room rocketed towards him. Nothing he could do would prevent the inevitable. His face hit the wall, accompanied by a loud crunch. The tip of his nose flattened like putty. His nostrils closed up and everything that once protruded out of his face, turned inwards. Blood spurted up into his eyes and down into his mouth. His teeth obliterated, one by one from front to back. He tasted his own blood, his own nose, and some chunks of tongue and teeth. The contents of his head slowly slid down his throat and into his lungs.

The Bourbon Kid pulled Albatross's head back from the wall. The cannibal's messed up eyes were still absorbing images, fuzzy, blurred, swaying images, like the wall zooming in towards him again.

And then again.

And again.

And again.

The Bourbon Kid rammed Albatross's face into the wall eight times in all. The Skinner was brain dead after the second blow. His heart carried on beating for a while, but after the eighth time of being bludgeoned by the wall, his skull had transformed into a million tiny pieces of bone, floating around in a bag of skin. The annihilation of Albatross ended with the Bourbon Kid ripping him apart with his own Gut-spiller knife. The blade slit open his heart and sliced down through his guts.

When the disembowelment was complete, the Bourbon Kid took a step back and away from his victim. Albatross fell apart, his innards sliding out through his open torso. The stench was worse than the toilets in the Tapioca.

There was no time for the Kid to savour the kill. In spite of it being a quick and relatively silent murder, it had attracted the attention of a passer-by in the corridor. The enormous shape of the Grim Reaper appeared in the frame of the doorway. The Reaper leaned down, his skeletal, yellow face peered inside the room. He saw the remains of Albatross on the floor, then looked up into the eyes of the Bourbon Kid.

The Kid launched himself at the eight-foot tall, hooded horror and thrust Albatross's Gut-spiller into its face. The blade of the knife did not penetrate the Reaper's skin at all. It didn't even make a dent. Instead it buckled and bent back out of shape. The Kid dropped it and butted his head into the Reaper's chest. The butt had more of an impact than the blade. It knocked the Reaper off balance and he stumbled back into the corridor. The Kid unholstered his Headblaster gun and stepped out after him.

The Reaper was quick to compose himself. He straightened up in the corridor and unclipped the handle of his sword from his belt. He pointed it up at the ceiling and wrapped his bony fingers around it. A blade made of bright red and yellow flames burst forth.

The Bourbon Kid had never been one to loiter around and wait for his enemy to strike first. He straightened his arm and pointed his gun at the Reaper's head.

BOOM!

The shot blasted the Reaper in the face. But unlike the many other targets of the Kid's infamous gun, the Reaper's head did not vanish, or turn into red goo. The blast snapped his head back, sure, but he shook it off like he'd merely been hit in the face by a basketball.

'Your feeble weapons cannot hurt me,' the Reaper said, twisting his neck one way and then the other. 'I am the Reaper, and I cannot be killed.'

Forty Five

It took Jasmine a while to realise she was dreaming. For a minute or so she was stuck in that strange zone between dreaming and waking up, where the people talking in her dream were also talking in the real conscious world. A sudden bump that felt like she had fallen out of bed, woke her up.

She was lying on the floor in the back of a moving truck. Two men were arguing nearby. Or was it one person, with two personalities, arguing with himself? The voice sounded the same regardless of who was talking, but at times it sounded like two people talking at once.

'It's the President's daughter!'

'I know that. She's been telling us that for two days.'

'She never told me.'

'Bullshit! It's all she's been saying since we picked her up.'

'Well what do we do with her now?'

'I don't know, but Calhoon says there's a ten-million-dollar reward for finding her. That's a reward worth claiming. It's more than we'll get for this other one.'

'There's a big difference though. We were told to *kidnap* Jasmine, whereas we were asked to *find* the President's daughter.'

'And we've already found her.'

'Yes, but if we hand her in, she'll tell everyone what we did to her. And that can't happen.'

A young woman's voice called out. 'I won't tell anyone, I swear.'

'What have we told you about talking?'

The woman did not speak again.

'What are we gonna do then? Kill her, and kiss ten million goodbye?'

'Leo, shut up. This is serious. Forget the ten million, forget all about it. We've gotta get rid of her, and quick.'

'This is Renwar's fault.'

'How is it his fault?'

'He chose her.'

'He didn't have a lot of choice. It was either her or her mother.'

'The mother wasn't bad looking.'

'Shush, the one dressed like a cop is waking up.'

'They're both awake. Look!'

'Okay, no more talk about Arizona. Understood?'

'Fine.'

Jasmine's hands were bound together behind her back with a taut wire, and she was curled up against the inside of the truck. Her belt had been removed, and with it, her gun. She wriggled into a more upright position and got a better look at the men who were arguing. No wonder they sounded the same, *they were the same.* Two men, identical in look and clothing. Skinhead mercenaries, dressed in black with sleeveless shirts.

'Jas, are you okay?'

'SHUT UP BITCH!'

The first voice definitely belonged to Flake. The second came from one of the idiots who had punched Jasmine in the face and drugged her with a shitty rag.

'Flake?' said Jasmine. Her vision blurred as she moved her head around to look for her friend.

'YOU SHUT UP AS WELL!'

One of the men marched over to Jasmine and lifted her up by her throat. He slammed her against the wall of the truck and pressed his ugly face up against hers. She recognised him as one of the nurses who had attacked her at the hospital. Whether or not he was the one who had punched her in the face, she couldn't tell, but her cheek was swollen and sore.

'Hello, Jasmine,' the man said, his foul breath wafting over her face. 'You have been captured by the world famous Bastard brothers. I am Vegas Bastard. I take it you've heard of us?'

'Nope.'

'Well, if you knew who we were, you'd know that if you piss me off, I'll knock all your teeth out, so I suggest you keep your fucking mouth shut, understood?'

Jasmine didn't reply, just in case it was a test. The man released her and stepped away. She slid back down the wall, giving her an opportunity to check out her surroundings. There was a young woman in a pink bikini tied up against the opposite wall further down the truck, closer to the cab. She had bruises around her eyes and blood on her chin. She gazed at Jasmine with pleading eyes, as if she were hoping to be rescued.

At the other end of the truck by the back doors, the other Bastard brother was standing over Flake.

'You okay, Jas?' Flake said, rephrasing her earlier question.

Speaking without permission earned Flake a kick in the ribs. She curled up in a ball and let out a low grunt. Like Jasmine, she had her hands bound together behind her back.

The man who had kicked her was Leonardo Bastard. He wrapped his hand around her neck and lifted her up. He pressed her against the wall, her feet six inches off the floor. 'I told you to shut up,' he said, spitting saliva in Flake's face as he spoke. 'Now watch what happens when you disobey me.' He turned to his brother. 'Vegas, make sure the other one is watching.'

Vegas leaned down and grabbed Jasmine by her hair, and whispered in her ear. 'Watch this.' He wrenched her head around and pressed it against the wall, forcing her to watch what his brother Leonardo was about to do to Flake.

Leonardo pulled his fist back and punched Flake in the head, busting her right eye. To her credit, Flake only let out a low groan. Leonardo released her and she slumped to the floor. While she was still dazed, he reached over to the back doors and flipped one of them open. It was still dark outside, and they were driving along a busy, snow-covered road with parked cars on either side. A blue car was following behind them, snow pelting down onto its windscreen, making it difficult for the driver to see what was happening inside the truck.

Leonardo returned to Flake and wrapped one of his hands around her throat again. He slid his other hand between her legs, then he lifted her up and carried her over to the open door. With one big swing he hurled her out into the road in front of the blue car.

Jasmine yelled, "NO!" and received a punch to the gut from Vegas for her troubles. She doubled over in pain, struggling for breath. The sound of screeching tyres and beeping horns floated in from outside, but then Leonardo closed the back door. The sounds faded. Flake was gone.

Vegas grabbed a clump of Jasmine's hair and straightened her up. 'So you're Jasmine, the dumb bitch who killed the Pope, huh?' he jeered. 'I thought you'd be tougher than this.'

Leonardo came over to join him. 'What are we gonna do with her?' he asked.

'You searched her, didn't you?' Vegas replied.

'Oh yeah. I gave her a very thorough search. She's got nothing. No phone, no ID, just the gun she had on her belt.'

Jasmine spat at Vegas. It wasn't entirely successful but she did get a bit on his cheek. He wiped it off, and curled his lip like he was going to spit back.

'That wasn't a wise thing to do,' he said.

'I can see why you have to kidnap women,' Jasmine replied with some hostility. 'With a face like that you definitely ain't getting it for free.'

Vegas pretended to laugh at her wisecrack, but then he leaned in close and poked out his tongue. He licked Jasmine's face from her chin up to her forehead. It was a warm, slobbery tongue that smelt like stale beer. When he was finished with all the licking, he smirked at her. 'Want some more?' he asked.

Leonardo, who seemed a little dumber than his brother, moved in closer and ran his hand up the inside of Jasmine's thigh. He pressed his face in close to hers. 'Did you *really* kill the Pope?' he asked.

'Shot him six times,' Jasmine replied, before spitting in his face too, with much more success than her attempt at Vegas. Leonardo got a big splodge in the eye. He wiped it off with his fingers and then licked it up, *the weirdo*. He leered at Jasmine in a way that suggested he was into the whole the spitting thing.

'ENOUGH!' yelled Vegas. He pushed his brother aside and squeezed Jasmine's arm. 'Your old boss Scratch hired us to find you,' he said. 'He's paying us and our brother, Renwar, a lot of money to hand you over to the FBI. And the Feds will pay us another million.'

Jasmine ignored Vegas and glanced over at the young woman in the pink bikini. 'Hello, what's your name?' she asked her.

'I'm Arizona,' the woman replied.

'Never mind her,' said Vegas. 'You should be worried about yourself.'

Jasmine continued to ignore him. 'Are you really the President's daughter?' she asked.

Arizona nodded frantically. 'Yes. You gotta get me outta here.'

Vegas grabbed Jasmine's face, squeezing her cheeks with his fingers. 'You're starting to piss me off,' he said.

Talking with her cheeks squeezed made Jasmine's reply come out in a kind of weird *Donald Duck* voice. 'You realise if you hand me over to the FBI, I'll tell them you kidnapped the President's daughter,' she said, her voice irritating Vegas so much he let go of her face.

Leonardo moved in again and flicked Jasmine on the ear. 'We rescued Arizona from a Mexican drug cartel,' he announced. The smell of bullshit wafted off his breath.

'If you rescued her, then why is she tied up?'

Vegas tensed up like he wanted to hit her again, but he restrained himself. 'Leo,' he said. 'Hold her down.'

Leonardo grabbed the back of Jasmine's head and pushed her down onto the floor, on her knees. He removed the binding from her hands, which came as a surprise, but then he positioned himself behind her and pushed her face closer to the floor. He pulled off her sneakers and cast them aside, then he started stroking and tickling her feet.

Vegas knelt down in front of her and grabbed a hold of her left arm. He squeezed her wrist and pulled her hand towards him, then he caressed her fingers as if he was about to kiss her hand, which he wasn't.

He leaned forward and spoke softly into her ear. 'We can't have you trying to escape, so we're gonna play a little game. Do you like games?'

'No.'

'Good. Because you're not gonna like this one.'

Vegas wrapped his fist around her little finger and bent it right back, snapping it at the joint.

CRACK!

Jasmine screamed, which put a smile on Vegas's face. His brother, Leonardo, laughed like a chimp behind her, then started licking the soles of her feet.

'One down,' said Vegas. 'Nine to go.'

'What do you want?' Jasmine pleaded.

'I want to break all your fingers and thumbs so that they're all pointing in the wrong direction.'

CRACK!

Vegas was true to his word. One by one he broke each of Jasmine's fingers and both of her thumbs. She cried in pain each time, and her eyes filled with tears. All through the finger-breaking, Leonardo stayed behind her, licking her feet and sucking her toes because he was a dirty creep.

Forty Six

Fucking vending machines!

Sanchez had been kicking the bloody thing and shaking it from side to side with absolutely no success whatsoever. The reason why his Chubby bar had not fallen had only just become clear to him. It wasn't just hanging off the end of the metal ring in the machine, it was impaled on it. The predicament reminded Sanchez of how his bodyguard Frank had been impaled on a bull's horn earlier in the day. Only this wasn't as funny. Sanchez had tried every possible way to get the candy bar to drop, except for one, the most dangerous method, a strategy reserved only for emergencies. It was something only Flake had ever successfully achieved. On one of the many previous occasions that Sanchez had been diddled by a vending machine, Flake had risked her life by pulling the machine forward and taking the entire weight of it on her shoulder. It had required a tilt of about 30 degrees to make the snack fall. And even though Sanchez wasn't sure he could handle the weight of the machine on his shoulder, he was fucking starving, and the Chubby was taunting him, so it was a risk worth taking.

With his hands on the upper corners of the machine he leaned back and pulled it towards him, just like he'd seen Flake do in the past.

Christ, it was heavy!

He managed to wrestle it forward at an angle of about ten degrees, but the Chubby bar still didn't budge. It didn't even wobble. The pressure on Sanchez's weak wrists was already too much to bear, so he slid one arm down from the top corner and pressed his shoulder against the glass screen. Shouldering the weight allowed him to bend his knees a little, lowering the machine a few more degrees. The Chubby bar began to jiggle, and after teasing him for a couple of seconds it finally dropped. It hit the glass screen on the front of the machine, right by Sanchez's face, then slid down to the dispensing tray at the bottom. Jackpot!

As was often the case for Sanchez, the triumph was short-lived. He now had to push the machine back up into its original position, only he didn't have the strength in his knees, or arms, or shoulders, thighs, calves, wrists, or anywhere for that matter. Plus, his shoulder was aching like crazy. To add to his misery, the song "Fall On Me" by R.E.M. came on the hospital radio, blasting into his ears through his headphones. And it seemed like the deejay had turned the volume right up. The bastard.

There was only one thing left to do. Move aside and let the machine fall. But even that was going to be difficult. Sanchez had visions of the machine landing on his feet and breaking his toes. In order to make it work, he was going to have to produce a sideways dive, the kind Riggs and Murtagh pulled off in *Lethal Weapon 2* when Murtagh was stuck on an exploding toilet. Sanchez pretended he was Riggs. He closed his eyes and counted to three in his head, then spun away and dived to the floor. He kept his eyes clenched shut, fearing the worst. But to his eternal delight, the machine didn't hit him.

He sat up and took a few moments to catch his breath. His heart was beating fast and he felt light-headed. He tentatively opened his eyes to see what had become of the vending machine. It hadn't landed on the floor like he expected. It had landed on a heavily tattooed man with a dodgy Mohican haircut, who looked like he wasn't wearing any clothes. The poor bastard was pinned beneath the vending machine, with only his head and shoulders visible.

Sanchez grimaced and pulled off his headphones. 'Cripes, are you okay there, buddy?' he asked.

'You fucking fool!' the man hissed, while wriggling back and forth in a futile attempt to free himself.

'Sorry, I didn't realise anyone was queuing behind me,' Sanchez admitted. 'Had my music on a bit loud.'

'Fuck you!'

In spite of the other man's hostility, Sanchez didn't want to be unreasonable just yet. 'Say, while you're down there, is there any chance you could reach around for my Chubby and pull it out?' he asked. 'It should be somewhere down by your knees, behind a metal flap.'

The man yelled something back in a language Sanchez didn't understand. The overall gist of what he was yelling was fairly clear though. He was a bit annoyed about the vending machine falling on him. Sanchez was about to describe what a Chubby looked like, when he caught sight of the other man's horrific black teeth. There was also a chain around his neck, made of tiny, jagged bones.

With the hospital's annoying, upbeat music no longer in his ears, Sanchez finally heard all the screaming and yelling that was going on, mostly from the floor below. The hospital had descended into chaos. A million thoughts raced through his mind. What had become of Flake and Jasmine? And what about Rex? Sanchez was supposed to be guarding him. He climbed to his feet and peered down the corridor to Rex's room. He was greeted by a bizarre sight. Since he'd been struggling with the vending machine, the hospital had gone bananas. The Bourbon Kid was outside Rex's room, squaring up to a man dressed just like him, only the other man was two-feet taller, and wielding a sword with a blade made from fire.

The angry nutjob underneath the vending machine snarled at Sanchez. 'Your time is up, fat man. When the Reaper kills your friend and frees me, I will peel your skin off and eat you alive!'

Sanchez winced. 'If you're really that hungry you can have my Chubby bar,' he said, generously. 'I've lost my appetite anyway.'

It seemed like a good time to make an exit. Sanchez had no intention of going anywhere near the Bourbon Kid and the Reaper so he hot-footed it along the adjacent corridor towards a set of double doors. That route was soon blocked off. A middle-aged male doctor burst through the doors with three semi-naked cannibals chasing after him. Sanchez's butt tightened. One of the cannibals leapt onto the doctor's back. Another helped drag the screaming doctor to the floor, and then they both began stabbing him repeatedly with bone handled knives. To Sanchez's great dismay, the third cannibal ignored the doctor. He had seen Sanchez and fancied a heartier meal than his friends. He sprinted along the corridor brandishing a knife and a hungry look on his heavily tattooed face. Sanchez turned and ran back the other way.

To make matters worse, the floor suddenly shook like an earthquake had struck. Sanchez lost his balance and stumbled towards the vending machine. He stayed upright for as long as he could, until he eventually lost his footing and tumbled onto the vending machine. He tried to steady himself on it, but his feet gave way underneath him and he fell "ass first" onto the face of the angry cannibal dude who was pinned underneath it.

The reason for the huge tremor became clear. Outside Rex's room, the Reaper was swinging his blade of fire at the Bourbon Kid. The Kid was ducking and dodging, and firing shots from his Headblaster gun. Every time the Reaper missed with a swing of his sword, its fiery blade ripped through a chunk of the floor, walls or ceiling, depending on where he was aiming. Chunks of plaster were falling from all directions and there were gaping holes in the floor. The hospital was crumbling.

The cannibal who was chasing Sanchez had also fallen over, but he wasn't going to let a crumbling building deny him his prize. He climbed to his feet and let out a loud scream, then he sprinted towards the vending machine. Sanchez clenched his butt cheeks and launched himself back onto his feet. There was only one way out of this mess. He ran as fast as he could along the corridor towards the Grim Reaper.

Forty Seven

Riding an invisible bicycle in mid-air while losing the battle against gravity. This was not the best time to come up with a plan. Elvis was going down fast, the street getting nearer by the moment. He had to time this perfectly. He whipped out his gun, took aim at a window and fired three shots. There wasn't even time to tuck the gun back in its holster. The glass of the six-foot by four-foot window he'd fired at began to shatter. A chunk of glass dropped out of the window and started the long drop to the ground below. Elvis, having leapt blindly from the rooftop of Sally Diamond's building had gone down at a 45 degree angle. He'd been hoping to find a metal staircase, a drainpipe or a window frame to grab onto. But all he'd found was the window two floors below the roof he'd just jumped from.

He crashed into the remaining glass in the window frame. His upper body flew majestically through it in a superhero pose, but his shins banged into the wall below.

'FUUUUCCCCKKKK!'

His momentum, and the weight of his head, carried him through the window, but from looking cool a second earlier, he was suddenly bouncing onto a wooden surface that was covered in glass. He dropped his gun and skidded along the floor, picking up chunks of glass with his face, hands and knees, while yelling obscenities. His forward motion came to an end when he thudded into the legs of a wax statue. He looked up. He was lying at the feet of a waxwork statue of a Predator from the *Predator* movies.

'Woah.'

Elvis sat up and flicked glass from his hair and shoulders, and took a quick inventory. He hurt like a motherfucker, but he'd live. He scrambled across the floor to retrieve his gun, and shook some specks of glass from it. All in all, the jump had gone as well as he could have hoped.

Assured that he was safe for a minute, that nothing was broken, and that he wasn't going to die from a femoral artery haemorrhage or an unlucky date with the ground below, he was finally able to take in where he was. He was in a huge exhibition hall filled with wax statues of characters from films. He'd been to this place once before on a Christmas Eve, when he'd helped Sanchez fight some rubbish Italian terrorists. He'd always wanted to come back, but not under these circumstances, and not through a window. He stared back across the room at the hole in the wall where the glass had once been. A rush of cold air was coming in through it, whistling like a toothless hobo. It wouldn't be long before someone else came hurtling through that window, whether it be Scratch or one of his pesky skeleton friends. Elvis stood up and dusted some more glass off his shoulders while he looked around for a way out. There was an elevator at the end of the hall, and set of doors next to it that led to a stairwell.

He limped towards the doors, still short of breath from all the running and jumping. The limping didn't last long though. He was forced to pick up the pace when he heard someone dive through the glassless window and bounce onto the floor behind him. He glanced back over his shoulder and saw a skeleton rolling across the floor.

Fucker!

No more looking back. He limped even faster than before.

Judging by the cackling and rattling sounds coming from outside, a bunch of other skeletons had tried the jump and not made it. But then came a louder thud. Someone wearing boots had landed on his or her feet inside the hall. It had to be Scratch.

Elvis didn't bother to check. He kept running, knowing he had a head start. But outrunning Scratch was one thing, outrunning the power of the Eye of the Moon was another thing altogether. A flash of red light lit up the hall for a brief moment, so brief that Elvis thought he'd imagined it. The repercussions of the red flash soon became clear.

As Elvis neared the end of the hall, a waxwork statue came to life and stepped out from its place in the display. It had a funny walk. It also had a gun holstered on its hip. Elvis recognised the Stetson wearing, bandy-legged cowboy right away. It was a waxwork model of Woody, the cowboy from *Toy Story*. Woody squared himself in front of Elvis, blocking the path to the exits.

"Goddammit," Elvis muttered as he slowed up. Fucking statues coming to life, whatever next? It didn't really surprise him, this was Santa Mondega after all, but it was bloody annoying. And behind him, he could hear the clank and clap of skeletons arriving on the scene.

Elvis drew his own gun and sped up. He fired a bullet right into Woody's face from about seven metres away. It was a total waste of time. Bullets don't hurt statues.

Elvis closed the gap between him and Woody, lowered his shoulder and barged into the waxwork cowboy. The fucking thing was as solid as it looked. Even so, the blow from Elvis knocked it off balance and it staggered back. Elvis skirted past it and looked back to check on Scratch. By now, a few more skeletons had made it through the window. And the waxwork statues were coming to life too. The Predator was on the move, and so was its nemesis the big, black alien creature from the *Alien* movies. It was a terrifying sight. Further back in the hall, Wayne and Garth from the movie *Wayne's World* were alive and running too. And if Elvis wasn't mistaken he also saw Elle Woods and her Chihuahua, Bruiser from *Legally Blonde*. In fact, it was looking like every single waxwork statue in the hall was waking up, ready to take orders from Scratch.

Elvis had intended to take the stairs, but he was so fucked-off with all the running, he gambled and headed for the elevator first. He pressed the button in the wall, hoping to see the doors open instantly. They didn't. The gears churned and the elevator carriage began slowly chugging up from the ground floor.

Fuck!

Valuable seconds were lost. Elvis hobbled over to the doors and burst through them to the stairwell. He hurried down the stairs, chased by an army of click-clacky skeletons and plodding waxwork models. And Scratch.

Forty Eight

Every enemy has a weak spot. It's just a case of finding it. Locating the Grim Reaper's weak spot was proving to be quite a challenge. The giant hooded freak with the yellow face and the flaming sword was an emotionless character. And he was impervious to the blasts from the Bourbon Kid's Headblaster gun. The Kid had encountered other seemingly invincible villains in his time. Like Frankenstein. That big dunce had also been bulletproof. His weakness had been his asshole. Slipping a Kinder egg loaded with explosives up his butt had blown his insides to smithereens. The Reaper though, did he even have an asshole?

It didn't really matter because the Bourbon Kid didn't have a Kinder egg to shove up there anyway. All he had was his Headblaster gun and his incredible dexterity. Every time the Reaper swung his flaming sword, the Kid dodged it, ducked under it, leapt over it, or rolled away from it. But the Reaper never lost his cool, he just kept swinging, always making the right move, never allowing his opponent a chance to get close.

As the Bourbon Kid ducked under another violent swing of the Reaper's sword, he considered the possibility of sliding between the robed giant's legs and shooting up at the bullseye. He had three rounds left in the Headblaster, and he had to make them count.

He fired one of his precious bullets at the Reaper's head. It knocked the giant off balance again, pushing him back against a window. But, as before, the Reaper shrugged it off and launched another attack with his sword. He missed the Kid again, but this time the tip of the fireblade struck the floor, ripping a gaping black hole in it. The building shook, and a thunderous rumble all around offered more evidence of the hospital's weakening foundations. But then an unexpected solution to the problem suddenly presented itself. *Sanchez.*

The tubby mayor of Santa Mondega was stumbling along the shaky corridor behind the Reaper. He had an ugly, bloodthirsty cannibal on his tail. Strange though it might seem, it was in that moment that the Kid finally saw the Reaper's weakness.

His overconfidence.

The man with the sword of fire saw the Bourbon Kid as his only threat. He paid no attention to Sanchez or the cannibal guy. And even if he *had* heard Sanchez sneaking up behind him, he wouldn't have recognised the danger.

The Bourbon Kid moved away, positioning the Reaper right where he wanted him, in the middle of the corridor. But before the plan could be put into action, he first had to get rid of the cannibal that was on Sanchez's tail.

'Your time is up!' the Reaper snarled. He swung his sword wildly at the Bourbon Kid's head, an easy move to avoid. The Kid ducked and moved to one side, and in one fluid move he fired a shot. His aim was true. The bullet whizzed past the Reaper, past Sanchez and into the face of the cannibal behind him. The impact took the Skinner's head off, transforming it into a lump of red goo that flew down the corridor and splattered into the wall above the overturned vending machine. Sanchez looked around to see what had happened, but in doing so he lost his balance and fell over.

The Reaper paid no attention to any of it. With the Kid's latest shot not hitting him, he seized on the opportunity to finish the fight. He closed in and lifted his sword high above his head. The Kid made no attempt to duck out of the way this time. He gambled and fired his last shot instead.

BANG!

Perfect!

The blast from the gun hit the Reaper in the chest, and right on cue the yellow-skinned psychopath took a step back. Only this time when he stepped back, his foot kicked against something on the floor behind him. Sanchez was crouched down on his hands and knees in the middle of the corridor. The result was inevitable. The Reaper lost his balance and toppled backwards over Sanchez. His robe flew up, revealing a pair of brown long-johns underneath. His head smashed against the floor, followed by the elbow of his sword-wielding hand. The sword slipped from his grasp and rolled across the floor. Its fiery blade extinguished as soon as it left his grasp.

The Bourbon Kid yelled at Sanchez, 'Get the sword!'

Sanchez rolled into action. He crawled across the stricken Reaper's robe as he headed over to the sword handle. At this point, the Bourbon Kid knew something that the Reaper didn't. He knew Sanchez was a fucking idiot and would never get to the sword first. To Sanchez's credit, he had already done as much as could be expected of him, but the Reaper didn't know that. While Barazima wasted valuable time and energy trying to stop Sanchez getting to the sword handle, the Bourbon Kid sprinted for it himself.

Even though the Reaper was infinitely stronger than Sanchez, the tubby Mexican was crawling across his robe, tying him up in knots, and making it difficult for him to get up. Barazima reached out and grabbed the collar of Sanchez's jacket with his bony fingers, only to discover it was covered in streaks of shit and damp patches of stale piss from an incident at a farm earlier in the day.

Sanchez reached for the cylindrical metal object but it was tantalisingly out of reach. The Reaper scampered over him to get to it for himself. The Bourbon Kid beat them both to it. He made a quick parkour-style move along the wall followed by a forward roll, which ended with him picking up the sword handle.

He clasped it in his hand and spun around to attack with it. The Reaper pushed Sanchez aside and sprung back to his feet ready to face the Kid.

The situation had changed considerably. The Bourbon Kid had Barazima's only weapon. There was just one problem. The fires of Hell were not shooting out from the handle like they had when the Reaper wielded it.

The Reaper wagged his finger. 'You cannot use my sword,' he hissed. 'The blade will only come forth when *my* hand is clasped on the handle. It is *useless* to you.'

The Kid shrugged. 'Fine. Have it back.'

He tossed the sword handle back to the Reaper. It arced through the air towards the other's man's bony yellow face. The Reaper saw it coming and reacted instinctively, snatching it out of the air before it hit his face. As soon as he wrapped his fingers around the sword handle, a look of horror appeared on his face.

'Shit!'

He barely got the word *"shit"* past his lips because as soon as the sword handle recognised its owner's grasp, the flaming blade erupted from the end of it. The fire ripped through the Reaper's face, passed through his brain and came out through the back of his skull. His head exploded into flames that rapidly spread, engulfing his whole body in a matter of seconds. His sword slipped from his grasp and clattered onto the floor by his feet, its hot blade extinguished. The Reaper's whole body disintegrated into dust and ash. The remains of his robe dropped to the floor, smouldering like an old camp fire. The Kid took a step closer to what remained of the Reaper and stared, satisfied.

Sanchez peeled himself off the floor and stood up to check out the carnage. It looked like a job well done. There were a few holes in the floor and the walls were missing in places, letting in a bit of a draft. But overall, things had turned out okay, even though he still hadn't got his Chubby bar.

The stench of decaying Reaper guts was quite unpleasant though. Sanchez waved his hand in front of his face to waft away the smell, as well as the black smoke.

'We sure dealt with him, didn't we?' he said, standing over the Reaper's melted remains.

'I guess we did,' the Kid replied.

'You know, I also threw a vending machine on top one of those jungle savages just now because he tried to mess with me.'

The Bourbon Kid looked at Sanchez and turned his nose up. 'Is that bullshit?'

'Yes, it is. I fell in some earlier. It's on the collar of my jacket. The Reaper got some under his fingernails too, I think.'

The Kid reached inside his coat for some ammo to reload his Headblaster gun. 'Where's everybody else?' he asked.

'Flake and Jasmine went for a piss together,' Sanchez replied. 'But they've been gone ages. Jasmine might be having a dump, I suppose?'

'Ever consider the possibility they might be dead?'

Sanchez's face dropped. 'I hope not. I'd better call Flake. I'm fucking starving, you know. Have you got anything I can eat?'

'Duck.'

'Duck? I was thinking of something more like a candy bar, really.'

The Bourbon Kid finished reloading his Headblaster and pointed it at Sanchez's face. He repeated the word, '*Duck.*'

Sanchez finally worked out what "duck" meant. He threw himself to the floor just before the Bourbon Kid fired off several ear-bleedingly loud shots from his gun. A bunch of cannibals in the corridor behind Sanchez lost their heads. Sanchez covered his ears and closed his eyes, confident that he had no need to get up and run.

As the echo of the gunshots faded, and Sanchez removed his hands from his ears, the sound of squelching corpses sliding around on the floor behind him became more prominent. The trailing smoke from the Kid's gun, coupled with the Reaper's smouldering remains, turned the hallway into a cloud of black fog.

Sanchez stood up and waved some more smoke away from his face. 'There's no duck is there?' he said.

The Kid tucked his gun back inside his coat. 'You're gonna have to take the credit for all this,' he said. 'I don't want anyone knowing I was here.'

Sanchez took in the sight of all the smoking corpses lying around. 'I suppose it's believable,' he said, dusting himself off. 'Before you go anywhere though, I'm pretty sure there's a whole load more of these cannibal freakshows downstairs. I'd help you kill them all, but I don't have a gun.'

The Bourbon Kid walked over to Rex's room and closed the door. 'Just do one thing for me,' he said. 'Stay here and guard Rex's room until the others get back. Got that?'

'Okay. Where are you going?'

'I'm going to go kill the rest of these cannibal fuckers, aren't I?'

Sanchez breathed a sigh of relief and pointed down the corridor. 'Good, because there's one under that vending machine over there. If you could kill him first, and push the vending machine off him, that would be a good start.'

The Kid ignored Sanchez. His focus was on something else, something further down the corridor. He reached inside his jacket and pulled out a large, jagged-edged knife.

'What's that for?' Sanchez asked.

The Kid did not reply. He had a look in his eyes that Sanchez had seen before. Some kind of killing spree was about to take place.

Back down the corridor, four more cannibals had arrived. Word had gotten out that the Bourbon Kid was in the building. The flesh-hungry savages began converging on the second floor from all directions.

Sanchez grabbed the handle on Rex's door. 'Perhaps I should wait in here,' he suggested.

Forty Nine

Being chased through the floors of Waxwork Tower by an army of skeletons and wax statues wasn't doing much for Elvis's health. His heart and lungs weren't used to this much running. Or limping. Come to think of it, nor were his legs. Or shoes. Running sucked.

In the midst of all the bizarre horror, one small positive emerged. It turned out skeletons weren't that good with stairs. As Elvis bounded down the stairwell, he could hear the bonies falling over each other and creating a pile-up that slowed down the waxwork statues. But, just when it looked like he was catching a break, he heard the elevator moving again. It was heading down to the ground floor. It had to be Scratch. The Devil would want to block off Elvis's escape route. A new strategy was required. Elvis had been running, jumping and crashing through things for too long. And the fucking things chasing him, clumsy though they were, none of them had lungs or a heart, so they weren't likely to get tired anytime soon. With that in mind, Elvis made a decision. *Find somewhere to hide*. A shit plan, of course, but it wouldn't require much more running. With any luck, it would involve a lot of sitting down, or lying down, maybe even sleeping. Enough with all the running shit!

He left the stairwell and burst through a set of double doors on the second floor, into another waxwork display hall. It was instantly obvious what the theme was. There were models of *Star Wars* characters everywhere. And in the middle of the giant hall was a huge replica of the Millennium Falcon spaceship. Elvis headed straight for it. The boarding ramp was down, inviting him in. He checked behind him to make sure he hadn't been followed by any skeletons or statues, then ran up the ramp into the ship.

When watching the Star Wars movies Elvis had never paid much attention to what the Falcon looked like inside, so he couldn't tell if the life-size model was accurate or not. He ducked down out of sight in a corridor at the top of the boarding ramp, and watched the doors at the front of the hall to see if any of his pursuers followed him in.

For just a minute things were looking good, but then the doors at the front of the hall opened and the bastard Woody waxwork walked in. He was soon followed by the Predator and its Alien friend, and a handful of skeletons. No sign of Scratch.

The statues and skeletons made their way through the Star Wars display looking for Elvis. Woody was sniffing lots of the other waxworks. The Alien kept bumping into the Predator, which was causing some friction between them. As for the skeletons, they began inexplicably attacking the Jar Jar Binks statue, which wasn't even moving. Fortunately for Elvis, none of them had enough brainpower to think about boarding the Falcon.

After a few minutes, the motley crew of Scratch's henchmen passed through the display, completely bypassing the spaceship. It left the way open for Elvis to make a run for it. He was debating whether to stay or go, when to his frustration, the situation changed again.

Scratch marched into the hall. He looked pissed. *Really pissed.* After scanning the hall, looking for any sign of Elvis, he raised his right hand. A red beam of light emanated from his palm. He directed it at a group of stormtroopers. A sharp flash of red lightning reached out from his hand and struck each statue in the squad, bringing them all to life.

'Find him!' Scratch barked at the Stormtroopers. 'He's here somewhere. I want every part of this building checked.' He looked across at the Falcon. 'Start with that spaceship!'

Three stormtroopers, armed with useless wax blasters jogged over to the Millennium Falcon. Elvis groaned. *Assholes.*

He moved away from his hiding place just inside the entrance and scuttled along the Falcon's corridor. His shoes seemed to make an enormous echo every time he took a step, but with all the waxworks and skeletons running around outside making lots of noise, he was hopeful no one would hear it.

The main problem Elvis had was that the Falcon wasn't all that big inside. It was no Tardis, that's for sure. In fact, it was the total opposite. It looked massive from the outside but inside it was just one shitty corridor that led to the cockpit, with a few other rooms just off it. He was cursing his dumb luck for hiding in such a rubbish place when he remembered something from one of the movies. There was a scene where some of the good guys hid under the floor in a secret compartment.

With the stormtroopers arriving at the foot of the boarding ramp, Elvis dropped to his knees and felt around on the floor for anything that could be lifted up. He slid his fingers into a gap between two tiles.

Jackpot!

The replica of the Millennium Falcon had clearly been designed by nerds. He lifted the floor tile and lowered himself into a small compartment beneath it, sliding the tile back into place just before the waxwork stormtroopers arrived on board.

The question now was, how long could he hide down there for? He pulled out his phone and switched it to silent, then made a call to Jasmine. After several rings it went to her voicemail. Elvis whispered her a message.

'Jas, I'm in the waxwork building. Scratch has got a giant Woody and some skeletons chasing after me. I'm gonna try and sneak out. Any chance you can get a car and pick me up out front?'

He ended the call and stayed as quiet as he could while the wax stormtroopers marched back and forth on the floor above him.

Fifty

Flake had never been more grateful for a downpour of snow. Without it, her skull would have hit the tarmac on the road when Leonardo Bastard threw her out of the *Cooler Cola* truck. Instead, she landed on a soft bed of snow that was almost ten inches deep, and speckled with salt. The snow had more than one benefit too. The thickness of it had slowed down the incoming traffic. It gave the driver of a blue Ford Focus just enough time to hit the brakes before she hit Flake. The Focus's front grill stopped inches from Flake's face. Behind the Focus, a bunch of other drivers were beeping their horns, which made the whole experience even more surreal. Flake was still dazed from being drugged, and her hands were bound behind her back, making it difficult to move.

A car door slammed and someone trudged through the snow. 'Are you okay, officer?' a female voice asked.

Flake looked up and saw a grey-haired old lady in a green dress and white cardigan standing over her. Rather than confuse the poor old dear, Flake kept up the facade that she was a member of the police force.

'Yes, thank you, ma'am,' she replied, rolling herself into a seated position in the snow. She showed the old woman her back, so she could see that her hands were bound together. 'Can you untie me please?'

'Of course, yes,' the woman replied. 'My name is Betty by the way, Betty Frostrup.' She reached into her purse and started rummaging around. 'Why *are* your hands tied?' she asked.

'Criminals,' Flake replied. 'They took my friend.'

Betty pulled out a four-inch long silver object. She pressed a button on the side of it and a sharp blade flicked out. 'Those fuckers,' she muttered. 'I hope the new mayor is gonna clean up this town.'

'He's a good man,' Flake said, leaning forward to give Betty a better angle to cut the binding. The old lady crouched down and set about cutting through the taut wire.

Flake attempted to tell Betty her name, only for her words to be drowned out by the beeping of a car horn. A bearded man in a white van behind Betty's blue Focus had his hand pressed on the horn and was showing no sign of releasing it.

Betty yelled into Flake's ear, 'I'm sorry, just give me a moment, please.'

To Flake's surprise, Betty reached into her purse again. This time she pulled out a handgun. She stood up and pointed it at the bearded driver of the van. He was a fat guy in his thirties, wearing a red baseball cap. At the sight of the gun, he stopped beeping his horn and ducked down out of sight. He was wise to do so. Betty was no slouch. She fired her gun, blasting a hole right through his windscreen. 'SONOFABITCH!' she yelled. 'Can't you see I'm fucking busy!'

The man in the van did not reappear, so Betty replaced the gun in her purse, whilst muttering obscenities under her breath.

'He was asking for it,' said Flake.

'Fucking right he was, the cunt.'

Betty got back to work cutting Flake's hands free. 'How come you got tossed off?' she asked, slicing through the last of the binding and freeing Flake's hands.

'I'm not sure,' said Flake, rubbing her wrists. 'My name is Flake by the way.' She looked around to gather her bearings. The truck she had been thrown from was now a dot in the distance. She thought of Jasmine. Her friend was being driven to God-knows-where. 'Shit! I've gotta go. Betty, thanks for everything, you're a real star.'

'No problem, my dear. I used to be a cop myself, back in the days when it meant something in this city.'

It looked like Betty was about to launch into a long-winded monologue about the good old days of shooting suspects and planting evidence on them, but then another foolish driver showed up. A heavy-set guy in a thick red and black checked coat had left his car and marched past the other vehicles on his way to give Betty a piece of his mind.

'What the fuck is the hold-up here?' he asked, an angry snarl on his face.

Betty muttered the word, *"motherfucker"* under her breath and pulled her gun from her purse again. She pointed it at the man's head. 'GET OUTTA MY FACE, YOU COCKSUCKER!' she yelled. 'CAN'T YOU SEE WE'VE GOT AN OFFICER DOWN OVER HERE?'

The tough guy was long gone before she even finished berating him. Betty fired a warning shot in the air and then set off in pursuit of the fleeing man. Flake saw the opportunity to make a break for it herself.

'Seeya, Betty. Gotta go, thanks!' she called out.

She staggered to the side of the road, still finding her feet after the recent ordeal. By the time she set foot on the sidewalk, she remembered that Sanchez was all alone at the hospital. She started running through the snow, heading back to Saint Jude's. She had no idea how long she had been unconscious for, but as she got closer to the hospital it was obvious a lot of things had changed. People were crying in the streets, telling tales of how Saint Jude's had been ransacked by a gang of cannibals. It sounded like a lot of people had been killed.

Flake had to see for herself. She would have phoned Sanchez, but those bastard Bastard brothers had taken her phone. The bastards.

When she arrived at the hospital, she saw a river of blood flowing down the steps outside onto the sidewalk. As she climbed the steps up to the entrance she received a warm round of applause from a crowd of people on the other side of the road. They obviously thought she was a real cop, the first to arrive on the scene, possibly.

The reception hall looked like something from a zombie horror movie. The bloodied and mutilated remains of doctors, nurses and patients were strewn across the floor. There was also a bunch of naked Latin men scattered all over the place. They had to be the cannibals Flake had heard about. Every single one of them had been butchered. Arms, legs, heads, hands, feet and innards were scattered everywhere. It was a bizarre sight.

"How long have I been gone?" Flake asked herself.

There were about twenty of the naked savages strewn around on the floors and tables. There was only one possible explanation she could think of. Sanchez must have killed them all. She stepped over several bodies and headed for the stairs.

She walked over to the stairwell where she and Jasmine had been abducted earlier. There were two more mutilated cannibals laid out halfway up the stairs. One of them was missing an arm and a leg, and the other had lost the top half of his head. There was blood all around them, dripping down the stairwell towards Flake. The trail of bodies and blood was leading somewhere.

'Sanchez!' she called out. 'Are you here?'

A gravelly voice replied from behind her. 'Flake?'

She spun around and raised her fists. Relief. The Bourbon Kid had snuck up behind her. The hood on his coat was down and his face was speckled in blood.

'Oh, thank God it's you,' she gasped. 'Is Sanchez here?'

'He's upstairs guarding Rex. Where have you been?'

'Me and Jasmine were drugged and kidnapped by three men. They've still got Jasmine.'

'What three men?'

'They were Bastards.'

'Yeah, but who were they?'

'The Bastard brothers. That's their name. There were three of them, and they were identical. Triplets.' Flake's head was fuzzy but she still remembered plenty about the kidnappers. 'They threw us in the back of a big trailer-truck. But then they chucked me out into traffic. I don't know what they're gonna do to Jasmine.'

The Bourbon Kid showed no emotion. 'Go upstairs,' he said. 'You and Sanchez should get Rex out of here. Scratch knows he's here, so get him somewhere safe, and stay off the phones. Don't call anyone.'

'Why not?'

'Because I said so.'

The Kid's calm demeanour was actually stressing Flake out. He didn't seem to be grasping the urgency of Jasmine's situation. 'You gotta go after Jasmine,' she said. 'They're gonna do horrible stuff to her. They already had one girl tied up in the back of their truck.'

The Kid didn't reply. He looked like he was deep in thought, his eyes inappropriately focussed on Flake's chest. She clicked her fingers in front of his face. He snapped out of his trance and his stare returned to eye level.

'What were you saying?' he asked.

'I said you've gotta go get Jasmine. She's in the back of a great big truck. If you leave now you can catch them before they leave the city. It's our only chance of getting her back!'

The Kid shook his head. 'Fuck Jasmine.'

'What?'

'Janis is dead because of Jasmine. You think I give a fuck what those guys do to her?'

Flake was flabbergasted. 'You what? They could do all sorts of horrible things to her. They're probably working for Scratch. One of us *has* to go after her.'

'No we don't.' He pointed at one of the dead bodies on the floor near Flake's feet. 'Take a look around you. There are bigger things going on right now than Jasmine, so *no,* I am not going after her. She's on her own.'

A lump built up in Flake's throat. 'You heartless piece of shit.'

The Bourbon Kid did not reply. He turned around and headed for the exit. Flake watched, aghast, saddened at the state of the mutilated bodies, but also by the betrayal of the one man who could have rescued Jasmine before it was too late.

When he was gone, she turned away and wiped a tear from her eye. Her beloved group of friends were dropping like flies. Only one man could reassure her now, and that man was Sanchez. She ran up the stairs to find him, hurdling the dead bodies as she went. When she walked through a set of busted doors at the top, she saw more mutilated bodies all along the corridor. But she also saw Sanchez. The sight of him warmed her heart and made her forget everything else for just a brief moment. The love of her life was standing outside Rex's room gazing lovingly at a Chubby bar he was eating. The dead bodies all around him hadn't affected his appetite. Flake ran towards him, leaping over several mutilated cannibals as she went.

'Sanchez!' she called out.

Sanchez put his Chubby down on a window sill and breathed a sigh of relief at the sight of Flake walking towards him. 'Oh, thank God you're okay,' he said, smiling. The smile soon turned to a frown. 'You look like shit!' he remarked. 'What happened?'

'I was sucker-punched, drugged and thrown out of a moving truck,' Flake replied. Saying it all out loud brought a lump to her throat. She needed a hug. She ran to Sanchez and threw her arms around him. He embraced her and pulled her in close enough that she could smell his collar. She didn't care. She squeezed him as hard as she could. Hard enough that he coughed a bit of his candy bar onto her shoulder. She didn't mind that either.

'Where have you been?' he asked, picking the candy crumbs from her shoulder and eating them.

Flake stepped back. 'Me and Jasmine got kidnapped by three guys.'

'Did you kill them?'

'No. They threw me in front of a car. They've still got Jasmine!'

'You should have stayed with me,' Sanchez replied, nonchalantly. 'I could have protected you. Did you hear I killed the Grim Reaper? Look, that's what's left of him over there.' He pointed at a pile of ash on the floor. Smoke was fizzling out of it.

'Wow,' said Flake. 'Is that what the awful smell is? Or is it your suit collar?'

'It's a bit of both.'

'We've got lots of catching up to do. And we need to come up with a plan to rescue Jasmine.'

Sanchez rubbed his stomach. 'Can we do it in the toilet? I am absolutely busting, but I'm afraid to go on my own.'

Flake kissed him. 'Okay, but we'll have to take Rex with us too. JD says we've got to get him out of here.'

'Three of us in one toilet? That'll be a bit cosy won't it?'

'Yes, but we can't leave Rex on his own. He's defenceless.'

A voice called out, 'I'll be okay.'

Flake and Sanchez rushed into Rex's room. His good eye was open, and he was no longer hooked up to any bags of blood or fluids. His oxygen mask was gone too. He was still covered in bandages though. He had the look of a one-eyed Mummy.

'Rex!' said Flake, beaming at him. 'You're okay?'

'I don't feel okay. I feel like shit.'

'You unhooked your blood bag,' Flake said, pointing at the disconnected tubes.

'Did I?'

Sanchez barged Flake out of the way. 'Hey, Rex. Listen, I need to go for a shit. Flake thinks we should all go together. Do you wanna come with us, or are you okay here?'

It was hard to tell from Rex's eye how he felt about it. He soon cleared the matter up though. 'I'll take my chances here. Just don't take forever.'

Flake sat down on the side of Rex's bed and stroked his head. 'We thought you were a goner,' she said. 'The doctors didn't think you'd make it through the day.'

'I nearly didn't. I think I was in Heaven talking to God, but then something pulled me back.'

'Pfft,' Sanchez scoffed. 'You were dreaming.'

'It *seemed* real,' said Rex. 'I was surfing the big waves. I felt totally free.'

'And where was God?' Flake asked.

'He was surfing too. We were riding the waves together.'

'God is a surfer?' Sanchez asked, sniggering.

'He looked exactly like Patrick Swayze in *Point Break*.'

Flake smiled. 'You dreamt that you were in your favourite movie!'

'I guess,' said Rex. 'But it wasn't a dream. It was so real. God was telling me I'll be okay. And he was granting me a wish, but then a big wave hit me. I went under the water, but then I woke up and I was here.'

'Yeah, that's definitely a dream,' said Sanchez. He tapped Flake on the shoulder. 'Come on, we've got to go. I'm touching cloth.'

'What?'

'I've got turtle's head.'

Flake leaned down and planted a kiss on Rex's forehead. 'We'll be quick, I promise. When we get back I'll fill you in on everything that's happened.'

As she pulled away, Rex reached up and grabbed her arm. He put his index finger over his lips to signal for her to be quiet, then he pointed at her chest. She looked down to see what had caught his eye. One of the buttons on her shirt looked different to the others. It only took a moment to figure out why. It wasn't a button. It was a small recording device shaped to look like a button. Someone was listening to everything they were saying.

Fifty One

Jasmine's fingers and thumbs were all broken, bent, and pointing the wrong way. From the moment she'd been punched in the face and drugged, everything had been a crazy mess. Her brain was frazzled and she felt delirious.

One thing keeping her going was knowing that the Bastards hadn't found her phone. She had even managed to stay cool when it vibrated to indicate she had an incoming call. The call had come in while Vegas was busting her fingers, and Leonardo was licking her feet. Her screams had drowned out the quiet buzzing from her phone.

With the torture temporarily over, she was laying on her front with her arms outstretched, unable to move much because of her broken fingers. The truck was parked up at a roadside while Vegas nipped out to buy takeaway burgers and fries. When he returned he bent down in front of Jasmine and fed her one of his French fries. Leonardo was slightly more generous to Arizona. He gave her a piece of pickle from his burger, although only after he had licked it first. The other Bastard, Renwar, didn't share his food with anyone.

All three of the brothers sat down in the back of the truck, eating their burgers and fries while huddled around a small wireless speaker. The speaker was relaying a live feed from a recording device they had planted on Flake before they threw her out of the truck. While they ate their food, they heard Flake arrive back at the hospital where she met up with the Bourbon Kid and relayed to him everything that had happened to her. The conversation didn't go well.

'Fuck me,' said Vegas, shaking his head when the conversation ended. 'Did you hear that, Jasmine? Your friend the Bourbon Kid ain't coming to rescue you. That's a damn shame, because you know, we had a whole trap set for him, and you were the bait. But I guess you're not as popular with your friends as you thought, huh?'

Jasmine had heard the conversation between Flake and the Bourbon Kid. The part that hurt the most was hearing the Kid say to Flake, *"Fuck Jasmine,"* and, *"Janis is dead because of Jasmine. You think I give a fuck what those guys do to her?"*

Vegas switched off the speaker. 'Leo, you keep listening in on your headset. If anything interesting happens, give us a shout.'

Leonardo slipped a set of headphones over his ears and carried on listening in on Flake's hidden microphone.

'So what are we gonna do now?' Renwar asked.

Vegas screwed up a plastic food wrapper and stood up. 'First of all, we're gonna have to get rid of this rubbish,' he said. 'Then, we're going to have to drive somewhere quiet and get rid of Arizona.'

'Can't we keep her a bit longer?' asked Renwar. 'We've never had two girls in the truck at the same time before. We should do something special.'

'Just clean up this shit!' Vegas replied.

Renwar collected up all the empty food wrappers and carried them over to the back doors.

'Hey, wait,' said Leonardo, waving at him. 'Don't move. I can hear something.'

Renwar was about to open the back doors to chuck the rubbish out, but he held off. 'Hear what?' he asked, his face revealing his bewilderment.

Leonardo tapped his headphones. 'Flake and this guy, Sanchez,' he whispered. 'They're doing something weird.'

'Weird? Like what?' asked Vegas, approaching him.

Leonardo frowned. 'I can hear someone playing a trombone. It's really out of tune.'

'A trombone?' said Vegas. 'Let me listen.'

'No, wait.' Leonardo's jaw dropped. 'Now I can hear a tuba, and I think someone is playing the bongo drums.'

Vegas finally lost patience. He leaned down and turned the portable speaker back on, and cranked the volume all the way up, which made the sounds on Leonardo's headphones go up to ear-bleeding levels. Leonardo yanked them off and glared at his brother. The sounds he'd been hearing through his headphones began blasting out of the speaker on the floor again. A mix of trumpeting sounds and rat-a-tat noises echoed around the inside of the truck, accompanied by some splashing sounds. Then Flake's voice came through loud and clear.

'Jesus, Sanchez! Flush it, please. It stinks!' she yelled.

Vegas slapped Leonardo across the face with the back of his hand. 'Jeez, you're fucking stupid sometimes. He's having a dump, you fucking moron!'

The sound of Sanchez flushing the toilet was more than Vegas could stand. He shook his head in disgust and pressed a button on the speaker's control panel. It switched the device over to a local radio station.

'It sounded like a tuba,' Leonardo protested.

'You dick!'

Jasmine scoffed, which prompted Vegas to storm over to her and kick her in the ribs. 'I don't know what you think is so funny,' he growled. 'Your friends didn't even care enough about you to try and rescue you. You're just a worthless little skank.'

Renwar shouted back to Leonardo. 'Hey, turn up the radio. I like that song.'

Leonardo duly obliged and turned up the volume on the speaker. Johnny Cash was singing "When the Man Comes Around".

Vegas reacted angrily. 'Turn it back down. This isn't a fucking disco!'

KNOCK, KNOCK.

'What was that?' said Vegas.

Renwar replied, 'Someone just knocked on the doors.'

Vegas put his finger to his lips indicating for everyone to be quiet, particularly Jasmine and Arizona. He made a throat cutting gesture at each of the women to ensure they got the message, then he glared at Leonardo and pointed at the speaker. Leonardo reached for the volume button to turn down Johnny Cash, but before he had a chance, a voice called through the doors at the back of the truck.

'Hey, this is a no parking zone!'

Vegas rolled his eyes. 'Fucking traffic warden,' he muttered.

Renwar was closest to the doors, so he leaned against them and shouted through. 'Sure thing, man. Just give us two minutes.'

BLAM!

A huge hole appeared in the door as if a bomb had gone off. Renwar's head exploded. His body crumpled to the floor, and a pile of red gloop splattered all over the inside of the truck. A chunk of flying brain hit Vegas in the face and slid into his open mouth. The bounty hunter spat it out onto the floor and put his hand to his lips to wipe some gunk away, then he stared at his fingers, wondering how his brother's brain tissue had ended up on his face.

While the shock took time to sink in, the back door swung open and the Bourbon Kid climbed into the truck. He had his Headblaster gun in his right hand. Smoke was filtering out of the barrel. He stepped over Renwar's bleeding corpse and pointed the gun at Vegas.

BOOM!

Vegas's left leg took the brunt of the shot. Jasmine had a front row view of it. The blast cut his leg off below the knee, leaving him standing helpless on one leg with blood gushing out from his new stump. A second later he overbalanced and landed on his back, screaming like a bitch, holding his severed leg.

Leonardo jumped up and charged at the Bourbon Kid, yelling a bunch of nonsensical obscenities. A third shot from the Headblaster took care of him. It hit him in the shoulder and spun him around. His arm separated from his body and flew off. It landed on the floor with a thud, not far from Jasmine's face. The blood from the arm squirted all over Vegas who was writhing around nearby, squealing like a pig. Johnny Cash was in full flow by now.

The Bourbon Kid tucked his gun back inside his coat and pulled out a large hunting knife. The blade already had patches of dried blood on it. He walked up to the one-armed figure of Leonardo and slammed him up against the wall. The Bastard was in shock and had no idea how to respond. The Kid pressed the tip of his blade into the corner of Leonardo's mouth, cutting his lip.

'OH GOD, MAN, PLEASE NO!' Leonardo wailed through gritted teeth.

The plea fell on deaf ears. The Kid dragged the knife from the corner of his mouth up to the bottom of his ear. Then he did the same on the other side of his face, giving him the biggest smile in Santa Mondega. The whole procedure was accompanied by screams, not just from Leonardo, but also his stricken brother, Vegas who was watching on from the floor while trying to hold his leg together.

And then came something quite unlike anything Jasmine had ever seen before. The Bourbon Kid put his knife back in its holster and repositioned himself behind Leonardo. He reached over the sobbing Bastard's head and stuck two fingers into his nostrils. With one extremely violent tug, he ripped Leonardo's nose up over his eyes. And he didn't stop there. He peeled the top half of the bounty hunter's face back over his scalp. When he eventually let go, the upper half of Leonardo's face was just a pair of eyes staring out of a blood-soaked skull. It looked like he had a hoodie hanging behind his head, made from his own scalp and face. The lack of eyelids made him look super-terrified too, which was fun. Leonardo dropped to his knees, gawping at Jasmine for a moment before he face-planted on the floor like a rag puppet.

And then it was Vegas's turn.

The Kid hauled the one-legged Bastard up from the floor and slammed him up against the wall.

'Do you know who I am?' the Kid asked him.

Vegas regained just enough composure to respond through an ocean of tears that welled up in his eyes and streamed down his cheeks. 'We were just hired to do a job,' he blubbed. 'We never laid a finger on her, I swear.'

'Do you know who I am?'

At this point, Vegas's face reminded Jasmine of the "crying Dawson" meme, which cheered her up a lot.

'I'm sorry, man,' Vegas whimpered. 'We didn't know she was your woman.'

'She's not my woman,' the Bourbon Kid replied. 'She's my friend.'

That was the cue for Vegas to suffer some delightful horrors. The Kid stuck four fingers into Vegas's mouth and pressed his thumb underneath his chin. With one spitefully vicious tug, he ripped the Bastard's bottom jaw off. It made a delightful crunch, like a tree snapping in half. The skin around Vegas's mouth tore like paper. Blood seeped out all down his chest and down parts of the Bourbon Kid's hand and arm. The Kid released his grip on the Bastard and stepped aside. Vegas's bottom jaw was hanging down in front of his chest, giving him the rather splendid look of the creepy mask worn by the killer in the *Scream* movies.

Vegas turned cross-eyed. Every part of his body began to quiver. Some magnificent gurgling noises followed, and a few seconds later he toppled over. His fucked-up face smashed against the floor next to his brother, Leonardo.

Whether the jaw removal was enough to kill him, Jasmine wasn't sure. But to remove any doubt about his condition, the Bourbon Kid stamped on the back of his head. His boot crunched through the back of Vegas's skull and obliterated it, squashing the contents across the floor in a puddle of filth.

Jasmine looked up at the Bourbon Kid, the tears in her eyes twinkling now with happiness. He stepped over the remains of the dead Bastards and took hold of her wrists. He hauled her to her feet and wiped some hair away from her face, then he took a look at her hands.

'These are fucked,' he said.

'I don't care,' she replied. 'I'm so happy. Arizona, this is my friend, JD.'

Arizona was tied up on the other side of the trailer. She had speckles of blood all over her legs and torso. She was staring open mouthed at the three corpses on the floor. 'That was fuckin' awesome,' she gawped.

The Bourbon Kid ignored her. He studied Jasmine's hands closely. 'These will have to be amputated,' he said. 'You're gonna need a pair of metal hands like Rex's.'

The joy of being rescued hadn't lasted long. Jasmine wailed. 'NOOOO! Not hands like Rex!'

The Bourbon Kid raised his eyebrows and smiled at her. 'You realise I'm kidding, right?'

Jasmine rolled her eyes. 'Oh my God. I have all my fingers broken and *now* you decide to make jokes?' A smile broke out on her face again, lighting up the truck. 'See,' she said. 'I knew you liked me!'

Fifty Two

Flake was used to hearing Sanchez's incredible butt symphonies. On many occasions in the past, she had heard him play a tune from his ass while he was on the toilet. It usually happened in the morning while she was brushing her teeth. Sanchez's ass could imitate almost any musical instrument, but his speciality was the horn section. Today's instrument of choice was the tuba.

They had found a Disabled toilet on the ground floor of the hospital. Flake freshened up over the sink and checked out the bruises on her face in the mirror while Sanchez conducted his symphony on the toilet. The deep notes from his epic tuba solo were perfect for drowning out the sound of Flake unhooking the recording device that had been planted on her shirt. It was a highly specialised device and it looked expensive. Flake wanted it gone as soon as possible. The thought that the Bastard brothers had been listening in on everything she had said and done gave her the creeps. Her intention was to drop it into the toilet when Sanchez flushed it. In the mirror, she could see him sweating and straining as he finished conducting the wind section, and prepared for his big finale.

'Jesus, Sanchez. Flush it, please! It stinks!' she snapped at him.

Sanchez stood up and turned around, giving Flake a great view of the orchestra while he flushed the toilet. She held her breath and moved around him, then she dropped the microphone into the bowl and watched it flush away with the swell of brown filth.

'What was that?' Sanchez asked as he sat back down, preparing for his encore.

'A microphone!'

'You were recording me?'

'No, dumbass. Those guys who kidnapped me, they stuck the mic on me. Rex pointed it out when we were in his room. Didn't you see him do it?'

'Aaaah,' said Sanchez, nodding his head. 'That makes sense. I thought he was just being creepy.'

Flake covered her mouth and nose. 'Would you mind finishing up,' she said through her fingers. 'And hurry up please! We've got to get back to Rex. He's on his own, remember.'

Sanchez completed his performance with a mighty blast from the tuba, followed by half a roll of toilet paper. When the show was over, Flake forced him to wash his hands, then she hurried over to the door to let the smell out into the rest of the hospital. But there was a problem. The door to the Disabled toilets wouldn't reopen.

'Sanchez, the door is stuck,' she groaned.

'You're probably turning the handle the wrong way,' said Sanchez. 'Let me do it.'

'Turning it the wrong way?'

Sanchez barged her aside and grabbed the handle on the door. He tugged at it for about ten seconds with no success. 'It won't move,' he announced.

'I just told you that.'

'Weird,' said Sanchez. 'It was okay when we came in, wasn't it? Is there a lock on here that we haven't seen?'

'I already turned the lock switch,' said Flake, turning pale. 'If we don't get out of here soon, I'm going to faint.'

Sanchez flipped the locking switch back and forth numerous times as he tried to turn the door handle. Nothing worked.

'Has someone locked us in from the outside?' he asked, puzzled.

'There is a keyhole,' said Flake. 'Maybe someone came past and locked it while you were making all that noise?'

Sanchez pulled a handkerchief from his pants and mopped his brow with it. As he patted his sweaty forehead, a key fell out of the hanky and landed on the floor.

'Hey!' said Flake, reaching down to retrieve it. 'Isn't this the key Levian gave you? He said it would unlock any door in the city, didn't he?'

'He was joking,' said Sanchez.

'We should at least try it. Here, move aside. I'll give it a go.'

'I'll do it.' Sanchez snatched the key from her and slid it into the lock. It fitted perfectly. He turned it and the lock clicked. 'Wow! It actually worked!' he said, triumphantly. 'Maybe Levian wasn't such a cock after all?'

Flake grabbed the door handle and twisted it. The door swung open, so she shoved Sanchez through it and hurried out after him, desperate for some clean hospital air. The door closed behind them. But they were no longer in Saint Jude's hospital. They were somewhere completely different.

'Where the fuck are we?' Flake asked.

They were standing at the top of some steps that led down into a bar. It was similar to the Tapioca, only this place was cleaner and didn't smell as bad. There were about fifty people in the bar, all drinking and having a good time.

Flake had seen this place before, many times. *On television.* 'Sanchez, this looks like the bar from that movie you're always watching,' she said.

222

Sanchez was gawping like he'd just seen his breakfast. '*Road House!*' he exclaimed. 'This is an exact replica of the Double Deuce bar!'

'Why would Levian's key take us here?' Flake asked, mystified.

'Maybe this is Heaven?' said Sanchez.

'That's stupid.'

Sanchez shrugged. 'It's exactly how I always imagined Heaven would look.'

Flake rubbed her head. 'We can't really be in Heaven though, can we?'

'I dunno, but it definitely looks like we're in Road House.'

He had a point. Even though Flake hadn't seen *Road House* as many times as Sanchez, she had walked in on him watching it plenty of times, so she knew what the Double Deuce looked like.

As if to confirm that they were in the middle of Sanchez's favourite movie, a female customer by the bar picked up a glass bottle and smashed it over the head of a man sitting on a stool close by. What followed was a bar fight like nothing Flake had ever seen. And she'd seen a lot of bar fights.

Customers who had been sitting around drinking and minding their own business suddenly leapt to their feet and started punching each other. Glasses were thrown, chairs were smashed over people's heads. Absolutely everyone was getting stuck in, and no one seemed to care who they were fighting, or why.

In the middle of all of it, Flake spotted one man who wasn't involved in the brawl, a tall, well-tanned dude with wavy brown hair, wearing blue jeans and a brown suede jacket. He was standing at the bar, drinking a cup of black coffee, and he was staring right at her. Flake nudged Sanchez in the ribs and whispered in his ear.

'Is that Patrick Swayze over there?'

Fifty Three

Hiding in a compartment below the floor of a replica spaceship wasn't as much fun as it sounded. It was a really cramped space, and Elvis's legs were starting to stiffen up. To make matters worse, the battery on his phone had died, so he had no way of knowing if Jasmine had returned his call. On the plus side, he hadn't heard anything of the wax stormtroopers for at least fifteen minutes, and no one seemed to be moving around outside the Millennium Falcon either. It felt like a good time to make a move.

Elvis pushed the hatch up and poked his head out of the smuggling compartment. There were no stormtroopers in sight, so he hauled himself up out of his hiding place and tiptoed over to the ship's entrance. There was no sign of Scratch or any of his skeletons in the hall. The waxwork statues had returned to their positions and none of them looked alive anymore.

He took a tentative stroll down the Falcon's boarding ramp, checking all around for any lingering danger. Nothing in the hall was moving. The place looked exactly as it should do. Elvis rolled his shoulders back, his confidence returning. He'd outwitted Scratch, and it had actually been pretty easy. He snuck along the edge of the hall, past a group of droids and bounty hunters on ten-inch high podiums. Each waxwork had its name embossed in gold letters on the podium beneath it. They had some really strange names too. Elvis couldn't even pronounce half of them. One of the names he *could* pronounce was Boba Fett. Unfortunately, the statue wasn't on its podium. Elvis took a look behind him to see if the masked bounty hunter was following him. Boba Fett was nowhere to be seen. *Jeez*, these statues could make a guy paranoid. It was time to go. No more looking at statues.

Elvis picked up the pace and scuttled over to the exit. He pushed one of the doors open and peered through it. All good. No one around. He breathed a sigh of relief and walked through the door. Then he headed over to the stairwell for a peek over the bannister. The stairs were empty. The whole building was deathly quiet.

He took his time descending the stairs, careful not to make any noise, whilst also listening out for anyone on the floor below. Still nothing.

He stepped off the last of the stairs onto the ground floor. One last set of double doors to pass through into the reception hall. He pushed one of the doors open a few inches and peered through the gap. The ground floor was the length of a football pitch. There were rows of crappy statues lined up along the sides. A reception desk was halfway down the hall with some turnstiles on either side of it for the suckers that actually paid to come in and look at the shitty statues. Elvis set his sights on the big glass frontage of the building. There was still some light snow falling outside, but no sign of Jasmine in an escape vehicle. Better than that though, there was no sign of any skeletons, and definitely no Scratch.

He was almost home free. He stepped into the hall and took a close look at a few of the nearest statues to make sure they weren't alive. None of them looked his way, which was good. There were no cool movie characters, rock stars, or monsters on the ground floor. The statues were all of historic local figures. One in particular did catch Elvis's eye though. In a section devoted to city leaders there was a brand new statue of the city's current mayor, Sanchez Garcia. It was horribly out of proportion, shorter than the real Sanchez, and a good deal slimmer. The people who had sculpted and designed it had done one thing right though. They had Sanchez's new suit down to a tee. Elvis was drawn to it, fascinated by the shitness of the statue, but equally fascinated at how the waxwork staff had dressed it in the same clothes Sanchez was wearing that very day. Then it hit him.

The lazy fuckers!

They hadn't built a new statue for Sanchez at all. This was a Danny DeVito statue, from the movie *Twins*. The sign on the base of the statue said, *Mayor Sanchez Garcia,* but Elvis wasn't fooled. Someone had just taken the Danny DeVito statue from upstairs and made a few lazy alterations to it. It had a different haircut, and its eyes were looking in different directions. Despite the obvious flaws, it was still quite a good likeness for Sanchez. If Elvis's phone wasn't dead, he would have taken a photo of it.

But then the statue blinked and one of its eyes looked right at Elvis.

Shit!

Elvis bolted. He headed straight for the glass doors at the building's entrance. All around him statues were waking up, and they all had their eyes on him. Fortunately, the wax fuckers were all slow and cumbersome, so Elvis whizzed past them all and vaulted over the turnstiles in the middle of the hall without any of them getting near him.

But then came the laughter. A hearty, booming laugh from the back of the hall. Elvis glanced over his shoulder. Scratch was in the middle of the gang of clumsy statues, casually strolling through the hall. He had Boba Fett walking by his side.

Skeletons were flooding in through the doors at the back of the hall, like water through a burst dam. Where the fuck had they all been hiding?

As he sprinted towards the doors his limp became more prominent with every step. He knew he'd get to the doors before anyone else, but they were certain to be locked. The big question was, how well would they be locked? High-tech shit, or just a traditional key?

He pulled out his gun and fired off two shots. The first bullet broke a small hole through one of the doors. The second was worthy of a gold medal. It hit the same door and blew it apart.

"High-tech my ass!"

The glass door shattered and splintered onto the snow on the sidewalk outside.

Waxwork statues, terrifying though they were when they came to life, weren't quick enough to catch anyone. Elvis had left them all behind.

POW!

But not the witch.

He hadn't seen her. Where the fuck had she come from? The question went through Elvis's head as he floated backwards, his feet rising up at the same speed as his head fell back. Trixie, the purple-haired witch had walloped him across the chest with a baseball bat.

He landed flat on his back, dropping his gun and hitting his head on the marble floor. It wasn't enough to knock him unconscious but it did leave him dazed and confused. The image of the witch standing over him, her gap-toothed grin smirking, wobbled in and out of his vision.

'So close!' Scratch gloated as he strolled up to join Trixie.

Elvis couldn't even sit up, he was too shaken by the blow to his chest and the smack on the head from the marble floor. Scratch leant down and grabbed a clump of Elvis's hair. He dragged him up from the floor, almost ripping his hair out. Elvis was too dazed to fight back, and his feet were unsteady beneath him.

'Hello there!' Scratch beamed.

'Fuck you,' Elvis replied, his vision still swimming around.

'That's very thoughtful of you,' said Scratch. He straightened Elvis up, and kept a tight grip on his quiffed hair. 'Elvis, have you met Trixie? She's the lady who glued Rex to a burger stall. You know, she and I made a mistake with Rex. We left the scene of his murder before it was complete.' He ran one of his sharpened finger nails down the side of Elvis's face. 'But we won't be making that mistake with you.'

Fifty Four

The man in the brown suede jacket and tight blue jeans walked through the crowd of brawling drunkards towards Flake and Sanchez. None of the fighting customers threw a punch at him. Likewise, all of the missiles that were being hurled back and forth across the bar missed him too. He didn't even flinch when a high-heeled shoe whizzed past the end of his nose. This guy was cool, and he was a dead ringer for a young Patrick Swayze.

'He's coming over here,' Sanchez squeaked out of the side of his mouth.

'I can see that,' said Flake. 'I'm not fucking blind.'

'Do you think we're in trouble?'

'How the fuck should I know?'

The Swayze lookalike stopped in front of Sanchez and Flake and gave a wry smile. 'I think it's time for you to leave,' he said.

'I knew it!' said Sanchez, grinning like a goof. 'You're Dalton from Road House!'

'Actually, no I'm not.'

Flake agreed. 'He's Patrick Swayze.'

'Actually, I'm not Patrick Swayze either,' the man replied. 'I just look like him.'

'Then *who are you?*' Flake replied, her face revealing her disappointment.

'I'm God.'

'Fuck off,' said Sanchez, without thinking.

'Be nice,' said the man. 'This is your idea of Heaven, is it not?'

Sanchez was dumbstruck. But the guy was right. This *was* his idea of Heaven. 'How did you know that?' he asked, when his voice finally returned.

'Because I'm God. You used the secret key that Levian gave you. It brought you to Heaven. And to you, Heaven looks like the Double Deuce, because you're an idiot with a Road House obsession.'

'That's true,' said Flake. 'He is obsessed with Road House.'

'And he is an idiot,' God reminded her.

Sanchez was having his doubts about God. The guy seemed like a bit of a dick. If it wasn't for the fact he looked like Patrick Swayze, Sanchez would have considered confronting him about his snide remarks. As it was, he chose to let it slide, for now.

'Do you know why you're here?' God asked.

Someone in the bar area threw a glass bottle that whizzed past God's shoulder and headed towards Sanchez's face. Flake reached out and caught it when it was just inches away from hitting Sanchez on the nose. She was about to hurl it back into the crowd of brawlers, but God suddenly raised his hand and clicked his fingers in front of her face. The fighting stopped immediately, and everyone went back to drinking and having a good time, as if nothing had happened. God took the bottle from Flake and set it down on the floor.

'Wow, that was impressive,' said Sanchez.

'Well, I am God,' the Swayze lookalike replied, with a shrug.

'No,' said Sanchez, shaking his head dismissively. 'I was talking about Flake catching the bottle in mid-air. *That* was impressive.'

God looked a bit cheesed off, which pleased Sanchez. He was tempted to ask the Swayze wannabe, *"Who's the idiot, now?"* but he decided not to push his luck, what with God being all powerful and stuff.

Fortunately for Sanchez, God was quite forgiving, and moved on swiftly. He pointed at the drinking area behind him. 'See this place,' he said. 'It's full of people you've met during your journey through life. That's what Heaven is, a bar full of people you met while you were alive.'

'Hey look,' said Flake. 'There's the Red Mohawk!'

Sitting at a table in the corner was a man in black jeans and a red leather jacket. He had short dark hair, and even though he wasn't wearing a yellow skull mask with a red mohawk on top of it, Sanchez still recognised him. Sitting next to the Red Mohawk was a slim, young, brown-haired woman in a coral dress, drinking a blue cocktail through a straw. Her name was Baby and she was the Mohawk's girlfriend.

'Holy shit,' said Sanchez. 'You put Baby in a corner?'

God closed his eyes and took a deep breath through his nose. It looked like he was counting in his head. Flake elbowed Sanchez in the ribs.

'Ow, what was that for?' Sanchez grumbled.

'Stop making shit jokes.'

God opened his eyes and winked at Flake. 'Have you worked out why you're here?' he asked, for the second time.

'Hey look,' said Sanchez, nudging Flake. 'There's Kyle and Peto, and, *oh my God*, that's Candy Perez!'

Flake ignored him and answered God's question instead. 'Are we here so that you can tell us how to beat the Devil?'

'That is correct.'

'Oh, thank God. I mean, thank *goodness*,' said Flake, losing her cool momentarily. 'Umm, before we go any further, do you know what happened to my friend, Jasmine?'

God smiled. 'Come, follow me.'

He walked over to an empty table with three crappy wooden chairs around it. He pulled out a chair for Flake, and another next to her, for himself. The two of them sat down. Sanchez pulled out the third chair, but made no attempt to sit down because he was watching Candy Perez dancing on top of the bar for a group of guys below her.

Candy was the hot blonde judge from the infamous *Back From the Dead* show that Sanchez attended once, many years earlier. He'd always had a bit of a thing for her. She was wearing a sexy pink dress and it looked like she was about to take it off. She was drunk and slurring the words to her hit song, *"I Love Chubbies"*, a favourite song of Sanchez's. A group of guys, including the two monks, Kyle and Peto, were standing below her, egging her on.

Flake grabbed Sanchez's arm and pulled him down onto his seat. 'Don't make me embarrass you in front of everyone,' she warned him.

Sanchez shifted around in the chair, trying to get comfortable. 'I don't rate these chairs,' he said. 'I've got better than this in the Tapioca.'

'Don't blame me,' said God. 'This is your idea of Heaven, remember?'

Flake kicked Sanchez under the table, then smiled at God. 'You were going to tell us about Jasmine?'

'I would love to,' God replied. 'But I'm afraid holy law means I cannot tell you anything about Jasmine's predicament.' He offered a conciliatory smile. 'But, put it this way, if she was dead, she'd be here in Heaven, right?'

'I don't know about that,' said Sanchez. 'I'm not sure she qualifies for a place in *my* personal Heaven.'

A huge cheer went up over by the bar. But before Sanchez could see why, his view of proceedings was blocked by Flake's hand covering his eyes. A loud thud followed, which sounded like someone falling off the bar. With the drama over, Flake removed her hand from Sanchez's eyes. He had missed an incident where Candy Perez removed her dress, but then lost her balance and fell off the bar top, landing out of sight behind the bar. She did not reappear, no matter how much Sanchez stared.

'Don't worry,' said God. 'She'll be fine.'

'We should go and check,' said Sanchez.

'No we shouldn't,' said Flake. 'God won't let any harm come to her.'

Sanchez was livid, and he suspected Flake was trying to curry favour with God. Typical.

'So, God,' said Flake. 'Can you tell us how to defeat Scratch?'

God took her hands in his, and looked deep into her eyes, *the weasel.* 'I can offer you guidance,' he said.

'Guidance?' Sanchez scoffed. 'Is that all?'

God ignored him and focussed on Flake. 'I already denounced Scratch's immortality, so he is no longer invincible. All you need to defeat him is faith and some holy water.'

Flake didn't want to piss on God's parade, but she had to share something with him. 'The thing is,' she said, grimacing, 'he's got the *Eye of the Moon*, which sorta makes him invincible anyway.'

'He has the Eye of the Moon?' God was incredulous. 'What fool gave him that?'

'Sanchez did.'

'Hey, don't blame me,' said Sanchez. 'I wanted to keep it.'

God handed Sanchez a bowl of peanuts. Quite where the bowl came from, it was hard to know. One minute it wasn't there and then suddenly it was in Sanchez's hand. He popped a handful in his mouth. They were very salty and surprisingly chewy. Consequently, Sanchez couldn't join in the conversation for a while. Another of God's sneaky tricks.

'Hmmm, Scratch has *the Eye*,' said God, stroking his chin and mulling the situation over. 'I see it now. He has used it to cover Santa Mondega in snow, and also to raise an army of the dead. *Zombies and snow, hmmm.* If you are to defeat him you must use one against the other.'

Sanchez spat some peanuts out, and a few of them hit God's brown suede jacket before they fell to the floor. 'Use the snow to defeat the dead?' he scoffed.

God threw him a sideways glance. 'Or maybe use the dead to defeat the snow?'

'What does that mean?'

'My guess is, Flake will figure it out,' said God.

'This is shit,' Sanchez complained. 'Aren't you supposed to grant us three wishes or something?'

'If you wanted wishes you should have chosen an *Aladdin* setting, not *Road House*. We sell booze in this place, not wishes.'

'How about *one* wish?' Sanchez suggested.

'Okay,' said God. 'I will grant you one request. You may ask for *one thing* that you think will help in your fight against Scratch. But think carefully because you only get one request, and once you've made it, you cannot change your mind.'

'That's easy,' said Sanchez.

'Take some time to think about this,' said Flake grasping him by the arm.

Sanchez shook her off. 'I want a fire truck!' he declared. 'That ambulance I've been driving around in is good, but I've always wanted a fire truck, ever since I was a kid. One of the big ones, you know? With a siren and everything.'

Flake slapped herself on the forehead. God's eyes diverted her way. He seemed to be thinking the same thing.

'Flake, what do you make of that request?' he asked her.

'I think it's great,' Flake said sarcastically. 'Can I make a request too?'

God smiled. 'It's already done.'

'But I didn't tell you what I wanted.'

'You don't need to.'

'Do I get the fire truck, or what?' Sanchez asked.

'Okay, but to get to it, you have to stand up and close your eyes,' said God. 'Then click your shoes together three times and repeat the words, "There's no place like home."'

Sanchez was eager to get the fire truck, so he leapt to his feet and followed the instructions even though it seemed stupid. He closed his eyes, clicked his shoes together and recited the words, *"There's no place like home,"* three times out loud.

When he opened his eyes, nothing had changed. He was still in the bar, but now all the other customers were staring at him, and sniggering.

'Were you pulling my chain?' Sanchez asked angrily.

God laughed. 'I just wanted to see if you'd do it.'

Sanchez glared at Flake. 'What are you smiling at?'

'Come on, we gotta go,' she said, standing up. She was holding a piece of paper in her hand.

'What's that?' Sanchez asked.

'It's a letter from God,' said Flake, folding it up and slipping it into her breast pocket.

'It's probably rubbish then.'

God clicked his fingers again. The doors at the entrance swung open, letting a cold breeze into the bar. It was dark outside and there was snow falling, but Sanchez could see a number of vehicles in the parking lot, one of which was a huge red fire truck.

'Holy shit! That's awesome,' Sanchez said, beaming. 'Cheers, God!' He left Flake and God behind and raced out into the parking lot to get a good look at the truck. A loud cheer went up in the bar area, not because Sanchez had left the building, but because Candy Perez had regained consciousness and was up on her feet again, without her clothes.

Flake smiled at God. 'You know, you're pretty cool,' she said.

God winked at her and said, *"Ditto"*, which pretty much fulfilled a lifelong dream she'd had ever since she saw the movie *Ghost*.

While Flake was staring open-mouthed at God, he took hold of her hand and kissed it. 'It was an honour to meet you,' he said.

Flake wanted to say something cool in response, but nothing came to mind. God didn't seem bothered about it though. He gave her one last smile, then he turned away and walked back to the bar to keep the drunken guys from grabbing Candy. Flake watched him go. He had a cool walk. In fact, everything about him was cool. She savoured the moment for a while, even taking time to appreciate Candy's incredible hooters. They were quite mesmerising. But the sound of Sanchez beeping the horn in his new fire truck reminded her that there were bigger things at stake. She left Heaven behind and joined Sanchez outside in his new fire truck.

Fifty Five

'Please can you cut me down? My arms are killing me.'

Arizona had spent the best part of three days in the back of the truck, with her hands bound and tied above her head for much of that time. The Bourbon Kid answered her cry for help and cut her free with his knife. Tears of relief streamed down her face, and she flung her arms around him.

'You're so cool,' she sobbed. 'I love the way you fucked those guys up.'

The Bourbon Kid peeled her arms away from him and pushed her back. To her surprise, he offered her the knife he had used to cut Leonardo's face up. There was a fair bit of blood still on it. Arizona stared at it, unsure if she should accept it or not. The Kid pointed to the three mutilated Bastard brothers who were spread across the floor.

'See the one whose scalp is hanging behind his head? He's still breathing,' he said. He placed the handle of the knife in her hand. 'Go nuts.'

Arizona stared at the knife, then over at the scalped figure of Leonardo. His body was twitching ever so slightly. 'What should I do?' she asked, nervously.

'Stick it in him, anywhere you like.'

'I'm not sure I want to.'

'Just try it. You might find you get a taste for it.'

Arizona took a few baby steps across the floor and knelt down beside Leonardo. She whispered something into what was left of his ear, then she pushed the knife slowly through his pants into his scrotum, which made him twitch a little more ferociously.

'How did you find us?' Jasmine asked the Bourbon Kid. 'Did you know Flake had a recording device on her?'

The Kid was watching Arizona ripping Leonardo's sack apart, but he replied anyway. 'Yeah, I saw it on her shirt straight away.'

'So, you didn't really mean it when you told Flake I was an idiot, and you weren't going to come after me?'

The Kid threw a sideways glance at Jasmine. 'I don't remember what I said.'

'But how did you find the truck? Even I didn't know where we were!'

'I tracked your phone.'

Jasmine shuddered. Then she did some kind of weird body-popping dance, while making a light groaning noise.

'What's with you?' the Kid asked her.

'My phone is vibrating. I keep getting notifications.' She held up her hands to show him her crooked, broken fingers. 'Could you get my phone out for me?'

'No.'

'Please. I can't do it myself because of my fingers.'

'Arizona!'

Arizona was in the middle of giving Leonardo some kind of autopsy, but at the sound of her name she stopped and looked up. 'Yeah, what's up?'

'Can you get Jasmine's phone out for her?'

'Uh, okay. Where is it?'

Jasmine stopped writhing around and breathed a sigh of relief before replying, 'It's inside me.'

'Inside you?'

'Yeah. In my pussy. I've got no pockets on this catsuit.'

Arizona was done with the whole castration thing anyway. She stood up and handed the Kid his bloodied knife back. 'Thanks,' she said. 'That was quite therapeutic.'

'Right.'

Arizona stepped in front of Jasmine and unzipped her catsuit. While she got down to business retrieving the phone, the Bourbon Kid moved away and crouched down next to Leonardo. He wiped the blade of his knife clean on the dead Bastard's pants.

Jasmine looked down at the top of Arizona's head, which was positioned between her legs. 'What's it like being the President's daughter?' she asked her new friend.

'Nothing special,' Arizona replied. 'I hardly ever see him. And no one is supposed to know he's my dad. Especially his wife.' She stood up straight. 'Here's your phone,' she said, holding it up.

'Aww, thanks. Can you keep it for me, please? And zip me back up?'

The Bourbon Kid finished wiping the blade of his knife clean and tucked it back into a sheath inside his coat. He turned around just in time to see Arizona zipping Jasmine's catsuit back up.

'Are you all done?' he asked.

Jasmine nodded. 'You missed all the good bits.'

'We should go. By the way, did you know there's a young kid on the roof of this truck?'

'Oh, yeah, him,' said Jasmine. 'He was rude to me earlier because I knocked him out of a window. We should leave him up there. Teach him a lesson.'

Arizona was listening in on the conversation with a big smile on her face. 'Jasmine, can I ask you a question?' she said.

'Of course.'

'Did you really kill the Pope?'

'I sure did. Six shots in the chest. Thought he was a zombie.'

'That is *so cool*.' Arizona fluttered her eyelids at the Bourbon Kid. 'Is it true you've killed *millions* of people?'

'I only kill people who irritate me.'

'What a wonderful philosophy. I wish I could be more like you.' Arizona offered Jasmine's phone to the Bourbon Kid. 'Do you want this?'

'You can keep it,' he replied.

It crossed Jasmine's mind that Arizona was coping remarkably well with everything that had happened to her. She'd been in the back of the trailer much longer than Jasmine, and must have suffered dreadfully at the hands of the Bastards.

'Arizona, are you okay?' Jasmine asked. 'I mean, did those guys do anything bad to you?'

The happy look vanished from Arizona's face. 'Oh, them.' She shuddered as she looked down at the three mutilated men on the floor. 'You know, I thought they were going to rape me, but they didn't. They were *so weird*. After kidnapping me, they just took it in turns to have some private time with me, but they were all sissy boys.'

Jasmine's eyes opened wide. 'What did they do?'

'Oh, y'know, they all just took turns jerking off on my feet, and calling me *mommy*.'

The Bourbon Kid shook his head. 'I shouldn't have been so easy on these guys.'

Jasmine was less disgusted. 'Ha, I had a couple of customers who liked that sort of thing back when I was a hooker. Guys are so weird.'

Arizona giggled. 'This whole thing has just been crazy. First I get kidnapped by these three muppets and have my feet jizzed on six times a day, *then* I get rescued by, *no offence,* a fucking mass murderer.' She smiled at the Bourbon Kid. 'And I just pulled a phone out of the woman who killed the Pope. I can't wait to tell my mom.'

The Bourbon Kid glanced down at Arizona's feet, then announced he was going to step outside for some fresh air. The truck did smell like shit, not because of Arizona's feet, but because the dead Bastards were starting to go stale.

As the Kid stepped outside, Jasmine's phone vibrated in Arizona's hand.

'Ooh, can you check that for me, please?' Jasmine asked her. 'I need to know if Elvis has been calling me?'

'Elvis?'

'Yeah, he's my boyfriend. He's one of our gang too.'

'What's your PIN?'

'Four-seven-four-seven.'

Arizona typed in the code. The display on the phone flashed up with a bunch of notifications. 'You've got a missed call from him,' she said. 'And a voicemail.'

'Play the voicemail, quick.'

Arizona put the phone to her ear to listen to the message. She soon looked even more bewildered than before.

'What did he say?' Jasmine asked.

'He said he's in the Waxwork building and he's being chased by someone called Scratch. Apparently Scratch has a giant Woody, and some skeletons. Does that make sense?'

Jasmine's jaw dropped. 'A giant Woody?' she said. 'What's he doing with it?'

The Bourbon Kid was standing in the snow outside the back of the truck, but he heard what was said. He yelled back at Arizona. 'Did he say anything else?'

'Yeah,' she replied. 'He asked if Jasmine could get a car and pick him up outside the waxwork building because he's going to make a break for it.'

Jasmine looked at the Bourbon Kid. 'We have to go. Scratch will kill him.'

'Yep.'

Jasmine rushed over to the doors and crouched down so the Kid could help her out of the truck. He grabbed her by her hips and lifted her out, then he set her down on her feet in the snow.

'FUCK ME! That's cold!' she squealed. She hopped up and down in the snow in her bare feet. 'Arizona can you bring my sneakers with you?'

Arizona's eyes lit up. 'Am I coming with you?'

The Kid shook his head. 'It's not safe. Scratch is the Devil, which makes this a suicide mission.'

Arizona was unfazed. She picked up Jasmine's sneakers and jumped out of the back of the truck. The cold snow underfoot didn't seem to bother her. 'Five minutes ago I was certain I was gonna die,' she said, bending down and slipping one of the sneakers onto Jasmine's foot. 'Now I'm having the best day ever. And you guys are *so much fun!* You've gotta let me come with you!'

'Can she come with us?' Jasmine pleaded.

'It's not a good idea.'

Arizona stopped tying the laces on Jasmine's shoe and stood up. 'You'd better take this then,' she said, offering Jasmine's phone to the Bourbon Kid. 'Jasmine can't use it, and you don't want me tagging along, so I can't keep it.'

The Bourbon Kid looked at the phone and made a snap decision. 'Okay, you can come.'

Fifty Six

Elvis kicked out as he tried to find the floor. Instead, he just kept finding Scratch's shins, not that it seemed to bother Scratch in the slightest. All around him skeletons and wax statues were watching on with interest as Scratch held him off the ground with one hand, squeezing the air out of his lungs. Elvis grabbed Scratch's wrist with both hands and tried to pull it away from his throat. It didn't work. He tried pulling Scratch's thumb and fingers loose. That also was a waste of time. The Devil was too strong. Elvis threw a punch that caught Scratch on the shoulder. It was a pitiful effort because with his feet off the ground he couldn't get any weight behind the punch. The feeble blow only served to broaden the annoying smirk on Scratch's face.

'I like this one,' said Trixie, moving into Elvis's eye-line. 'I'd like him in my collection.'

'By all means,' Scratch beamed. He pressed his face closer to Elvis's. 'Do you know what Trixie's hobby is?'

'Not washing her hair? Smelling like cheese?' Elvis rasped, wasting some valuable oxygen in the process as Scratch tightened his grip around his throat.

'No. She collects men's private parts,' said Scratch. 'She pickles them in a jar, cooks them up and serves them as a delicacy in a restaurant she owns. A cock and balls cuisine, if you will.'

'Sounds like *your* kind of place,' Elvis retorted. He kicked Scratch in the shins again. This time just for fun.

Scratch pinched harder on Elvis's neck, choking the air right out of him. Trixie moved in close and wrapped her hand around Elvis's crotch, rubbing it and checking out the merchandise.

As the oxygen in Elvis's lungs vanished altogether, his sight blurred into a rainbow of nonsense. He was on the verge of losing consciousness, but at the last moment, Scratch opened his hand and dropped him. Elvis landed on his ass and rolled onto his side, coughing and gasping for air on the cold marble floor.

'WHAT THE FUCK IS THAT?' Scratch bellowed.

Elvis was wheezing in and out like a knackered bagpipe, but as the oxygen was restored to his lungs, his eyesight returned to a level of normality. He blinked a few times and looked up at Scratch. The Devil was staring in the direction of the front doors, absolutely transfixed. Boba Fett was standing just behind Scratch. The bounty hunter unholstered his wax blaster and pointed it at the entrance.

It had been hard for Elvis to hear anything while Scratch was choking him, but after a few sharp breaths, he heard the sound that had gotten Scratch worked up. It had also grabbed the attention of Trixie, the skeleton army, and all the creepy wax statues. Everyone was staring at the front entrance.

WEE-OWW, WEE-OWW!

It was a siren.

A fucking loud siren. Getting louder with each passing second. Getting closer. Elvis lopped his head to the side and saw what everyone else had seen. A huge, bright red fire truck was zooming along the snow-covered driveway that led up to the building.

'IT'S COMING RIGHT AT US!' Scratch yelled.

He was right.

The fire truck smashed through the glass frontage on Waxwork Tower. Its rear end skidded around, overtaking the front, spraying chunks of glass over everyone. Elvis scrambled out of the way as the truck eventually came to a halt, side on, blocking off half of the entrance. The driver of the fire truck was Sanchez, which probably explained why the truck had skidded into the building at a sideways angle. But the really good news was on the side of the truck. Flake was standing on a ledge behind a large and very powerful water cannon. Elvis blinked a few more times to make sure he wasn't seeing things.

Scratch's face contorted into a spiteful snarl. 'Those fuckers,' he muttered. 'GET THEM!'

Hundreds of skeletons and waxwork figures followed the order and charged at the fire truck.

Wrong move.

Flake was unfazed. She winked at Scratch, aimed the water cannon at him and said three words that struck the fear of God into him. And Trixie.

'Holy water, bitches!'

She released a lever on the cannon and blasted a thick stream of water at Scratch. It hit him in the chest and knocked him off his feet into a crowd of skeletons behind him. Every part of his skin that was touched by the holy water lit up on fire. His red suit ignited and sparked into flames, totally ruining it. With the Devil down on the ground, Flake swung the water cannon around and sprayed anything that came close to the fire truck. Every single skeleton or statue that she hit went up in flames. Boba Fett was one of the first to go.

Elvis stayed down, wary of taking a blast of water in the face. The witch, who only moments earlier had been feeling him up, dived onto the floor. But there was no escape. Flake turned the stream of water on her. It lit up the soles of her shoes, the hem of her dress, the nails on her fingers and the split ends on her shitty purple hair. Every drop of water that touched her burned into her skin, peeling it away, melting every cell in her body. She lit up faster than Michael Jackson in a soda commercial. The green bitch writhed around on the floor, screaming and scratching at her face. Tempted though Elvis was to give her a kick in the fanny, he chose the more sensible option and rolled across the floor, away from the cannon's aim.

Flake sprayed every corner of the hall with water, torching every last bastard of Scratch's dead army. It was off the scale in its awesomeness. Skeletons screamed, rattled and whistled away into puffs of steam and smoke. Waxworks melted like chocolate. The only downside, as far as Elvis was concerned, was all the fire. The hall was rapidly turning into a furnace, and the flames were spreading fast. Elvis's suit was wet and weighing him down, but he staggered to his feet and stumbled over to the fire truck, the cries from Trixie playing like music in his ears.

'I'm melting! I'm melting!' she screamed.

Elvis took one last look back and saw her transform into a pool of apple sauce. He climbed up onto the side of the fire truck and collapsed in a heap on a wide metal ledge behind Flake.

Flake was having the time of her life, swinging the water cannon around the giant hall like it was a Gatling gun. Elvis sat up and watched the last of the skeletons and waxwork figures melt away into nothing. One of the last to go was the short wax figure that looked like a cross-eyed Sanchez. In less than thirty seconds Flake had wiped out the entire undead army.

When she finally turned off the water cannon, only two people had survived the attack. Elvis. And Scratch. The Devil had been knocked off his feet and engulfed in flames just like the others. But he had the *Eye of the Moon* concealed within his body. While the fire had obliterated everything else, Scratch was kept alive by the healing power of the Eye. He staggered, half naked and badly burnt, all the way to the back of the hall, where he squeezed out through a set of doors, leaving a trail of smoke and traces of scorched red clothing behind him.

Elvis reached up and grabbed Flake's hand. 'You're fucking awesome, Flake, did you know that?'

'Yes I did,' Flake replied, helping him up. 'Are you okay?'

'I am now. Got kinda close there though. How the fuck did you get a fire engine with holy water?'

Sanchez hopped out of the driver's cab and strolled over. 'God gave it to us,' he said, kicking a skeletons hand out of the way.

'What?'

'We met God,' said Flake. 'And he looks like Patrick Swayze. He gave us this *pretty-fucking-special* truck, and filled the cannon with holy water!'

'And sent you here to rescue me?'

Flake fumbled around in her pockets. 'He gave me a note telling us to come here,' she said. 'I seem to have lost it though. That's weird.'

'Is that a joke?' Elvis asked. 'Because if it is, I don't get it.'

'Never mind. I'll explain it later.'

'Where is everyone else?'

'Rex is still at the hospital,' said Flake. 'He's conscious again. It's like a miracle or something. He did say he was surfing with Patrick Swayze though, which makes sense now.'

'Does it?' said Elvis frowning. 'What about Jas? Where is she?'

As if to answer the question, Sanchez's phone rang. 'Jasmine's calling me!' he said, waving the phone above his head.

'Answer it then!' Elvis snapped.

Sanchez took the call and for the next thirty seconds he was involved in a catch-up conversation in which he bragged about single-handedly rescuing Elvis. He also did a lot of *uh-huh-ing*, and *no-way-ing*" as he heard an even better story from the other end of the line.

When he ended the call he looked more confused than usual.

'Well?' said Flake. 'Where is she?'

'That wasn't her. It was someone called Arizona,' Sanchez replied. 'She's with Jasmine and the Bourbon Kid. They're going to the hospital to get Rex, then we've got to go meet them at the sea bridge on the edge of town. Apparently we're all getting out of Santa Mondega.'

'Great,' said Elvis. 'What are we waiting for then? Let's get moving!'

Fifty Seven

Scratch bounded up the stairwell, inwardly raging at what had just happened. The humiliation of being set on fire and having his suit burned to shreds was eating him up inside. Sprayed with holy water! Damn, the indignity of it! *Flake, bloody Flake!* Everyone always forgets Flake. *That bitch!*

Scratch wasn't nearly as angry at Flake as he was at himself for allowing her the chance to spray water at him. Where the fuck did she find a fire truck with holy water? Then there was that smug twat, Sanchez. Scratch tensed up at the embarrassment of having his plans scuppered by Sanchez. It didn't even matter that the fat Mexican had only been driving the fire truck. It was still humiliating. Visions of Sanchez boasting about the time he outwitted the Devil were racing through Scratch's mind. His credibility would be destroyed if the angels and demons of the world were to hear about what had happened. He'd be a laughing stock for all eternity. What he needed right now was an ego boost.

Halfway up the stairs he ripped off his tattered pants. His cell phone fell out onto a step by his feet. Thankfully it had survived the fire and the holy water, unlike his suit, which was destroyed. He was about to pick the phone up when he spotted a security camera on the wall, looking at him, smirking. Scratch raised his hand and blasted a bolt of red lightning from his palm. It hit the camera and blasted it into a thousand pieces. There was absolutely no need for any cameras to be filming him running up a stairwell in his *Thundercats* underpants. He bent down and picked up his phone. It was boiling hot but still working, so he made a hasty call to Einstein. The goofy scientist answered straight away.

'Hello boss,' Einstein said, cheerfully. 'Are they all dead yet?'

'FUCK OFF!'

'Is something the matter?'

'Who's left in Purgatory? Any of those Skinners or skeletons?'

'Err, no. There's just me and——'

'And who?'

'Zilas.'

'GODDAMMIT! Right, round up every fucking zombie you can find buried out in the desert.'

'What for? I thought you already had a load of skeletons and cannibals with you? Are they all dead?'

Scratch was livid. Having to admit to the staff that his glorious plans had failed was just the worst. But a small ray of joy came his way when a pair of skeletons appeared behind him on the staircase.

'They're not all dead,' he bragged to Einstein. 'But yes, most of them have just melted.'

'Melted? *Wow.* What about Trixie?'

'She's melted too. Bloody Flake showed up with a water cannon full of holy water.'

'Flake? Which one is she?'

'EXACTLY! Fucking Flake!' Scratch shook his fist. 'Just find every zombie you can.'

'Sure thing boss. Just tell me where you are and I'll send them through the portal to you.'

'No, don't do that.'

'I'm confused.'

'Listen to me, Einstein. I do want you to send the zombies through the portal, but not to me. Send them a few at a time into every bathroom in Santa Mondega.'

'That's a lot of bathrooms.'

'Yes it is. I want everyone in this city dead. The Dead Hunters will have no place to hide, and nor will anyone else. It's time for a massacre of apocalyptic proportions.'

'That'll take me a while, you know?'

'I DON'T CAAAAAARE!'

'Yes sir. I'll get right on it.'

'And send Zilas through the portal with a new suit for me. Mine's melted. I'm at Waxwork Tower.'

'What floor?'

'TOP FLOOR!'

Scratch ended the call. Things had gotten so bad he actually wanted Zilas for company. The hunchback was an idiot, and a very annoying idiot at that, but he was also an ass-kisser, and right now Scratch was in need of a lift. He stormed up the stairwell all the way to the top and marched out onto the roof in just his underpants.

Zilas arrived on the roof a short while later, carrying a dark red suit for his master. The hideously deformed hunchback looked really pleased to be called upon.

'Here's your suit?' he said, handing it over. 'Is there anything else I can do?

Scratch accepted the suit and started dressing himself.

'I like your underpants,' said Zilas.

'I hate your face,' Scratch replied.

'Would you like to see my underpants?'

'NO!'

Scratch buckled up his belt and then put on the red shirt and jacket Zilas had provided. He felt better immediately.

'Did you bring me a hat?' he asked.

'Yes, sir.'

Zilas reached inside his green velvet jacket and pulled out a flat piece of red material. Scratch snatched it from him and rearranged it, punching the middle of it up, switching it into a smart cowboy hat. He placed it on his head.

'How do I look?' he asked.

'Like the devil you are,' Zilas replied.

'Good.' Scratch marched across the rooftop towards the edge that overlooked the main street. Zilas hobbled along behind him, excited to be involved.

Scratch looked down at the snow-covered streets below. They were mostly empty. The residents of Santa Mondega were tucked up in their homes. They would all soon be in for a horrible surprise.

'How did you end up in just your underpants?' Zilas asked, as he stepped up to the roof edge next to Scratch.

'Elvis was so fucking lucky.'

'What did he do?'

'He got lucky, and that's all you need to know.'

'The Bourbon Kid got lucky too. Did you know he killed Albatross *and* the Grim Reaper?'

Scratch's face contorted like he was having a stroke. 'GODDAMMIT! FOR FUCKSSAKE! CAN'T ANYONE DO ANYTHING RIGHT?'

'Apparently not,' said Zilas nonchalantly. 'I heard the Reaper stabbed himself in the face with his own sword. How rubbish is that?'

'It's fucking shit. That's what it is.' Scratch was shaking his fist at the sky. 'Bloody Grim Reaper. Useless fuck.'

'So, what are you gonna do now?'

Scratch stopped shaking his fist and scoured the city landscape. The whole city was visible from his spot at the top of Waxwork Tower. It didn't take long to find what he was looking for. A bright red fire truck was speeding through the streets in the direction of the main bridge that led out of the city.

'It's time to use the Eye of the Moon,' he said, rubbing his hands together, getting his mojo back.

'For what?'

'Watch this.'

The Devil raised his arms to the sky. The black clouds above him began to quiver. A red glow emanated from the pit of Scratch's stomach, lighting him up, glimmering through his suit, making him look like a shitty low-budget CGI demon. Low-budget or not, the effects were real. A gentle rumbling, like a drum roll, built up in the sky. Bright red lights flickered within the black clouds, giving the impression they were on fire. The rumbling drums turned into claps of thunder as if a thousand giant drummers were playing in unison.

'What the shit are you doing?' Zilas yelled over the din.

Scratch ignored him and kept his focus on the clouds. He opened his hands and leaned back. Red lights burst out of his palms and shot up into the sky like bolts of electricity. And so began the storm of all storms. Hail stones burst down from the sky, rattling on the rooftops, the shopfronts and the cars in the streets. Scratch manipulated the weather like a conductor directing a cloud orchestra.

Zilas covered his head with his hands to protect himself from the downpour of hailstones. 'Fucking Hell!' he yelled. 'Can I borrow your hat?'

Scratch stepped away from the edge of the roof. He still had a huge current of electrical power from the Eye of the Moon surging through his body. He turned it on Zilas, blasting him with red electricity from his hands. The bolts hit the pathetic hunchback in the chest and legs, frazzling him, electrocuting him and eventually blasting him off the rooftop and down to the street below.

'See you back in Hell!' Scratch cackled.

The Devil drank in the images of chaos all around, revelling in the pleasure it brought. And this was only the beginning. He turned his hands over, aiming his palms at the streets.

'Let the dead rise from the ashes!' he cried. 'From the sea beds, from the ground and from every morgue in the city. In the name of the Prince of Darkness, I command the dead to reveal yourselves, abide with me, and *destroy my enemies!*'

All across Santa Mondega, mounds of earth trembled. From the coffins, the tombs, the rivers, the sea beds and the shallow graves all around the city, one by one the dead rose up to join the Devil's army.

There was still one more thing to do. He had to prevent his enemies from escaping, keep them in Santa Mondega, corner them, leave them with no place to hide. In the distance he saw the fire truck had come to a stop just short of the sea bridge at the edge of the city.

With one wild shot of electricity from his hand, Scratch turned a cloud above the bridge into a ball of red fire. The cloud emitted a loud clap of thunder, then a bolt of lightning reached down from within it and struck the foundations of the sea bridge.

The bridge was about half a mile long, and made of solid steel, but the power of the electrical blast shook its foundations. A huge crack appeared in the middle of the bridge. It wobbled and shook and then split in two, until it eventually crumbled into a million pieces that fell into the sea, generating an enormous tidal wave. The huge wall of water crashed onto the mainland and swept through the surrounding streets, washing away everything in its wake.

A smile reappeared on Scratch's face. No one was escaping from Santa Mondega. Not today.

Fifty Eight

Driving a fire truck was a dream come true for Sanchez. He was having a blast steering it through the streets towards the edge of the city. Flake was still out on the side of the truck manning the water cannon just in case. Elvis was beside Sanchez in the passenger seat, offering advice and directions. Sanchez ignored them all.

'Can this thing go any faster?' Elvis asked.

'Not in this snow,' Sanchez replied, swinging the truck around a corner. As the entrance to the sea bridge came into view, they encountered a new problem. The dark clouds up above suddenly started shitting hailstones down onto the city. The fire truck took a battering.

'Turn the wipers on!' Elvis yelled. 'Fuck! I hope Flake is okay out there.'

Sanchez didn't have a clue what all the buttons in the fire truck did. He pressed one on the dash that looked like it might be for the wipers. It wasn't. The window on Elvis's side of the truck wound down. Elvis slapped him on the arm.

'Which button did you press?' he scowled.

'One of those,' Sanchez replied, pointing at a bunch of buttons of different shapes and sizes on the dash.

Elvis pressed one. It opened up a fan on Sanchez's side and blasted cold air into his face.

'Idiot!' Sanchez yelled as the cold air blew his hair out of shape.

Elvis went to press another button, but Sanchez slapped his hand away. Elvis slapped back. The situation was on the verge of turning into a childish slapping match. It came to an end when a huge tremor shook the fire engine. Sanchez's side of the truck bounced up off the road, throwing him sideways into Elvis. When the truck landed back on the ground, Sanchez straightened up and hit the brakes. The truck skidded along on a patch of ice and snow for another fifty metres before it eventually came to a stop by a wall of metal railings beside the sea bridge.

'What the fuck was that?' Elvis asked as he held down a button on the door to wind his window back up.

'A mini earthquake, I think,' Sanchez replied, while checking his wing mirror for any sign of Flake.

'She okay back there?'

'I hope so.'

Elvis checked their position. There wasn't much to see apart from hailstones battering the windscreen. 'Where's the Bourbon Kid then?' he asked. 'Is this where we're supposed to meet him?'

'Maybe he's not here yet?' said Sanchez. 'We should just wait, I suppose?'

A hand slammed against the driver's window causing Sanchez to jump.

'Christ, what was that?'

A face appeared next to the hand. It was a bearded man with scraggly long white hair and dull red eyes. He was covered in snow. He pressed his face up against the window and pulled at the door handle, trying to get in. The sight of the flesh on Sanchez's neck was driving him wild. His mouth was open and he had saliva drooling down the hair on his chin.

'KILL IT!' Sanchez yelled. 'IT'S A FUCKING YETI!'

'It's not a Yeti,' Elvis said, calmly. 'It's a zombie.'

'THAT'S EVEN WORSE!'

The zombie problem was soon resolved. From further back on the truck, Flake blasted holy water at the crazy zombie man. It hit him and knocked him off the side of the truck. The power of the water sent him spinning over the metal railings that were supposed to stop people falling into the sea. His body erupted into flames and he plummeted down into the choppy waters below.

'See! Nothing to worry about,' said Elvis.

Another hand thumped on Sanchez's window.

'KILL IT!' Sanchez screamed.

'It's Flake, you idiot.'

Sanchez clutched his chest and breathed a sigh of relief. It felt like his heart was playing bongo drums. Elvis was correct though, it was Flake at the window. She signalled for Sanchez to wind the window down. He pressed a button on the door and wound it down a few inches to allow her to speak through the gap.

'Why are we stopping?' she shouted over the sound of hailstones.

'We're waiting for Jasmine and the Bourbon Kid,' said Sanchez. 'They're going to the hospital to get Rex, remember?'

'There's zombies appearing all over the place,' said Flake, ignoring Sanchez and trying to squeeze her face through the tiny gap at the top of the window.

'There's more of them?' Sanchez gasped. He was tempted to wind the window back up, but he had a feeling Flake wouldn't approve.

'Didn't you see them?' said Flake. 'They're climbing out of the ground all over the place! It's like there's dead bodies buried under every patch of grass.'

'There are a lot of shallow graves in this city,' Elvis reminded her.

'Yeah, thanks for that,' said Flake. 'Listen, I had an idea. Sanchez, seeing as how you're still the mayor, you could record a message on your phone warning people to stay in their homes. Send it to SMTV News. They'll broadcast it because you're the mayor. People will really appreciate it. You could save thousands of lives.'

'That's a great idea,' said Elvis. 'Gimme your phone, Sanchez. I'll film you.'

'Oh, for fuckssake,' Sanchez groaned. 'Is this really necessary?'

'Your salary is paid by the taxpayers,' said Flake. 'If they're all dead, you don't get paid.'

'Fine. I'll do a short message.'

Flake gave him a thumbs-up sign through the gap in the window. 'I'll go back and man the water cannon in case any more of these zombies attack the truck,' she yelled.

'Good luck!' said Elvis.

For the next couple of minutes, while Flake blasted holy water at anyone she saw who looked like a zombie, Elvis filmed Sanchez issuing a warning to everyone in Santa Mondega to stay indoors due to the bad weather. When it was complete, Elvis forwarded it to the local news channel.

'That wasn't bad for your first public address,' he said, handing Sanchez his phone back. 'You know, you might actually make a good mayor.'

'I'm going to be called President,' Sanchez replied. 'Mayor is a crap title.'

'Shut up,' said Elvis.

'You shut up.'

'No, I mean "SHUT UP". Can you hear that?'

'Hear what?'

'Up ahead. Turn on the wipers.'

During the time they were recording Sanchez's epic public address, the windshield had become covered in an inch of snow and ice. Sanchez pressed a few buttons before eventually finding the one that turned on the wipers. The noise Elvis was referring to was immediately obvious.

'Fucking Hell!' said Sanchez. 'The bridge is coming down!'

The bridge, a half a mile long and the only exit out of Santa Mondega was wobbling up and down like a snake doing aerobics. Deep cracks appeared all along it and then suddenly it crumbled and fell into the sea.

From the rear of the truck, Flake screamed. 'BACK UP! BACK UP!'

'What is she yelling about?' Sanchez asked Elvis.

'I think she's seen that,' said Elvis, pointing through the windshield at an enormous tidal wave that was building and barrelling its way towards them.

'We ought to back up a bit,' said Sanchez, his butt cheeks clenching. 'Any idea where the reverse gear is on this thing?'

'BACK UP!' Elvis yelled.

By the time Sanchez found the reverse gear, the huge wave had arrived. It crashed through the fencing and into the fire truck, pummelling it with sea water. The power of the giant wave pushed the truck back several metres. Lucky for Sanchez and Elvis they were inside the truck, whereas Flake had to duck into an alcove on the side, which offered minimal protection. She took a boatload of water in the face, and got soaked through to her skin. When the giant wave finally passed, the truck was still upright, but Flake was so wet it looked like her cop uniform had been tattooed on. Sanchez wound down his window and leaned out to see how she was. Hailstones from above were still pounding down on the truck, and on Flake.

'Did you see that big wave?' he shouted back to her.

She didn't reply.

'I'm gonna reverse back okay?'

Elvis slapped him on the shoulder. 'Sanchez, look at that! We've got to go. Now!'

'What the fuck now?' Sanchez groaned. 'All I ever hear is, *"Look over there, listen to this, did you hear that?"* It never ends!'

'Are you finished bitching?' Elvis asked.

'I believe I am.'

'Good, because look at that!' said Elvis, pointing at something up ahead.

Sanchez tried to see what he was pointing at, but whatever it was, it was concealed by a huge cloud of fog that was coming in from the sea and heading their way. And as fog goes, it was moving pretty quick.

'I can't see anything,' Sanchez complained. 'The fog is blocking my view.'

'Turn us around. Get away from the fog!'

'Why? What's in the fog?'

'FOG!'

'There's fog in the fog?'

Elvis grabbed Sanchez by his shirt collar and growled in a way that made Sanchez's toes twitch. 'Get us out of here, you moron!'

An awkward moment followed where both men realised Elvis had grabbed the shitty part of Sanchez's collar. It was never spoken of, but

Sanchez duly reversed the truck back to avoid riling Elvis any further. By the time he had turned it around, the fog had engulfed them.

'Have you ever seen that movie, *The Fog?*' said Sanchez. 'It's scary as fuck.'

'DRIVE!'

Sanchez checked his wing mirror. Flake was barely visible through the thick fog, but she was still manning the water cannon on the side of the truck. She was also yelling something and shaking her fist at Sanchez.

'Head for the Tapioca,' barked Elvis. 'It's the safest place because it's got that underground tunnel.'

'Got it.'

Sanchez hit the gas and drove the fire truck out of the thick white fog onto the main highway towards the city centre. The fog chased after them, never more than a bus length back.

'What the fuck happened to Jasmine and JD?' Elvis wondered aloud. 'Weren't they supposed to meet us at the bridge?'

'They should be coming from the hospital, so we might drive past them in a minute.' Sanchez suggested.

'Oh fuck. Look at that shit!'

'What shit?'

'The park. Look! Flake wasn't kidding.'

Up ahead, at the side of the road, there was a public park, the kind where old people go to sit down and throw bread at ducks. It looked like the grass in the park had been dug up. There were piles of dirt everywhere, like giant mole hills. Only these weren't created by moles. Decomposed bodies of humans were climbing out of the ground.

A violent tremor shook the truck. Sanchez struggled with the steering wheel as everything suddenly leaned to one side. Up ahead, a wide crack was developing in the middle of the road, swallowing up snow and anything else that came near it.

'Fucking FUCK!' Sanchez screamed. 'The fucking roads are snapping in half!'

'*Shit the bed*, this is bad,' said Elvis. 'Can you see Flake? Is she okay?'

Sanchez checked the wing mirror. Even though Flake was drenched in water, and hailstones were hitting her in the face the whole time, she was blasting holy water from her cannon at a bunch of zombies that were near the truck. Each one she hit burst into flames. She even managed to annihilate some zombies in the park before they finished climbing out of the ground.

Another mighty tremor made the ground beneath the truck wobble like jelly. Sanchez lost control of the steering wheel. It fizzed around so fast he couldn't get a grip on it. The truck swerved across the street and the passenger side crashed into a grey Ford Puma that was parked at the roadside.

'Keep your foot on the gas!' yelled Elvis. 'Don't stop.'

Sanchez had no intention of stopping. The fire truck dragged the Ford Puma along with it for a while until a sturdy lamppost got in the way and took out the Puma. It got left behind and swallowed up in the fog.

Elvis leaned across Sanchez to get a look in his wing mirror. 'Shit, I think Flake's cannon just ran out of water,' he said. 'Hurry the fuck up. She's a sitting duck out there!'

'That God fella is a right weasel!' Sanchez moaned. 'He's fucking stitched us up.'

'What are you talking about?'

'He hasn't given us enough holy water, the double-crossing cheapskate.'

'Keep your voice down,' said Elvis. 'I don't think God's gonna appreciate you dissing him like that.'

'What a sneaky bastard,' Sanchez ranted. 'Disguising himself as Patrick Swayze so we'd trust him. Fucking useless. Where is he now, eh? I mean, bloody Scratch is here somewhere, doing all his devil stuff. And where's God? Fucking around in a bloody bar, pretending to be a bouncer! He disgusts me.'

'Would you shut the fuck up for a minute!' Elvis yelled. 'Flake's in deep shit back there if any of these zombie things get aboard the truck. I'm gonna try to get out there to help her.

'Use the sunroof,' Sanchez suggested.

'Sunroof?'

'That thing up there.'

There was a hatch in the roof of the cab. There was no time to argue with Sanchez about whether or not it was really called a sunroof though. Elvis reached up and flipped it open. Sleet and hailstones poured in through it, along with a strong wind. Elvis climbed onto his seat and poked his head out of the hatch. Through the battering wind and hail, he saw Flake crouched down behind the water cannon. He yelled and waved at her until he caught her attention.

'FLAKE! CAN YOU GET UP HERE?' he shouted to her.

Zombies and skeletons were running towards the truck from all directions, and most of them were heading for Flake. One of them, a large male zombie in a torn grey suit, grabbed a hold of the base of her water cannon. Flake kicked out, catching the zombie in the face with her boot. It knocked him off his feet, back onto the road, where he was soon swallowed up by the cloud of fog that was chasing the truck. There were plenty more dead people closing in though, and they were all grabbing onto parts of the truck, desperately trying to climb aboard.

Elvis attempted to crawl out onto the roof, but the sheer force of the storm and the constant ground tremors throwing the truck from side to side made it impossible. The truck bounced around like a kid on an inflatable castle. One particularly sharp movement made Elvis lose his balance. He fell back inside the truck, landing beside Sanchez.

'We're fucked!' said Sanchez. 'I'm just driving over suicidal zombies. Look at them! They're throwing themselves at the truck.'

'Can you see Flake?' Elvis asked.

Sanchez checked his wing mirror again, but the fog had engulfed the back half of the truck, making it impossible to see anything. And it was moving up towards the front.

'GO FASTER!' Elvis yelled. 'If the fog overtakes us, we won't be able to see where we're going. Then we'll be totally fucked.'

Fifty Nine

Back at City Hall, the Chief of staff, Melinda Bone, was having a stressful day. Her brother Norman had been found dead in one of the building's elevators, and her mother, Yolanda had been shot and killed in the parking lot.

'This is the worst day of my life,' Melinda sobbed.

She was sitting at a desk in the dimly lit security office watching video footage of her brother's murder on a television screen on the wall. The video showed Flake leaping on his back and stabbing him to death with a letter-opener.

Melinda wiped some tears from her eyes with a hanky. The building's chief security guard, Eric, an overweight loser in an ill-fitting blue uniform, was standing over her, rubbing her back and offering words of comfort, while he slurped coffee from a paper cup. Much of the coffee ended up in his ghastly handlebar moustache.

'Oh, my poor, Norman,' Melinda sobbed. 'He was such a good man.'

'That Flake is a real bitch,' said Eric. 'Would you like to see what she did to your mother?'

Melinda nodded. 'Go on.'

Eric used a remote control to bring up some more video footage on the screen. The murder of Melinda's mom, Yolanda, had been captured on a security camera in the parking lot. Melinda watched through her fingers as the footage showed her mother accidentally reversing her car into Flake's ambulance. Eric fast-forwarded to the moment Flake showed up and shot Yolanda in the chest.

'That's enough. Turn it off,' Melinda said, weeping.

Eric tried to bring the video to an end, but he pressed an incorrect button on his remote, causing the footage to freeze on an image of Flake driving the ambulance over Yolanda's face.

'Don't worry, Melinda,' he said, pressing a few more buttons with no success. 'I'll see to it that the police are informed right away. Flake Munroe will not get away with this.'

'I don't know if I want the police involved,' Melinda sobbed.

'Why on earth not?' Eric asked.

Melinda had her reasons. Normally she wouldn't have shared them with anyone, especially not a goof like Eric, but her whole family was now dead, thanks to Flake and Sanchez, so it felt like a good time to confess.

'Eric, how would you like to earn yourself an extra fifty-thousand dollars on the side?' she asked.

'I'd love to,' Eric replied, his chubby face lighting up. He perched his ample butt on the edge of the desk, and looked into Melinda's eyes. 'What have I got to do?'

'Can you keep a secret?'

'Of course.'

Melinda looked around. The two of them were alone in the confined space of the security office. There were no windows in the room, and ironically it was one of the only areas in the building with no security cameras, so no one would see or hear what she was about to tell Eric.

'A few nights ago, I was visited by a really scary black man in a red suit. He came into my apartment through my bathroom. He said his name was Scratch.'

'You want me to track him down?' Eric asked.

'No, nothing like that. This man Scratch, he was okay. He told me about Sanchez and Flake killing Mayor Shepherd. Then he alerted me to an ancient law that stated anyone who kills the mayor must be beheaded at Mutner's farm and paraded around the streets to deter others from plotting to kill the mayor.'

'That's an actual law?'

'Yes.'

Eric took a loud slurp of coffee. 'It sounds fair, I suppose,' he said.

'I agree,' Melinda continued. 'Scratch suggested I put the law into action. Now, normally I wouldn't have had anything to do with something like this, but Scratch confirmed something else I've suspected for a long time.' She paused to dab her eyes with her hanky.

'What was it?' Eric asked.

'Do you remember my sister, Nora Bone?'

'Of course.' Eric lowered his head. 'It was tragic what happened to her.'

'It was,' Melinda agreed. 'You know, the night Nora was killed, she called me to say she had just carried out a hygiene inspection at the Tapioca. She'd finally found enough hygiene issues to shut that awful place down.'

'You think it was Sanchez and Flake who ate her alive?'

Melinda shook her head. 'No. But Scratch told me they arranged it. They paid the cannibals to kill her in order to save their horrible dive bar from being closed down.'

'That is evil,' said Eric, shaking his head. 'What's this got to do with my fifty grand pay rise?'

'Scratch gave me a suitcase filled with money to help me arrange the Mutner's Farm thing. I offered fifty thousand of it to two hitmen named Manuel and Frank. They were going to execute Sanchez at the farm, then come back and kill Flake too. But the whole thing has gone wrong. Manuel and Frank are dead, and now Flake has killed my mom and my brother!'

The emotion of the confession was overwhelming. Melinda broke down again and blew her nose into her hanky.

Eric rubbed her back and slurped some more of his coffee. 'Are you offering me the fifty grand to kill the mayor and First Lady?' he asked.

'Would you?' Melinda sobbed. 'You wouldn't be breaking the law. It's down in paper. They killed the last mayor, so they must be executed.'

'I'd love to kill Sanchez,' said Eric. 'You know that sonofabitch served me piss once when I went into his bar! I was sick for days afterwards.' The security guard got so passionate while remembering what Sanchez had done, that he squeezed his coffee cup so hard it crumpled, and the contents spilled over his hand.

'Shit! Fuck! That's hot!' he said, jumping up. He blew on his scalded hand and danced on the spot like a child that needed the bathroom.

While Melinda sobbed and Eric danced a jig, a young, dark-haired, female secretary named Alexandria burst into the security office, panting like she'd run up a flight of stairs. 'Have you seen the news?' she asked, before realising she had walked in at a bad time. 'Oh, I'm sorry, should I come back later?'

'It's okay,' said Melinda, drying her eyes with her snotty hanky. 'What's on the news?'

Alexandria closed the door behind her before replying. 'The mayor has put the city into lockdown!'

Eric stopped dancing and picked up his remote control. He pointed it at the TV and attempted to switch over to the news. After a mishap that led to them re-watching the ambulance driving back and forth over Yolanda's face a couple of times, he finally managed to switch to the local news channel. Sure enough, Mayor Sanchez Garcia was on screen in some badly recorded camera footage.

'What the hell is this?' Melinda asked. The sight of Sanchez's smug face was more than she could stomach right now.

'Listen,' said Alexandria. 'They're playing the message over and over on every channel.'

On the screen, Sanchez ordered all citizens of Santa Mondega to lock their doors and stay inside their homes or workplaces, and to avoid the streets completely.

'Does he have the authority to do that?' Eric asked.

'Don't listen to a word that man says,' said Melinda standing up. 'He's infringing the human rights of all the people in the city with this nonsense. We'll put out another message telling people they are welcome to go out into the streets, but to be careful because of the dangerous weather.'

Alexandria grimaced. 'Oh.'

'What's the matter?' Eric asked.

'It's just that, we've already secured the entire building. All exits have been locked by the central computer. We were just following the mayor's orders.'

'The mayor's a fucking idiot!' Melinda snapped at the young secretary. 'Let me out of here! I'll sort this out.'

Melinda marched past Alexandria and pulled the door open. A cacophony of noise filtered in from the corridor outside.

'What in God's name is all that shouting about?' Eric asked.

A stampede of people in the corridor outside bustled past the door, yelling and screaming a load of garbled nonsense. Melinda reached out and grabbed hold of one of them, a young Asian woman in a shiny silver suit. In spite of the woman's efforts to fight her off, Melinda dragged her into the security office.

'Gamu, what on earth is going on?' she demanded.

'Zombies!' Gamu replied, her face filled with terror. 'They're coming out of the washrooms, hundreds of them. They're eating people alive! And all the exits are locked!'

'What nonsense!' Melinda scoffed. She poked her head around the door to take another look at what was going on in the corridor. The look of scorn on her face soon vanished when the first of the zombies appeared around the corner. It was an unsightly, grey-skinned female with greasy blonde hair, dressed like a supermarket cashier. The zombie leapt onto the back of one of the stragglers, a young man Melinda knew as Donny the mail boy.

Melinda backed away and released her grip on Gamu. 'Oh my God! What *is* that thing?' she gasped.

'Told you!' said Gamu. She stamped on Melinda's foot then re-joined the fleeing herd of council workers in the corridor, running and screaming in a panic.

'I think she's right,' said Alexandria. 'Fuck this!'

The secretary sprinted out of the security office without so much as a goodbye to Melinda and Eric. Melinda slammed the door shut, muffling the sound of the horrors outside.

'Quick, lock the door!' she yelled at Eric.

Eric fumbled in his pocket for his keys. The delay was fatal. The door flew open and a zombie, dressed up to look like James Brown, burst into the room. Its eyes were drawn to Eric's chubby neck. It ran past Melinda and took a running jump at him. Before Eric had a chance to defend himself, it bit a huge chunk of flesh out of his throat. Blood squirted out all over the zombie and down Eric's shirt. Eric's knees gave way and he dropped to the floor, with the funky zombie on top of him, feasting on his ample flab.

Melinda froze, unsure what to do. She was too stunned to even scream. This was all too much. 'What's happening to the world?' she sobbed.

The answer was simple. Melinda's world was fucked. Zombies swarmed into the room. Two of them leapt on her and dragged her to the floor. A third soon joined them, and while Melinda screamed for help, the three of them began tearing at her clothes and biting any flesh that was on show.

All over Santa Mondega, similar scenes were taking place. Zombies were entering bathrooms in homes and offices, eating alive everyone they found.

Melinda suffered the same horrible fate that had befallen her sister, Nora Bone. Being eaten alive by a group of lunatics was a chilling, horrific nightmare. But for Melinda there was the added torture of the television playing Sanchez's recorded message over and over.

'Remember everyone, lock your doors and stay inside. It's the only place you'll be safe. This is your President, Sanchez Garcia speaking. Lock the doors, stay inside, and stay safe.'

Sixty

From her position on the ledge of the fire truck, Flake couldn't see shit. The thick white fog in the air and the even thicker white snow on the ground made for a terrifying experience, because every now and again the face of a skeleton or zombie would appear out of the whiteness, zooming towards her. The undead fuckers were hurling themselves at the truck, trying to climb aboard, *trying to get to her.*

With no holy water left in her cannon, she resorted to using her boots to fight the undead. When one of the skeletons grabbed a hold of one of the water cannon's legs, she kicked the sneaky fucker in the chops. It lost its grip and fell off the truck into the snow, but to Flake's irritation it bounced back onto its feet straight away and re-joined the chase, along with a bunch of other bonies. The problem with the skeletons was they had no blood, flesh or bodily organs, making it difficult to hurt the bloody things. They were quick too because none of the fuckers were overweight.

Flake heard Elvis call out her name. The fog made it hard to see him, but it sounded like he was somewhere on the roof of the cab.

'JUST KEEP GOING!' she yelled back. 'I'LL BE OKAY.'

The timing of the "I'll be okay," comment was unfortunately misjudged. A skeletal hand grabbed hold of her ankle and clung on tight. Flake wrapped her arms around the water cannon and kicked out with her other foot, catching the skeleton in the face. It didn't work out quite as well as she hoped. Her boot got wedged in its mouth, and the cheeky cunt bit down on her foot.

'Get off you little shit!' Flake screamed at it.

Matters took a turn for the worse when even more of the undead showed up. They were leaping from the upstairs windows and rooftops of the local shops and houses, trying to dive-bomb onto the truck. Many of them were dressed as dead rock stars. One of them, a possible Amy Winehouse impersonator, judging by its beehive hairstyle, leapt out of a third storey window on an apartment block and landed with a thud on the back of the fire truck.

'Fuck.'

Inside the fire truck, Sanchez was struggling to hold onto the steering wheel. Zombies were leaping onto the windshield, bouncing off it and falling under the wheels. They were coming from all directions.

'Look! They're jumping out of windows now,' said Elvis, pointing up at a high-rise building with zombies diving out of it.

'I know!' said Sanchez. 'I'm running over them like they're Eskimos.'

'What does that mean?' asked Elvis.

'I don't know. I didn't think it through.'

'Christ, we'd better think of something *fast*. Flake's a sitting duck back there.'

'Do you know what *any* of these buttons do?' Sanchez groaned, pointing at the dashboard.

'How the fuck should I know? It's your fire truck. Didn't God give you any instructions?'

'He was too busy sucking up to Flake.'

'Maybe he put some modifications in?' said Elvis. 'You know, weapons and stuff? I mean, he gave you a holy water cannon, right? Maybe there's other cool stuff in here? This could be like the car in *Knight Rider.*'

'That car was smug.'

'Smug or not, let's start pressing buttons,' said Elvis.

While Sanchez kept his foot heavy on the gas, and swerved to crush zombies, he and Elvis pressed every button and pulled every switch they could find in the truck's cab. Sanchez succeeded in turning on the hazard lights and the siren, as well as lowering the seats. Elvis had slightly more success. He pressed two buttons, one turned on the headlights, the other turned on the radio. The song, "Smack My Bitch Up" by The Prodigy blared out.

'Turn off the fucking siren!' Elvis snapped at Sanchez. 'Do you want them all to know where we are?'

Sanchez flicked the switch to turn off the siren. 'What about that thing up there?' he asked, pointing at a yellow handle above the windscreen. 'Pull that one!'

Elvis reached up and pulled the lever. It initiated the sound of some heavy-duty, metal gears grinding behind them.

'What the fuck did that do?' Elvis asked.

'I dunno,' said Sanchez. 'Just keep pressing stuff!'

Back outside, Flake was having no luck shaking off the skeleton that was trying to eat her foot. The bony bastard had succeeded in ripping both her shoes off. To add to her woes, another skeleton, a stinky, old, yellowy one with a crack down the middle of its skull, latched onto her. It grabbed a clump of material on her pants, clinging on with its bony fingers. Once it had established its grip, it started climbing up her leg. Flake had no choice but to take one hand off the water cannon to try and swat it away. Swatting with her hand had no effect, so she unclipped a can of pepper-spray from her belt. She knew it would be futile spraying the stuff at a skeleton, so she smashed the can into its face. The skeleton wrapped its teeth around the base of the can and snatched it away. It then spat the can back out and carried on climbing up her leg. No amount of leg shaking from Flake would get rid of it, and it wasn't long before it wrapped its bony fingers around her belt, which gave it more leverage to pull itself up. While the other skeleton was happy chewing Flake's foot, this bastard wanted some face.

The truck bounced over another deep hole in the road. The shudder loosened Flake's grip on the water cannon. It wasn't the best thing for her to be clinging onto anyway. She needed something higher up. With the two skeletons hanging off her, pulling her down, she reached up and grabbed a metal rail above her head. She clung onto it with both hands and dragged herself up, but at some cost. The skeleton holding onto her belt was so determined to stop her that it succeeded in pulling her soaking wet pants down to her knees.

Survival was Flake's number one priority, but even so, she was also desperate not to lose her underwear. She kicked out, which only succeeded in making her pants slide down to her ankles. But it gave her an idea. If she could shake her pants off, then the bony cling-ons would go bye-bye.

'YOU WANT MY PANTS?' she roared at the skeletons. 'YOU CAN FUCKING HAVE THEM!'

She shook her legs out of the pants. It worked. The two skeletons fell from the truck, clutching her dark blue police pants as their prize. She breathed a sigh of relief. They hadn't taken her underwear. The panties she was wearing had sentimental value. Sanchez had bought them for her on her birthday, and they had a picture of his face on the back.

She climbed up to safety on the metal rung. But, as was the way in Santa Mondega, when one problem was resolved another soon appeared. The beehived zombie appeared above her, crawling along the roof of the truck. It reached down and tried to grab a handful of Flake's hair. Flake leaned back away from the grasping, scaly hand. Before the zombie could make a second lunge, the metal rung Flake was hanging onto started moving. It rose up high above the truck and the zombies, and kept going. It climbed above the streetlamps, road signs, and in some cases, rooftops. From her new elevated position Flake was pelted even harder by the falling snow and hailstones.

As it turned out, the metal rung that she had latched onto was part of an extending long-ladder used by firemen. Someone in the driver's cab had pressed a button to extend the ladder to its full height. It kept rising, with Flake clinging onto it, hoping and praying there were no low bridges coming up. She wrapped her legs around the rungs of the ladder and held on for dear life. The dreadful weather, while less of a threat than the undead creatures trying to steal her underwear, was still a major pain in the ass. The wind was blowing hard all around her. The snow and hail pelted her all over, and occasionally the fog blinded her. Overall though, Flake had to count her blessings. The ladder had been a real stroke of luck.

'SUCK ON THAT YOU UNDEAD FUCKS!' she yelled triumphantly.

Of course, Flake had forgotten one of the other golden rules of Santa Mondega. *Never gloat, because there's always more trouble around the corner.* Her joy at escaping the undead was short-lived because one of the idiots inside the truck pressed the ladder button a second time. The ladder began retracting, lowering Flake back down towards the road and the swarms of bony shitheads that were clambering onto the truck.

Fuck!

As the hungry faces of the zombies and skeletons zoomed towards Flake, the loud roar of a car engine nearby caught her attention. The swarms of skeletons and zombies that were running alongside the truck were sent flying through the air like skittles. A black Cadillac Eldorado pulled up alongside the fire truck. And to Flake's immense relief, Jasmine poked her head out of the passenger side window.

'Hey Flake!' she yelled. 'What'cha doing?'

'I'm fucking stuck!' Flake called back as the ladder lowered her down even closer to the arms of a hungry zombie that was climbing up the truck.

'You wanna ride?' Jasmine asked.

'Yeah!'

Jasmine ducked back inside the car and a few seconds later the roof of the Cadillac began to peel back. The Bourbon Kid was driving and Jasmine was in the passenger seat. A young blonde woman in a pink bikini was sitting in the back, waving at Flake like she wanted to be friends. The weirdo.

'JUMP!' Jasmine yelled.

Flake took a deep breath and prepared herself for the life-or-death leap. What followed should have come as no surprise to her, but just as she was about to make the jump, one of the dickheads inside the truck pressed the ladder button again and she started moving up and away from the Cadillac, heading back up to the sky.

'WHAT ARE YOU DOING?' Jasmine yelled. 'DO YOU WANT A RIDE OR NOT?'

Flake made a hasty decision. Fuck it.

She jumped.

Sixty One

Flake's leap from the ladder on the fire truck coincided with a zombie that looked like Barry White, throwing itself in front of the Bourbon Kid's Cadillac. The car bounced over the big, bloated zombie, squashing it beneath the wheels. The collision knocked the Cadillac off course, deviating it away from the fire truck while Flake was in mid-air.

Jasmine yelled at Arizona in the back seat. 'CATCH HER!'

There was no time for Arizona to do anything of the sort because Flake didn't land near enough to her. She actually landed on the trunk of the car, and promptly bounced off it. Arizona stretched out her arm and managed to grab Flake's hand just before she slid off the back of the car. With hailstones pelting down on them from above, and hundreds of skeletons and zombies chasing after them, the Bourbon Kid had to keep his foot hard on the gas, and hope Arizona didn't let go of Flake's hand. Stopping the car for even one second would see them all swamped by the living dead.

'Arizona, pull her in!' Jasmine screamed.

Arizona wasn't physically equipped for holding onto a person while they dangled off the back of a moving car. In her determination not to let go of Flake, she ended up being dragged over the back seats herself, which lowered Flake far enough back that her toes were dragging through the snow.

While Arizona tried desperately not to let go of Flake, Jasmine could do very little to help because of her broken fingers. She wriggled around in her seat and managed to slide over into the back, where she dived onto Arizona's legs. She wrapped her arms around them and clung on to stop Arizona being dragged over the back of the car. At this point there was nothing to do but hope for some luck.

Out of the thick fog, another vehicle closed in behind the Cadillac. The driver beeped his horn to get their attention. Jasmine looked up. She recognised the driver and his jeep, and knew he was offering to help.

'FLAKE!' she yelled. 'AGENT SACK-WHACK IS BEHIND YOU!'

Flake was being dragged along behind the Cadillac with her bare feet zipping through the thick snow on the road. If she slid back another two inches she'd be done for. And at this point, she had no idea who Arizona was, but it was abundantly clear that the girl in the pink bikini wasn't strong enough to hold onto her for much longer.

Flake heard Jasmine shout something that ended with the words, *"Behind you!"* so she looked back over her shoulder. There was a blue, open-top jeep following them, a car length back. A young man behind the wheel was beeping his horn and yelling something at her. Whatever he was yelling, Flake was in no position to react to any of it. All her focus was on keeping her feet off the ground.

The guy in the jeep veered across the road and mowed down a couple of zombies as he mounted the kerb. From there he started driving along the sidewalk. He sped up alongside the tail end of the Cadillac, ploughing into skeletons and zombies as he went.

'Here!' the driver yelled, reaching out to Flake. 'Take my hand!'

Another shit plan! Flake was fed up with shit plans, but when were there ever any *good* plans on offer? Never, that's when.

With her free hand Flake floundered around trying to catch hold of the jeep driver's welcoming hand. After several swings and misses, she finally slapped her hand into his, just as her other hand slipped out of Arizona's grasp. The driver of the jeep had a phenomenally strong right arm, and a vice-like grip with his fingers. He hauled Flake into his open-topped jeep without any part of her touching the ground. It wasn't exactly a smooth landing though. Flake ended up face down with her head between the driver's legs and her thighs wrapped around his neck, giving him a good look at the soggy picture of Sanchez's face on her underwear.

It took some impressive wriggle work for her to reposition herself into a slightly more dignified spot, sitting on the driver's lap. From there she manoeuvred herself across to the passenger seat. Her heart was beating so fast she could hear it over the rest of the chaotic noise all around. She wiped some wet hair out of her face and checked out her surroundings. The jeep had moved off the sidewalk and was back on the tail of the Bourbon Kid's Cadillac, which was just behind the fire truck. They were finally outrunning the fog, and it looked like they had also left the majority of the undead fuckers behind.

'Fuck, thanks, man,' said Flake. 'You really saved my ass. I owe you one.'

The driver was a stocky young fella in a black shirt and grey sweatpants. His hair was covered in snow, and he had a big smile on his face.

'Hi, I'm Bradley,' he said. 'Is that Sanchez on your underwear?'

'Yeah. How do you know Sanchez?' Flake asked, weirded out by the knowledge that Bradley had been inspecting the picture on the back of her knickers while her ass had been pressed against his face.

'I'm a fan of Jasmine's,' Bradley replied. 'I recognised Sanchez from her porno video. I've seen it like a million times. I came to Santa Mondega to meet her. It's been the best day of my life, so far. Has she mentioned me? She knows me by my code name, Agent Sack-Whack.'

'Agent what?'

'Sack-Whack.'

Bradley drove the jeep over a bump in the road. It caused him to bounce up out of his seat and smash his crotch into the bottom of the steering wheel. He seemed to enjoy it.

'Is that why you're here?' Flake asked him. 'You're stalking Jasmine?'

Bradley was taken aback. 'No, I'm not a stalker. I'm just following her without her permission.'

Flake muttered the word, "psycho" under her breath then politely asked, 'Can you take me to the Tapioca?'

'Definitely. But in return could you let me have your underwear?'

'What?'

'I just love the picture of Sanchez on the back. It's *to die for.*'

'Just drive will you? *Christ!* Why does everyone in this city have to be such a fucking creep?'

'I'll give you fifty bucks for those panties, right now? And I'll give you mine in exchange.'

'I don't want your stinky underpants!'

Flake leaned across the jeep and punched Bradley hard in the groin, in the hope it would shut him up. It knocked the wind out of him and he squirmed in his seat, his head almost hitting the steering wheel.

'Owwww,' he groaned. 'That's fucking amazing.'

'What?' Flake punched him again, this time in the arm. 'Just get us out of here, you pervert!' she snapped. 'Otherwise, I'll rip your fucking nuts off!'

'Oh God,' Bradley groaned. 'This day just gets better and better.'

'Hey, you're slowing down,' said Flake, flicking his ear. 'Put your foot down! There's fucking zombies everywhere, remember?'

All the physical and verbal abuse from Flake had caused Bradley to ease off on the gas. He regained some composure and accelerated again. Up ahead, the fire truck took a right turn.

Bradley looked longingly at Flake. 'What's your name anyway?' he asked.

'Just follow the fire truck!'

'Are you a porn star too? Is that what the bottomless cop outfit is all about?'

'LOOK OUT!' Flake yelled.

Further ahead, at the roadside, a naked male zombie was standing on top of a bus shelter, just waiting for some sucker to drive past. The Bourbon Kid's Cadillac swerved away from it, but Bradley was too busy interrogating Flake to see it coming. As they drove by, the zombie leapt off the bus shelter and landed on the hood of the jeep. It reached over the windshield and grabbed a clump of Bradley's hair.

'SHIT!' he screamed. 'GET IT OFF!'

Flake had nothing to hit the zombie with. She reached over the windshield and grabbed a clump of the zombie's thick brown hair. Unfortunately, its hair was actually a wig and it came off in her hand. With valuable seconds wasted, the zombie was able to climb halfway over the windshield. From there, it leaned down, and with its mouth gaping, it bit a chunk out of Bradley's ear.

He screamed and battled frantically to push the naked zombie away, but it leaned in for another bite, this time with even greater success. It wrapped its teeth around his nose and bit into it. Bradley cried out in agony and forgot all about driving the jeep. His sole focus was to get the zombie off his face. His foot came off the gas pedal and the jeep slowed down. It swerved across the street, hitting another incoming zombie and bouncing over it. Flake leaned across the gearbox to try to push the zombie away from Bradley. She gave it a big shove on the shoulder and it lost its balance. The flesh-hungry creature slid over the side of the jeep, but refused to let go of Bradley. His side door popped open and the zombie dragged him out into the snow. Bradley could not be saved. The naked zombie was joined by more of its kind. The self-proclaimed Agent Sack-Whack became their mid afternoon snack.

Flake manoeuvred herself into the driver seat and took over the driving of the jeep. She raced after the Cadillac and the fire truck, leaving the fog and the army of the dead behind.

Sixty Two

Jasmine was out of breath. Dragging Arizona back into the car had been exhausting. But, with her new friend now safe on the back seat, she climbed back into the front next to the Bourbon Kid. She slouched back in her seat, sucking in air, and quite a few hailstones. Her arms were aching from all the pulling, and her fingers still hurt like fuck too.

Arizona was coping much better. She was kneeling on the back seat watching what was going on behind them. 'Your friend Agent Sack-Whack is dead, I think,' she called out.

Jasmine twisted around in her seat. 'What about Flake? Is she okay?'

'I think so. Sack-Whack got dragged out of the jeep by a naked zombie. I think Flake has taken over the driving.'

Arizona was proved correct when the jeep came into view again through the fog. Flake was driving, but Agent Sack-Whack was nowhere to be seen.

'It's a damn shame about Bradley,' said Jasmine. 'I liked him. He was so sweet.'

'Isn't this exciting?' said Arizona, twisting back around and poking her head between the front seats.

'We do cool shit like this all the time,' Jasmine assured her.

The Bourbon Kid suddenly yanked the steering wheel and the Cadillac swerved across the street. Arizona lost her grip on the front seats and fell into the back. The swerve also caught Jasmine out. Without a seat belt to stop her, she fell sideways, her head landing in the Bourbon Kid's lap. She looked up at him and smiled.

'Hi.'

He ignored her, and reached inside his coat. He pulled out his Headblaster gun and pointed it over the windshield. The reason for the big swerve became clear. A zombie had leapt from somewhere high up and landed on the hood of the car. It was clinging onto the windscreen wipers and trying to climb over the windshield. From her spot below, Jasmine had a good view of it. It was a grey-haired, old female in a filthy white dress. It was also the first zombie Jasmine had ever seen wearing glasses and lipstick.

The Bourbon Kid pointed his gun at the zombie's face. The barrel of the gun almost touched its nose.

BOOM!

Jasmine felt a few tiny splatters of blood land on her face. The zombie's head obliterated. Its body slid across the hood and fell off into the road. The Kid put his gun down by the side of his seat.

'Wow!' said Arizona, poking her head between the front seats again. 'This is *so* cool. Can I have a go with your gun?'

'No.'

'Can I press the button to put the roof back up then? I'm getting soaked back here.'

The Kid replied, 'Knock yourself out.'

'How do I do that?'

'Do what?'

'Knock myself out?'

The Bourbon Kid looked down at Jasmine.

'I'm sat on the roof switch, aren't I?' she said.

'Yep.'

'Hang on. I'll use my ass.'

While Jasmine tried to locate the switch with her butt, Arizona leaned across her. 'Can I turn on the ra—?'

She didn't finish the sentence. Her hand never touched the button she was reaching for on the radio. She vanished into the back of the car.

'What happened?' Jasmine asked, looking up at the Kid.

He checked his rear-view mirror. 'Skeleton's got her.'

'Can you help her?'

'I'm driving.'

'Is she okay?'

The Kid glanced in the mirror again. 'Yeah, it's just feeling her up. It's only a skeleton. It'll be good practise for her.'

'HELP ME!' Arizona screamed.

Jasmine couldn't see what was going on, but it sounded like Arizona was struggling. 'Please can you help her?'

'I can't shoot it. I'll hit her.'

Jasmine wasn't happy with the response. 'You know I can bite you from down here,' she warned him.

Without taking his eyes of the road, the Bourbon Kid reached back over the seats and grabbed hold of one of the skeleton's legs. He pulled it through the gap between the seats, which gave Arizona enough breathing space to push the bony freak's face away from her. Between the two of them, Arizona and the Kid managed to slam the skeleton into the windshield. It bounced back and its head landed on Jasmine's chest, it's horrific face staring into her eyes. It had a pink bikini top in its teeth.

'GET IT OFF ME!' Jasmine yelled.

The Kid stuck his fingers into the skeleton's eye sockets and lifted it away from Jasmine's chest. With one substantial swing of his arm he hurled the bony creature high into the air. As the car sped on, the skeleton flew past Arizona's head and bounced off the trunk before it vanished into the fog.

'Happy now?' the Kid asked Jasmine.

'Yes, thank you.'

He grabbed her head and pushed her off his lap, back into an upright position in the passenger seat. Removing Jasmine from his personal space only opened up a spot for Arizona. The topless blonde leaned through the front seats again, but this time, rather than attempting to switch on the radio, she leaned over and grabbed the Bourbon Kid's face. She twisted it towards her and planted a kiss on his lips.

'I think I'm in love with you!' she said, her eyes swelling up with affection.

'Christ.'

BEEEEEEEP!

'Hey look!' said Jasmine. 'Here comes Flake!'

The blue jeep pulled up alongside them. Flake was driving, and she looked pissed, which was hardly surprising. She had a skeleton in the back of the jeep pulling her hair. She glared at the Bourbon Kid. 'WHO THREW THIS FUCKING SKELETON AT ME?'

Jasmine yelled the answer, 'IT WAS JD! I SAW HIM DO IT!'

The jeep swerved and bumped into the side of the Cadillac, knocking Jasmine off balance again. Her face fell into Arizona's naked breasts. Before things could get any sillier, the Bourbon Kid pushed both women back into their respective seats.

Flake yelled from the jeep, 'HELP! I CAN'T SEE!'

The skeleton had wrapped Arizona's pink bikini top around Flake's head, covering her eyes. She kept her foot on the gas, but she couldn't see where she was going. Her jeep banged into the Cadillac again.

'Wow,' said Jasmine. 'This is like that race at the end of Grease, you know, when they're on Thunder Road?'

'Fuckssake,' said the Kid. He grabbed his gun again and straightened his arm across Jasmine, pointing it at the skeleton that was attacking Flake. It was a tough shot to make at high speed in a moving vehicle.

'Shoot then!' Jasmine yelled. 'What are you waiting for?'

'I can't,' the Kid replied. 'That thing's all over her.'

Arizona piped up from the back. 'Hang on. I'll help!'

Before anyone could stop her, Arizona leaned out of the back of the car and reached across into the jeep. She grabbed the skeleton by its spine and yanked it back away from Flake.

BOOM!

The Bourbon Kid didn't waste any time. One shot from the Headblaster was all it took. It knocked the skeleton's head off its shoulders. Arizona let go of it and cowered back in the Cadillac. The skeleton stopped attacking Flake. Its headless body crumpled into the back of the jeep. Flake peeled the pink bikini off her face and threw it over her head. It vanished into the fog.

'My bikini top!' cried Arizona. 'Can we go back for it?'

'No.'

Flake yelled across to Jasmine. 'HEAD FOR THE TAPIOCA!'

Arizona tapped the Bourbon Kid on the shoulder. 'Seriously, can we put the roof back up?' she asked. 'It's really nippy back here.'

While the Bourbon Kid put the roof back up on the Cadillac, Flake sped on ahead in her jeep and pulled up alongside the fire truck. She yelled some instructions at Elvis and Sanchez, then hit the gas again and sped off into the distance. That jeep sure could move. With the roof of the Cadillac back up, the Bourbon Kid put his foot down and overtook the fire truck too. Jasmine waved to Elvis as they went past.

Inside the fire truck, Sanchez was singing along to the song, "Drive" by The Cars. It was getting on Elvis's nerves.

'Can't you go any faster?' Elvis complained.

'It's not my fault,' Sanchez replied. 'This thing's fucking shit. God's given us a rubbish fire truck. I bet it's second hand.'

'Quit bitching. Just drive *faster!*'

'Who's that in the back of the Cadillac?' Sanchez asked, pointing up ahead at the Caddy which was rapidly vanishing from sight.

'I don't know,' Elvis replied. 'But she had great tits.'

'What?'

A flash of bright golden light fizzed down from the sky. Before Elvis could yell, "LOOK OUT!" the bolt of electricity struck the front of the fire truck. It made an almighty bang. The truck's engine cut out and Sanchez lost control of the steering wheel. The truck veered across the road and crashed into a lamp post on the other side. Elvis was jolted forward. His head thudded against the windshield. The glass was solid and didn't break, but he felt the full force of it. He slumped back into his seat and looked over at Sanchez who had just suffered the same fate, but had a fatter head that softened the impact.

Sanchez blinked a few times and rubbed his forehead. 'What the fuck was that?'

Elvis wiped some moisture from his face. Blood trickled down from just below his hairline. 'I think we just got hit by lightning,' he said.

'What are we gonna do?' Sanchez asked, panicking.

A sea of fog engulfed the fire truck, accompanied by the sound of cackling skeletons and groaning zombies closing in from all sides.

Elvis wiped some blood from his face. 'We're gonna have to get out and run.'

Sixty Three

It had been a long time since Scratch had taken part in a massacre. It was exhilarating, finally letting loose, unleashing all that pent up frustration. The city of Santa Mondega had seen some massacres in its time, but this was on an entirely different level. It baffled Scratch how anyone would want to live in this shithole city. Murder capital of the world, rife with the undead for centuries. What did anyone see in the place? He actually knew the answer. It was low taxes that attracted the wealthy, and a bungling police force with a low conviction rate that brought the criminals in.

There was all kinds of chaos going on in the streets below Waxwork Tower. Scratch couldn't see any of it though because he'd covered the whole city in thick fog. Bloody fog. Fog was cool and it no doubt scared a load of people, but it was also ruining his view of the carnage he had created.

He stood by the edge of the roof and gazed up at the sky once again. This time he closed his hands. The red glow in his stomach dimmed. The hail and snow that had been pelting down from above, gradually slowed and fizzled out. Over the course of several minutes, the fog beneath him gently dissipated, revealing a better view of the streets. It brought a smile to Scratch's face. The streets were still covered in snow, but now the snow was decorated with streaks of blood. Dotted all around were crashed cars, dead bodies, zombies feasting on the dead bodies, and skeletons roaming the streets aimlessly. Skeletons weren't such a great idea after all, he decided. They looked cool, and they were scary and stuff, but in actuality they didn't really do anything. They were incapable of actually eating anything, and unless they were armed with knives, they didn't do a lot of damage either. Mostly, it was all about biting and poking people. The zombies though, *they were good.* Lean, fast, hideous, ugly killing machines. And some of them had fun clothes. Quite a few of them had originally been contestants in the *Back From the Dead* show at the Hotel Pasadena in the Devil's Graveyard. Scratch normally only allowed them out of the desert once a year on Halloween. But this was a special occasion, and zombies are allowed out on special occasions. It's in the rules.

He scoured the city for any sign of the Dead Hunters. To anyone who didn't know them, it would be like looking for a needle in a haystack, but for Scratch it was simpler than that. He knew the Dead Hunters always left a trail of destruction in their wake. All he had to do was locate the trail.

And there it was. The fire truck. The one Sanchez and Flake had used to help Elvis escape from Waxwork Tower. It was a mile away, but from his heightened position Scratch saw it as clear as day. The truck had crashed into a lamp post. Zombies were swarming all over it. Scratch could tell from the truck's location what its intended destination was. The Tapioca was only a few blocks away from the crash site. Those stupid Dead Hunter fools were heading to the Tapioca, the most obvious place they could have gone. So obvious that Scratch hadn't even considered it, until now.

Once more he raised his hands to the skies and opened them, showing his palms. The Eye of the Moon glowed bright red inside him, reacting with the environment. Down below in the streets, the zombies and skeletons that were swarming over the fire truck, abandoned it and began streaming towards the Tapioca. They weren't the only ones. Thousands more of the undead felt the telepathic message from Scratch. It was a joy to behold watching them heading in their droves for the Tapioca. There was only one thing left for Scratch to do. Join them.

He stepped up to the edge of the Waxwork Tower rooftop and launched himself off it. It felt glorious, floating through the cold air. The power of the Eye allowed him to control his descent to the street below. He floated down like a butterfly, landing on the snow-covered sidewalk with gentle grace, like any great supervillain. Gentle though the landing was, the impact of his feet hitting the ground sent a tremor all around the city. Power was a wonderful thing.

The roads quivered and quaked. The houses shook. The high-rise buildings wobbled. The whole thing was glorious. All Scratch needed now was a ride to the Tapioca. It duly arrived in the shape of a black pickup truck that was speeding along the crumbling street. As the vehicle neared him, Scratch stepped off the sidewalk, into its path. He raised his hand, aiming his palm at the truck. The engine on the truck cut out, and to the driver's dismay, it slid gently to a stop in front of Scratch. The Devil walked around to the passenger side, opened the door and climbed in.

The driver of the pickup was a guy in his early fifties, wearing a thick black and green checked coat and a red beaver hat. He had a flappy turkey-neck, and black circles under his eyes. He scowled at Scratch. 'Who the fuck do you think you are?'

Scratch wasn't supposed to be killing innocent people because God had enforced all kinds of petulant, joyless rules upon him over the centuries. But he noticed the driver of the truck had a shotgun tucked in a compartment inside his door. If he could just coax the idiot into reaching for it, he could kill him and claim self-defence. Or better still, just kill him anyway. After all, it felt like a good time to remind everyone that he was *the fucking Devil,* and he could do what he fucking pleased.

'I am Satan, Prince of Darkness, Lord of Evil, Ruler of Demons, Father of Lies, Iblis, Lucifer, and Deceiver of the whole world,' he said in response to the other man's stupid, *"Who the fuck do you think you are?"* question.

The moron reached for his shotgun, fully intending to blast Scratch in the face with it. Unfortunately, by the time he turned it on his unwanted passenger, his time was up. Scratch struck him in the head and chest with a blast of raging hot, red fire from the palm of his hand. The flames burned the skin off the man's stupid, saggy face. He screamed and flailed around like a blind person being stung by a swarm of bees.

'Hurts like a motherfucker, doesn't it?' said Scratch. 'I'd say your best bet is to get out of my new pickup and bury yourself in the snow. Try it.'

The truck driver opened his door and hurled himself out into the street. There was a loud hiss as the fire on his head hit the snow.

'Thanks ever so much,' said Scratch as he squeezed into the driver's seat and restarted the engine. 'See you again soon!'

He hit the gas and left the truck's previous owner burning and writhing in agony in the snow. He switched on the radio. "Lorca's Novena" by The Pogues came on. Perfect. Scratch headed for the Tapioca with the images of his enemies flashing through his mind.

Look out, Dead Hunters. The Devil cometh.

Sixty Four

Flake noticed a lot less zombies on the streets as she neared the Tapioca. She steered the jeep around a corner into a backstreet and cruised up to the Tapioca's rear entrance. There was enough room for three cars to park out back. Flake drove into the spot normally reserved for Sanchez's ambulance. A few seconds later the Bourbon Kid's Cadillac pulled in alongside her. So far, no sign of any zombies.

The Bourbon Kid was out of his car in double-quick time. He ran up to the Tapioca's back door before Flake had set foot out of the jeep.

'Have you got a key to get in?' he called out to her.

'I lost them. They were in my pants.'

CRASH!

Problem solved.

Flake wasn't exactly chuffed that he'd smashed her back door in, but in the circumstances he'd had no other choice. She hopped out of the jeep and ran up to the busted door. She peered inside. The Kid had already passed through the kitchen into the bar area.

'Wait for us!' Jasmine called out.

Flake held the knackered door open for Jasmine and her young friend in the pink bikini bottoms. Once they were all inside, Flake closed the broken door and wedged a chair against the handle in an effort to stop any zombies from getting in.

The kitchen was untidy. Flake had been cooking a breakfast when she'd last been in it. There was a tray of cold breakfast items on a long metal table in the middle of the room.

'Help yourselves to some food,' she said to the others. She grabbed a hash brown for herself and took a bite. It was cold, but edible.

'Where did JD go?' Jasmine asked.

'He went through to the bar,' Flake replied. She caught sight of Jasmine's messed up fingers. 'What the fuck happened to your hands?'

'Those guys who kidnapped us did it. Broke all my fingers, one after the other.'

The topless blonde chipped in. 'They took turns jizzing on my feet too.'

'I'm sorry,' said Flake. 'Who are you exactly?'

'I'm Arizona,' said the blonde girl, as she picked up a slice of bacon and a sausage from the table. 'I held onto you when you were falling off the back of the car just now, remember?'

'Yes, I remember that, thanks. I just wondered how come you ended up with us?'

'I was a prisoner in the back of the Bastard truck.'

'Bastard truck?'

'Yeah, you know the three guys who kidnapped us all,' Arizona replied, while she fed a sausage to Jasmine. 'They were Bastards.'

'Oh, them. What happened to them?'

'They're dead,' said Jasmine. 'Very, *very* dead.'

'You guys are my heroes,' Arizona said, talking with a mouthful of bacon. 'I gotta tell you Flake, I was so happy when the Bastards threw you out of the truck into moving traffic.'

'Excuse me?'

'Because I knew you'd send help. And I was so excited when the Bourbon Kid showed up. He killed all three of the Bastards. He blew one guy's head off with his gun, then he shot another one's leg off, and—'

Arizona's rambling monologue was mercifully cut short when a severed head flew past her face and smashed into a fridge behind her. It came from the bar area.

'That's quite an entrance,' Jasmine said, almost choking on the piece of sausage she was chewing.

The head belonged to a male zombie. Blood was oozing out of its neck onto the floor. Its lifeless eyes gawped at Flake.

'Where did his body go?' Arizona asked.

'Stay here,' said Flake. 'I'll go find out.' She grabbed a saucepan from a hook on the wall and ran through to the bar area.

'We should go too,' said Jasmine. 'Grab me another sausage.'

In the bar area, the Bourbon Kid had encountered three zombies. The first, a female in a yellow tracksuit, was on the floor with a chair leg rammed down her throat. She was twitching a little, but she was as good as dead. The second zombie, a skinny male in red overalls, was staggering around the bar area with a knife wedged into its eye. There was blood all over its face and it couldn't really see where it was going. It tripped over an upside down table and landed face down on the floor, pushing the knife further into its eye until the tip of the blade poked out through the back of its skull.

Zombie number three was a big fucker, an eighteen-stone male blob with no hair, wearing just a pair of white underpants. The Kid stepped up and punched it in the face. The zombie took it like a champ, then with surprising dexterity it grabbed the Kid's arm and bit down on his fist, drawing blood.

Flake opened up the hatch on the bar and rushed through it, her saucepan primed and ready for action. The Kid held up his good hand, ordering her to stay put. It soon became obvious why.

The zombie made no attempt to attack again. It had tasted some of the Bourbon Kid's blood, and was not enjoying it. It started quivering, as if it were having a fit. As Flake stood by with her saucepan raised, the zombie started shaking its head violently, and its stomach made a loud gurgling sound.

SPLAT!

The zombie exploded, spraying blood and guts over everyone, and all over the walls and furniture. Some of the flaming guts landed on the other zombies on the floor. As soon as it hit them, they lit up in flames. A second or two later, they blew up too, spraying blood and guts in all directions. The Tapioca had rarely looked worse. Zombie guts were all over everything, and the stink was horrendous.

Flake lowered her saucepan and wiped some dead zombie guts off her face and shoulders. 'What the fuck just happened?' she asked, spitting some goo onto the floor.

Arizona and Jasmine were standing behind the bar. They too were caked in zombie guts. Arizona peered over the bar at the mess on the floor. 'Wow!' she said. 'Why did they melt?'

The Bourbon Kid flicked some zombie innards off his shoulder, and waggled the fingers on his injured hand to make sure they still worked. 'Holy blood,' he said eventually. 'Zombies can't live with holy blood. Vampires can, but zombies, they just blow the fuck up.'

'Can somebody clean me up?' Jasmine asked.

Arizona was happy to oblige. She gently stroked some zombie blood away from Jasmine's eyes and mouth.

'I think I need a shower,' Jasmine whined. 'But my hands are fucked.'

'I'll help,' said Arizona with great enthusiasm. 'I need a shower too. I'll wash us both.'

'Aww, would you?' said Jasmine. 'That's really sweet of you.'

'We're not really supposed to use the bathrooms,' Flake reminded them. 'That's probably how these zombies got in here. You'll have to make do with water from the kitchen.'

Jasmine groaned. 'But I've got zombie ass in my hair, and it's sliding down into my catsuit.'

Arizona ducked down below the bar, only to resurface a few seconds later holding a soda gun. 'This thing sprays water doesn't it?' she said.

'It does,' said Flake. 'But it'll be cold.'

'I don't mind that,' said Jasmine, her eyes lighting up. 'Quick, strip me off and wash me down.'

Arizona unzipped Jasmine's catsuit and carefully pulled her arms out of it. It made Jasmine squeal in pain a few times as her fingers caught on it, but once her arms were free, Arizona pulled the catsuit down to her feet and helped her step out of it.

'Of course, you've got to be completely naked,' Flake said, shaking her head.

Arizona missed the sarcasm in Flake's voice and took it as an instruction. She peeled her pink bikini bottoms off and then switched on the soda gun. She sprayed cold water over Jasmine's face to begin with, but when Jasmine protested at how cold it was she sprayed it in her own face to make sure. The pair of them started giggling.

'Do me again!' Jasmine cried.

Arizona turned the soda gun onto Jasmine's boobs. The screaming and giggling got worse.

'Great,' said Flake, rolling her eyes. 'All we need now is a camera crew and some dodgy music!'

The Bourbon Kid walked over to the bar's jukebox and kicked it with the toe of his boot. The song "Love Muscle" by The Sex O'Rama Band came on.

Jasmine waved at Flake with her fucked up hands. 'Come and join us!' she cried. 'This is great fun.'

Flake was conscious of the fact she was already dressed for porn. Her police officer shirt was stuck to her because it was so wet, and her underwear was so damp it was practically see-through. It was time to find somewhere private to clean up.

With the washrooms not an option, Flake returned to the kitchen. She grabbed some paper towels from a dispenser on the wall and wiped as much of the zombie guts off her face and legs as she could. She dumped the soiled towels in the trash and turned on the faucet above the sink. She grabbed some soap and started washing the stench off her hands and face. After a short while, the Bourbon Kid came out to the kitchen to join her. He ripped some paper towels from the dispenser and started wiping the blood and guts from his face.

'Do you need that hand bandaged up?' Flake asked him.

'It'll heal up on its own in a minute.'

'Holy blood,' said Flake. 'You're so lucky.'

'Yeah.'

Flake unbuttoned her shirt and peeled it off. It was drenched in rainwater, snow and zombie blood. She rolled it up and squeezed it out over the sink. In normal circumstances she wouldn't strip down to her bra and underwear in front of anyone other than Sanchez, but these were unusual times. She reached up to a cupboard above the sink and grabbed a roll of bandage tape. While the Kid was still wiping his face with paper towels, she walked over to him and grabbed his injured hand. It caught him by surprise, but she took a firm hold of his hand and wrapped some bandage around the injury.

'It's really not necessary,' he said.

'I know, but I just want you to know that, well, y'know, the stuff I said earlier about you being a dick, and not caring about anyone else, I didn't mean it.'

'Yeah, you did.'

Flake smiled at him. 'Okay, maybe I did at the time.'

He almost smiled back.

The sound of Jasmine and Arizona giggling in the bar area floated into the kitchen. Flake nodded at the doorway to the bar. 'Wouldn't you rather be in there watching the soft porn show?' she asked.

'I like it better out here. Sometimes it's good to take a break from the insanity.'

Flake looked through the doorway into the bar area. 'Shouldn't Sanchez and Elvis be here by now? And what happened to Rex? I thought you were picking him up from the hospital?'

'That whole part of town was covered in fog,' the Kid replied. 'But I wouldn't worry about Rex, he'll be okay.'

'We should go find him.'

'Flake, stop worrying. When the others get here, we'll all go find Rex together. No more splitting up.'

Flake finished bandaging up his hand and stepped back to admire her handiwork. 'You'll survive,' she said.

'So will you.'

Their private moment was interrupted when Jasmine walked in and stood in the doorway, naked and soaking wet. 'Flake, have you got a frying pan and a dildo I could borrow?'

Flake blushed. 'What makes you think I've got one of those?'

'I've seen you use it.'

'You what?' Flake turned an even darker shade of red. 'I don't even own one,' she muttered, embarrassed that the conversation was taking place in front of the Bourbon Kid.

'Yes you do,' said Jasmine. 'You cook Sanchez a fried breakfast in it every morning.'

Flake let out a deep sigh. 'Oh, the frying pan. Yeah, I've got one of those.'

'And a dildo?'

'No! I don't have one. And this really isn't the time.'

A naked Arizona appeared in the doorway next to Jasmine. She was holding up Jasmine's phone. 'I just took a call from Sanchez,' she said.

'Where is he?' Flake asked.

'He says the fire truck broke down.'

'Oh, for fuckssake! Where are they?'

'He says they made a run for it, but now they're stuck in a sex shop.'

'A sex shop?' Jasmine flashed a smile. 'Perfect. He can get me a dildo.'

The Bourbon Kid rolled his eyes. 'What do you need a dildo for at a time like this?'

'I was thinking you could strap it to me.'

'What?'

Jasmine held up her crippled hands. 'You could put a frying pan in one hand and a dildo in the other. Wrap tape around them to strap them into my hands. Then I can use them as weapons!'

Flake decided the dildo discussion should come to an end. She grabbed the Bourbon Kid's arm. 'We should go and get Sanchez and Elvis. They're probably in Jack and Jizz. It's the only sex shop in the neighbourhood. At least, that's what I've heard.'

The Bourbon Kid wiped a speck of blood from Flake's cheek. 'I'll go. You stay here.'

'I'll come too.'

'You're not dressed for it,' he reminded her. 'And these two can't look after themselves. You're gonna have to hang back here in case any more zombies break in. And don't forget, stay away from the bathrooms. I'll be back in five.'

Sixty Five

Sanchez and Elvis bailed out of the fire truck and made a run for it. Elvis led the way, not by design, but simply because he was fitter and quicker than Sanchez. He ducked into a side alley with Sanchez close behind, wheezing like an accordion. Elvis knew the area well and headed straight for a wooden door in the side of the alley between two big yellow dumpsters. After testing the door's strength with a shoulder barge, he stepped back and kicked it as hard as he could with the heel of his boot. The lock shattered and the door swung open, revealing a dark corridor behind it. Sanchez finally caught up, but before he could start moaning about all the running, Elvis pushed him inside and then pulled one of the dumpsters across the doorway as a token effort to hide the entrance from any zombies that might be on their tail. He closed the door and joined Sanchez in the creepy corridor. The place was deathly quiet, which was promising.

Sanchez flicked on a light switch. An eery red light lit up the corridor.

'What is this place?' Elvis asked. As his eyes became accustomed to the red light he saw the walls all around them were painted black.

'We're in Jack and Jizz,' said Sanchez, looking around.

'The sex shop?' said Elvis. 'I've never been in here before.'

'Me neither.'

Sanchez hurried on up to a door at the end of the corridor. He pushed it open and stepped into the shop's customer area. It was filled with interesting clothing, toys and gadgets. The windows on the shop front were tinted black, meaning no one outside could see in. It was the perfect place to hide.

'Is there a back entrance in here?' Elvis asked.

'Didn't we just come in the back entrance?'

'Hmm, I guess we did.'

'Did you hear that?'

'What?'

'That.'

Back out in the alleyway, someone, or some*thing* was trying to move the dumpster that Elvis had used to block off access to the door.

'You got a phone on you?' Elvis asked.

'Yeah, why?'

'Make some calls. Get us out of here.'

'Right.'

'While you're on the phone, you can keep an eye on the back door. I'll stay here and look for some weapons.'

'Weapons? In here?' asked Sanchez.

'This place could be a gold mine.'

While Sanchez returned to the black corridor, Elvis started hunting around in the shop's front rooms for anything that could be useful in a fight. There were numerous sex toys around but none of them looked like they could do much damage to a zombie without getting up close, *intimately close*. Just when he was about to give up looking, something caught his eye on a shelf behind the counter. He used a small step-ladder to get to it. The gadget was inside a large rectangular box. He lifted it from the shelf and placed it down on the counter. It was exactly what he was looking for. He dusted off the box and lifted the lid. Inside was a powerful heavy-duty drilling device with a handful of interesting attachments. The best option for fighting zombies had to be the rubber fist attachment. Elvis picked up the drill and screwed the fist onto the end of it. It looked impressive. He fired up the drill and was surprised by how powerful it was. It made a loud buzzing noise and vibrated in Elvis's hand, making him shake too. It was very difficult to hold on to.

'What are you doing?'

Elvis hadn't seen Sanchez sneak back in. He turned around and showed Sanchez the formidable gadget that was vibrating in his hands. 'Uh, I just found this, and I thought it might make a good weapon,' he said, truthfully.

Sanchez's eyes lit up. 'Is that *The Anal Intruder?*'

'Yeah.'

'From the movie, *Top Secret?*'

'Yep. Wanna try it?'

'What?'

'I mean, do you wanna hold it?'

Sanchez stared at the jabbing fist on the end of the drill. 'Err, no. It's okay. You keep it. I just called Jasmine's phone and spoke to Arizona again.'

'Arizona?' said Elvis, a look of realisation on his face. 'Was she the girl in the back of the Cadillac, with the great tits?'

'I didn't ask.'

'That's too bad. Why does she keep answering Jasmine's phone anyway?'

'I didn't ask that either. But she talks at a million miles an hour. If I heard her correctly, she's sending someone to come and pick us up.'

'Thank fuck for that.'

Sanchez slipped his hand into his pocket and started fiddling around.

'What the fuck are you doing?' Elvis asked.

'I just got a text.' Sanchez pulled his phone out and checked the message. 'It says the Bourbon Kid is on his way, and also can you grab a couple of sexy outfits for Jasmine and Arizona?'

'Okay.'

'And a dildo.'

'What?'

'It says they want a dildo as well as two outfits.'

'I guess the dildo must be for Flake?' said Elvis.

'Why would you say that?'

'No reason.' Elvis put the Anal Intruder down on the counter and looked around. 'Any idea where the sexy outfits are in this place?'

'Back room, far corner,' Sanchez replied. 'Just past the Gimp masks.'

'Right.' Elvis considered leaving the Intruder behind but sensed Sanchez would do something stupid with it, so he took it with him.

'I guess it's up to me to grab the dildo then?' Sanchez called after him.

'Yeah, be quick.'

Elvis found the sexy outfits exactly where Sanchez said they would be. With time in short supply he grabbed a naughty nurse outfit and a dark blue catsuit that looked like it would fit Jasmine. He slung them over his shoulder and headed back to the front of the store. Sanchez was waiting for him, holding a large brown carrier bag. He opened it up for Elvis to place the clothes in. At the bottom of the bag was a box containing a dildo. Elvis shoved the clothes in on top of it.

'Okay, so now what?' Sanchez asked. 'I guess we just wait in here?'

The answer was emphatic, although it didn't come from Elvis.

BOOM!

The door at the front of the store was blown off its hinges by a blast from the Bourbon Kid's gun. A sliver of light from a nearby streetlamp breezed into the store. It had stopped snowing outside, and the fog had almost cleared, but it was still dark. Elvis ventured over to the open doorway. The Bourbon Kid's Cadillac was parked outside in the snow.

Sanchez barged past and hurried outside, carrying the bag of goodies. As he stepped out onto the slippery sidewalk he was clattered into by a passing zombie who hadn't even seen him. The impact of the collision knocked Sanchez over. He dropped his bag and landed on his ass in the cold, wet snow. The zombie landed nearby, but it sprung back up straight away, its eyes set on Sanchez. It was a naked, middle-aged male, covered in blood and filth. It eyed up Sanchez for its next meal. It stood over him showing off its rotting teeth and black tongue. Sanchez lay still in the snow, working on the assumption that the Bourbon Kid would blow the zombie's head off. But that didn't happen.

It was the Anal Intruder that came to the rescue.

Elvis stepped out onto the sidewalk with the formidable sex device in his hands, primed and ready for optimal fisting. He smashed the zombie in the chops with it. The rubber fist pummelled the surprised creature, repeatedly hitting it in the mouth. The ferocious fisting inflicted upon the zombie gave Sanchez enough time to pull himself together, gather up his big sex bag, and crawl across the sidewalk into the back of the Bourbon Kid's car.

When Elvis's attack on the zombie came to a shuddering climax, he left the battered creature spreadeagled in the snow, and jumped into the front seat with his new toy still vibrating.

The Bourbon Kid hit the gas and pulled out into the street. There were zombies everywhere, but they were all running away from the Cadillac.

'Look at them all running away!' said Sanchez, jeering.

The Bourbon Kid sped up and drove the Cadillac into the back of a gang of the undead fuckers who were sprinting down the middle of the street. A few of them fell under the wheels, squealing like pigs as they were crushed. It caused the Cadillac to bounce up and down like a pimp's car as it bulldozed its way down the street.

'That serves 'em right for ignoring the highway code,' Sanchez commented from the back seat. 'Look at 'em go. Cowards!'

'I'll tell you something,' said Elvis, while he tried to find the OFF switch on the Anal Intruder. 'They're not running from us. They're heading for the Tapioca.'

Sanchez's phone buzzed in his pocket again. 'I've got another text,' he groaned, feeling around in his pants for the phone. He retrieved it and read the message. 'Bad news!' he shouted.

'What is it?' asked Elvis.

'Scratch is at the Tapioca.'

Sixty Six

When Scratch pulled up outside the Tapioca in his new black pickup, the place was already swarming with zombies and skeletons. They had ripped the front door off its hinges, which allowed Scratch the luxury of exiting his vehicle and strolling in unannounced.

Inside, the zombies were running amok, looking for any living creatures to feed on. All around the drinking area, tables and chairs were overturned. Scratch took a moment to soak in the sights, looking for any sign of the Bourbon Kid or his friends. The first thing to catch his eye was a tattered yellow tracksuit laid on the floor, burned at the edges and covered in zombie remains. Not far from it, the mashed entrails of another zombie were splayed across the floor. Steam was escaping from its sludgy remains, floating up to the ceiling where a propellor fan covered in zombie gloop was wobbling around on its axis. This had to be the work of the Bourbon Kid. And it was recent.

Scratch walked around the bar and headed into the kitchen. It was filled with zombies sniffing around for flesh. There were trays of breakfast food on a metal table in the middle of the room. The zombies weren't interested in that kind of stuff. It was high quality food too. The kind Scratch would normally associate with Flake. The sort of stuff she cooked for Sanchez every day.

Upon further inspection of the area, he noticed the kitchen sink was half-filled with water, and there were bloodied paper towels dotted around the place. A roll of bandage tape was left on a sideboard too. But most telling of all, to a detective like Scratch, was the back door. Its lock was busted, and someone had wedged a chair against it to prevent anyone from getting in.

'They're still here,' Scratch whispered aloud. 'But where?'

He returned to the bar area with the intention of checking upstairs, but as he approached the staircase, he noticed an excess of water on the floor behind the bar.

"What has happened here?" he asked himself.

Looking around for more clues, he saw one of the zombies, a young male in a green vest and shorts, sitting on the floor in the bar area. While the others were looking for food, this idiot was sniffing a pair of pink bikini bottoms. Scratch stood still and scoured the area for more out-of-place items. He found one under the bar, tucked into a shelf of empty glasses. A purple catsuit. It had to be Jasmine's. Scratch pulled it out and sniffed it. He recognised Jasmine's scent.

"This catsuit has only recently been discarded."

Scratch was puzzled. As far as he knew, Jasmine had been snatched by the Bastard Brothers, hadn't she? If that was the case, then how was her catsuit back in the Tapioca, smelling like she'd been wearing it only minutes ago? Those dumb fucks! *The three Bastards must have fucked up their one and only job!* Scratch pulled out his phone and made a call to Vegas Bastard. No answer. He made another call, this time to Alexis Calhoon. She answered after one ring.

'Hello,' she said.

'Bastard brothers. What's happened to them?'

'Last I heard, they'd captured Jasmine. I've heard nothing from them since.'

'Assholes. What about your other guy, Falco someone?'

'Falco Logan. I haven't heard a word from him, which is normal, but I was able to trace his phone. He's just arrived in Santa Mondega.'

'Good. Find out what happened to the Bastard brothers and call me back.'

Scratch ended the call without another word. Was it really possible that his army of bounty hunters and assassins had failed to kill or capture *any* of the Dead Hunters? *Useless fucks.*

He turned away from the bar and bounded up the stairs, taking them two at a time and barging some zombies aside on his way up. The rooms in the upper level were all unoccupied. He stormed from room to room, trashing everything, rummaging through cupboards and closets, desperately looking for anyone hiding. He found nothing. The upper floor showed no sign of any recent activity. If anyone was still in the Tapioca they were most definitely downstairs.

He descended the stairs kicking a few zombies on the way to make himself feel better. He arrived behind the bar and looked around again for something he might have missed. All he could see were upturned tables and chairs, clothes on the floor, blood and water everywhere, and dead zombies.

DAMN IT!

He needed some alcohol to calm himself down, help him think. He grabbed a bottle of liquor from a shelf under the bar, flipped the lid off it and took a swig.

He retched and quickly spat it out, his eyes bulging.

It was piss.

'FUCKING SANCHEZ!'

He hurled the bottle across the drinking area. It smashed against the wall next to the Disabled toilets and splintered onto the floor along with the warm piss. Steam hissed back up from the floor, floating up to the ceiling.

Of course! The washrooms! Scratch marched over to the Disabled toilet and pushed the door open. *Empty*. The men's toilets. Smelly, but also empty. And so to the Ladies toilets. He burst through the door and kicked open all of the stall doors. Nothing. There was no one home. No one in the Tapioca. Except there was. *He knew there was*. But where? Where the fuck were they hiding?

He marched out into the drinking area again.

And there it was. The clue he was looking for. Handprints on the floor. Wet handprints, next to wet footprints. The footprints could have easily been dismissed as belonging to the zombies, but not the handprints. The zombies weren't touching the floor with their hands. This was something else. The handprints were bunched together and they belonged to more than one person. He crouched down and ran his hand around the floor. Amidst all the dirt and crap that usually existed on the floor of a bar, there was an outline of a square imprinted in the dust. Scratch dug one of his long fingernails into the outline. His nail sunk into the floor.

Trapdoor!

Sneaky fuckers.

He lifted up the hatch and flung it open. There was a metal-runged ladder built into the wall below, leading down to a tunnel. Scratch knew right away where the tunnel ended. Papshmir's church. It explained how Janis had evaded capture earlier in the day. Well, he'd gotten her in the end, and he would soon get all the others too.

He stood up, put his fingers in his mouth and whistled loudly. The zombies that were roaming aimlessly around the bar area all stopped and looked at him. Scratch pointed into the tunnel. His undead servants instinctively knew what he meant. They swarmed over to the hole in the floor and began climbing down into it.

Scratch had no intention of joining them. Messing around in a dark tunnel was for fools. There were quicker ways to get to the church. He headed for the exit and hopped into his new pickup truck.

Sixty Seven

The secret underground tunnel that ran from the Tapioca to the church of Saint Ursula was cold and damp. It was also unlit, so the three women were in total darkness as they travelled along it.

A few minutes earlier everything had been going fine. Jasmine and Arizona were having a cold shower and Flake was eating Sanchez's breakfast. But then half the zombie population showed up at the Tapioca. A hasty escape had to be made. The tunnel was the only option. Flake allowed Jasmine and Arizona to climb in first. Jasmine couldn't use her hands so she hitched a ride on Arizona's back, making the whole thing take much longer than it should have. By the time Flake stepped onto the ladder, the zombies were almost done kicking the front door in. If that wasn't bad enough, just as she lowered the hatch down above her head she saw Scratch pull up outside in a pickup truck.

Once they were in the tunnel, it was Flake who had to lead the way because she wasn't afraid of spiders. Jasmine and Arizona kept close behind her. Arizona kept giggling while she sent texts to Sanchez to let him know what was going on. And Jasmine kept bumping into the back of Flake and complaining that she'd hurt her fingers.

'Christ, would you be quiet!' Flake hissed at the other two. 'Scratch is going to find this tunnel sooner or later, and I gotta tell you, I'd rather it was later!'

'Jeez, what's with her?' Arizona whispered, loud enough for Flake to hear it.

There was no point in getting into an argument, so Flake bit her tongue and carried on. When they reached the other end of the tunnel, she climbed a set of metal rungs in the wall up to another trapdoor. She pushed it open while the others waited below.

'Can you see anything?' Arizona called up to her.

Flake poked her head out through the hatch and looked around. Judging by the size of the room, and the desk and chairs nearby, she guessed it was Papshmir's private study. No zombies. That was a promising sign. Flake cocked her ear and listened. Peace and quiet. Just what she was looking for.

'Is it safe?' Jasmine whispered up from the bottom of the ladder.

'It looks like it. I'm in Papshmir's study. There's no one here.'

'We just got a text,' Arizona whispered.

'What does it say?' Flake asked, doing her best to keep her voice down.

'It's from Sanchez. He says they're coming straight to the church to meet us.'

'Great.'

Flake climbed through the hatch into Papshmir's study. It was only slightly warmer than the tunnel, but she could hardly complain. After all, there was snow outside, she was soaked wet through and wearing only her underwear. At least she was better off than the two naked idiots down below, bickering about how best to climb out of the tunnel.

'I can't climb up this!' Jasmine called up from the bottom. 'One of you will have to pull me up.'

'Use your wrists!' Flake groaned. 'Press them down on the rungs of the ladder.'

'It's too close to the wall. I'll hit my fingers!'

'Use your elbows then.'

'I'll give you a push if you like?' Arizona offered.

Flake left the hatch open for them and checked outside the study door. There was no sign of any zombies, skeletons, or potential bounty hunters roaming around the church. Not yet anyway. She stepped back into the study and closed the door. Her eyes were drawn to Papshmir's desk. To calm her nerves while Jasmine and Arizona bumbled their way up the ladder, Flake did some snooping around. She found a small photo on the desk. It was of Papshmir and Janis. In it, Janis was about twelve and already showing signs of becoming a hippy. Flake picked it up and took a closer look. She wondered if one day she and Sanchez would have any children. And what kind of world would they be bringing a child into?

A series of thudding sounds from the tunnel snapped her out of her maudlin thoughts. She returned to the hatch in the floor and peered down into the tunnel. It was exactly as she expected. Jasmine and Arizona were in a heap at the bottom.

'What are you two doing?' Flake grumbled, her impatience obvious.

'I lost my footing!' Jasmine called back.

Arizona's muffled voice then said something that sounded like, *'My nose is in your ass.'*

Flake rolled her eyes and left them to it. There were more interesting things to look at in the study. A yellow poster on the wall caught her eye. It was made from old parchment and it had some black italic writing on it. It was entitled *"How to bless water and make it Holy"*. Flake moved closer and read the instructions.

Take a handful of salt and a bowl of water. Use the salt to make the shape of a cross in the water and recite these words -

"May this salt and water be mixed together in the name of the Father, and of the Son, and of the Holy Spirit."

Flake unhooked the poster from the wall and rolled it up. Blessing water and making it holy was something she was keen to try, having seen how successful the holy water cannon had been earlier. Water and salt. Easy things to find. Salt would be in the kitchen.

She snuck out of the study and headed along the corridor towards the church kitchen, leaving the bickering voices of Jasmine and Arizona behind.

As she passed through the main hall in the church, she paused to look around. It was a mess. The front doors were busted, and an ice cold wind was blowing in. There was blood on the floor, and on the walls and some of the pews. Some bad shit had gone down in that hall today. Flake shuddered and hurried across to the kitchen. It was only a small, very basic kitchen, barely half the size of the one in the Tapioca. She opened a few cupboards and eventually found a salt shaker. She took it and headed back to the main hall to find the font.

The roar of a car engine pulling up outside made the hairs on her neck stand up. She was unarmed, apart from the salt. She need not have worried. The car that parked outside the gates at the end of the churchyard was a black Caddy. The Bourbon Kid jumped out and jogged down the path that led up to the entrance. Elvis and Sanchez were in the back of the Caddy fighting over a brown bag. It was almost as irritating as watching Jasmine and Arizona trying to get out of the tunnel.

The Bourbon Kid jogged into the church and made his way down the aisle to Flake. She was happy to see him again.

'You okay?' he asked.

'Yeah, fine.'

'Where's the other two?'

'Stuck in the tunnel.'

The Kid looked at the rolled up poster Flake was holding. 'What you got there?'

'I took this from Papshmir's wall. It tells you how to bless water and make it holy. I thought maybe we could give it a try?'

'Can I see it?'

Flake handed it to him. He unrolled it and started reading.

Elvis arrived in the church and stopped just inside the doors. He winced at the sight of the remains of Stunky the axeman. The top half of the bounty hunter's head was embedded in the wall on top of an axe.

'Jeez, what happened to that guy?' Elvis asked, moving briskly past it.

'He's dead,' Flake replied with a shrug. She pointed to the poster the Kid was reading. 'This thing shows us how to bless water and make it holy,' she said. 'I thought it might be useful.'

Elvis walked up to join them. 'I'm not sure,' he said. 'Me and Rex tried blessing water once. It didn't work, *and Rex is an ordained priest*. Only person we ever met who could bless water and make it holy was Papshmir.'

The Kid agreed. 'I used to take holy water from the font in here. Never found another place anywhere in the world with water that could kill the dead.'

'I reckon *you* could bless it,' Elvis suggested, peering over the Kid's shoulder at the words on the parchment. 'You're Papshmir's father, and he was the only person in the world that could bless water. You must be able to do it too, surely?'

Flake liked the idea. 'Scratch went up in flames and ran like a bitch when I blasted him with holy water earlier today. This has to be our best bet for taking him down.'

'Papshmir's got a few water guns round here somewhere,' said Elvis. 'If we can find them we could fill them up with it.'

The Kid studied the words on the parchment again while he mulled the idea over. 'It's not a bad idea. First thing we gotta do is find some salt.'

Flake held up the salt shaker and waved it in front of the Kid's face. 'Ta-da!'

Elvis raised his eyebrows. 'You've got no pants, but you've got salt?'

'Eyes up, soldier,' Flake replied.

The Bourbon Kid took the shaker from her and walked up to the font. He filled the font with water from a large jug that had been left on the floor beside it, then he held the salt shaker over the water.

'Here goes nothing,' he said.

As he poured the salt into the water in the shape of a cross he recited the words from the parchment. When it was done, he handed the salt shaker back to Flake, and stared at the water. Nothing much happened.

'Did it work?' Elvis asked.

'I have no idea.'

'Can we test it on anything?'

'Yeah, the zombies…. when they get here.'

'Shit. Man, if this doesn't work, we're fucked.'

Sanchez finally entered the church, yelling Flake's name at the top of his voice. He ran as fast as he could down the aisle towards them, carrying a brown sex bag, and waving his phone in the air.

'Hi, honey,' said Flake. 'What's the matter?'

Sanchez stopped to catch his breath. While wheezing heavily, he said, 'I just spoke to Arizona again. She's stuck in a tunnel with Jasmine, and there's loads of zombies down there.'

Sixty Eight

The sound of the zombies running along the tunnel had been getting louder for some time. They were invisible in the darkness but their presence was obvious, and their arrival imminent. Things weren't so funny anymore. Arizona had been trying to push Jasmine up the ladder into Papshmir's study without success. On two occasions, Jasmine had fallen just when it looked like she was climbing out at the top. Both times the two naked women ended up entangled at the bottom of the ladder. On the first occasion, Arizona's nose ended up wedged between Jasmine's butt cheeks, and on the second occasion, Jasmine's cell phone, which Arizona was holding onto, almost went the same way. Realising time was not on their side, and with Flake nowhere to be found, Arizona made another phone call to Sanchez, begging him to send help.

'Is he coming?' Jasmine asked her.

'I'm not sure, but he was breathing heavy. He said he'd send Elvis.'

'They'd better get a move on. Those zombies sound like they're twenty seconds away!' The panic in Jasmine's voice was obvious.

'Sanchez was just entering the church when I spoke to him,' Arizona replied, trying to stay calm.

'We can't just wait down here,' said Jasmine. 'We've got to keep trying, but I just can't grab onto anything when I get to the top.'

'Let me climb out first then,' said Arizona. 'When I get to the top I can pull you out!'

Jasmine moved aside. Arizona grabbed a rung on the ladder and stuck Jasmine's phone between her teeth so she could start climbing. Jasmine waited her turn, then stepped onto the ladder too, and clawed her way up using her elbows. The growling from the zombies was now accompanied by the pounding of their feet on the ground as they closed in.

There were roughly thirty rungs on the ladder. By the time Arizona reached the top, the arrival of the zombies was imminent. She poked her head through the open hatch and spat Jasmine's phone out onto the floor. Crawling out of the tunnel wasn't so easy. She was finally able to appreciate how difficult it would have been for Jasmine to do it with no usable fingers. As soon as she was out she turned around and looked back into the tunnel. Jasmine was a few rungs down, climbing up on her elbows. Arizona dropped to her knees and reached down to her.

'Hurry!' Arizona squealed. 'I can see them behind you!'

Jasmine pumped her elbows and feet on the rungs of the ladder until she was close enough to reach up and offer Arizona her left hand.

Arizona grabbed her wrist and pulled, while Jasmine carried on using her legs to ascend the ladder.

'Shit! Pull me out. Quick!'

Arizona grabbed Jasmine's other arm and pulled with all her might, dragging her new friend up. But just as Jasmine's head poked through the hatch into the study, a giant, cold zombie hand grabbed her foot and pulled it off the ladder.

'SHIT! They've got me!'

Arizona pulled as hard she could, but it was clear that something else, something much stronger than her, was pulling hard the other way, and it had gravity on its side. Jasmine slid back down several rungs, pulling Arizona partway into the hole with her.

Arizona refused to let go, even when her upper body was dragged into the hole. She screamed for help, praying that someone would come to her aid.

Someone did.

Elvis.

He burst through the door into Papshmir's study. He was greeted by the sight of a naked ass staring at him from the hole in the floor. Normally, he would have taken a moment to admire such a fine specimen, but Jasmine's terrified cries from below meant he had to leap into action immediately.

He dived down onto the floor and grabbed Arizona's ankles. A second later would have been too late. An epic tug of war ensued. Elvis pulled on Arizona's ankles while a zombie below pulled on Jasmine's. The zombie had the easier task, so in spite of Elvis's best efforts, Arizona continued to slide further into the hole.

Help arrived in the shape of Flake. Elvis yelled at her.

'Grab a leg, quick!'

Flake dived down onto the floor next to him and grabbed one of Arizona's thighs. She wrapped herself around it, anchoring it to the floor. It gave Elvis the opportunity to edge his way up Arizona's other leg until he had a firm grip on the other thigh.

Sanchez arrived in the study just in time to see Flake and Elvis on the floor attempting to pull a naked ass out of a hole. All kinds of grunting noises were going on, mostly from the people doing the pulling. There was some animalistic growling going on down in the tunnel too. Sanchez ran over to the hole and peered down past Arizona to see what was going on. He couldn't see much because it was dark, but Jasmine was down there on the ladder with a zombie wrapped around her legs.

'GRAB SOMETHING AND PULL!' Flake yelled at him.

Sanchez pondered the situation for a moment. There wasn't much left to grab, not legally anyway. He chose the option that was least likely to land him in hot water. He ran back and grabbed a hold of Arizona's feet, which were unusually sticky. The extra weight he provided made all the difference. With Sanchez as the anchor, Flake and Elvis were able to pull the legs and ass out of the hole.

'There's a huge growler down there,' Sanchez warned them.

Elvis slid one hand up to Arizona's shoulder and pulled her up through the hole. Jasmine's hands appeared, wrapped inside Arizona's fists. Elvis grabbed one of Jasmine's arms with both hands and pulled.

'Come on, Jas,' Arizona cried. 'You can make it!'

'It's climbing up my legs!' Jasmine yelled. 'Quick, it's trying to eat my ass!'

With one mighty tug, Elvis leaned back and hauled Jasmine clear of the horny zombie. He dragged her up through the hole and kept pulling until she was all the way out and her face was up against his chest, at which point he lost his balance. The two of them fell into an erotic heap on the floor.

The zombie that had been nibbling Jasmine's legs and ass, poked its head up through the hole. It was a toothless old bastard with thinning grey hair. Before it could grab hold of anything, Flake stamped on it, forcing it back down. She flipped the trapdoor shut and sat down on it. It rumbled beneath her feet as a zombie below banged on it, trying to push it open.

'Hey!' she yelled at the others. 'Pull Papshmir's desk over here. We need to keep this hatch closed.'

Arizona and Sanchez dragged the big wooden desk across the floor. Flake moved aside so they could position one of its legs over the hatch. The table leg bounced up a little as the zombies banged on the trapdoor from below, but they couldn't force it open.

Arizona took a moment to catch her breath, then looked around at her new friends. She was excited about being involved in the action, and having just played a big part in saving Jasmine, she felt like she was a bonafide member of the gang. It was a thrill to finally meet Elvis too, after hearing Jasmine talk about how cool he was.

'Hi, I'm Arizona!' she said, grabbing Sanchez's hand and shaking it. 'You must be Elvis. So pleased to meet you. Jasmine was right, you are a stud.'

Flake grabbed Arizona's arm and pulled her away. 'That's Sanchez,' she said. '*He's mine.* That guy over there who looks like Elvis, *he's Elvis.*'

Elvis was still on the floor, underneath Jasmine. The two were having a private moment.

'Oh,' Arizona gasped. 'I see what you mean. He's even more like Elvis than Sanchez is!'

Jasmine took a break from kissing Elvis and looked over her shoulder at Arizona. 'Thanks, you guys,' she said. 'I thought I was a goner. Something definitely bit me. How does my ass look?'

'You've got a big gash down there,' Sanchez replied.

'It's just a graze,' said Flake. 'Nothing to worry about.'

The desk bounced up an inch as the zombies banged harder on the hatch beneath it. Arizona hopped up onto the desk and sat on it to add some extra weight to it. 'Isn't this great?' she said, bobbing up and down on the desk. 'I feel like I'm in one of those low-budget horror movies that's written by a pervert.'

Sanchez nodded in time with Arizona's boobs as they bounced up and down. 'It is great,' he agreed.

Flake's face appeared in front of him, blocking his view of Arizona.

'Why don't you go and get those outfits we asked for?' she suggested. 'I'm sure Jasmine and Arizona are keen to get dressed.'

'Outfits?'

'The ones you were bringing from the sex shop.'

Sanchez snapped back to reality. 'Oh yeah, those.'

'Go on then.' Flake ushered Sanchez over to the door and shoved him through it. When she turned around Elvis and Jasmine were back on their feet. Elvis had his arm around Jasmine's shoulder, but his head was nodding up and down in unison with the bouncing desk just like Sanchez had done a minute earlier. Flake waved her hand in front of his face.

'Perv much?' she said.

Elvis threw a sideways glance at her. 'You jealous?'

'No.'

'Why exactly are you ladies naked anyway?' he asked Jasmine.

'We were showering,' she replied. 'But the zombies showed up, and there was no time to get dressed.'

Elvis looked at Flake. 'And how come you kept your underwear on?'

'I had no reason to take it off,' Flake replied, giving him an icy stare.

'It's still wet though,' said Jasmine. 'I can see right through it.'

Flake turned to leave the room, but bumped into the Bourbon Kid on his way in. He was carrying two axes. He tossed one to Elvis, who caught it with his free hand.

'What's this for?' Elvis asked, staring at the bloodstained axe.

'We gotta chop some wood.'

Sixty Nine

Flake left Arizona and Jasmine in the study and followed Elvis and JD out into the corridor. While the two guys went to chop some wood, Flake went to find something to wear. She passed Sanchez on his way back to the study carrying a brown sex bag.

'Where are you going?' he asked her.

'To find some clothes,' she replied. 'Unless there's anything in that bag for me?'

Sanchez shook his head. 'There's just the two outfits for Jasmine and Arizona. You can probably find one of Papshmir's dresses down that way though,' he said, nodding down the opposite wing.

Flake grabbed Sanchez and kissed him. 'Just make sure the girls dress themselves,' she said. 'No helping!'

'Got it.'

Flake left Sanchez with what she considered to be clear instructions and headed down the other side of the church. She came to a corridor with a private room in it where she found a bed, a dresser and a closet. The closet was full of women's clothes that she presumed belonged to Janis. She grabbed a green and red flowery dress and slipped it over her head. It was a good fit, if not a perfect style choice.

Through the bedroom window she could hear the screams of innocent people nearby being eaten alive by zombies. She tried to ignore the sounds while she looked for some shoes. Eventually she found a pair of Janis's ankle boots and slipped them on, then headed back out to the church hall. The sounds of the zombies were getting louder, and closer.

She found Elvis and the Bourbon Kid chopping up the wooden doors that once stood at the church entrance.

'What's the plan here?' she asked, as she ran down the aisle to join them.

'We're gonna start a fire just outside the entrance,' said Elvis, taking a break from the wood cutting. 'It's the only way we can realistically hope to keep the zombies out.'

'Can I help?'

The Bourbon Kid looked up. 'Find some accelerant, and anything that'll burn easily. Bibles might be a good start.'

'Got it.'

Flake sprinted off to find anything that could be of help. She returned a short while later with a bunch of books, some posters, and a can of lighter fluid, by which time the guys had chopped the doors up and built a woodpile just outside the front entrance.

****

When Sanchez returned to Papshmir's study with his big brown sex bag, Jasmine and Arizona were sitting together on Papshmir's desk. The zombies were still banging on the trapdoor below, making the desk (and the two naked women sitting on it) bounce up and down. It was quite a mesmerising sight.

'Have you got some clothes for us?' Jasmine asked him.

Sanchez tried to think about Elton John while he reached into his bag and pulled out a sexy white nurse costume. 'I think this is for you,' he said, offering it to Arizona.

Arizona's eyes lit up and she snatched it away from him. 'I always wanted to be a nurse,' she said. 'This means if anyone gets hurt, I can take care of them now. How cool is that?'

Sanchez didn't respond. He'd forgotten all about Elton John already, and was just nodding along with the bouncing desk.

'Hello!' said Jasmine. 'What have you got for *me?*'

While Arizona started the awkward task of putting on the nurse's outfit without getting off the bouncing desk, Sanchez regained his composure and reached into the bag again. He pulled out a sparkly blue catsuit.

'Elvis chose this for you,' he said, offering it to Jasmine.

'Can you help me put it on?' she asked. 'We're not supposed to get off this desk, so can you slide it up my legs?' She laid back on the desk and lifted her legs up so he could slip the catsuit over her feet.

Sanchez panicked. He looked at the catsuit, then at Jasmine. 'I dunno,' he said, backing away. 'If Flake comes back and catches us, she'll kill me.'

'Ugh,' Jasmine groaned. She sat back up. 'You're such a wuss. Did you get me a dildo?'

'I sure did.' Sanchez put the blue catsuit on the desk next to Jasmine and reached into his sex bag again. He pulled out the final item, a box containing a dildo.

'Open it up!' said Jasmine.

Before opening it up, Sanchez had to ask a question that had been bugging him. 'What exactly do you need it for?'

Arizona finished sliding the nurse's outfit over her head and answered on Jasmine's behalf. 'We're going to strap it to Jasmine,' she said.

Sanchez took a sharp intake of breath. 'Really?'

'Yeah,' Jasmine nodded. 'I need it strapped into my fist. Take it out of the box. Let me see it.'

Sanchez fumbled around with the box, taking an age to open it. When he eventually got it open he pulled out a large brown dildo. It was shaped and moulded to look like an enormous turd.

Jasmine screwed up her face. 'What the fuck is that?'

Arizona clapped her hands together with excitement. 'Holy shit! That's a Steamer isn't it?'

'You've heard of it?' Sanchez asked, surprised.

Jasmine stuck out a leg and used it to drag Sanchez over to her. 'Turn it on,' she said. 'I wanna see it in action.'

Sanchez held the big brown device out in front of him and looked for a button to switch it on. Unfortunately for him, right at that moment, Flake walked back in. She was wearing a flowery dress and she had an angry scowl on her face. The sight of him standing in front of Jasmine, pointing a huge brown dildo between her legs did not go down well.

She marched over and snatched the dildo from Sanchez's grasp. 'What the fuck is this?' she asked.

'It's a dildo,' said Jasmine.

'I know it's a fucking dildo!' Flake snapped. 'Why does it look like a turd?'

'It was the only one I could find,' Sanchez lied.

'Bullshit!' said Flake, shaking the dildo at Sanchez while she rebuked him. 'Of all the dildos in the world, why did you have to get one that looks like a piece of shit? What is wrong with you?'

'I heard that ladies like the big brown ones,' Sanchez replied, nonchalantly. 'Besides, I believe they're quite popular. They're known as Log dildos.'

Arizona agreed. 'Yes, that's right, and *the Steamer* is the number one seller.'

'Are you sure it's not the number two?' said Sanchez, giggling to himself.

Arizona took the dildo from Flake. 'This is the vibrating model,' she said. 'It has five different speeds and it makes some amazing noises and smells too.' She switched it on and it started vibrating and wobbling in her hand. It also made some amusing farting sounds, accompanied by some unpleasant aromas.

'Can I have a go with it?' Sanchez asked, his face lighting up.

'Sure thing,' said Arizona, turning up the speed on the dildo. 'Drop your pants and bend over.'

Flake snatched the dildo back from her. 'That's not what he meant,' she snapped. She switched off the vibrating instrument. 'Sanchez, go out into the hall and see if the guys need any help. *I'll* help Jasmine get dressed.'

For the next few minutes, Flake and Arizona did their best to help Jasmine into her new catsuit, which was a tough task on account of her busted fingers and the fact she was sitting on a bouncing desk. When the job was done, Flake picked up the dildo again.

'Okay, we need to strap this into your hand,' she said, pointing the device at Jasmine.

Right on cue, Elvis walked in with some industrial tape and an aluminium frying pan. He was swinging the pan around as if he was swiping invisible zombies with it. He stopped in his tracks when he saw Flake holding the turd-shaped dildo. 'Cripes,' he said. 'Is that a Steamer?'

'Who cares!' said Flake. 'Can we just strap it to Jasmine, please?'

It took a few minutes to strap the dildo and the frying pan into Jasmine's hands. When the job was done, the gang left Papshmir's room and locked it shut in case the zombies managed to make their way out of the trapdoor beneath the desk.

Back in the church hall, the raging fire outside the entrance was keeping the zombies out of the church, but their wails and groans were filtering in through the flames.

Twenty metres back from the entrance was a barricade made up of overturned wooden pews. A selection of weapons were stacked up inside the barricade. The Kid was standing inside it, spraying water from a high-powered water-rifle onto the floor just inside the entrance.

'Are there many zombies out there?' Flake asked him as she approached.

He nodded at her but said nothing.

Arizona walked up beside Flake. 'Why is he spraying water everywhere?' she asked.

'It's holy water,' Flake replied. 'If the zombies get through the fire, the holy water will burn them alive. If they get through that, then we shoot them.'

The Bourbon Kid stopped spraying water at the floor and elaborated on Flake's answer. 'Some of us shoot them,' he said. 'And some of us fight them.' He looked at his water rifle and added, 'I'm not even sure this water is holy.'

Arizona raised her hand. 'Can you tell by tasting it?'

Flake pulled her hand down.

'Okay, folks,' said Elvis, addressing everyone. 'Grab your weapon of choice, because any minute now, the zombies are gonna come through the fire, or through the windows, or any other entrance they can find. We've gotta stay together. Any questions?'

The selection of weapons he was referring to didn't inspire confidence. There was a Skorpion machine-gun, a ten-inch high silver cross, a chair leg with a nail in it, a candelabra, and a drilling device with a rubber fist on the end. Other than that, there was just what the Bourbon Kid had inside his coat, the two axes Elvis was holding, and Jasmine's dildo and frying pan combination.

'Are these really all the weapons we have?' Flake asked.

''Fraid so,' said Elvis. 'We've got what we've got, and that's it.'

'Then we're fucked.' Flake looked at Elvis, then at the Kid, then back at Elvis. 'Do we have a backup plan?'

'Not exactly,' said Elvis. 'We're kind of hoping that if we kill Scratch, all the zombies will just die, you know, like they do in the movies?'

'You mean like they do in *bad* movies?' said Flake.

'Yeah, that's it in a nutshell. That's our plan.'

Flake looked to the Bourbon Kid for a better answer. He placed a cigarette between his lips and sucked on it, lighting it up.

'I think what Elvis is saying,' he said as he blew some smoke out of his nostrils, 'is that we're hoping for a miracle.'

Seventy

The scramble for weapons hadn't gone as well as Sanchez hoped. Flake snagged the Skorpion gun and the chair leg, which left Sanchez and Arizona to fight it out over the rest of the items. Arizona may have looked weak, but she outmuscled Sanchez in a fight for the silver cross. She grabbed the candelabra too, leaving Sanchez with the Anal Intruder. The Intruder was only ever going to be useful for close combat, but it was better than nothing, Sanchez supposed. He fired it up and crouched down next to Flake behind the barricade. It was the place he felt safest. Flake had military focus. Her eyes weren't shifting away from the fire at the entrance.

Zombies began surrounding the church, banging on its windows and doors. It was only a matter of time before they found their way in. The fire at the front of the church wouldn't keep them at bay for long. They were zombies after all, fire shouldn't bother them too much.

Sanchez looked along the line of people behind the barricade. He had Flake next to him, the Bourbon Kid was beside her, then Elvis, Jasmine and finally Arizona on the other end. Everyone was staring at the fire, waiting for something to come through it.

Sanchez prodded Flake with the rubber fist on his weapon. 'Psst, Flake. Is it possible we've barricaded ourselves into a building that's going to catch fire?'

Flake threw a sideways glance at him. 'Would you feel safer outside with the zombies?'

As the sound of zombies outside grew louder, the Bourbon Kid addressed the group one last time. 'Okay everybody,' he said. 'If you've got anything you wanted to say to each other, now's the time.'

Flake rubbed Sanchez's back. 'Don't worry,' she said. 'We've been in worse situations than this. We're gonna be just fine.'

Sanchez kissed Flake on the cheek. 'You make the best breakfasts in the world,' he said. 'There's no way I'm letting anything happen to you.'

Further down the line, Elvis and Jasmine exchanged a passionate kiss. When it was over, Jasmine shared a kiss with Arizona too, so she didn't feel left out. The Bourbon Kid stayed silent, his eyes on the entrance.

And then the first zombie took a chance with the fire. A scrawny female charged through the flames into the church. By the time she was inside she was lit up like a Molotov Cocktail. She staggered on towards the barricade, screaming and waving her arms around. Elvis leapt over the row of upturned pews and charged at her with an axe. The zombie never saw him coming. He slammed the axe into her skull and split her in half down to her waist. As the flames on her body started licking their way up the handle of Elvis's axe, he yanked it out and retreated back to his position. The split zombie fell back into the patches of holy water on the floor, and lay there burning to a crisp.

Sanchez raised his hand. 'Are we taking it in turns to kill these things?' he asked.

'Just do what you can,' Elvis replied. 'Stay close and watch out for each other.'

The dying zombie in front of them was just the test pilot. The others soon followed. Zombies and skeletons began making suicidal runs through the fire. The zombies came through with their skin, hair and clothes engulfed in flames. The skeletons, who were useless most of the time, fared much better. The fire didn't light them up because they had no skin or hair. The holy water on the floor didn't seem to hurt them either.

Arizona followed Elvis's lead and jumped over the barricade to take on the first skeleton. She smashed it on the skull with her candelabra, then followed up by slamming her silver cross into its ribcage. At the touch of the cross, the skeleton's bones ignited in flames. Where the blow from the candelabra hadn't hurt it, the mere touch of a silver cross melted the fucker into the ground. Sanchez never saw what happened next for Arizona because a big skeleton charged his way. It leapt over the barricade, its arms above its head, and its jaws wide open like it was laughing. Sanchez gave it something to put a smile on its face. He thrust his Anal Intruder at it. The rubber fist on the end of the sex drill pummelled the skeleton's head. With the skeleton's forward motion halted, Flake smashed in the back of its skull with her chair leg.

There were small fires breaking out all around them from the burning zombies, so the gang were in retreat almost from the off. The heat from the fires was problematic enough, but then came the biggest problem of all. Scratch.

The Devil walked through the wall of fire at the entrance. As zombies flailed all around him, Scratch remained unfazed and untouched by the fire. Even his red suit and cowboy hat seemed to be impervious to the flames on this occasion.

This was the Bourbon Kid's fight. He rose to face Scratch, armed with his water rifle. There was no time for speeches, he just opened fire. A stream of water spurted from the rifle and splashed all over Scratch, hitting him in the face and chest.

Sanchez took his eye off the skeleton he and Flake were doing battle with and watched to see how Scratch reacted to the holy water.

Nothing.

Flake stopped hitting the skeleton. 'Oh, shit!' she said. 'It's, not working. He should be on fire by now. The water isn't holy!'

She was right. The Bourbon Kid's attempt at blessing the water and making it holy hadn't worked. He was firing a gun filled with plain old H20 at the Devil.

Realising his folly, the Kid stopped firing and hurled the water rifle at Scratch. The man in red swatted it away like it was nothing. He grinned at the Bourbon Kid.

'You thought you could bless the water and make it holy didn't you!' he cackled. In typical smug fashion he then pointed at the Kid and burst out laughing.

Flake finished bashing in the skeleton's skull with her chair leg, and turned to her other weapon, the Skorpion gun. She pointed it at Scratch and opened fire, hitting him with everything she had. The rat-a-tat of gunfire was deafening. But none of the bullets did anything to Scratch, except anger him and take his focus away from the Bourbon Kid for a moment.

The Devil turned his wrath on Flake. He lifted his hand, showing her his palm. It glowed red with electrical fire. With a sharp thrust of his arm he hurled a ball of lightning at Flake. It hit her in the shoulder and launched her back toward the church font. She cracked her head against it and slid to the floor, unconscious.

'FLAKE!'

Sanchez forgot everything else and rushed over to help her. In his desperation to get to her he tripped over a pew and stumbled onto the floor, faceplanting a metre short of where she had fallen. It was lucky that he did, because Scratch, having heard Sanchez cry out Flake's name, had hurled a ball of lightning his way too. With Sanchez down on the floor, the ball of energy flew over his head and blasted into the stone wall behind the font, ripping a huge hole in it, big enough to ride a bike through. A gust of cold air surged into the church.

Sanchez scrambled to his feet. The only person he truly cared for was Flake. She was down, and out of the game. On many occasions in the past, she had come to his rescue. It was time for him to come to hers. As the zombies and red hot skeletons swarmed into the church through the front entrance, Sanchez got down on his knee and grabbed Flake. He hauled her up and slung her over his shoulder. With fire and zombies all around, and armed only with his sex drill, he carried her out of the church through the hole in the wall that Scratch had just created.

It was bitterly cold in the graveyard. From walking on a stone floor inside the church, Sanchez was suddenly wading through eight-inches of snow.

And a thousand zombies.

Sanchez pressed his finger on the trigger of his sex drill and barged into the first zombie he came across, knocking it over. He barrelled on through the snow, barely able to muster anything faster than walking pace.

He had caught the eye of every zombie within the churchyard. They closed in on him from all sides. Sanchez lowered his head to try and charge through them, holding his sex drill up like a joust. It was no use. Zombies started grabbing at Flake, pawing at Sanchez. It was impossible to fight them all off at once.

A zombie hand grabbed his shoulder from behind. As Sanchez tried to pull free of it, his foot sunk into a hollow patch of snow in the ground. He stumbled and lost his balance, dropping Flake. She landed on her head in the snow just in front of him. The snow parted and she fell right through it, vanishing from sight. Sanchez, in his efforts to reach down and grab her, lost his footing and sank through the snow too, like it was quicksand. The snow had been covering a deep hole in the ground. Not just any hole either. Flake had fallen into an open coffin six-feet below ground. Sanchez landed on top of her. The two of them were trapped in a wooden box below ground. A box that had once been inhabited by one of the undead creatures looking down at them from above.

With Flake unresponsive beneath him, Sanchez rolled over and pointed his Anal Intruder upwards, ready to impale anything that leapt upon him.

Seventy One

The final showdown was everything Scratch hoped it would be. The Bourbon Kid had screwed up, shooting a water gun at him that was filled with nothing but plain water, then throwing it at him in desperation. Flake on the other hand... *that bitch had shot bullets at him!* They hadn't hurt, but even so, Scratch still hadn't forgiven her for spraying him with holy water earlier in the day. He dealt with her accordingly, firing a blast of lightning at her. It lifted her off her feet, and she smashed her head against the font, putting her out of the game.

Scratch fired a shot at Sanchez too, but the lucky sonofabitch tripped over and inadvertently ducked under it. The lightning bolt blasted a hole in the wall instead, which was no bad thing as far as Scratch was concerned. As the cold air raced in, Scratch brewed up another fireball in his hand to try again.

BOOM!

The Bourbon Kid's Headblaster gun put paid to that plan. The blast hit Scratch's hand and redirected his fireball up at the ceiling. A set of chandeliers took the brunt of the impact. The fireball obliterated them and took a big chunk out of the church roof at the same time. Chunks of the ceiling rained down from above. It was snowing outside again too, so drops of snow floated down with the debris. By the time Scratch regained his composure, Sanchez had fled through the hole in the wall, with Flake slung over his shoulder. The fool. He ran straight into trouble.

Scratch allowed himself a wry smile at the sight of the undead streaming in through the busted wall, joining the skeletons and burning zombies that were already inside the church. Things were going well.

BOOM!

A second shot from the Kid's gun hit Scratch full in the face. It barely registered. Thanks to the Eye of the Moon, Scratch felt nothing. He shook it off like he'd been hit by a sponge ball.

The next fool to attack him was Elvis. Brave and stupid as ever. The King leapt over the barricade of pews, knocked a skeleton over and ran at Scratch with an axe. He swung it at Scratch's head. But the Devil was seeing everything in slow motion by this time. He had plenty of time to deal with Elvis. With a flick of his hand he shot a bolt of lightning at him, hitting him in the chest. The blast knocked the axe from Elvis's hand and sent him spinning head-over-heels through the air all the way to the back of the church hall. He crashed into the altar and slumped to the floor in a heap, not moving.

This was momentous, the most fun Scratch had had in centuries.

BOOM!

His head snapped back again, courtesy of yet another blast in the face from the Bourbon Kid's Headblaster gun. Damn, that was getting annoying. Scratch shook it off again and responded by hurling another lightning bolt, not at the Kid, but at the ceiling. It was a strategy he hoped would surprise his enemies. The lightning bolt ripped the shit out of the church roof. Huge chunks of plaster, snow and stone fell from above, showering down on the barricade of pews. The Bourbon Kid was knocked to the floor by the falling debris.

It was time for some gloating.

Scratch approached the Kid, a wry smile on his face. 'HOW DOES THAT FE—'

The word "feel" never quite made it out of Scratch's mouth. Out of nowhere he was blindsided by a big brown dildo. Jasmine, of all people, had snuck up on him and shoved a twelve-inch Steamer into his mouth. She pressed it right into his throat too. The stinky device vibrated and writhed around inside Scratch's mouth, making strange noises and clanking against his teeth. *Oh, the humiliation!*

Before Scratch could rip her hand away, he was clanked on the back of the head by a frying pan. That certainly caught him by surprise too, and it forced the dildo further down his throat. The indignity was more than the Devil could stand.

With one swing of his arm, Scratch swatted Jasmine away as if she were a fly. The power of his fist lifted her off her feet, and sent her, and her stinky dildo spinning back down the church aisle. She crashed into a big white concrete pillar, which shook her to the core and spun her over. She bounced onto the floor and slid along the aisle until her unconscious body ended up next to the motionless figure of Elvis.

Snow was pelting down into the church through the gaping holes in the ceiling. It caused the skeletons and zombies to slip and slide around as they made their way down the aisle towards the unconscious figures of Elvis and Jasmine.

Scratch allowed himself a quick fist pump. Aside from the embarrassing dildo incident, everything was going great. All his enemies were out of the game already. Too easy!

The Bourbon Kid was struggling to fight his way out of a pile of bricks and rubble that had fallen on him. The hood of his coat was down, his face and hair were covered in blood, grey dust and droplets of snow from above. Scratch approached him, a smirk on his face.

'Is this how you saw this—'

CLANK!

HISS!

'FOR FUCKSSAKE!' Scratch was getting seriously pissed off with people attacking him while he was in the middle of gloating. This time he was under fire from a blonde nurse with impressive tits. She'd smashed a candelabra over his head, which knocked his hat off. And she'd followed it up by pressing a ten-inch high silver cross onto his scalp, which was the reason for the hissing sound. It fucked his soul-glo hair up in a big way. He could feel it smouldering. On top of all that, she rammed her knee into his balls. Scratch winced and closed his eyes.

'Take that, dickwad!' the nurse yelled, clanking him with the candelabra again.

'Who the fuck are you?' Scratch asked, opening his eyes.

'I'm Arizona.'

'Well, Arizona, say goodnight.' Scratch wrapped his hand around her throat and lifted her off her feet. He hurled her down the aisle towards Elvis and Jasmine. Her arms flailed around above her head and she smashed into the back of a group of zombies and skeletons, knocking them all over like bowling pins. Arizona ended up in a tangled heap on the floor.

'STRIKE!' Scratch yelled, for his own amusement, before turning away from her.

And so just one remained. The Bourbon Kid.

The Kid climbed out of the pile of rubble. He stood up straight and shook some debris off his shoulders. He staggered towards the Devil like a man who'd drunk his own body weight in alcohol, which it was possible he had. Scratch boogied towards him, dancing along to some imaginary funk music in his head.

The Kid peeled off his long black coat and cast it aside. He was wearing a sleeveless black undershirt that showed off his ripped muscles. 'I guess it comes down to this,' he said. 'Just you and me.'

'A fist fight?' said Scratch. 'You realise I could rip your head off right now if I wanted to?'

The Bourbon Kid charged at Scratch and threw a right hook at the side of his head. It connected sweetly and twisted the Devil's face sideways. He followed it up with a left uppercut. Scratch staggered back a few steps. More punches rained in on him. The Kid unleashed all his anger and fury. Scratch hadn't expected the attack to be quite so sudden, or so ferocious. But after the initial shock, he took a step back to compose himself and caught the Kid's next punch in his open hand. Too easy.

'Did you really think you could beat me?' Scratch laughed, squeezing the Kid's fist. 'I'm the Devil, you fool. I *cannot be killed*.' He twisted the Kid's arm around, then grabbed him around the throat with his other hand, lifting him off his feet.

'I'm still gonna kill you,' the Kid replied, choking the words out.

Scratch allowed himself another of his famous hearty laughs. 'What are you gonna do? Bless some more water and make it holy?'

'Nope.'

The Kid reached up with both hands and grabbed Scratch's hand. His strength was impressive. He peeled the Devil's fingers away from his neck, planted one foot down on the floor, then launched himself forward, and cracked a headbutt on Scratch's forehead. He followed it up with a punch to the chest that knocked Scratch off his feet and sent him sprawling back into a flaming zombie that was spinning around behind him. The two of them ended up on the floor in a tangled mess. Scratch pushed the zombie off him and stood up. The fight was supposed to be easier than this. He could feel his rage building. It was time for a demonstration of strength to remind the Bourbon Kid who was number one.

He unleashed fire bolts from his hands. At this point, such was his rage he wasn't even aiming at anything in particular. He just wanted to destroy some stuff, make a statement. He blasted a few more holes in the ceiling. By now the roof was so fucked that it gave way completely. Almost all of it collapsed in. Chunks of stone and rubble fell down all around the hall, flattening half of Scratch's undead army. Piles of snow that had settled on the roof slid down from above too. A huge drift of snow fell down on Scratch, irritating him some more. He shook it all off, his rage clear for everyone to see. But then his eyes settled on the Bourbon Kid again and he relaxed. A smile even broke out on his face. The Kid was no longer a threat, He was buried beneath another huge pile of rubble and snow. His head and arms were visible, but the rest of his body was concealed beneath a mixture of rocks, dust and snow.

Scratch flicked away some snow that had landed on his head and shoulders, then approached his fallen enemy.

'It's time to end this,' he said, raising his hands, revealing the red fire glowing in his palms. 'You know, for a while I was worried that you might have come up with a plan to defeat me, but all you had was the holy water thing. Did you really think you could bless water and make it holy? You might have holy blood, but that's not enough. You've got to be a priest too. Now you know why your son became a man of the church.' Scratch laughed to himself. 'I enjoyed killing him. It was glorious.'

The Bourbon Kid pushed some rubble away from his chest. 'You're boring,' he said. 'And I'm still gonna kill you.'

'I don't think so,' said Scratch, a broad grin on his face. 'Only one of us is dying today, and in case you haven't figured it out yet, it's you!' He raised his hands and unleashed more blasts of electricity at the Kid. The lightning struck him in the chest, lighting him up and pinning him to the floor. Scratch took great pleasure seeing his enemy struggle. He had time for one last gloat before finishing things.

'I'll see you again,' he sneered, 'IN HELL!'

Seventy Two

Elvis opened his eyes. His head was pounding. There was chaos all around. Two thirds of the church roof had caved in, bringing with it an avalanche of snow and debris that covered everything. Elvis was lying on the floor by the altar, which was one of the less affected places. There were piles of rocks and stones around his legs and feet, all covered in a layer of snow. Jasmine was lying beside him. She was conscious but staring into space like a drunk person.

Elvis sat up and blinked a few times. Where was everyone else? He saw Arizona a few metres away, laid face down in a pool of blood, surrounded by more fallen debris. There were zombies and skeletons scattered around the floor too, their limbs visible through the piles of rubble. Some were still alive and trying to free themselves so they could get on with the job of eating the living.

The last of Elvis's senses to wake up was his hearing. It came back like someone had unmuted a million televisions all at the same time. Suddenly every noise came through loud and clear. Above all else, the sound of Scratch laughing filtered into Elvis's consciousness. The Devil was further down the church, standing over the Bourbon Kid, gloating, and firing bolts of lightning at him. The Kid was pinned down, unable to get to his feet as the electrical storm rained down on him. Elvis wanted to get up and help, but he wasn't ready to stand up. This was like waking up from the world's worst hangover, with snow and zombies for company.

Fleeting thoughts flooded into his mind. What had become of Sanchez and Flake? He looked around for them. They were nowhere to be seen.

Was this it? The end of the gang? Had Scratch really triumphed? It would make sense, he was the Devil after all. But Elvis remembered many previous occasions when all hope was lost. Someone in the gang always came through to save the day. He hoped it wasn't supposed to be his turn because he was all out of ideas.

Scratch must have seen Elvis sit up because he took a break from firing electricity at the Bourbon Kid and stared down the hall at him. He couldn't resist the urge to gloat.

'Elvis! Nice to have you back with us,' he called out. 'In case you missed it, I won! So start preparing yourself for an eternity of agonising pain. That goes for *all of you!*'

As if to signal Scratch's victory, a car horn honked loudly outside.
BEEEEEEEEEP! BEEEEEEEEEP!

'Hear that?' said Scratch. 'That is the sound of victory. This day will be remembered for the rest of time!'

The tooting of the car horn was followed by an almighty ruckus outside in the churchyard. The beeping became just one of many sounds. There were screams, snapping bones, the roar of an engine. The ground quivered as something big barrelled across the snow towards the church.

'What the fuck is that?' said Scratch, a puzzled look on his face.

As if the church wasn't already decimated enough, a huge silver truck blasted through the hole in the wall that Scratch had created when he fired a bolt of lightning at Sanchez. The entire wall collapsed. More rocks and stones fell from above, piling up on top of the rubble and mutilated zombies on the church floor.

Scratch was up to his shins in rocks and fallen debris, so when he saw the enormous truck driving straight at him, he was unable to get out of the way. He only managed to lift one foot out of the rubble before the truck ploughed into him. As the front grill smashed into Scratch's face, the driver hit the brakes. The vehicle ground to a halt just after one of its huge front wheels rolled over Scratch's legs, pinning him down beneath it. A huge sheet of snow slid off the roof of the truck and landed on Scratch, turning him into a snowman.

'What the fuck was that?' he said, wiping snow off his face. He blinked a few times as he took in what had just happened to him.

The driver of the truck killed the engine. Elvis's heart skipped a beat. He recognised the truck, and the driver. The truck was known around town as, "The Bum". Its driver was Elvis's best buddy, the one and only, Rodeo Rex.

Rex opened the driver's door and jumped out. He looked totally different to when Elvis had last seen him. From being a bloodied mess, lying in the snow with chunks of his skin missing, he was now dressed in his usual attire, black jeans, sleeveless black leather jacket, Stetson hat, and a newly acquired eye patch over his left eye.

On the top of the truck, a long pipe was swivelling around at 360 degrees spraying salt all around the church. Rex had a handful of it in his gloved hand. He walked over to Scratch, grains of salt slipping through his fingers onto the rocks and snow all around the church floor.

'What are you doing here?' Scratch asked, the surprise on his face palpable, as he worked to push the wheel of the truck back off him.

Rex's reply was unexpected to say the least. *May this salt and water be mixed together; in the name of the Father, and of the Son, and of the Holy Spirit.'*

Scratch paid him little attention. He had more important things on his mind, like climbing out from under the truck. With both hands he pushed back against the wheel of the truck. The truck rolled back a metre, allowing Scratch to climb back to his feet.

'YOU CLOWN!' he yelled at Rex as he dusted himself off. 'You're as stupid as him!' He pointed at the Bourbon Kid, who was himself fighting his way out from under some rubble. 'Neither of you two can make holy water,' Scratch went on. 'He's not ordained as a priest, and *you don't have holy blood!*'

Rex smiled and said one word. *'Amen.'*

The salt he had dropped into the snow began to sizzle like fat in a hot pan. Every drop of snow in the church started to sparkle a mix of shiny red and gold colours, like pixie dust.

'What the fuck is that?' said Scratch, his eyes darting around the floor, taking in the odd sight of the chemical reaction between the snow and the salt.

'You know, I *should* be dead,' said Rex, exuding an impressive level of calm. 'But while I was lying in a hospital bed, taking my last breath after you had me attacked by cannibals, someone snuck into my room and donated some blood. Can you guess who it was?'

'How the fuck should I know?' Scratch grumbled. He lifted his hands, expecting to see his palms glow red. They didn't.

'It was a friend of mine,' Rex continued. 'He injected some of his blood right into my veins. It's amazing stuff. They call it Holy Blood. It has healing power just like the Eye of the Moon.'

The usually smug look vanished from Scratch's face. 'Holy blood?' he said, confused.

'Yep.'

'You have holy blood *in* you?'

'I do. And in case you forgot, I'm also an ordained priest.'

'Fuck off. It's a lie!'

All around Scratch, the salt and snow melded together, the red and gold sparkles spreading fast in all directions like fire on a trail of gasoline. A zombie, half buried under some rubble not far from Scratch, suddenly lit up like a firework. Its body burst into flames. It let out an anguished scream, a scream that was extinguished a second later when its whole body crumbled into ash and smoke. Not far from it, another zombie suffered the same fate, then another, and another. The skeletons all went the same way. Throughout the church and the graveyard outside, zombies and skeletons lit up in flames as they came into contact with the holy snow. Each of them swiftly disintegrated into ash and smoke.

The holy snow Rex was generating spread like wildfire in all directions, through the churchyard and into the streets. It raced around the city, splintering off into every street and alleyway, picking up speed as it went. The trails of salt Jasmine had showered the streets with earlier in the day, combined with those Rex had covered on his way to the church, acted as an accelerant, igniting the snow all over the city, making it holy. Across Santa Mondega, zombies and skeletons were burned to a crisp by the lethal mix of snow and salt.

No matter where he looked, Scratch was surrounded by sparkly snow. His feet felt the effects first, his shoes erupting into flames. The fire swept up his pants and onto his torso. In no time at all he was engulfed in red and gold flames. He flailed around, throwing his suit jacket off and trying to extinguish the blaze that was consuming him. Normally fire did nothing to the Devil, but this was a different kind of fire. *It burned only the dead and the Devil.*

Scratch's clothes and shoes melted away into nothing. His skin would have melted away too, had it not been for the Eye of the Moon. Its miraculous healing powers kept him alive in the face of the boiling heat from the fire.

From his perceived triumph only moments earlier, Scratch was suddenly naked and on fire. Flames danced all over his body. He was stranded, a solitary figure, robbed of his undead army in a matter of seconds.

There was only one thing he could do. Run!

CLANK!

Before Scratch took even one step, Rex's metal fist caught him under the chin. So much for running. Elvis could happily vouch for the fact that it's hard to run when your feet aren't on the ground. The sheer power of Rex's punch would have knocked most men into next week. It lifted Scratch off his feet and sent him horizontal through the air. He landed several metres away on his back in a thick patch of snow. A terrible hissing sound filled the air as smoke billowed up from his naked body. Every part of him that touched the snow began to sizzle and cook. The heat from the blessed snow was hotter than anything he'd ever felt in Hell.

The Eye of the Moon continued to keep Scratch alive, but the pain from the holy water burning his skin was excruciating. He crawled back up onto his knees and looked up at Rex, his eyes pleading for mercy. But his humiliation was only just beginning. The Bourbon Kid had freed himself from the pile of rocks and rubble that had fallen on him. He joined Rex, standing over their stricken enemy.

Over by the altar, Elvis also climbed to his feet. He helped Jasmine up. He couldn't exactly take her by the hand because she had a giant dildo in one and a frying pan in the other, but even so, they made it work. The two of them staggered over to Arizona to check on her. Aside from some cuts and bruises, she was doing okay too. She had a bloodied lip and a deep gash on her forehead.

'You okay?' Jasmine asked her.

'Yeah, I think so.' Arizona reached up and touched the deep wound on her head. It made her wince. 'Ouch, what is that?'

'It's just a nasty cut,' said Jasmine. 'Don't worry, we'll get it sorted.'

'Anyone see what happened to Sanchez and Flake?' Elvis asked.

'We're here!' Sanchez called out.

Elvis looked around and saw Sanchez and Flake re-enter the church through the hole in the wall behind Rex's truck. Flake was still in a bad way, leaning on Sanchez for support.

'Where did you guys go?' Jasmine asked.

'We fell into a coffin,' said Sanchez. He held up the Anal Intruder. 'I was going to use this to fight all the zombies off, but then I figured it would be easier just to close the coffin door. It got a bit hairy for a minute but then they all melted. Anyone know why?'

'You can thank Rex,' said Elvis. 'You guys are just in time too. Scratch is about to get fucked.' He pointed at what was happening in front of the salt truck.

Rex and the Bourbon Kid were beating the shit out of Scratch. The Devil was begging for mercy, but none was on offer. While the holy snow kept him weak and unable to defend himself, the Eye of the Moon was inside him, doing its best to keep him alive in spite of it all. The Devil had become a human punchbag. And his suffering was about to get a lot worse.

Seventy Three

Sanchez had seen some shocking things in his time, but the public torture and ruination of Scratch was brutal, violent, disgusting, humiliating, extremely creative and utterly magnificent. The Bourbon Kid dragged the Devil up to the corner of the church where Papshmir was killed. From there he carried out the brunt of the nastiness, cutting off pieces of Scratch's body and feeding them to him, stubbing out cigarettes in his eyes, ripping off his fingernails, setting fire to his hair and slicing off chunks of his skin with a jagged edged knife. He took a lot of pleasure from hearing Scratch shriek and beg for mercy.

The rest of the gang helped out at times too. Rex used his metal fist to knock a few of Scratch's teeth out, and Jasmine got really creative with the big brown dildo, using it on Scratch in ways that Sanchez had never thought possible. Flake, Elvis and Arizona all chipped in from time to time by kicking Scratch in whichever parts of his body they could get to. Sanchez didn't want to be left out, so he took a private moment to refill his damaged hipflask with his special homebrew. And when it was his turn to join in the fun, he poured the contents of the hipflask onto Scratch's injuries to make them sting a bit more.

Time does tend to fly when you're having fun, and the torture of Scratch went on so long that after a while the local townsfolk, now free from the army of zombies, began venturing out into the streets again to see what exactly was going on. Many people understandably headed for the church. And they were shocked by what they found. Consequently, word of the gang's torture of Scratch began to spread. A crowd of people began to gather around the crumbled church to see what all the screaming was about. The two local activists showed up with their *"Black Lives Matter"* and *"Mayor Garcia Sucks Balls"* banners. Then came the local news crews. At that point Sanchez decided it was time to make a hasty exit, what with him being the city mayor, and all that.

'I hate to interrupt,' Sanchez said to the others, 'but I think it's time we finished this.'

'I'm not done yet,' said the Bourbon Kid.

Elvis sided with Sanchez. 'He's right. It's time to end it. Cut the Eye of the Moon out of him and let him die. We've done enough. I know he's the Devil, and he's a cunt and everything, but it's time to put him out of his misery.'

The others all voiced their agreement, so even though the Bourbon Kid could have carried on for a few more days, he acknowledged that it was time to kill the Devil once and for all. He used his hunting knife to cut a gaping hole in Scratch's stomach, then he reached in and ripped out the Eye of the Moon. The magical blue stone was covered in thick, black blood. He dropped it into some snow, and then plunged his knife into Scratch again. This time the blade ripped open the Devil's chest. The Kid stuck his hand in and tore out Scratch's black heart. It was still pumping, but its beat was fading. He held it up in front of Scratch.

'This is for Janis, Vincent, Annabel and Beth,' he said. He closed his fist around the heart, squeezing the blood out of it. The heart turned to pulp and trickled through his fingers. He smeared the remains over Scratch's face and said one last thing to him. 'Time to die.'

Blood oozed from Scratch's mouth. He had time for one pathetic look of self-pity, then he slumped forward, faceplanting in the divine snow. His body sizzled as the holy water and snow that had been kept at bay by the power of the Eye gradually took hold of every part of his skin and bones. The fire burned his insides, melting every tiny part of him into nothing, with the exception of the huge Steamer that had been inserted into his asshole. That thing was fire resistant, adding to its already impressive list of features.

'Come on, let's go,' said Rex.

A mob of local residents were gathered at the entrance of the church, but they parted like the red sea to allow the group to make their way out. There was no cheering, no applause, just looks of bewilderment and confusion. No one was about to mess with the gang of killers, but equally, no one quite understood what they had just done.

As they walked down the path to the church gates, Flake took a little time out to beat up the guy with the offensive banner about Sanchez. She wrestled his banner from his grip and started smashing him over the head with it. It made the assembled crowd of local folk think twice about hanging around.

'Is it over now then?' Arizona asked Elvis as they watched Flake beating up the protestor.

'The Devil is gone,' Elvis replied. 'So yeah, it's over.'

'What happens now then?' Arizona asked, her voice filled with disappointment.

'I don't know about anyone else,' said Elvis, looking around, 'but I could use a drink.'

'Me too,' Jasmine agreed.

Flake dropped the banner she had successfully broken over its owner's head. 'Is everyone coming back to the Tapioca?' she asked. 'Drinks are on me and Sanchez!'

Arizona groaned. 'I'm not sure I've got the energy to walk that far.'

'No problem,' said Jasmine. 'I'm sure Rex would love to take you in The Bum, wouldn't you Rex?'

Arizona looked surprised. 'Really?'

Rex hadn't even been properly introduced to Arizona. 'I'm sorry,' he said. 'I didn't catch your name.'

'I'm Arizona,' she replied.

'And how did you end up hanging out with this lot?'

'It's an amazing story,' said Arizona. She then launched into one of her super-fast-not-pausing-for-breath monologues. 'You see, I was walking home one night when I got kidnapped by these three guys, and they were all identical, like triplets, you know? And they tied me up in the back of their truck and took turns jizzing on my feet because they were weirdoes. And then they kidnapped Jasmine and Flake, but they threw Flake out into the street in front of some moving traffic. I knew who Jasmine was because she'd killed the Pope, but they broke all her fingers. And then the Bourbon Kid showed up and he ripped one guy's head off. In fact he kind of ripped all their heads off but in different ways, you know what I mean?'

Rex placed his gloved metal hand across her mouth. 'Why don't you tell me all about it on the ride back to the Tapioca?'

'Okay. Are we going in your big truck?'

'Yeah, that's The Bum,' Rex replied. 'The city salt truck.'

'What a great name for a truck,' said Arizona.

'I had a ride in The Bum this morning,' said Jasmine. 'I salted half the roads and sidewalks in the city. People said I was stupid, but it's really paid off, hasn't it?'

Elvis slid his arm around Jasmine's waist. 'That's my girl,' he said, kissing her on the top of the head. 'Just think, if it wasn't for you, Rex wouldn't have been able to turn the whole city into a pool of holy water.'

'So, I'm the hero?' Jasmine said, a broad smile on her face.

'You are,' said Rex. He walked up to her and took hold of her wrists so he could inspect her busted hands. You really had all your fingers busted?' he asked.

'Yeah, hurts like fuck.'

Rex shook his head. 'You realise you're gonna have to have these amputated and replaced with metal hands like mine, don't you?'

Jasmine rolled her eyes. 'Pfft, Rex you're too slow, *as usual*. JD already did that joke.'

'Goddammit!'

Arizona snuck up to Rex and took hold of his gloved hand. She felt the solid steel fingers inside it. 'Wow,' she gawped. 'This is awesome! Do you jerk off with it?'

Rex gritted his teeth. 'Do you want me to take you in The Bum, or what?' he asked.

'Let's do it!'

Arizona slid her arm inside Rex's and the two of them walked back to the salt truck. 'I love your eye patch by the way,' Arizona said. 'Did you know my dad is the President?'

While Rex and Arizona hopped into The Bum to get acquainted, the others made their way back to the Tapioca on foot. It was a pleasant walk through the snow and the blood and the charred remains of the zombies and skeletons, and the ravaged corpses of many of the local citizens.

With the Devil no longer in existence, the snow stopped falling and the dark clouds above the city gradually parted. A rainbow appeared on the horizon. It inspired Jasmine to begin singing the song "Rainbow" by Kacey Musgraves. She wasn't too hot on the words, so Flake joined in to help her out. By the time they reached the chorus, Elvis and Sanchez joined in too. For a few minutes Santa Mondega seemed like a nice place to be.

When the singing ended, Sanchez and Flake walked arm in arm the rest of the way home. Flake occasionally leaned on his shoulder and got a good whiff of his bullshit. Behind them, Elvis and Jasmine walked together and exchanged stories about the adventures they had both been through that day. The Bourbon Kid walked alone at the rear, smoking cigarettes and listening to the stories the others told.

Seventy Four

The Tapioca was a shithole. In general it was a shithole, but today it was an even bigger shithole. And it smelled like dead zombies. Sanchez groaned when he walked through the front doors and saw the mess. It would take Flake ages to clear it all up. But being the all-round decent guy that Sanchez was, he assured her that the cleaning could wait until the morning. The only thing that mattered right now was getting drunk with their friends. Sanchez located a crate of beers in the storage room, and Flake carried them out into the bar area. A few tables and chairs were arranged and then the whole gang sat down for some quality time together to catch up on the tales they all had to tell.

'How did you guys all become friends?' Arizona asked, snuggling up to Rodeo Rex on a cushioned bench by the wall.

'Shit, that's a long story,' said Rex. 'Me and Elvis, we've been friends since way back.'

'Yeah,' Sanchez agreed. 'The three of us go back a long way.'

'What about Flake and Jasmine?'

Jasmine was over by the jukebox picking out some tunes. She had the Steamer strapped into her hand again, and was using it to press the buttons on the machine. It was left to Flake to answer Arizona's question. Flake was sitting on Sanchez's lap on the opposite side of the table to Arizona. She took a swig from a bottle of beer and thought about how to answer.

'I worked at a café in the city for a long time,' she said, remembering it fondly, 'so I got to know Rex and Elvis when I worked there. Sanchez came in for his breakfast every morning, and then one day me and him became cops and, along with JD and our friends, Dante and Kacy, we saved the city from being taken over by vampires. Then Sanchez asked me to move in with him. But Rex and Elvis were dead at that point, I think.'

Arizona spat some beer out through her nose. 'Dead? What do you mean, dead?'

'Yeah, we were dead,' said Rex. 'But that's another story. Me, Elvis and JD, we all had contracts with Scratch, so we worked for him hunting down the undead. On one of our jobs we picked up Jasmine at an airport in Romania, and we never managed to get rid of her.'

Jasmine shouted out, 'I heard that!'

The jukebox started playing the first song Jasmine had selected. It was "Start Over" by Hans Zimmer. The relaxing tune floated out of the speakers, providing the perfect background music for the conversation that was taking place.

'How did you all meet the Bourbon Kid though?' Arizona asked.

The Kid was sitting at the end of the table drinking beer. It was possible he'd had enough bourbon for one day. He had a cigarette hanging from the corner of his mouth as usual.

Rex showed Arizona his gloved hand again. 'First time I met him, he gave me this,' he said, throwing a glance at the Kid.

Arizona ran her fingers over the glove. 'It's really nice,' she said. 'Is it real leather?'

Rex groaned. 'Not the glove, the metal hand. I beat him at arm wrestling so he broke all my fingers because he's a bad loser.'

'Are you still bitching about that?' said the Kid, blowing smoke in Rex's direction.

'Hey, she asked how we met,' said Rex, waving the smoke away. 'I'm just answering the question.'

Jasmine returned to the table and sat down next to Elvis. She leaned forward and sucked on a straw that was sticking out of her bottle of beer. 'JD never likes anyone at first,' she said. 'But deep down he loves us all really.'

'I'll drink to that,' said Rex. 'If he hadn't showed up at the hospital and injected some of his blood into my veins, I wouldn't be here right now. Seriously, I was talking to God at one point. My number was up.'

'Don't forget Elvis saved your ass from the cannibals first,' Jasmine reminded him.

'I guess I'll drink to that too,' said Rex. He raised his bottle to Elvis. 'Cheers, bud.'

'And *I'll* drink to that,' said Elvis. 'But I'll also raise a glass to Flake who saved my ass with her holy water cannon.'

'Me and Arizona would be dead too,' Jasmine added. 'And our feet would be covered in jizz, if JD hadn't showed up and saved us from the weirdo brothers.'

'To us all,' said Elvis, holding up his beer.

Everyone leaned in and chinked their bottles together, apart from Jasmine, who used her big brown dildo instead. That Steamer sure was useful.

'To Janis,' said the Bourbon Kid. 'And Papshmir.'

The others repeated the words and chinked their bottles against Jasmine's Steamer again, but this time the mood was more sombre as they remembered those they had lost. For a while afterwards no one spoke, until Rex asked a question that had been bugging him for a while.

'Does anyone know what happened to Sally?'

All eyes turned to Elvis. He swallowed a mouthful of beer, almost choking on it.

'She died,' he said.

'You killed her?' Rex asked.

'Yep.'

'Fuck her,' said Jasmine. 'She deserved it.'

'Who was Sally?' Arizona asked.

'A cop,' said Elvis. 'She almost became part of the group, but then she fucked up. She double-crossed Rex and nearly got him killed.'

Arizona shook her head. 'What a cunt. I mean, I've only known you guys for half a day, and you're already the best friends I ever had. I would never give any of you up.'

'None of us would ever give each other up,' said Elvis.

Rex leaned back and puffed out his cheeks. The skin on his arms was still raw in places where he had been attacked. When he stretched out his arms, it served as a reminder to the others how close they came to losing him.

'Does that still hurt?' Flake asked him. 'Because it looks really sore. I could rub something on it for you if you like?'

'I'll be all right,' he said. He looked over at Elvis. 'You know, if anyone ever sold *you* out to an enemy, I'd kill 'em, and I wouldn't think twice about it.'

'Yeah,' said Elvis. 'I know.'

As the song on the jukebox came to an end, the sound of someone playing a harmonica floated in from the Ladies room.

'What the fuck is that?' said Sanchez, twisting his chair around to ensure Flake was shielding him from whoever came out of the Ladies.

The washroom door opened and a familiar face poked his head out. Jasmine called out his name. 'Jacko!'

'Room for one more?' he asked.

'Fuck yeah,' said Elvis. 'Pull up a chair. Where you been, man?'

'Glad you asked,' said the bluesman. He was wearing a new black suit, with a matching Fedora hat. He breezed over and grabbed a beer from the crate on the floor, then pulled up a chair at the table next to Sanchez and Flake. 'God's given me a new job,' he said. 'As a reward for my efforts in keeping you guys alive, I'm in charge of Purgatory and Hell from now on.'

'Cool,' said Rex. 'Good for you, buddy.'

'Sounds like a shit job to me,' said Sanchez. 'I reckon God's stitched you up there. You'll be all on your own most of the time, or hanging out with Zilas.'

'Are you kidding?' said Jacko. 'Hell is where all the interesting people go.' He looked across at Arizona. 'Who's this nice young lady?' he asked.

'I'm Arizona,' she replied. 'I was kidnapped a few days ago. And now I'm here.' For a brief moment it looked like she was going to say something else, but she stared at her beer bottle with a blank expression on her face. Eventually, she said, 'I should probably call my mom and tell her I'm okay.'

Jasmine tapped Jacko on the shoulder with her Steamer. 'Did you say you met God?' she asked.

'Yeah.'

'What did he look like?'

'It's the strangest thing,' said Jacko. 'He looked like Eddie Murphy in that movie *Coming To America.*'

Jasmine's eyes lit up. '*Holy handjobs!* Can I meet him?'

Jacko smiled. 'He said he'll take you to a basketball game when your fingers are healed up. And he asked if you wouldn't mind wearing your new Harry Potter outfit. Does that make sense?'

'It does.'

Sanchez butted in. 'God does not look like Eddie Murphy!' he argued. 'I've met him. He looks like Dalton from Road House.'

A loud knock at the front doors ended what was about to become a ridiculous conversation. And because the front doors of the Tapioca were fucked, the person who had done the knocking walked into the bar area without waiting for an invite. He was a tall black man in a police uniform. By the time he saw the group at the table, several of them were pointing guns at him. He took off his hat and lowered his head.

'I come in peace,' he said. 'I'm Adrian O'Hara, the new Chief of Police.'

'What do you want, Chief?' Flake asked.

'I just wanted to come and thank you all for what you did today. I know you all saved the city, or at least, you saved what was left of it. Thousands of people died today, but if it hadn't been for you guys, it could have been a lot more. And, well, I just want you to know that for as long as I'm the Chief of Police here, you guys are welcome to come and go as you please. You'll get no trouble from the law.'

'Thank you,' said Rex. 'We appreciate that. Care to join us for a beer?'

'Er, no. It's okay. There's one other thing,' said O'Hara. 'It's about Sanchez and Flake.'

'What about us?' asked Flake.

'Well, the whole thing about you being Mayor and First Lady of Santa Mondega, you know it was bullshit, right? I mean, you don't really get to become mayor by killing the previous mayor. That's just stupid. So, there will be an election held to choose the new mayor in a few weeks. You're welcome to apply, of course.'

Sanchez scoffed. 'I could have you fired, you know,' he said.

'I am aware of that,' said O'Hara. 'But then you'd get a new police chief, and he might want to make an issue of you going on the local news and telling the whole city to stay indoors during the zombie invasion. Thousands of people died because of your message. The zombies were coming out of people's bathrooms. Did you know that?'

Sanchez waved a dismissive hand. 'That can't be proven…. *can it?*'

'Maybe not,' said O'Hara. 'But earlier today, someone at City Hall emailed me some video footage of Flake murdering a security guard in an elevator, and an old lady in the parking lot. Fortunately for you, the person who emailed me the footage has since been eaten alive by zombies, like everyone else at City Hall for that matter, so what I'm saying is, I can make that footage disappear.'

'You'd *better* make it disappear,' Flake warned him.

'That's what I thought,' said O'Hara. 'Anyway, I'll bid you adieu, and once again, I'd just like to thank you all for whatever the fuck it was you did today. It's much appreciated.'

Chief O'Hara left the Tapioca and the gang carried on drinking into the night. And at some point, just after midnight, Arizona remembered to phone her mom to say she was okay.

****

The Ranch

Alexis Calhoon was sitting in her armchair in the lounge, waiting for her phone to buzz. It had been hours. She had tried calling the Bastard brothers for an update. None of them were answering. It wasn't hard to work out what that meant. The dumb fucks were probably dead. Kidnapping Jasmine was never likely to work out well for them. But for Calhoon, not knowing what had become of them, or anyone else for that matter, was a problem. She wouldn't be able to sleep without knowing what had become of the Bourbon Kid. When midnight came and went, she picked up her phone. There was only one person who could help her now. She sent a message to the world's best assassin, Falco Logan. Five words.

"Did you kill him yet?"

Seventy Five

It was inevitable that the black Mercedes G-Wagon would show up at Alexis Calhoon's ranch again. It was eleven o'clock on a bright sunny morning and her husband, Roger, had taken the dogs out into the woods for a walk. Calhoon was sitting in a rocking chair on the porch, staring out at nature. The Mercedes G-Wagon made its way down the long dirt track to her house. She knew who was in the back seat. It was Mike Raffone. She knew why he was coming too, so she was pleased that her husband wouldn't be around to see it.

The driver of the G-Wagon parked up outside the house and Raffone exited the vehicle. He was wearing military combat gear, which was unusual, but he was here to do some dirty work, so maybe he felt a suit wasn't appropriate. Two military soldiers, dressed in blue, also exited the vehicle. They accompanied Raffone up to Calhoon's porch.

She stood up and saluted Raffone, even though he was a prick. He waved the salute away and she lowered her arm.

'Can I get you something to drink?' she offered.

'No. Let's go inside, please.'

Calhoon opened her front door and Raffone marched past her into the kitchen. She followed him in and closed the door behind her, leaving the two soldiers outside on the porch.

'Can we go to your office, please?' said Raffone.

'It's through there,' said Calhoon, pointing to a door at the end of a short hallway off the kitchen.

Raffone led the way and entered the office first. He gestured for her to take her seat behind the desk, as if he owned the place, then he sat down in one of the two chairs on the other side. Calhoon walked behind the desk and sat down with her back to a large window that overlooked a green field that led down to the river. Raffone stared at her, a look of steely determination in his eyes, like a Headmaster preparing to discipline an unruly pupil. Calhoon ignored it and started up the pleasantries.

'I heard you got the President's daughter back,' she said. 'He must be pleased.'

'He is. He's ecstatic. But enough about that. You obviously know why I'm here?'

'Social visit?'

'Don't be funny Alexis. It doesn't suit you. You fucked up, and you fucked up big. I've never wanted to know who your people are. But since it turned out you had the Bastard brothers on the payroll, I'm afraid things have changed. I'll be taking over your operation.' He shook his head, his face filled with disgust. 'What the fuck were you thinking?'

'I was doing what you asked me to do.'

'Your people kidnapped the President's daughter, then you hired them to find her! Could you be any more fucking inept?'

'I could.'

'I told you, don't be funny. You know what makes this all even worse, is that the girl, Arizona, claims she was rescued by the Bourbon Kid and Jasmine, *the Pope killer!*'

Calhoon was already growing tired of Raffone's macho bullshit. 'What exactly do you think I do here, Mike? Do you honestly think I have boy scouts working for me? I don't. I have people working for me that *you* can't know about. That's how it's always been. And just because you found out who they are, doesn't give you the right to be upset about it.'

Raffone leaned forward, his teeth gritted. 'I have every right to be upset about it. You screwed this up, royally. You hired three guys who turned out to be the fucking serial foot-jizzers we've been looking for. And then you hired the fucking Dead Hunters, the people at the top of the FBI's most wanted list, to find the Bastard Brothers. I don't mind telling you, Alexis, I'm very disappointed, and very, *very* fucking angry.' He took a moment to compose himself before continuing. 'Now, here's what's going to happen. You're going to give me all your passwords, your devices, and access to any fucking thing I might need, and then you and I are going for a ride.'

'My husband is out in the woods walking the dogs,' Calhoon informed him. 'He'll be back any minute now.'

'Then we'd better make this quick, hadn't we?'

'I guess so.'

'First of all. I want to know how you contact the Dead Hunters. If I can see to it that they get caught, then I might, just might, ensure that you get a military funeral.'

Calhoon leaned back in her chair and looked at her watch. 'You did get one thing wrong though,' she said.

'What's that?'

'The Dead Hunters don't work for me.'

'That's not how it looks.'

'Maybe so, but the truth is, *I* work for *them*.'

Raffone's expression flipped from irate to confused. 'What's that supposed to mean?'

'It means what it means.'

'Don't play games with me, General. I want all their contact details. And you can give me the details for that other guy you hired as well, what's his name, Falco Logan?'

Calhoon sat forward again. 'Falco Logan? No, I can't do that.'

'You can, and *you will.*' Raffone shook his head in disgust. 'Anyway,' he went on, 'if this guy was as great as you said he was, then how come *he* didn't find the President's daughter?'

'He did.'

'What?'

'Falco Logan rescued the President's daughter. And he killed the three Bastard brothers.'

'Don't play games with me, Alexis.'

'I'm not.'

'Then I don't know what you're talking about. Explain yourself.'

'You don't understand because you're an idiot. You should get more fruit in your diet.'

'Don't!' Raffone was pissed. Calhoon's flippant remarks were getting on his nerves. 'I'm warning you, don't test me. Where do I find this Falco Logan?'

Calhoon leaned back in her chair again, and pointed. 'He's behind you.'

'Is that supposed to be funny?'

'No. It's tragic. For you anyway.'

Raffone felt a hand on his shoulder. His blood turned cold and he looked up. A man, his face concealed beneath a dark cowl was standing over him. There was a smell of bourbon on his breath.

'What the fuck is this?' Raffone blurted out, his confidence evaporating.

Alexis smiled at him. 'This is goodbye.'

Seventy Six

Mike Raffone was removed from Alexis Calhoon's study. As she closed the door she could hear him acting like he was still a big shot, hurling abuse and threats at the Bourbon Kid. His threats soon stopped and turned to sobs when he realised the soldiers who had accompanied him to the ranch had already been executed, along with the driver of his G-Wagon. Raffone's planned elimination of Calhoon hadn't worked out the way he expected. Taking her out into the woods and shooting her like a lame horse, wasn't going to happen. It was Raffone who was taken outside and disposed of.

Calhoon carried on with her work, checking emails and news updates until her husband Roger returned home from walking the dogs. He poked his head around the door to check in on her. He looked a little nervous, which was unlike him. He was a stocky, six-foot tall, middle-aged black man who had chopped down hundreds of trees in his time, so he was rarely unnerved by anything.

'Is everything okay?' he asked, his eyes darting around the room.

'Yes, it's all sorted now. Did you have a good walk?'

'Usual drama,' Roger replied, breathing a sigh of relief. 'The dogs chased a squirrel, like they do. Logan is covered in mud, and Falco's hurt his paw again.'

'Need any help with them?'

'No, it's fine. I've got it all under control.'

Calhoon started tapping away on her laptop again, but out of the corner of her eye she noticed Roger still hovering by the door.

'What?' she asked him.

'I know I'm not supposed to ask,' he said quietly, 'but, isn't that the Dead Hunters outside?'

'Yes, it is. Recognised them, did you?'

'Yeah, seen them on the news enough times. Do they work for you?'

'Kind of.'

'Did you ask them to kill the people from the White House?'

'I did.'

Roger never normally asked her about her work, but then, they'd never had a bunch of mass murderers on their front lawn murdering White House staff before. He stepped fully into the office and closed the door behind him, but he didn't approach her desk. 'You absolutely have to tell me what's going on,' he said, like an excited teenager.

'You wouldn't believe me.'

'Oh, go on, please.'

'It's kind of a long story, but the short version is this, Mike Raffone and the military guys came here to kill us this morning. And the Dead Hunters dropped by to ensure that it didn't happen. Could you make me a sandwich when you're done washing the dogs?'

'Kill us? *Both of us?*'

'And the dogs.'

'No fucking way!' Roger fumbled around behind him trying to get a grip on the door handle. 'I thought we'd agreed that you weren't going to tell me about your work stuff!'

'I told you never to ask.'

'I'll be out the back washing the dogs if you need me.'

'Don't forget my sandwich, or I'll set my people on you.'

Roger laughed, but made a hasty exit all the same.

Calhoon went back to working on her laptop. A few minutes later there was a knock at the door.

'Come in.'

Although disappointed that it wasn't Roger coming back with a sandwich for her, she was pleased to see Rodeo Rex open the door and walk in.

'Is it all done?' she asked, closing her laptop.

Rex stayed by the door, holding onto it with one hand. 'It's done,' he said.

'Thanks, that's good to know. Is there anything I can get for you while you're here? I like the eye patch by the way. It suits you.'

Rex reached up and touched the eye patch with his gloved metal hand. 'I'm turning into a fucking cyborg,' he joked. 'Seriously though, I just wanted to say thanks for what you did the other day, copying the Bourbon Kid in on your group chat. If it wasn't for you, he wouldn't have known I was in hospital, and I'd be dead. That took guts because I'm guessing you were under some serious pressure from Scratch.'

Calhoon laughed. 'You could say that. It wasn't just Scratch either. I also had the Government demanding I find the President's kidnapped daughter.'

'Weren't you worried Scratch would work out who Falco Logan was?'

'I'll be honest, Rex. When the Devil showed up in my home I was certain I was going to die. And I asked myself, *"What's my best play here?"* I mean, I've got the Devil listening into my calls and monitoring my messages, so I can't contact you guys to warn you what's going on. For a minute I thought I was going to have to give you up, but then Scratch made one tiny, little mistake.'

'What was that?'

'He let slip that he didn't have the Bourbon Kid's phone number.'

Rex rubbed his brow. 'Wow, that's a heck of a gamble. But I'm glad you took it. Scratch hasn't had the Kid's number for a long while now, but even so, copying him in on messages that Scratch can read, jeez, you've got some balls!'

Calhoon pretended to wipe sweat from her brow. 'You know what, Rex? If it had gone wrong, Scratch would have killed me. But if I have to take sides, and my options are *the Devil,* or *you guys*, then I choose *you guys* every day of the week, and twice on Sundays.'

Rex gave her a warm smile. 'And that's why we're here for you today, Alexis. Anytime you need us, we'll be here, I promise.'

Calhoon rolled her chair back from the desk and stood up. 'Are you guys staying for lunch?'

Rex shook his head. 'We can't hang around. These days we've gotta keep moving.'

'Well, before you go, I've got a proposition for you.' Calhoon walked around the desk and perched her butt on the corner of it.

'Business?' said Rex.

'Uh huh, remember your little friend Arizona, the President's daughter?'

Rex remembered her well. She was hard to forget. 'I certainly do,' he said. 'She's quite a character.'

'Yes she is,' Calhoon agreed. 'And she's got her father's ear. When she talks, he listens. If you guys ever want any well paid government work, I can keep you in business for a long time. You know what the government are like, we've always got someone that needs killing!'

Rex grinned. 'I think I like the sound of that. I'll run it by the others.'

Calhoon approached him with her hand outstretched. The two of them shook hands.

'You know, whether you like it or not, you're one of us,' said Rex.

'That's nice to know, I think. Call me when you've spoken to the others. Come, I'll show you out.'

Calhoon opened the door and she and Rex headed out onto the front porch. Rex wrapped a stars and stripes bandana around his head, and jogged down to a Chopped Harley Davidson that was parked on the dirt track outside the house. He climbed on and revved the engine.

A black Cadillac pulled up behind him with the song "Alive" by Pearl Jam blaring out of its stereo. The roof of the car was down. Elvis was sitting behind the wheel, and Jasmine was in the seat next to him, half asleep with her head on his shoulder. Flake and Sanchez were sitting in the back playing a game that seemed to involve Flake slapping Sanchez around the face a lot.

A third vehicle, a black Ford Mustang with its roof down, rocked up behind them on the dirt track. The driver was the Bourbon Kid. He was wearing a pair of dark sunglasses, and he looked pretty chilled considering he'd just murdered some important government people.

Rex started up the engine on his Chopper and waved at Calhoon. 'Until we meet again!'

She waved back, not to just to him, but to the others too. They all acknowledged her, then the Chopper and the two cars pulled away and drove down the dirt track to the main highway.

Calhoon's dogs, Falco and Logan, joined her on the porch. She made a fuss of them while she watched the three vehicles ride off into the distance. As they vanished over the horizon, she allowed herself a contented smile. The Dead Hunters were good friends to have. Dangerous. But good. And she had no idea if she would ever see them again.

The End.

Printed in Great Britain
by Amazon

67374356R00199